DEPARTED ACTS

a novel
by Barbara Griffith

FOREWORD by Bill Griffith

When I completed my graphic memoir, *Invisible Ink* in 2015, I thought I'd dealt with all the real and fictional aspects of my mother's long and secret love affair. My book relied on two main sources for its factual accuracy: my mother's diaries and her 380 page unpublished novel, *Departed Acts*.

In *Departed Acts*, using fictitious names that were all readily apparent to me, my mother laid out in great detail her mostly unhappy marriage to my father and her sixteen year affair with Lawrence Lariar.

I used scenes in her book, sometimes verbatim, to illustrate her relationship with my father, my sister and Lariar. This is especially true in my depictions of the places in which the affair was conducted and in scenes where the two lovers have conversations, do things together and have sex.

In press interviews since my book's publication, I've been talking a lot about how important my mother's book was to writing and drawing *Invisible Ink*.

It seems only fitting that, for those who might be interested in the original source material, that I make it available.

My mother tried, unsuccessfully, to find a publisher for *Departed Acts*.
This then, is her published novel.

Note: This book is printed directly from my mother's typed manuscript.
I did not change a word. It contains a few corrections made by her.
I let stand the markings I made to the manuscript in the course of doing my own book.
*This is a facsimile edition of **Departed Acts**.*

"DEPARTED ACTS" by Barbara Griffith (1919-1998) Unpublished. Last revised: 1997

Pages in manuscript related to scenes in "INVISIBLE INK" by Bill Griffith (pub. 2015)

Equivalent names in real life to names in the book:

BEE (JORDON) SHEPARD = Barbara Griffith

PHIL SHEPARD, Bee's husband = James L. Griffith

ANNE SHEPARD, Bee's daughter = Nancy (Griffith) Marriott

JACK JORDON, Bee's father = Clarence S. Jackson

WILLA JORDON, Bee's mother = Ethel (DeMott) Jackson

MAURICE GREENWOOD, Bee's lover = Lawrence Lariar

HARRIET FROST, Bee's "Aunt" = Gladys Pierce

Also see: **Family Trees** on last pages of "Invisible Ink"

KEY SCENES IN "DEPARTED ACTS" WHICH WERE USED or REFERRED TO IN "INVISIBLE INK"

Page 144 - Sex between Bee and Phil
Page 151 - Sex between Bee and Phil
Page 181 - Bee's dissatisfaction with Phil & life in the suburbs
Pages 205 - 208 - Bee meets Maurice Greenwood
Page 209 - More Maurice Greenwood
Page 212 - Sex between Bee and Phil
Page 212-223 - Maurice & Bee begin their relationship
Page 221-223 - First sex between Bee and Maurice
Pages 236-240 - Bee and Maurice become lovers and friends
Pages 266-268 - Phil discovers Bee's affair
Pages 270-271 - Phil molests Anne
Pages 277-278 - Bee's affair enters a rocky stage
Pages 291-294 - More trouble in Bee & Maurice's relationship
Pages 310-218 - Maurice begins the break-up with Bee
Pages 319-323 - Bee and Maurice break up

Departed Acts ©2015 Bill Griffith
Contact: griffy@zippythepinhead.com
To order a signed copy of **"Invisible Ink: My Mother's Secret Love Affair with a Famous Cartoonist"**
(Fantagraphics Books) go to the zippythepinhead.com home page.

Barbara J Griffith
3365 Sacramento St #424
San Francisco CA 94118

DEPARTED ACTS - Synopsis

Principal characters:

Bertha Harriet Jordon, known as "Bee."
Willa and Jack Jordon, Bee's parents.
Harriet Frost, Willa's girlhood friend and the family's "benefactor."
Phil Shepard, Bee's husband.
Anne, Bee and Phil's daughter
Maurice Greenwood, Bee's lover.

PART ONE: Chapters I-III, V-IX. 1926-1945.

In the opening chapters, young Bee Jordon lives with her parents, Jack and Willa in a shabby Brooklyn tenement, and spends weekends with her mother's friend Harriet Frost, who is unmarried and wealthy. Bee's life in the 1920s is affected by the Depression and, more intimately, by the conflict she senses between her parents and Harriet.

In a flashback to 1909-19 (Ch. IV), the basis for this arrangement is set up. Jack, a cocky small-time adventurer, pursues Willa but she rejects him, having set her sights, not on marriage but on a business career - a brave plan, given the prevailing attitudes of the early 20th century. Inexperienced sexually, she fights a losing battle with seduction. When she furiously rejects his plea to marry him, he turns to her friend Harriet. A few weeks later, Harriet tells Willa she and Jack will soon marry.

Willa finds herself pregnant. Her Catholic upbringing rejects the stigma of unwed motherhood and she demands that Harriet release Jack so he can be legal father of her child. Harriet now confesses bitterly that Jack never married her, that he is no good for either of them. But Willa must "take her medicine." Abortion is out of the question. Jack must marry her, and she must give up her hopes and plans for a career. Harriet tells her she's making a big mistake, but Willa's rigid morality sees no other way.

Jack is elated, sure now that he can win Willa's affection. He abandons Harriet and he and Willa marry. Willa assumes the role of cold, unloving partner that will characterize her life as his wife. Harriet offers Willa material help in raising Bee, her hidden agenda to repay Jack for his defection - she will keep his daughter for herself. She and Willa, acting from different motives, reduce Jack to impotence over the years.

The remainder of Part One shows the joys and sorrows of growing up in Brooklyn in the early 1930s, as Bee is tugged between her parents and Harriet.

Jack dies in an accident. Bee learns the lessons of survival as adolescence begins to shape her future. The resulting emotional dysfunction sets the pattern as she moves on into her own marriage.

In Part Two, Bee and Phil, having married in wartime New York after a romantic courtship, embark on married life with high hopes but little skill. When their daughter Anne is born, Bee, not having learned from her own mother, is shown as an inexpert parent. The war over, she and Phil move to live near his parents in another state. Bee delights in her young wife/mother role. Shortly after this, Willa dies.

Harriet persuades the young couple to move back to New York, promising rewards and help in many forms if they will only live nearby. They find a small house in a bedroom community on Long Island and settle in.

By the time Anne is in school, Bee and Phil's marriage has lost flavor. Bee begins a love affair with Maurice Greenwood (engineered by Harriet, who nurses jealous resentment against Phil for having taken away "her baby.") a New York art dealer and gallery owner. Drawn as before to romantic attachment, Bee believes she has found true love at last. The affair brings many joys and satisfactions, but her sexual withdrawal from Phil opens the door for trouble.

→ 265-268 IN NOVEL

Ever vengeful, Harriet arranges for Phil to discover his wife's infidelity. Abandoned by his wife, Phil has begun to drink. Proof of Bee's affair drives him over the edge. Defeated by alcohol and rejection, he turns to his 12 year old daughter for sexual satisfaction. This lasts for 2-3 years, during which Anne suffers in silence, afraid of her father and unable to get close to her mother, whose absorption with her lover has taken over her life.

A crisis occurs in Maurice's life and he tells Bee they are through as lovers. Bee is devastated.

Her careless mothering has distanced her from Anne, who finally reveals to Harriet that her father has abused her. Harriet lets Phil know she knows about this, and threatens to expose him if he does not arrange for her to take Anne away. She sends Anne to a private school in Connecticut.

When Anne is caught smoking pot she is expelled from school. Phil believes he has finally conquered his addiction to his daughter, but when he learns she will come home to live, he knows he cannot trust his own feelings, and leaves.

Bee berates Anne for her behavior at school, tells her she is ungrateful for all that Harriet has done for her. Unable to deal with her disordered life, Anne attempts suicide. Bee saves Anne's life, but in a furious scene, accuses both Phil and Anne of ruining her life. This makes clear to Anne that she can no longer live with them. She runs away - to become a flower child in San Francisco in the sixties.

Bee is alone, leaves the Long Island home and finds an apartment in Manhattan. With time for self-evaluation and painful recreation of the events of her past, she decides to fly to California and try for a reconciliation with her daughter. They meet and together examine their history, the wrongs done, the role of Harriet, and, at last, Phil's part in the final tragedy.

Surviving the breakup of her marriage, the loss of her lover and, finally, estrangement from her daughter, Bee finally is brought face to face with her own failures. Though Anne is doubtful that the past can be mended, she is willing to suspend hostilities as they struggle toward understanding, and, possibly, forgiveness for Phil and even Harriet.

DEPARTED ACTS - INDEX OF CHAPTERS

DEPARTED ACTS - PART ONE

Chapter I

1926-1929

On Sunday, Willa got them up early, made breakfast and had the dishes done by eight. There was no containing Bee's excitement. In all her six years she had never been out of Brooklyn, and seldom off the street where she lived.

"What's Rockaway?" she asked.

"It's the name of the beach."

"What else?"

"You sit on the sand and have lunch. A picnic."

"Can I go in the water?"

"Yes."

Jack blinked angrily over his coffee cup. "Why do we have to go to the beach? None of us can swim."

Willa didn't answer at once but continued to gather towels and stuff them into a paper bag. "I think it's the new automobile," she said finally, holding Bee off with one hand as she tucked a Saturday Evening Post in beside the towels. "It's a Pierce Arrow, very expensive. She wants to take it out for a trial."

"And to flaunt it in front of us." Jack's face reddened and he slammed his hand against the table, glared at his wife and picked up his cup and saucer. When it clattered in the

sink she turned and looked at him, then past him through the
curtained window.

"She's here. Let's not keep her waiting."

Bee jumped up and ran to look. "It's Harriet! In the
new car! It's blue!" She waved joyously, her eyes wide with
anticipation. "A brand new car! To ride to the Rockaway in!"

She missed Jack's scowl and Willa's answering shrug, her
attention on the tall woman who got out of the new blue
automobile and waved back at her.

Harriet had brought a folding card table and after pressing
the legs firmly down into the sand, spread a cloth and laid
out plates and cups. Willa helped her take sandwiches and fruit
from a large basket and arrange them on the table next to the
thermos containers of coffee and milk. Jack opened a big black
umbrella and spread a blanket under it. No one had spoken since
leaving the car.

Barefoot, entranced with sun and sand, Bee darted among
the adults, crowing with delight. She was small and pale, a
city child in a gray tube of a bathing suit, seeing wide beach
and endless ocean for the first time.

"When can I go in the water?"

"In a few minutes." Harriet laid out silverware and napkins.
"Wait until I'm finished here, then we'll go down together."

"Soon?" Bee pleaded. She tugged at Harriet's skirt and
stared at the line of surf a few yards away.

"I'll take you." Jack held out his hand, avoiding Harriet's eyes. "Let's go test the water."

Scuffing sand, they crossed the beach to the water's edge. Around them children dashed into the waves, squealing as the cold licked their shins, turning to see the effect such daring had on anxious parents. Bee pranced on thin, knobby legs, ankle-deep, gripping Jack's hand. A wave caught his rolled-up trousers and he jumped back. Bee tumbled against him, beside herself with excitement.

"Jack! Jack! Don't let it get me!" she screeched, kicking at the incoming wave.

"I'll watch her now." Harriet's voice came over his shoulder. "You can go back and sit with Willa."

Jack turned. "Like hell I will!" He yanked at Bee's arm, swinging her around behind him. "She's having fun - with me! And I can watch her as well as you can!"

His sudden move killed the happy dance. Bee's face crumpled and she wailed disappointment.

"Where your daughter is concerned," Harriet said, her eyes narrow with contempt, "you can't do anything better than I can, Jack." She reached for Bee's hand and pulled her away. "Sssshh, now, it's all right. Come back and Harriet will give you a cookie."

Subdued, Bee followed her back up the shingle to where Willa sat on the blanket, watching. Only a small, fleeting twitch of her lips, not enough to be called a smile, indicated her interest in the scene.

Jack planted his feet where the pull of receding waves sucked

them down into sand and stood there, scowling out over the water.
After a while he pulled a small bottle from his back pocket
and drank, then turned and went back to the others.

"I've poured coffee," Harriet said. "Help yourself to
sandwiches."

Spooning sugar into her cup, Willa didn't look up. Bee
munched chocolate cookies, her eyes following Harriet.

The sun rose higher, breezes fell to little gusts and the
beach sand, cool when they arrived, began to warm. Other family
parties trudged onto the beach, carrying baskets and blankets,
squinting in the heat. Children raced for the water with tin
pails and shovels. Here and there a dog loped after them to
the surf's edge, barked frantically and splashed in the shallows.

Willa removed her shoes and stockings and rolled her sleeves
to the elbows. Harriet sat beside her and they talked in low
tones, eating sandwiches and sipping coffee. Jack took a
position some distance from the umbrella and blanket, brought
his knees to his chest and closed his eyes. Only Bee's incessant
movement - jumping from blanket to sand, hopping around the
table - disturbed the tableau.

Finally, patience worn thin, she pulled on Harriet's arm.

"You said I could go into the ocean," she begged. "You said
I could get wet. I've got the bathing suit on. Please?"

Harriet drained her cup. "Not all the way, Bee. Not way
out. You have to stay close to the edge. It's very dangerous
to go far out."

"You, too, Willa?" Bee asked. "You coming too?" She leaned in over the blanket and peered into her mother's face.

"No. Go along now, mind Harriet." Willa glanced at Jack,
who had turned away from them and once more pulled out his
bottle. "Go along now," she said again, and went back to her
magazine.

The afternoon passed. Happily wet, coated with beach sand,
Bee played at the water's edge, vigorously digging channels
and piling up terraces to protect them from the creeping tide.
The adults watched her, only Harriet smiling.

The breeze returned and, chilled now, they packed the lunch
things and went back to the car. Willa complimented Harriet
on her new purchase and received figures on the automobile's
cost and specifications. In the back seat Bee, exhausted, slept
against Jack's shoulder while beyond the window telephone poles
and roadside architecture passed swiftly as Harriet drove the
big new car back to Brooklyn.

Willa, Jack and Bee lived in a four-room walk-up apartment
in the Flatbush section of Brooklyn. Jack's job in an industrial
warehouse downtown paid bare-living wages but gave him Saturdays
and Sundays off. He turned his pay envelope over to Willa each
Friday and on Monday received carfare and drinking money for
the week. Her four days behind the hosiery counter at The Avenue
D Ladies' Wear brought in enough to supplement his earnings
and with the two she bought food, paid the rent and the gas
and electricity bills.

Furnishings were shabby, clothing shared closet space with

broom and mop. Bee's bed lacked a leg, the fourth corner

supported by bricks, and she had a dresser whose drawers stuck,

yielding only to brute force. ~~On~~ The kitchen, where the three

met for silent meals, ~~held~~ a metal table and chairs, a dingy

porcelain sink and some dish closets.

The streaked and pitted linoleum floor and the faded green

walls told Bee nothing about poverty, about hard times. This

was simply the way things were, here and in the tenement

apartments of her friends on the block, and possibly, everywhere

else in the world. She watched Willa coax life to the cranky

gas stove, empty the drip pan behind the ice box and scrub the

stained sink with Bon Ami, and asked no questions.

Harriet Bertha Frost was Willa's best friend, or so it

appeared. Bee believed this because of overheard telephone

conversations and because gifts arrived occasionally from

downtown department stores, like the gray bathing suit, and,

just before her first day of school, a package containing skirts

and sweaters.

She knew her mother and Harriet had been classmates at Girls'

High School, on Nostrand Avenue, and that Harriet was rich and

lived far away, on the very edge of Brooklyn. She also knew

about the Tea Room Harriet owned, somewhere "in the Village,"

where she served tea and sandwiches, to local students. Willa had talked about

it briefly, just once, saying, "She has no need of any more

income, it's just a pose with her," in answer to some remark

of Jack's.

Harriet's visits to the Flatbush apartment were rare, and in Bee's memory no return visit had ever taken place. Perhaps the recent picnic was a sign that Harriet was now coming into their lives in a more intimate way. Perhaps she would now invite them to visit and Bee would see the castle her imagination had created from pictures in one of Willa's magazines.

The one piece of notable furniture in the apartment was an old upright piano, highly polished, a relic of Harriet's basement, given to Willa because Harriet had no use for it. On the rare occasions when Willa sat down to play, Bee edged in and perched warily on a corner of the bench.

"Who taught you to play?" she ventured one evening.

"Nobody. I taught myself."

Persisting: "How?"

Willa stopped in the middle of "Annie Laurie". "I listened a few times, and after that I could play it." She finished the piece and stood up. "That's enough. We've got dishes to do."

Bee stared at the keyboard. "Would you teach me to play?"

"Don't be ridiculous," Willa said tartly. "There's no time for such nonsense. I have to earn a living."

Dragging her feet, Bee followed her mother into the kitchen. "How about, maybe, I could try by myself, all I need is a little help."

The sulky tone reached Willa's ears as she leaned into the steamy sink and rattled dishes together. "Get a dish towel and dry, and when you finish, you might turn a hand to cleaning your room." She talked into the suds, not turning her head.

"And don't say anything more about the piano."

Arriving home from school at three fifteen, with Willa still
at The Avenue D Ladies' Wear, Bee invested half an hour for
a couple of weeks and reconstructed the melody of "The Old Oaken
Bucket" with one finger, singing the words from the copy of
"Old and Familiar Songs" that Willa kept beneath the bench lid.
When at last she felt confident about her skill, she chose an
evening that had begun without supper table recriminations,
and played the piece.

There was silence for a moment. Bee stared at the keyboard,
back stiff, and waited.

Jack put down his newspaper and blinked at her, a bleary
smile angling one corner of his mouth. "Sounds pretty good,
pretty good," he said, and went back to his reading.

Willa crossed the room and stood beside the piano. "You
learn that all by yourself?"

"Yes."

"Fine." She went back into the kitchen without looking
at Jack and banged the cupboard door hard.

Bee jumped up, hands on hips. "What's the matter with her?
What's she got against playing the dumb old piano, anyway?"
she said in a fierce whisper.

To her astonishment, Jack dropped his paper and glowered
at her. "You don't talk about your mother that way, hear?"

Accustomed to his usual non-participation in family events,
Bee took the unfamiliar words seriously and moved away from

the piano. "Well," she began, then thought better of it. In
her bedroom she reviewed what had just happened. Jack had paid
her a compliment of sorts, but Willa had been unmoved, even
hostile. Was it not much of an accomplishment to play with
only one finger? Was it because he liked it that Willa didn't?
It was normal for them to disagree, when they bothered to talk
to each other at all. A safer course of action would be to play
the piano when she was alone in the apartment, Bee decided.

Willa's hair had gone gray before she reached thirty-five,
and because only "flashy" women bleached, she let it stay that
way, frizzing it with a Woolworth's curling iron heated on the
gas stove. Her dresses were short in the fashion of the
Twenties, hip-hugging and cheap. She claimed to have hazel
eyes, but Bee saw sharp green and often had trouble meeting
their steady gaze.

Bee was eight the year they moved into the flat on 37st
Street. Willa played Gilbert and Sullivan that year: "Tit
Willow," and "Three Little Maids From School Are We," and songs
from "H.M.S. Pinafore." After the supper dishes were cleared,
she sat for half an hour, her face withdrawn, eyes half closed,
and played the songs from memory. Bee watched Jack, in his corner
near the window, his eyes fogged from the hour spent at the
speakeasy down the street, to see if the songs or the playing
meant anything to him. With the newspaper on his lap he stared
across the room at Willa, his face slack and without expression.
Formal education took place in P.S. 89, on Newkirk Avenue.

The building was old, its corridors cheerless, smelling of chalk
dust and wet wool. The Principal's office was on the third
floor, a place of dread, where, on a long bench, miscreants
sat, often for an hour or more, while the Principal studied
the nature of their crimes. Mrs. Sampson was imperially tall
and silver-haired, wore lace collars and long black skirts.
New in the neighborhood, Bee had been warned against behavior
that might lead into her clutches, but entering the third grade
classroom on a September morning, she got off to a bad start
in a matter of minutes.

"What is your name?" The teacher ran her eyes down the
attendance list, then looked up.

"Bee. And my last name is Jordon. Bee Jordon."

Miss Schaffman said impatiently, "No, child. That's not
a name, it's a nickname. Do you know what a nickname is?"

"No."

"Say, 'No, ma'am.'"

"No man."

"Ma'am. No ma'am. Say it."

"No mam, please. My name is Bee. Bee Jordon."

Miss Schaffman came around in front of her desk and loomed
over Bee's seat at the head of the second row. "Your name is
Bertha Harriet Jordon," tapping the roster in her hand."Not
Bee Jordon, not Bee anything. Now repeat after me:'My name is
Bertha Harriet Jordon and I have been disrespectful to my
teacher.'"

Bee raised her eyes and blinked back tears. "I'm not

Bertha!" she cried. "I hate being Bertha! My name is Bee -
Willa says so! You can't make me be Bertha!" And fearing a
sudden blow from the terrible figure above her, she catapulted
from the seat and dashed for the classroom door. Sheer bad
luck drove her into the knees of a teacher about to enter the
room and together they fell to the floor, while the class hooted
with nervous laughter.

Ten minutes later, towed by Miss Schaffman, Bee arrived
at the Principal's office, a sign hanging from her shoulders
With
~~bearing~~ the message: "I am a cry-baby" in tall red letters.
At Miss Schaffman's suggestion, the class had gleefully created
it with crayon and foolscap. Wearing this albatross, Bee was
marched through the dreaded door.

"Sit there." Miss Schaffman pointed to the bench. "I'm
going in to see Mrs. Sampson and tell her all about you."

Heart pounding, Bee sat down to wait for punishment. In
a few minutes Miss Schaffman emerged, stalked past her and out
into the hall. The door to the inner office remained closed
and there was no sound from within. After a while Bee got up
and knocked timidly on the frosted glass. Nothing happened.
She bent to squint through the keyhole. Suddenly the door sprang
open. The black and white apparition in the doorway frowned
in disbelief.

"Go back and sit down!" the voice boomed. "What do you
think you're doing, child? Sit down at once!"

Bee slunk away from the door and went back to the bench.
Another half hour passed. Then the door opened again and Mrs.

Sampson sailed past her and out to the corridor without a downward glance. Bee jumped up and ran to see where she had gone, but the hallway was empty. Authority had vanished. This, then, was to be her punishment: to be abandoned, left to sit forever on a hard wooden bench outside an empty office. No one would ever come for her. No one would know she was missing. She would sit here until she was old and then she would die. Panic flooded over her. She ran to the window and looked down at the pavement far below. Could she survive a plunge to the sidewalk?

She whirled at a sudden noise behind her. Seeing Mrs. Sampson in the doorway, Bee fled like a hunted rabbit, around the tall figure and out into the hall, down the stairs, out of the building. Home was seven blocks away. She raced for it, sobbing.

Willa met her at the door. "They've already called from school. They say you ran away and I was to look for you and report when I found you." She stood aside as Bee bolted into the kitchen and fell on a chair. "What did you do so terrible that you had to run away?"

Exhausted by fear and the mysteries of the morning's events, Bee put her head down on the metal surface. "They won't call me Bee! They're going to call me Bertha!" she howled from inside the circle of her arms.

A moment of silence.

"What's that thing on your sweater?"

Bee looked down at the remnants of the paper sign. "They

put it on me - they - made me stand against the blackboard -
and the teacher put it on me - " Her heart broke. She looked
up at Willa, eyes overflowing. "Why didn't you name me Cynthia?"

"I'll get my coat," Willa said. "I want to see what's going
on in that school."

Willa prevailed, in a way, after promising to bring the
matter of the sign to the attention of the Board of Education,
City Hall, the Mayor, and a number of officials in local
government. Miss Schaffman, however, would never fully comply
and when calling on Bee in class would say, with venom, "Miss
Jordon, please!"

In later years, Bee would recall this as a rare and
astonishing act of parental support, uncharacteristic and
difficult to fit into the memories of her childhood.

Soon after the family moved to the flat on 37st Street,
Willa told Bee she would be spending weekends with Harriet.
No reason was given, and Bee knew enough not to ask for one.
It was a chance to see the world outside the Flatbush
neighborhood, and the prospect was exhilarating. At eight and
a half, she would be venturing out into the wider world on her
own.

The trip on the Brooklyn streetcars took an hour and wound
in and out of the mid-borough slums and warehouse areas. The
round trip fare was ten cents. Willa presented Bee with a
quarter, leaving 15¢ for options.

"Don't spend it all on candy," she said.

Riches in hand, Bee watched her mother's back recede toward the kitchen. Fifteen cents would buy any number of pleasures, not excluding candy. She stared lovingly at the coin, then dropped it into the pocket of her skirt and packed a nightgown and clean underwear into a small satchel for the journey.

At last introduced to the big house on Hendrix Street, in the section of Brooklyn called East New York, Bee found her imagination had not given her a false picture. The formal parlor, with tall windows draped in mauve velvet, a lavender and pink carpet and satin brocade side chairs was a dazzling sight. White plaster rosebuds and cherubs trailing ribbons decorated the high ceiling, where a chandelier with crystal prisms sent colors dancing over the walls. The family living room, just beyond and separated by a set of sliding doors, was furnished with a plain sofa, some upholstered chairs and small tables holding china figurines and bud vases.

Harriet led an inspection tour for Bee's benefit: "You will be doing the dusting here, and you must be very careful of the bricabrac."

"How come you keep the doors shut?" Bee whispered, overawed by such opulence.

"The parlor is for celebrations, parties, at Christmas and Thanksgiving. It's closed the rest of the time to keep out dust." Harriet advanced through a long hall into the kitchen, where Bee saw for the first time the new-fangled refrigerator, a marvelous invention "that does away forever with horse-drawn

ice delivery," Harriet said proudly. Bee was allowed to peek
into the cold-pantry, and saw sacks of vegetables and barrels
for flour and rice. On into the dining room, a place of
no-nonsense Mission furniture, with a mirrored sideboard for
silverware and linens. Bee had never seen such luxurious
furnishings, and walked past the pink tiled fireplace that
straddled a corner of the room in stunned silence.

Harriet led the way upstairs, where Bee was shown the three
bedrooms, the bathroom and the narrow, winding stairs to the
"attic," which wasn't a real attic, Harriet told her, but three
small rooms for storage.

Bee's domestic education, arranged in a private conference
with Willa, was about to begin. Over the next months there
were lessons in bed-making, how to set a table, how to purchase
produce from a street vendor and the preparation of simple dishes
like macaroni and cheese and butterscotch pudding. As these
were mastered, the lessons expanded to include bread-making,
omelettes and pastry.

Saturdays began with chores. In order to simplify things,
Harriet gave her housekeeper the day off to visit relatives
in New Jersey, and after tying Bee into one of her own big
aprons, led her into the front parlor and gave her a dust rag.

"Everything here and in the living room," she told Bee.

"Brickabrackabrickabrack," Bee hummed, working her way past
bookcases and small tables decorated with lace doilies,
pretending that she was an heiress like Harriet and owned this
magnificent mansion, filling it, of course, with many servants

so she wouldn't have to "dust the bricabrac."

Below, there was a dark cellar where trunks and boxes of
unknown contents gathered dust. The stairs to this region were
off limits and Bee, learning early that in Harriet's curriculum
the first subject was obedience without question, complied.

On Sunday mornings there were no chores. They went to church,
St. Andrew's Episcopal, four blocks away. Bee was enrolled
in Sunday School, Willa and Jack not having been consulted.
Persuaded into the Junior Choir, she lent her tinny soprano
to the hymn singing, dressed in a black gown, starched white
cotta, and skullcap.

As weekend duties and instructions became routine, Bee began
to feel a new sense of belonging, of having a place in this
world. Discipline from above was a familiar condition, but
here, with Harriet, it was imposed with thought to the future,
to the faraway time when she, Bee, would be in charge of her
own destiny. She moved into Harriet's guardianship with a sense
of anticipation, the learning duties leading to a goal, one
which she wholeheartedly endorsed.

If she found it unusual that Willa never asked about the
visits to Hendrix Street, Bee saw it as simple lack of interest
or, perhaps, that Willa's job at the Avenue D Ladies Wear and
keeping house for Jack, both of which filled her days and nights,
left no time for other concerns. The new two-part life beginning
for her quickly brought relief from the bleakness of the Flatbush
apartment and Willa and Jack's cursory parenting.

Following with dust rag and furniture polish, Bee listened

to Harriet's sly references to Jack's incompetence and bad
habits, woven into conversation about the uses of cleansing
agents and how best to restore a high gleam to silver.

"How come you don't like him?" Bee asked finally, having
listened once again to a lecture on the evils of sloth and what
a man was expected to do to provide for his family. Questions
she had never asked of Willa crowded her mind: like, why were
her parents together when no signs of affection were ever
demonstrated? Why did Jack drink and why did he despise Harriet,
benefactress, Lady Bountiful, without whom life would be, instead
of bearable, totally barren?

The morning's lesson was bread-making. They stood side
by side at the long counter while Harriet measured flour and
salt and Bee mashed yeast into warm water.

Harriet didn't hesitate, as though the question had been
expected. "We don't get along."

"But why?"

"I don't like drunks."

"Sometimes he doesn't drink." She tried to remember such
an occasion, but only scenes of Jack's dinner-time arrival,
red-faced, smelling sour and unclean, came to mind. "Sometimes
he just listens to the radio."

There was a pause while Harriet reached into the cupboard
for bowls. "He's a drunk, Bee, and how he dares to spend money
on whiskey when you and Willa go without things..."

Persisting: "Is that the only reason you don't like him?"

Sharp eyes now fastened on Bee's face, waking a vivid memory

of Miss Schaffman, grade school tormenter. It was the same
message: something venomous was about to issue from her mouth.

"Your father is a lazy bum who hasn't the gumption to earn
a decent living. I told your mother he'd never amount to
anything, but she didn't listen." She shoved the big brown
bowl toward Bee. "Now turn that out on the board and start
kneading." A short intake of breath. "And he doesn't like me
because I know all about him."

Now that the ice was broken, Bee couldn't hold back. "But,
ever since I was a little kid you've been doing things for us,
for me. How come, if you feel that way about him?"

"It's for you, Bee. You're the one I care about. You're
more my family than his!" She seized the mound of dough and
flung it down on the floured surface, working it furiously.
"Finish with this, now, then put it back in the bowl and cover
it with a towel. And don't ask me any more questions, you hear?"

Stubbornly, "He's my father. Don't I have a right to know
something about him?"

Harriet grabbed her shoulder and spun her around. "Listen
to me. That man doesn't deserve to be your father. He didn't
want you to be born, you - you were just the result of something
bad he did! Now we're going to drop this subject right here
and now!" She yanked off her big white apron and left the
kitchen in a rush.

For a long moment Bee stared at the bread dough, thinking
about what Harriet had said. Something Jack did - something
bad he did way back when she was little? Or maybe before she

was born? The bad things about Jack, she felt, were what went
on daily, like coming home not quite sober, like sitting around
not offering to help, like not caring about anything. Harriet
had talked about that often enough. This was something new,
some memory of hers that hit a sore spot. And any more questions,
of course, were out of the question.

Chapter II

1929-1932

The year Bee turned nine Jack roused himself briefly and took an interest in her presence.

"I'm going to teach you the foxtrot," he announced one spring evening. A rare smile started to life on Willa's face, but when Bee glanced questioningly at her, it disappeared and she went back to work.

For a few minutes they blundered around the room to the accompaniment of a scratched record, "Harvest Moon," none of the movements, as far as Bee could tell, corresponding to the rhythm of the song. Jack had big feet, and there was a lot of gyrating as she tried to avoid his heavy tread.

"Why do I have to learn this?" she asked, when the record finally came to an end and she could lean away from the rank smell of whiskey.

"It'll be useful when you grow up." He went back to his chair near the window and sank into it, breathing heavily.

"I don't think I'll ever need to foxtrot," she said over her shoulder as she picked up a sweater and headed for the door. "And nothing else you could teach me," she added after the door had closed.

Then for a while he talked. Not general conversation, not joining in when they were all together. Not about why he lived the way he did, but about men who had been famous when he was young, heroes of his.

"J.P. Morgan. He was a giant, Bee, saved the whole damn
country, we'd have gone down the drain if he hadn't stepped
in and saved us." When Bee asked him what"we" had been saved
from she got something about finances and bankruptcy, and other
long words she didn't understand. Blinking furiously, he went
on to name others. "Teddy Roosevelt, now there was a man!
And that explorer guy - Peary." He looked over at Willa,
knitting on the couch, a paper bag of yarn at her feet. She
didn't look up. "He went up there to the North Pole and stuck
a flag in it - an American flag! What a guy!"

His eyes went off into a private distance and he began to
hum and shuffle his feet in a soft shoe routine, grinning
sideways. It all ended soon enough. When his efforts stirred
up no response in Willa or Bee, he went back into his hazy shell
and they could have marched through the room blowing bugles
and he wouldn't have noticed.

Bee's chores at home were dishes after supper, errands in
the neighborhood (a pack of Luckies for Jack, a loaf of Bond
white for Willa), pulling in the wash and folding it, and once
a week dusting the living room furniture. There was homework
and sidewalk play and a best friend down the block and, always,
the trauma at school. Then it was Friday, bringing entry to
Harriet's world where things came her way, instead of passing
her by. And the weekends provided subjects that could be brought
into conversation with the girls at P.S. 89, when they talked
about their families.

If she took notice of Willa and Jack, aside from daily unavoidable contact, she wondered once in a while why her mother put up with this lump, who was never quite sober, who sat by himself and took no part. How could she be such a dishrag? Why didn't she flare up, insist on help with the housework, the food shopping, even the laundry? Why, at least, didn't she say something about the drinking? What went on between them that somehow kept them together in this shabby place that held no happiness or fun, ever?

At school there was a hierarchy of predators. The stronger and/or older a child was, the greater the number of unfortunates he/she could bully or subdue. When the younger ones gathered in the schoolyard the phrase often heard was, "He's after me! I gotta hide!" as rash actions drew abuse down on someone's head.

The land around P.S. 89 was open, an area two blocks west and south was brown and dusty, a weedy field crossed by well-worn footpaths. To reach safety, a fugitive had to cover this at a run, streak past the ugly brick buildings of the city pumping station that stood at its edge, and on into the Farragut Woods. The Woods was a half mile long and a couple of blocks wide, a narrow band of trees and grimy grass that sank in the middle and separated the Avenue D section from the Farragut section. In the morning, children crossed it to get to school, and fathers to reach the subway station at Nostrand Avenue. Along the floor of the Woods there was a wide, flat place where rain water collected and froze in winter. Neighborhood children ice-skated there, dodging roots and bottles sticking up through the dirty ice.

Brooklyn winters were blustery; snow was frequent, requiring a heavy coat, knit cap and galoshes. The gloves were Willa's, too big, cold and wet most of the time. When Bee removed the safety pins that secured them to her sleeves she was kept in the house while the street outside erupted in snowball fights, forts were built and defended and sleds dropped down the lumpy slopes to the bottom, spilling their shrieking riders into drifts. The second time, Willa gave in. There would have been a third time and a fourth time, because Bee had enough to live down without appearing in the street pinned into gloves like a baby. Willa must have sensed this and so capitulated. That was the year Bee had someone "after" her once a week.

Having beaten a big girl, Shirley Pratt, in a spelling contest, Bee made the fatal error of gloating over the loser.

"I'm going to get you, Jordon," Shirley promised, as they left the classroom. Menace hung in the air as she leaned over Bee's shoulder. "I'll be waiting for you outside."

The meaning was clear. She would hide somewhere along the homeward route and jump out and plunge Bee face down into a snow bank. Choking and gasping, Bee would be pinned against the ground while Shirley packed snow down the back of her coat where it would melt and trickle into her underwear and she'd have to explain to Willa why everything was soaking wet. The only way to avoid this was to find a new way home, even going blocks out of the way. There were a dozen exits from school.

A frequent choice in this situation was the basement door through
which coal delivery was made. With luck and good timing, Bee
could outrun pursuit by a dash up Newkirk Avenue, skirting the
Woods, with a final shortcut across a few backyards, and arrive
home, safe. Every once in a while this worked. More often,
she was found and victimized by whoever was "after" her that
week.

     A sultry August afternoon. Sun-baked weeds and wilted grass
suffered on the slope above the makeshift diamond (winter's
skating field), where some little boys were going through the
motions of a baseball game. Bee leaned against the trunk of
a tree and pulled her knees to her chest, watching the scene
below. After a few minutes she lifted her eyes and peered
skyward through the dusty leaves. A small plane was passing
overhead, burping and stuttering, and she followed the unfamiliar
sight for a moment, wondering if it would crash, maybe right
here in the Farragut Woods, maybe down on the field, scattering
the baseball teams, tearing up the ground, a real catastrophe,
fire engines racing to the scene, people crowding along the
rim of the hill, watching as the fearless firefighters pulled
the pilot from the smoking wreckage, still alive somehow - "Thank
you, God!" - his leather helmet fire-blistered, face black with
soot and oil, but a happy grin on his face, waving to the
spectators to show he'd made it, a real event, a movie, for
the entertainment of the neighborhood...
     A face appeared above her head, blocking her view of the

little plane as it wobbled away through the hot sky. Joe Payton,

from over on Glenwood, known as "The Pig" among the younger

kids on the block.

"Watching the game?" He sat down beside her on the grass.

Shoulder to shoulder, they leaned against the scratchy bark.

Joe was a sixteen-year-old ruffian who held girls in contempt.

From his territory in front of the candy store on Nostrand Avenue

he treated them to a stream of obscene comment that sent them

scurrying off with red faces.

"Hey, you in the green sweater! Come on over and let me

pinch your tits! How about it, kiddo? Then you can tell all

your friends Joe Payton gave you a feel!"

The victim would break into a run while Joe and his buddies

sent raucous shouts after her. At ten, Bee had not yet qualified

for these attentions.

"Yeah," she said without looking at him. "The Peewees are

winning, I think."

"Been here long?"

She edged away. "What's it to you?"

"Oh, I just wondered. Does your Ma know you're here?"

He moved against her, his thigh hot on her bare leg.

The players below had reached a point of fists and screams.

The noise trickled up the slope as Joe put a hand on her knee

and let it slide down to the edge of her khaki shorts.

"Wanna have some fun?" he said, grinning.

"I've got to go and set the table - " She started to get

up, but he pulled her back against the tree.

"Wait - here, let me show you something, kid." Now his hand reached up into her underpants and grimy fingers blundered over her private parts. Twisting in sudden fear, Bee saw his other hand buried in his own crotch. The fly buttons were open and he had pulled out a roll of flesh that, as she watched, grew huge. His head was low over his chest now, his breathing heavy. Then, as she looked on in frightened fascination, something spurted into his hand and he gasped, loosing his grip on her leg.

"Ugghhhhhh..." spilled from his mouth as he fell back against the tree. Bee was unable to tear her eyes from the incredible sight. Nothing in her experience came even close to what she had just seen. Sure, girls at school talked, pretending knowledge they didn't have, but speculation and sly confidences had never added up to this. A year ago there had been Kenny, eight years old, who had taken it upon himself to give her an anatomy lesson in the basement of the apartment house. Giggling and prancing around her, he came to a breathless halt and dropped his knickers to display his small thing, which he took between thumb and forefinger and waved jauntily at her. Unimpressed, she stepped back, made a rude noise at him and ran for the stairs. It was not, however, an event of any great significance because it involved Kenny, the neighborhood "sissy," and was soon forgotten. Today's awesome performance was far more serious. This was a sixteen-year-old, a Big Boy. He had singled her out for this attention, and she was uneasy, suspecting danger.

She got up cautiously, backed away as he began to button

his pants. At the edge of the brown grass she turned and ran.

Sleep held off at night, her mind a jumble of words and worries. The one she heard frequently on the street was "fuck." In a rash moment, weeks ago, Bee had slipped it into an answer she made to Willa, watching for reaction. It came swiftly. A bar of brown laundry soap was rubbed vigorously across her lower teeth, leaving a taste that took hours to clean out. Did that word have anything to do with what Joe Payton had done? Who could be safely asked about this? Maybe Lucille, best friend down the block. She lived with a lot of sisters and brothers and undoubtedly saw more than most girls.

Opening the subject on the way to school the next day, Bee said, "Why do boys always, uh, try to poke around, try to get their hands into - places? Why do they ask if 'you wanna have some fun?'" She postured, smirking, to show that this was of course a rhetorical question.

Lucille laughed. "My mom says it's because they have dirty minds."

"What do you think?"

"I think - maybe it is fun!"

Bee scuffed pebbles on the path. "This is about..." She waited, hoping for questions. When none came, she went on: "...Joe Payton. Something he, uh, did over on the hill, yesterday."

"Oh?" Lucille turned with interest. "To you, you mean?"

"Yes."

"Well, what?"

"He took his - you know - his 'thing' out of his pants and then, oh boy, this is really crazy, he did something to it and..."

Lucille leaned close, grinning. "Did what? What did he do, Bee?"

"He kind of shook it, then it just - you know - went whoosh! All over his pants - like he was peeing, or something."

"But - you said he did something to you?"

"His other hand, he put it into my, uh, underpants and touched my - me while he was doing this other thing." It was getting easier, and Lucille's bright interest helped. "Lu, could I ask you a question?"

"Sure. What?"

"Does what he did have anything to do with that word, the one we're not supposed to say?"

"You mean the 'F' word?"

"Yeah."

Lucille's grin faded and she looked serious. "I don't think so," she said. She took Bee's arm and they walked along in silence for a moment. "He was just playing with himself, is all. Mom says boys do this a lot. Did he do anything else?"

"No, that's all."

"If he didn't do anything else, if that was all, absolutely all he did - was it, Bee?"

"Absolutely! I got up and ran as soon as I could."

"Then I guess it doesn't have anything to do with that word. Like my Mom says, it was because he's got dirty things on his mind."

Trudging along beside her, Bee thought about what she had learned, putting yesterday's events and Lu's explanation, patchy though it was, into some kind of continuity. What seemed to be the lesson in all this was not to let a boy get so close he could act out "dirty things" in his mind. Why Joe had done what he did remained a mystery. Fun, like Lu suggested? His gravelly groan at the end surely didn't mean it was fun? Well, maybe when she was twelve she'd know more about these things. For now, file it away with other strange events in the back of her mind.

Jack was the enigma, the inexplicable presence. Nightly he returned from work, ate in silence, then sat in the big chair and listened to his radio - Rudy Vallee, Ted Weems - with eyes closed and no sign of interest or movement, until bedtime at ten o'clock.

Harriet's evaluation had the ring of truth. As a father, he wasn't very useful. Sunday afternoons parents in the neighborhood took kids to the Bronx Zoo, or to Coney Island for Nathan's hot dogs and a ride on the Ferris Wheel. Some even took the family on a ferry ride to Staten Island, for a picnic on a grassy hill. Jack did nothing much, not with Bee, not with Willa. His personal recreation took place in the speakeasy,

where his drinking money allowed him a few ponies of cheap
whiskey after work each night. On Sundays Willa ironed, cooked
dinner, and went to bed early. Before the weekends with Harriet,
family entertainment was nothing to expect or hope for. Bee
deeply envied Lucille and her brothers and sisters, who had
a busy, rambunctious family life, and on Sunday piled into their
big Essex and headed off to the countryside with noisy humor.

Watching Jack for signs of life, Bee tracked his eyes, when
they opened, to Willa and fantasized a scenario for herself.
Willa had been a rich man's daughter, kidnapped and held for
ransom in a dark cellar, maybe. Jack was the janitor, or the
caretaker, and one day he heard her moans and offered to rescue
her while the kidnappers were off somewhere, if she would marry
him. To save her life, she agreed, and they lived unhappily
ever after.

She tried this out on Lucille one afternoon as they walked
home from school.

"Really," Lucille said, with raised eyebrows. "How sad.
You're making this up, right?"

Bee sighed. "You can tell, huh?"

"Every time, with you." Lucille gave Bee's arm a poke.
"Why don't you just ask them what really happened, like how
they got married, all that stuff?"

"They'd only give me dirty looks and tell me to mind my
own business." Bee stared at her shoes, one of which had begun
to separate from its sole. "My parents don't answer questions."

"God, that's awful!" Lucille slowed, looking at Bee with

damp eyes. "Mine never stop talking about themselves, how they first saw each other at a high school dance and fell in love right on the spot, and how they couldn't wait for a wedding but eloped and found a priest and got married."

"How about inviting me to dinner, Lu? I could call Willa from your house, say I got asked to stay."

"You know my Mom, she never counts how many are sitting around the table. Sure, come on, you can help me peel potatoes."

Jack left for his warehouse job every morning at seven, carrying the lunch pail Willa had filled the night before, and rode the Flatbush Avenue streetcar down to the industrial area, a mile of warehouses and factories fanning out from the Navy Yard. The work involved ladders and heavy boxes, but he said it was nothing he couldn't handle. One winter day he fell from a high ladder, struck his skull on the concrete floor and died a few hours later at Kings County Hospital, without regaining consciousness.

From never having to give him any real attention, Bee now had to think about his dying. What was expected of her? Tears, probably. Maybe a solemn face. Harriet would wear black, of course. And Willa? How would she act at the funeral? What could his death possibly mean to her?

At Sullivan's Funeral Parlor Willa didn't cry but greeted her few acquaintances with dry eyes and a calm, bleached face. She placed a small bunch of roses on the casket, next to the giant mass of carnations Harriet had sent, and before the lid was closed she leaned in and kissed his forehead. Watching

this act, which she had never seen her mother do while he was

alive, Bee choked suddenly. Bent over her own lap, between

two strangers, she wailed without words until someone patted

her and said, "There, there, little girl. Don't cry. There,

there, he's with God now, nothing can hurt him any more." It

was one of the women who worked at the store with Willa, a nice

old lady with thick glasses and heavily powdered cheeks.

Bee lifted her head and cried into the kind face above her:

"He didn't give a damn about God! And I'm not crying for him

anyway!" She jumped out of her seat and ran to the back of

the room and stood behind the chairs with her eyes on the floor

until it was over and the mourners filed past the casket and

out to waiting cars.

That afternoon Jack was put into the ground in a Brooklyn

cemetery and they all went back to Harriet's house for a funeral

supper. Bee's first experience with death, it was a revelation

to her to see how much people ate on such an occasion. The

men from the warehouse were given beer and a bottle of gin.

They ate ham sandwiches and potato salad and cake, and talked

in low voices about their work. The ladies from The Avenue

D Ladies Wear had coffee with their sandwiches, and gave Willa

wan little smiles when she looked their way. Harriet used her

best china, but not her best silver. She moved through the rooms,

insisting that everyone eat and drink, smiling, smiling, smiling.

After the clean-up she drove Willa and Bee back to their

apartment. She offered to stay a while but Willa said No, she would be all right.

Bee was glad when Harriet left, wanting, for some reason she hadn't examined, to be alone with her mother. Willa looked fragile, suddenly. Her face was pale, her eyes without light, darting here and there, looking through things, not at them. She walked around the living room touching surfaces, stroking the back of a chair, patting a cushion, smoothing a doilie, stopping to look out the window at the cold Brooklyn street where darkness had begun to blur the edges of buildings.

When Willa stood quietly for a minute before the old blue chair that had been Jack's, Bee did something she had never thought of doing in all her twelve years. She put an arm around her mother's shoulders, clumsily, and their cheeks just touched. Neither spoke. The day ended, finally, over teacups at the kitchen table, in silence.

The year Jack died at 44 years of age, when Willa was evicted from the flat for failure to pay the rent, Bee went to live with Harriet and was given one of the small attic rooms for her bedroom.

Having disposed of the shabby furniture in the apartment and sold the piano for $20 to a local church, Willa found a furnished room in Manhattan and a job at Gimbel's department store.

The goodbyes took place at Harriet's.

"You'll like living with me all the time, won't you?" Harriet's voice was soft, not her usual strident tone, appropriate to the gravity of the occasion.

Bee looked at Willa, standing at the front gate with a bulging paper shopping bag and an ununreadable look in her eyes. "Sure," she said, and tilted her cheek tentatively in case her mother felt moved enough by this separation to offer a kiss. She didn't.

"Be good and do what you're told," Willa said, her goodbye eyes for Harriet.

"Sure," Bee said again and stared hard at the iron gate.

With an awkward sweep of her hand, Willa turned and took to the sidewalk, her last words trailing behind her. "Thank you, Harriet, thank you for this. I'll keep in touch."

Harriet and Bee went into the house, closing the heavy glass door against the memory of Jack and the reality of Willa as she marched off to do battle for survival in Gimbel's Basement. I don't belong to them any more, Bee told herself. Not to Jack, for sure, and not any more to Willa. I'm Harriet's now, maybe forever. It was not a gloomy prospect, considering the past few years of weekends. Harriet could be manipulated, was vulnerable because she admitted to caring. At the very least there would be good times, movies, restaurants, vacation trips — and not much required beyond obedience to a few rules and a general admiring attitude, with heavy thanks for what was given her.

Harriet reached into her handbag.

"An allowance?" Bee stared at the coins Harriet had dropped

into her hand. Five quarters. "Can I spend it any way I want to?"

"That's your lunch money, for school." Harriet added five dimes. "These are for carfare." She counted out three more quarters, shaking a finger playfully. "And this is spending money. Don't buy junk with it. Save it for something you'll want later on."

Willa and Jack had never mentioned an allowance. At school Bee pretended: "Oh, I spent my allowance on the movies last week," to a classmate who wanted to know why she didn't have a nickel for an Eskimo Pie.

There were shopping trips to the downtown stores: Abraham & Straus, Namm's, Loeser's, where Harriet bought her a wool skirt, sweaters, sensible shoes, a heavy coat and mittens. Bee wanted high heels, a chiffon dress, silk stockings. These ugly things, she knew, would last forever, unlike Willa's purchases which were cheap and could be depended on to wear out quickly.

Harriet enrolled her in the confirmation class at St. Andrew's and when instruction was completed, bought her a frilly white dress and a veil for the great occasion. To commemorate the event, snapshots were taken and inserted in Harriet's big leather photo album. In the pictures, Bee stood on the steps of the church, a bunch of wilting roses in her arms, a graceless, gangling 12 year old, whose mother hadn't bothered to show up for the ceremony.

Harriet closed the Tea Room in June (University students and faculty off for the summer) and they traveled to Connecticut in Harriet's new Packard, a classy blue sedan with velvet upholstery and a little glass vase for flowers at the side window. It was like riding on a cloud. They sang "Old MacDonald Had a Farm" and "My Grandfather's Clock," Harriet in a rusty alto and Bee in her wavering soprano.

The eight-room beach cottage was old and solid, weathered by winter storms from Long Island Sound, perched on a low dune sixty feet from the water. The nearest neighbor was a mile away. Harriet, an only child, had spent vacations here with her parents, in the early years of the century.

With no one her age nearby, Bee spent the weeks in Harriet's company. Unescorted exploration in the dunes or along the shore was discouraged, although Bee argued her ability to take care of herself. Harriet said: "You don't know how to swim. You might drown. You might get lost. I don't want you going off by yourself. Anything could happen to you."

In shallow water, under Harriet's watchful eyes, Bee taught herself a variation of the crawl and after a while this lifted the water ban.

Together, in the July heat, they painted bedrooms and washed window screens and weeded flower beds. Harriet like to "work with my hands," she said often. "It's good honest work," and "never hurt anyone to keep busy." Bee sang "Lazybones, sleeping in the sun"... but Harriet didn't take the hint and gave her another bucket of paint and told her to put a second coat on the porch railing.

Lady Bountiful assembled her court of weekend guests after careful selection among friends and acquaintances. Willa was not among them. Because of her job, Harriet said. Bee

remembered the empty bedrooms in the house on Hendrix Street
and Willa trudging off to a furnished room in Manhattan. What
kind of friendship was this? On the surface it appeared
unremarkable, two women who had known each other since girlhood,
no strong affection but a casual, uncomplicated relationship.
What went on behind the conversations they held was a mystery.
But speculation didn't last long. There was beach to play on,
waves to run into, shells to collect and endless blue days of
summer. Flatbush Avenue and the flat where Willa and Jack had
lived their joyless lives was far, far in the past.

The Fourth of July brought the Reverend and Mrs. Carter
Plumb from St. Andrew's. Harriet, Bee understood, liked to
keep her account with God in the black. The summer invitation
was additional security.

The next weekend it was Agnes Foster, one of the elderly
teachers who patronized the Tea Room, and after that, George
and Alice Meeks, who didn't like children and wanted to sleep
until noon. They wouldn't be asked back. Breakfast wasn't
offered after 9:30, to clear the decks for the big events of
the day: cocktails at four and a lavish dinner at seven.

Bee made peanut butter sandwiches and took them to the beach
with a book and sunglasses. She liked being alone, not having
to "be seen and not heard" among the invited adults.

Occasionally Harriet joined her on the sand, venturing down
to the water in her voluminous bathing dress. Barging in, she
would float for twenty minutes, splashing idly, then back to
the cottage for a shower and a fresh cotton dress.

On a hot afternoon after a swim they sat together on the porch, fanning themselves, subdued by the heat. The latest visitors had left and five days of peace lay ahead.

Harriet was in a nostalgic mood. "When I was fifteen we spent a whole summer here," she mused as her rocker creaked and her straw fan stirred a small breeze. "My parents never went near the water, just walked along the sand fully dressed, strewing crumbs for the seagulls."

Bee stared at her. What was the point of coming here, making the long trip from the city to this house? Summer was for fun, for being outdoors in shorts, in a bathing suit, on the beach. Hard to understand people who came only to feed the seagulls. She herself was a water rat, her skin brown, nose freckled, eyes salt-rimmed. How could one not dash into the waves, float on an inner tube, blissfully, under the hot sun?

Bee offered to teach her how to swim, but Harriet said No, she hadn't come here for that. For her, the summer meant lobster dinners, appreciative guests, the "happy hours," not the sea.

Harriet lowered her fan and leaned toward Bee with a tender smile. "You like being here with me, don't you, Bee?"

"Sure."

"And you like staying with me, in Brooklyn?"

"Sure."

Harriet looked off toward the shore and resumed fanning her warm red face. "Some day I'll get old, Bee. Some day, when you're all grown up. I'll be an old, old lady."

Bee didn't like the way this was heading. People got old, but she didn't want to know how they felt about it. She wanted to go into the kitchen for a cold drink.

"Suppose I ask you if you would live with me when you grow up. Would you think about it, that is, not going off and getting married, but coming to live with me when I'm an old lady, and taking care of me? Suppose I asked you to do that?"

Here it was. Surprised that it wasn't something hard to do, something that would curtail her present freedom, Bee grinned. Years and years ahead, not anything to worry about now.

But Harriet wasn't waiting for an answer. "We could do wonderful things, Bee. Like traveling to Europe, having a fine life, just the two of us. I have all the money we'd ever need..." Her voice trailed off and she stopped fanning and looked at her lap.

It came through to Bee that this was an emotional moment, a tender subject, maybe even an embarrassment for Harriet. "I don't have any plans to get married," she said hurriedly. "I don't even have a boyfriend yet, Harriet." Was this going to be a commitment, a bounden duty? "Sounds great, traveling. And I could do the taking care. Sure, I guess I could." Anything to get that strange look off Harriet's face.

"Promise me?"

"Sure, I promise." Bee jumped up. "I'm going to get some lemonade. Want some?"

Harriet's eyes were brimming. "Sure," she said.

Chapter III

1933 - 1935

A week after her 13th birthday, Bee returned to Willa and a new kind of life began for them. They moved into a three room furnished apartment a few blocks closer to P.S. 89 than the earlier one had been. The rent was low, the place shabbier, reflecting Willa's state of mind as well as her finances. The job at Gimbel's was still her only source of income, but the year had produced a modest raise and the sewing she took in from neighborhood families enabled her to keep her small household together. From having spoken rarely to Bee about anything other than what daily necessity called for, she now communicated hardly at all and it was a surprise if a situation produced conversation. Rules of behavior having been laid down, Willa considered the topic closed to discussion and choosing the wiser course, Bee didn't challenge the curfew hours or balk at errands in the neighborhood.

Harriet had not been happy about it, raising questions about Willa's ability to provide adequately for a growing girl, mentioning expenses connected with the approaching graduation from grammar school and introduction to higher education. Willa had listened without comment and then taken Bee home with her.

Two bedrooms, a kitchen-dining room-living room comprised their quarters, with a miniscule bathroom between the bedrooms.

It was a third floor walk-up, the stairs dark and smelling of disinfectant. Bee's feelings about returning seesawed - she would miss the good times with Harriet, but she would be back in her old neighborhood, where Lucille and family lived. She had missed their friendship more than she realized. Weekends at the Hendrix Street house probably would continue for a while. The year had changed her, Willa would say "spoiled" her, but she felt no different, really, about her life and about the women who still controlled it.

In the last days before leaving, Bee received a sermon on sex from Harriet. Preliminary remarks included a half-hearted apology for taking this upon herself, her excuse Willa's up-to-now unavailability. Opening the subject seemed to exhilarate her, and she rushed through the introductory speech before sitting down opposite Bee at breakfast on the last Friday.

"I'm going to tell you about this, Bee, because forewarned is forearmed, because sooner or later some young man is going to try to talk you into something." She drew a breath, squared her shoulders and looked meaningfully at Bee. "And you need to understand what he means so you can protect yourself."

Bee broke a piece of toast into small pieces and began to butter each one carefully. Harriet's speeches were to be endured patiently, if you wanted to get on with your business. The preamble was always the same: "I'm telling you this for your own good." When one was delivered on a school morning, like today, the point might not be reached in time for Bee to catch the 8 o'clock streetcar that took her back to Flatbush and P.S.

89. She sighed and crunched a crust without looking up.

Harriet's voice deepened and she stood up dramatically. "You must never, never, let a boy touch you - down here!" She jabbed a long finger at a spot in the center of her skirt. Bee raised her eyes, mildly interested. "He'll ask you - he'll say things like, 'Want to have a party?' which is just a euphemism for asking if you'll get into bed with him. Do you understand what I'm saying, Bee?"

"No," Bee answered, "euphemism" not yet a part of her vocabulary, which had only recently expanded to include menstruation and its appurtenances. That, too, had come from Harriet, while Willa was still in her Manhattan furnished room. So now, in addition to something uncomfortable that was due to happen to her soon, there was something else, probably even more unappealing. This was growing up. It was what you had to put up with now, teen years being ahead of you. She watched Harriet's face change color and her eyes take on a brittle glitter.

"That's what married people do, in bed, at night, when they want to have a baby. It's not anything to do before you get married. Am I making myself clear?"

"But - what do they do?" Bee allowed a little impatience to dilute her respectful tone.

"It's - it means getting into bed and getting very close to your husband and letting him - getting very, very, close and then his lower parts, his - you know - yours and his come together and - that's how you make a baby."

Bee stared at her. "Is that all? Just doing that makes a baby?" This couldn't be true, this could only be another of Harriet's cautionary stories, created to subdue children and keep them on the straight and narrow.

Harriet hadn't finished. "You've got something all boys want, Bee, and you mustn't let them have it!"

Okay, this would be going on for a while yet. "What is it I have? What is it they want?"

"It's your body! They want to use you - take you and use you, and then go off and leave you!" Her voice cracked and Bee, horrified, saw sudden tears start down her cheeks. "They want your body, that's all they want!"

"My body?"

"They have that - that disgusting thing between their legs, it's all they ever think about, how to get it into you." She looked blindly down at Bee, then turned and hurried into the kitchen, and Bee heard dishes and pans rattle in the sink. Should she follow? Should she stay where she was, finish her breakfast and go to school? What was expected of her now?

Before she could decide, Harriet reappeared in the doorway holding a cup of hot chocolate. Her face was still flushed but she seemed to have pulled herself together. "Drink this - it's cold outside and this will warm your innards."

Bee took the cup silently and sipped.

Harriet sat down. "I'm sorry I got upset a few minutes ago. I didn't mean it to sound as bad as it did, really. Let's start again, shall we? Ask me some questions and I'll try to answer them."

Anxious to leave and not really wanting to hear any more "euphemisms" Bee said: "Are you talking about what people do, like when they're in love - in the movies - they kiss, only you don't see what goes on after the kissing?"

"It's what you do when you love someone, but always, always, you wait until you're married to do it. If you remember that, Bee, you'll be a virgin on your wedding night, just as you're supposed to be. Now, you can come to me if you have any more questions. Don't listen to what children at school tell you - I'll give you the right answers."

Seeing the end in sight at last, Bee said: "I'll remember what you said, Harriet."

At home, when she had helped Willa to arrange furniture and put dishes into cupboards, she compared the new information with what she had gleaned from other sources, but the understanding didn't do much to make sense out of the facts. The basic difference between boys and girls wasn't new information, but the function of the differences had only been hinted at.

A few nights later Willa said: "What's that look mean?"

"Nothing." Bee squirmed. Discomfort was a daily condition in this kitchen.

Willa was not pleased with the answer. "Nothing? Not when you give me that kind of look." She stirred something on the stove, glancing at Bee over her shoulder.

After a minute, "It's what Harriet told me."

"What."

"She told me about - it."

"It?"

"What people do, you know, to get a baby. In bed."

"Really."

They were having words again. Bee had picked up the
expression somewhere and it described what went on when they
were together. Willa didn't talk, didn't hold conversation,
and never chatted. With Bee, she had words.

"Can I go now? I have homework - "

"Tell me what she said."

"I don't want to talk about it," edging toward the door.

Very loud: "Tell me!"

No way out now. Her eyes on the floor, Bee started. When
she got past "when two people are in love and want to have a
party" Willa snorted as though she had heard the phrase before.
Bee stumbled on, hoping she had remembered it right. Then she
said: "Can I ask you a couple of questions? Like, where the
legs go? She didn't tell me that." Her face was hot.

Willa told her to stop fidgeting. "The legs take care of
themselves," she said flatly. She lifted a pot from the stove,
poured the contents into a bowl and went to the ice box.

Bolder now, because it was coming easier, Bee had another

question. "Is that why in the movies when they kiss, they never show anything more? Is that what's supposed to be going on after the kissing?"

But Willa wasn't to be deflected. "What else did she tell you?"

"I really don't - "

Very loud: "Tell me!"

"Well, she said not to let anybody - any boy - touch me any place. Something about I've got what they want and I shouldn't let them have it, stuff like that. I'd just like to know - " hurriedly, before Willa could shut her down, "if this is really true, is this exactly what people do, or is it something Harriet made up, you know, to scare me into doing what she says?"

"It's true, as far as you're supposed to know right now. When you get older, you'll find out the rest." Another swift glance over her shoulder. "How come you never asked me about this?"

"I didn't ask Harriet - she just told me."

"I see. Anything else?"

What Bee wanted to know - how all this felt while you were doing it, came too close to the area where she and Willa couldn't meet. If they stuck to facts, it was possible to keep going. Feelings and opinions were No Man's Land. Bee grumbled: "Can I go now? That's all there was."

"Go." The interview was over. Willa lit a cigarette and puffed hard.

For a short, startling moment there had been a softness in her eyes, only a flash, then hidden. Bee left the kitchen, wondering how her mother had felt during this strained, strange exchange. Did she care that Harriet had been there to talk about these things, when she wasn't? Were her feelings hurt?

After this the distance between them didn't narrow. Willa went back to being annoyed by Bee's failings and Bee went back to resenting the short shrift she received. Much later, Willa offered what amounted to detailed sex advice, coming from her: "There's no way you can get pregnant if you don't do it."

Lucille Engel's family had moved, too, and now lived in a big white house on Glenwood Road. At fifteen she was allowed to wear high heels, make-up, and flowered dresses to school. Erasmus Hall, with its racy reputation, had been declared off limits by Willa and Harriet when Bee graduated from P.S. 89. They chose Girls' Commercial High for her, all business, no boys to become distractions to study. Lu brought back tales of after-school activities and rumors of student dissipation - beer drinking, smoking in the washrooms. Lu had already dated, talked about French kisses and petting. Bee listened, shivering in admiration and awe. In her plaid wool skirt and navy blue cardigan (the remains of the wardrobe Harriet had bought her) she felt far removed from such a scene, young and raw and deprived.

Lu's mother Stella was a hairdresser and occasionally gave her a blonde rinse, the height of sophistication in Bee's eyes, an appearance she yearned for, anguished over.

"You've got to help me," she moaned. "I hate the way I look! What can I do?" She slapped at the brown jumper and white shirt, scowled at the ugly, square-toed Coward shoes Harriet had bought her recently.

"Maybe...your hair." Lu looked at her critically. "It's too straight. You need a perm."

"You know I couldn't talk Willa into that."

"Let's try something," Lu said, and went for scissors, a curling iron and bobby pins.

While Bee watched the mirror in front of her, Lu squared off bangs, then heated the iron and created a bunch of tight little curls which she brushed out and pinned back behind Bee's ears. The finished product rather resembled a dandelion gone to seed, but Bee was ecstatic.

"I can't believe it! I look at least nineteen!"

On Friday evening Lu phoned. "I've got some news, but before I tell you, you've got to promise me you'll do it."

"How can I promise if I don't know what it is?"

"It's something you'll like. You've got to start somewhere, Bee! It's a shame to waste your new hair-do!"

"What are you talking about?"

"Hold your breath. I got a date for you for tomorrow night!"

"A -   what?"

"You remember Tony, the guy I've been going with? Well,
he's got a friend and this friend asked him if he knew a good-
looking girl and Tony asked me and I said I did!"

"You're crazy, Lu! How can I - what could I tell Willa
- she wants me in the house by nine!"

"It's for tomorrow night, silly. Your mom always works
late on Saturday nights, doesn't she? The boys will come for
us at seven-thirty and we'll walk up to the Park, maybe have
a soda afterwards, you can leave a note for Willa that you're
over at my house and my mom will cover for you if she phones,
she'll say we went down to the corner for a cone or something.
Bee, you've got to do this!"

"Oh, God, Lu - " Bee breathed. "Okay, okay, but you'll
have to help me get ready."

"I'll lend you one of my dresses, and shoes, you'll look
peachy!"

Saturday at six o'clock they stood in front of the bathroom
mirror in Lu's house.

"Tell me again, Lu. How do I act? What do I say? Oh,
why did I ever say I'd do this?"

"Don't ever talk about school, it makes you sound too young.
Wait and see how he starts a conversation, and try to act
natural, like you're used to dating. You've got to do this
yourself, Bee, all I can do is point you in the right direction."
Lu dusted Bee's nose with face powder, added a round spot of

rouge to each cheek, then held out a small red box. "Here, watch me and do what I do." She took out a tiny brush, wet it under the faucet and rubbed it across the black strip in the box. "Now brush up on your lashes, that's right, look at your eyes. That's what mascara does for you!"

Make-up finally done to her satisfaction, Lu took a pale yellow flowered chiffon from the closet and laid it on the bed, then brought out a pair of patent leather shoes with Cuban heels.

When Bee looked at herself in the mirror again, she sighed. "Oh, Lu, I feel like a movie star! I can't believe that's me!"

Lucille pulled out another pastel chiffon, ducked into it and smoothed it over her hips. "Now, let me give you a piece of advice. First, when he wants to kiss you, you tell him you don't do it on the first date. He'll respect you if he's not a total boob. And second, if we go for sodas, they pay. This is a date, Bee, not just a walk in the Park with a couple of boys from the neighborhood."

Bee was rigid with anxiety. Would he be short? Would he have pimples? What could she ever find to say to him? Suppose he didn't like her. How would she get through the evening?

Finished at last, they turned and surveyed each other.

"You look like Marion Davies," Bee said. "Gorgeous!"

Lu held out a paper gardenia. "Here, pin this in your hair, and you'll look just like Claudette Colbert!"

"Yeah. and my date's going to look like Clark Gable!" Bee giggled.

They grabbed each other, shrieking with laughter.

Stella came in waving a cigarette. "You look real cute, you two," she commented genially. "But get your little fannies back here by ten or I'll have Willa banging on the front door."

When the bell rang, Stella welcomed the boys and they stepped inside, ruddy-faced and grinning.

"They'll be out in a minute," she told them. "You can wait in the living room."

His name was Jimmy Farrell. He was tall, with dark hair, no pimples, a deep voice. Bee looked up at him mutely, tried a little smile, and was rewarded with, "Pleased to meet you, Bee. Hey, that's a ritzy dress. You look swell." He poked Tony with an elbow. "How about taking these girls out for a stroll, okay?"

Crossing Flatbush Avenue, he took her hand and they walked into the summer dusk in Prospect Park. Lu and Tony, ahead by a few yards, stopped at a bench in the shadows and sat down, melted into one silhouette and nuzzled each other in silence.

What now, Bee agonized. Do we sit down too? Or do we find another bench, and am I supposed to do the same thing? No kissing, Lu had advised. What, then? Will he want to do other things? Memory of a day long ago in the Farragut Woods, Joe Payton with his searching hand. Why do boys want to touch you? And Lu's answer, My mother says it's because they have dirty minds.

Still holding hands, they sat down. He didn't seem to have any immediate plans toward intimacy but Bee remained stiffly alert.

"You go to Erasmus too?" he asked. "Like Lucille?"

Don't talk about school. But what if he brings the subject up? Nothing was going according to expectations. Well, if that's what he wants to talk about...

"Girls' Commercial, over near the Botanical Gardens," she answered. "My mom says boys would keep me from studying, so I'm going to an all girls school."

"You like it?"

"It's okay."

"What're you taking?"

"The usual - math and bookkeeping, English, typing, stuff like that."

"What d'you like best?"

Oh God, this conversation was impossible, how could he possibly be interested in what she did at school?

"Not math, for sure," she said finally, "but the rest of it isn't too bad."

"I quit before I graduated," he said, letting his arm drop around her shoulder. "I had to get a job. My old man gave me hell, said I should stick it out but I told him I wanted some money in my pocket, that was more important than any damn diploma."

"Where do you work?" The question might get him away from the subject of school.

"I deliver flowers for a shop over on Church Avenue. Got my driver's license last month, so they let me drive the truck to make deliveries. It's not a bad job. I get tips, sometimes."

Bee glanced furtively at the other end of the bench, where Lu and Tony were still wrapped around each other. No help from that direction. She was on her own, and not in charge of anything that was going on.

The arm around her shoulder stayed there while Jimmy continued talking about his job, about how some day he'd like to learn the business from inside. She murmured some encouraging words and a silence developed, grew, became uncomfortable. Then a low moan from the other end of the bench caught his attention and he tightened the arm around her and leaned in.

"I don't - " she said, but the words blurred against his lips and something warm and wet slipped past her own. She tried to pull away, twisting against him, but his arms held her and she couldn't move. Out of breath, angry and frightened, she broke away at last and jumped to her feet. "That's enough!" she yelled, wiping her mouth with a sweatered arm. "You didn't even ask!"

The two at the other end suddenly came to life.

"Hey, what's going on?"

"Nothing," Jimmy answered with a low laugh. "I just got me a little tease here, that's all."

"Lu?" Bee called, close to tears. If friendship wouldn't come to her rescue, there was only once course left. She would have to make a run for it.

"Hey, fellas," Lu's voice rose in the darkness. "We're thirsty. How about treating us to a soda?"

After a strained moment, Tony stood up and came toward them. "Fine with me. Okay with you, Jim?"

Lu came up and took Bee's hand. "Tell your friend not to rush things, okay, Tony? Bee's a nice girl, not the other kind."

On his feet now, Jimmy mumbled something by way of apology and they moved on down the path toward the lights of the Avenue, Bee keeping a careful two feet away from danger.

Refreshments softened the strain and in a lighter mood they strolled along with the Saturday night shopping crowd, looking into store windows, Lu tactfully steering talk to areas where Bee could join in. And after a while, when Jimmy took her hand and gave her a wink and a grin, she relaxed and smiled back at him.

54

Chapter IV

Willa and Harriet

1909-1918

New York City, hub of the universe, splendid with opportunity
and golden promises, beckoned to Willa McConnell, recently
graduated from Girls' High School in Brooklyn, and she answered
its call without hesitation.

July of 1909 found her job-hunting on Manhattan streets.
When she learned that work was being offered in the Personnel
Department of American Pharmaceuticals, she applied at once.
The interview with the supervisor went well.

"Are you willing to learn how to operate a typing machine?"
John Lake looked at Willa over his eyeglasses and saw a slender,
fresh-faced Irish girl with gold-green eyes and straight brown
hair pulled into a bun at her neck. She wore a crisp white
shirtwaist and a dark skirt, her hands were gloved and she
carried a small leather purse. There was a real carnation on
the brim of her straw sailor hat.

"Yes, sir."

"And will you be satisfied to work for ten dollars a week,
Miss McConnell?"

"Yes, sir." She tried not to blink at so handsome a salary.
Schoolmates who had found work behind sales counters or as
waitresses were getting along on far less.

"You'll be expected to learn the rudiments of our filing

system, as well as the typing." He pushed his chair back and stood, a tall, spare man with a kind face. He held out his hand. "Report here on Monday morning at eight. You'll have twenty minutes for lunch and the closing bell rings at six."

She was dismissed.

Triumphant, she walked past busy desks, whispering, "I have a job! I'm going to work - for a fine salary!" She ducked out the door and ran down the stairs to the street. A steady paycheck meant she could now help her mother with expenses, even have something left over for frivolity, if it tempted her. Jennie McConnell made a marginal living from ironing, sewing and occasional housecleaning jobs in her Brooklyn neighborhood. She would be glad for any help Willa could give. For her, it would be a step up from bare survival; for Willa, a step forward into the sunshine of New York City's business world. It was opportunity, adventure, a future of infinite possibility. She was tired of being poor. She would have a career, a fine life, and happiness. "I shall not go Jennie's way," she promised herself. "I shall make a name for myself, I shall be somebody!"

Willa McConnell was four days into her nineteenth year. She believed that all you had to do for the path of success to open before you was to set your feet in a forward direction.

Following Jennie McConnell's death a year later, Willa arranged with a local charity to empty the flat and turned her back on Brooklyn. Three months in a Manhattan lodginghouse, while she scraped together the money for Jennie's interment, freed her to move into a furnished room above a tailoring shop

in Greenwich Village and at last reach her primary goal - to
live independently and pay her own way.

By 1917 infinite possibility had shrunk considerably and she found
herself still at American, her work no more challenging that it had been
from the beginning. For a few years, patriotic hysteria gripped the
city, with rationing discomforts and Irving Berlin tunes inescapable.
With no personal stake in the situation, Willa watched the years run
back into each other without significant change. When she became
aware of this at 26, she told herself there was still time for
opportunity's golden doors to open. Life was long, wasn't it?

An event occurred early in 1918 that offered the chance to move up
a rung and this opened her eyes once more to the future. John Lake
had risen to a managerial position and now approached her with an offer
of promotion to assistant manager of Personnel, with a substantial
raise in salary.

"You have made yourself a valued employee, Miss McConnell," he told
her. "The firm wishes to recognize this. Let me be honest with you.
In the event you decide to make your career with us, American is
prepared to give you an office and an assistant to help with your
new responsibilities."

Willa heard the warning behind his words. Marriage and babies was
one career. Assistant Department Manager at American was another.
Choose. Her head still ringing with the promises of her own office,
her own "assistant" and, loudest of all, a raise in salary, Willa
saw no choice at all.

The promotion, however, would not be without a negative
aspect. No longer one of the "young ladies" in the clerks'

room, she would be removed from anonymity and elevated. There would be no more comfortable camaraderie, no more cozy gossip over coffee cups. Without doubt, a gap would open up between her and the women with whom she had worked for eight years. She would be one of "them," no longer one of "us." In addition, the new position carried with it the possibility that male employees in administrative jobs would not take kindly to a woman joining their ranks. Willa considered: if John Lake had reviewed these facts and decided she could handle the situation, he must have confidence in her abilities.

"Thank you for this opportunity, Mr. Lake. I'll do my best to meet your expectations." Formalities over, she walked back to her desk, avoiding the questioning eyes of her co-workers, confident that the steps she had taken so hopefully toward a bright future all those years ago were at last approaching their destination.

Willa chose a table near a window and sat down to wait for Harriet, her handbag and gloves on the other chair marking the space as reserved. The restaurant was big and drafty, with a cold tiled floor, white tablecloths and heavy utilitarian china, a working person's eating place. Cooking odors were inviting, however, and Willa was satisfied with her choice. Idly, on the steamy windowpane, she traced the words 'Assistant Manager' and drew a line under them. Then she picked up a napkin and cleared a small area. Through this little window she saw the crowded sidewalk, people in heavy coats and mufflers sliding

and slipping in the melting snow of yesterday's storm. From
each winter-pinched face warm breath rose and followed its source
out of sight.   Harriet would be dashing from her nearby office
through icy wind and slush, arriving any minute. Half an hour
for lunch. That will change, too, Willa thought as she looked
up at the clock over the cashier's counter.

The two women had kept a tenuous friendship alive since
their school days. Harriet was the product, the only remaining
one now, of a well-to-do Brooklyn family with a minor city
official or two on its roster. She had grown in youth to be
a big girl at a time when small bones and delicate features
were prized. Tall, heavy-breasted and saddled with an aggressive
nature, she developed a formidable personal charisma that
compensated for her lack of girlish charm. No one of the opposite
sex, so far, had presented himself as a possible suitor, and
now, at twenty-eight, she suspected that her chances of marrying
were slim. She had a strong, jutting jaw, piercing eyes, a
high-bridged nose and to go with these, a resonant voice that
was only marginally feminine. But she was rich, and this meant
a lot, both to her and to her contemporaries. No one mocked
her. She thought idleness a sin, and had come to Manhattan
when Willa did, to look for a job. Higher education for women
was a waste of time, she believed, and hadn't given college
a thought. A family connection had helped her find employment
and she joined the crowds of Brooklyn travelers who headed for
the city each morning.

Harriet entered the restaurant in a rush, shaking cold

fingers. "The wind goes right through you!" she announced,
settling into the vacant seat, from which Willa's handbag and
gloves had been whisked away. Harriet's fur coat, casually
draped over the back of her chair, caught Willa's attention.
Not through that, she thought and glanced at her own, a bulky
damp black thing on a peg near the door. Next year, Willa
promised herself, I too shall have a fur to throw nonchalantly
over a chair.

They chose soup and rolls from the menu and sat back.
Harriet's enthusiasm for the Howard Publishing Company, where
she was in charge of a pack of young clerks, was ebbing. She
was thinking of resigning.

"I've been there too long," she said, buttering a piece
of roll and popping it into her mouth.

Willa said: "Are you thinking about some other kind of work?"

Harriet now leaned forward eagerly. "I've been looking
into the possibility of opening a small restaurant over near
the University, a place for teachers and students to get little
cakes and sandwiches, tea and coffee." She talked on for another
few minutes, her long, big-jawed face alive, eyes glistening.

Willa listened attentively, trying to visualize her friend
in an apron slicing bread and spooning out jam.

Harriet said, "What do you think of the idea?"

Willa shook her head, smiling to soften the words. "You've
already made up your mind, haven't you? What difference could
my opinion make?"

Harriet raised her eyebrows. "Well! I think you might show

a little more interest. After all, I might even be able to
offer you a job - something to take you away from that office
drudgery you've endured all these years."

The moment had arrived. She had not known how she was going
to introduce her great good news, and suddenly Harriet had
given her an opening. "I've been offered a position as assistant
office manager," she said, lifting her voice. "John Lake's
been promoted. He's recommended me for his old job."

"How nice," Harriet said, impatient to resume.

"Harriet! I've got a future with American. If I stay with
them, who knows how high I can go?"

Harriet laughed sharply. "You're a woman, Willa. What's
your salary? Fifteen dollars a week? You don't think they're
ever going to give you a position of real authority, do you?"

Willa's spirits sank. She said peevishly, "You don't have
to dash cold water on my good news, Harriet. I think it's just
as important as your tea room."

Advantage, the undercurrent in their relationship, like
tennis, a game neither had ever played. The serve, the return,
the failure to score, the point gained. For a few strained
moments they ate soup and munched rolls, patted crumbs from
their lips, sipped water.

"When do you start your new job?" Harriet asked, no hint
of apology in her voice.

"Next Monday." None in Willa's either. "Have you picked
out a location for the tea room?"

"There's a shop for rent a block from the Square. I'm to

see it this evening, after work." Harriet picked up her story. Financing the project would be no problem, of course. She talked about food and furnishings, rent and overhead. "I do need to find someone to help out in the kitchen. I had hoped it would be you, Willa."

Willa shook her head, thinking of her future. Working as Harriet's kitchen maid was not part of her dream. "It sounds as though everything will work out fine for you. And help isn't hard to get these days."

It would be another week before they met for lunch again, and by then she would have more news and a fine new salary figure to throw into the conversation.

They finished the meal and rose to leave. No question of who would pay the cashier. They took money from their respective purses, left a modest tip and went their separate ways.

Back at her desk, Willa took up her ledgers and the afternoon waned. Mr. Lake had mentioned that he would interview applicants for the assistant's position today, and if he selected one, would bring the person to be introduced.

At three John Lake appeared, followed by a clean-shaven young man with dark hair slicked to his skull and a confident smile on his face.

"Miss McConnell, this gentleman's name is Merriwether Jordon. He has accepted the position we spoke about last week and will start work with you on Monday." His mouth bent into a smile.

Willa got up with a confused glance at both men, then remembered her business manners in time to shake hands with the new employee.

"Miss McConnell, may I make a request?" The young man's
grin held as a couple of seconds ticked by. "Merriwether gave
me a lot of trouble back in my school days. I try to get
everyone to call me Jack now. Middle name's John."

Mr. Lake nodded at Willa. "I think we can make that
accommodation," he said. "If you'll see me in my office, Miss
McConnell, when you've had a word with - ah - Jack, here, we
can go over your new duties."

It was an uncomfortable five minutes for Willa. Expecting
a girl, younger and far less experienced than herself, she felt
misgivings about this good-looking, anything but ill-at-ease
young man. He seemed anxious to display his abilities, mentioned
other positions he had held, told her his age - twenty eight
- and his marital status - single - and why he had accepted
the job when it appeared he had earned better wages previously.

"I've worked in commission sales for the last three years.
Shoes, dry goods. I think it's time to raise my sights toward
a business career." With a casual wave of his hand he finished,
"Some time in the future I'll be thinking of settling down,
finding a wife, having a family..."

Willa sat back as the speech ended. "Jack Jordon, is it?"
she said dryly. "Is there bookkeeping in your background?"

"Yes ma'am. And figuring payrolls, and filing, and I can
make coffee, too, if that should be your pleasure."

"I plan for you do a little of everything for a while,"
she said, resisting his blandishing tone, "until the job develops

a routine and we see whether you can cut the mustard."

Jack Jordon put his hand out again. "Miss McConnell, ma'am, I plan to do everything I can to earn your good opinion." The words were ingratiating, the confident smile still in place. "And may I say, you're the prettiest boss I've ever had!"

Willa pretended not to see his outstretched hand and turned away. Without a break in his cheekiness he bowed deeply and walked away, down the long room to the stairway, with a swing and a swagger that made her even less pleased with the way things were working out.

From the beginning, Jack's goal was conquest of Willa. He used whatever came to hand. If she dropped something, he rushed to pick it up. If he could anticipate a need, he was there to fill it. When work kept her at her desk through lunch or after six, he saw to it that she got refreshment. A cup of tea would appear at her elbow, with a small biscuit. Once a bag of chocolates was left for her with a note: "Sweets to the sweet." At his own desk outside Room 324 he did his work. He was quick to learn and eager to please. Grudgingly, she conceded this point. How he dressed and managed to lead a man's life on what they paid him, she had no idea. Since Willa was now out of the big room and away from its gossip, she heard nothing of how other employees saw him. Occasionally she caught sly glances turning to follow them if they walked together through the room to another office, and she knew it should have amused her, but it didn't. *Very soon* she knew he would be a danger. He was persistent, single-minded and unshakable in his intentions.

Passing her in a corridor, he would manage to brush against her sleeve. Bringing her a cup of coffee, he would linger a shade too long, looking down at her while she worked. He stood daily at the door when she left, to open it and follow her down the stairs and out onto the pavement. And his "Goodnight, Miss McConnell" always had more in it than a simple farewell. His eyes, above the unwavering smile, sought hers whenever they were together and this became her greatest problem - how to work with this man and ignore the purpose radiating from him every minute.

He waited a week before asking.

"Miss McConnell, there are a few things about this work I'm still not sure about. May I invite you to lunch so we can talk?"

Her immediate refusal brought only a wider smile and left her with a feeling of uncertainty. Had she been less than businesslike? How far could she go, officially, to keep him in his place? He had to be discouraged. But how? She found herself regretting the curt response, but knew it would have little effect on his brashness.

A week later Jack tried again, with an invitation to a vaudeville performance. Once more, he didn't succeed. She said she had a previous engagement. A few mornings after that she found a pot of geraniums at her desk when she arrived, with a note attached:

> If I have offended, my apology is sincere.
> My intentions are honorable, my admiration is
> genuine. My hope is to demonstrate all of the
> above.

This is what happened. Jack slipped into Room 324 as Willa

relaxed into a smile.

He took her to a restaurant a few blocks from the office, and they ate broiled lamb chops with mint jelly and mashed potatoes. She felt uncomfortable, edgy, while he pressed her with further information about himself, his ideas, his feelings about the work he was doing, and finally his desire to see her socially, away from American Pharmaceuticals.

"Jack," she said wearily. "If you are looking for a companion, I'm not the one." She met his eyes squarely. "You're a bright young man. I'm sure you can see why I feel this way. My job is just beginning to move upward and I don't want to do anything to jeopardize it. I've got plans for my future, and they don't include a friendship, or whatever you want, with you."

He looked away for the first time. There was silence between them. He drank coffee, she twisted a napkin. Then he sighed. "You're a very smart, very pretty and very dedicated lady, Willa. Please - let me call you that. I won't do it in the office. I'd just like to get to know you." He held up his hand as she started to speak. "Lunch now and then, maybe a show - " His smile was back in place, jaunty as ever.

She looked down at her hands, folded the napkin and patted her lips with it. "Let's finish our lunch. I don't want to discuss this any further right now. And please," she wasn't smiling, "try to behave yourself in the office. If Mr. Lake should notice what's going on -- "

"I'll be as good as gold," he said. Reaching across the

table, he took her hands in his. "I'll stay in my place, Miss McConnell, while we're at work. But I plan to do my best to persuade you to change your mind about the rest of it."

She thought about him, at home in her room over the tailoring shop, and admitted reluctantly to herself that he was amusing, even charming in a way. But she refused to admit that his hands were warm and his eyes challenging and that something stirred in her whenever she met them. The possibility that she was beginning to like him was firmly rejected. There was no way she could fit him into her plans. He represented failure. If she listened to his blandishments, she would end up as Jennie had, in a cold water flat.

Now the rare occasion when she capitulated and they had lunch together developed a dangerous aspect. Once he put his arm around her as they walked along Fifth Avenue. She shook it off. He held her hand, until she snatched it away. He did his work adequately, if not as enthusiastically as at first. His attention appeared unfixed, he side-stepped minor duties and followed her with his eyes whenever she was near. She debated with herself about putting a firm end to their meetings, and while she was thinking about this, someone saw them leaving the building together, his arm through hers, and gossip reached John Lake. This frightened her.

She was confused. At twenty-seven years of age, sex was largely a mystery. She believed, however, that its urges could be controlled by a resolute effort. With a steadfast refusal, the next time he asked, she tried to convince both of them that he was being kept at arm's length. He grinned at her, standing in front of her desk, when she delivered a fierce ultimatum.

"If you keep this up, Jack Jordon, I'll have to tell Mr. Lake you're stepping out of line."

Instead of answering, he turned and closed the office door.

"What are you doing?"

He came back and put his hands on the desk and leaned in. "Willa, I'm going to ask you and keep asking you until you give me the right answer. Will you marry me?"

"Oh, my God..." She put her head in her hands. "Jack - don't do this - open the door and go away!"

Now all Willa's pride in her new position, her confidence in the brightening future, began to dim.

"I really don't deserve to be treated this way," he told her. "I'm in love with you -- "

"Be quiet!"

" - is that a crime?"

She got up and with a rough shove against his chest, went to the door.

He turned. "Second, I've kept my attentions out of the office. You'll have to give me credit for that."

She glared at him. "Stop it!"

He was grinning again. "I can't. Every time I'm near you I want to reach out and take you in my arms."

"Stop it!"

"And third -- "

"Get out!"

* * *

*   *   *

"What a nice surprise!" Jack said.

Willa and Harriet looked up from their chicken salad to see him standing beside them, hat in hand, his eyes for Willa only. She knew the rush of warmth to her cheeks would not slip by Harriet.

"Ah...."

"Miss McConnell, ma'am. Isn't this a coincidence! I didn't expect to see you here at Mulvaney's." He glanced toward Harriet who, fork on way to mouth, watched with interest.

No way to avoid it. "Miss Frost, this is my assistant at American, Merriwether Jordon." There was perverse pleasure in broadcasting the name he preferred to forget.

Harriet nodded and gave him a brief smile, then looked at Willa. "And where have you been keeping him these past weeks?" she said under her breath.

Willa ignored the sly comment and said firmly: "There's a stack of attendance records on my desk. Do you think you could get them in order before I return, Merriwether?"

His eyes laughed at her. "Why of course, ma'am. I'll do it right away." And he took off briskly, whistling.

"Merriwether?" Harriet said. "I hope he has a nickname."

"He wants to be called Jack. And he has a lot of nerve, believe me." Willa hoped she sounded disparaging but something in Harriet's expression told her it wasn't coming off. "He's becoming a real nuisance," she said, and bent over her salad.

"Nice looking nuisance."

"Handsome is as handsome does, my mother always said."

"He seems cheerful and friendly. Is he any help with those dreary departmental records?"

"Yes."

Harriet appeared to be waiting for more than a monosyllable.

After a minute Willa said: "He's been bothering me, pestering, for weeks. He won't leave me alone!" She felt the blush coming again and wished she knew how to handle a situation like this. "I made the mistake of having lunch with him, well, once or twice and after that -- "

Harriet's eyes sharpened. "You've been going out with him?"

"It's not like that at all. He can't take no for an answer. I went to lunch with him just to shut him up, don't you see?"

Harriet stared at her for a moment before she said: "That doesn't make much sense, now does it, Willa?"

Willa wrapped the start of a smile in her napkin. "No, I guess it doesn't." She met Harriet's gaze with a deep frown. "I'm not going to be his 'girl' or anything like that. I can't let the likes of Jack Jordon figure in my plans."

This seemed to satisfy Harriet and they finished lunch and parted on the sidewalk. But the chance meeting started a train of speculation that was obvious by her questions from time to time. "Are you still seeing that Merriwether chap?" she would inquire, eyes on her plate.

Bristling, "Not any more than I can help."

Another time: "Anything new with Merriwether - I mean, Jack?"

"Harriet, can't you forget about him?"

"He's a nice fellow, good-looking, you could do worse."

"I'm not going to 'do' anything with him, least of all think about him seriously."

"Bring him next Friday for dinner at my house. A few friends are coming from the office for a farewell dinner. I plan to resign the end of the month to get the tea room started."

"I'd much rather come alone."

"Nonsense. Everyone else will come with an escort. You'll stick out like a sore thumb." She tapped Willa's wrist. "There's safety in numbers, Willa. He'll be far less of a bother in a crowd than by himself. Besides," she now looked at her own hand, and quickly lifted it from Willa's, "I think he's rather nice. Maybe I'd like to know him better..."

Willa looked up in surprise. "You?" she said before she realized how the bare pronoun sounded.

Harriet said only: "Come about eight, both of you. I'm serving sherry before dinner."

I'm making a mistake, if I ever hope to shake him off. Then again, later, in her room before bedtime, Why am I doing this? Why don't I just stand up to her and tell her I'm coming by myself? Then, out loud: "I'm not going to get tied up with someone like Jack Jordon! Not now, not ever!"

In the office on Monday morning, Jack received a phone call from Harriet, inviting him to escort Willa to dinner at the Hendrix Street house. He accepted with enthusiasm. Feeling as though she were the victim of a conspiracy, Willa slept restlessly the next few nights, dreaming she was undressed, grabbing at curtains to hide behind while someone who looked like Jack Jordon watched, grinning, from the sidelines.

On Friday when Jack came to her door carrying a tiny bouquet of violets, she frowned at him, got her coat and, for the moment, gave up the fight.

An evening at Harriet's was a staged event. She appeared in magenta velvet and bugle beads, dark hair piled high, pearls over her bosom, and moved majestically through the rooms greeting her guests. The sherry was imported, the menu elaborately French and the silver and china heirlooms from past generations of Frosts. There was an aproned maid to serve, hired for the occasion, and crystal candelabra on the long dining table. Alice, the new young housekeeper, presided over the wine and hors d'oeuvres in the formal parlor. The guests stood with glasses in hands and chatted in low voices, smiling cosily when Harriet passed among them. The scene that Willa and Jack came into reflected Harriet's past and her future, and both appeared to provide her with deep satisfaction. Mr. Bardini, whose rental property would become Harriet's Tea Room, had come with his wife and his attorney, and the talk at one end of the room was all facts and figures.

Willa wore peach chiffon, an extravagance she had felt was justified when the promotion had brought with it the promised raise. She was, in Jack's breathless words, "pretty as an Irish spring!" He gave up after several attempts to hold her hand during the evening and appeared content to feast his eyes on

her face. On her way to the powder room, Willa saw Harriet
take him in tow, her arm through his, and introduce him to the
rest of the gathering. Moving at her side among the guests,
Jack was obviously enjoying himself.

74

His face glowed, his glance was bright and sharp and when he
looked at Harriet there was just the right amount of reverence
in his eyes. Like a pet poodle, Willa thought irritably, he's
trotting along beside her and wagging his tail.

During dinner he whispered to Willa: "This must have cost
a fortune!"

She gave him a chilly smile and turned to talk to the man
on her left.

At eleven they said goodbye and walked the three blocks
to the elevated line that would take them back to Manhattan.
Twice during the wait for the train Jack tried, and somewhat
succeeded, in giving her a fervent kiss: once on the cheek,
the next time on the neck, having missed her lips when she turned
impatiently away.

"Please don't, Jack." Even in her own ears, it didn't sound
like displeasure. She was weary, had drunk too much sherry
and the wine during dinner had been poured liberally. She pushed
against him, but in the swaying car   found it impossible
not to lean against his shoulder as her eyes drifted closed.
He said nothing, but sat quietly, holding her as she napped
beside him. It was midnight when they arrived at her doorstep.
When she extracted her key from her purse he took it and unlocked
the street door. Inside, he followed her up the stairs to the
second floor and again unlocked the door, then moved aside to
let her enter.

She wasn't quick enough. Inside the dark room, before she
could push him away, he pulled her fiercely against him and

covered her face with kisses.

Her protest was faint. "No, Jack - don't - "

His hands fumbled at her clothes, he moved her back with a force she couldn't resist and they fell on the bed. Now she fought him, but randomly, as his rough strength cancelled her efforts. She cried out, but he covered her mouth with his hand and whispered: "Don't fight me, Willa, please - please - sweet girl - I've wanted you for so long - " His breath was hot and smelled of wine and his voice was choked. "You can't go on saying no forever - "

"Don't!" She believed she was screaming but the sound was a moan, and when it died he had managed to pull the peach chiffon away and his hands were working her undergarments loose. She shoved against him frantically, but it was useless. Twisting in his arms, she reached for something to strike with - a book, a lamp, anything. He caught her arms, pinning her to the bed and his mouth came down on her breasts hungrily, his tongue stroking her nipples. The sensation left her breathless, unable to move. Then he was over her, his own clothes undone, his body hot against her. She gasped. "No - no!"

He forced her knees apart. .
"Let me do this, Willa, you have to let me - "

Then a kind of darkness came over her, vision blocked, cries stifled, as he thrust himself into her with a tremendous surge. Briefly, she whimpered beneath him then stopped fighting and, unconscious of the act, put her arms around his heaving body. When he burst inside her she finally screamed, in ecstasy and fear and loathing.

For two days she barely moved, leaving her bed only to use
the toilet. She ate nothing, drank a little water and went back
to bed. It was as though waking would make it all happen again.
She pulled the covers up to shield her eyes from daylight and
slept, dreaming she heard a voice: "I'm sorry, I never meant
to hurt you, I'm so sorry..." In sleep her mind suffered and
awake her body hurt. Once, she thought she heard the doorbell
ring but violent dreams blanketed the sound.

On Sunday night she got up and warmed some soup on the hot
plate and cut a slice of bread. With cup in hand she pulled
a chair up to the small metal table near the window and gathered
her wits together. Common sense told her she would survive.
The experience, in one form or another, was one most females
underwent when they matured. Done roughly or with tenderness,
the first time was a physical shock. She had known she was
struggling to preserve something precious, and when that proved
ineffective, she expected pain and humiliation. She was totally
unprepared for orgasm. No word had reached her, from Jennie
or any female friend, to tell her of such a thing. In subsiding,
it had left her limp, and when he lifted himself and began to
gather his clothes, she shuddered, a long, total body tremor
that couldn't be controlled. Then she had wept, her face in
the pillow, overwhelmed with shame and misery, with no way to
understand why she had been unable to fight him, or why she
had, at the end, embraced his body and given up the struggle.

Thoughts surged painfully as she drank the soup and swallowed the dry bread. Where, along the way, could she have escaped from him? A dozen times, surely. What had come over her? How could she have allowed this to happen? The only answer that fit the facts was one she refused to face.

Before leaving for work on Monday morning, she made a solemn vow. Jack Jordon, if indeed he showed his guilty face, would be treated with the contempt he deserved. There was only one way to handle things now. She must make his life in the office unbearable and force him to leave. It was unthinkable that he should remain and continue to harass her.

He was at his desk outside Room 324 as usual, and to her consternation, had no trouble meeting her eyes. Rather, something newly confident radiated from him. She walked into her office and shut the door. At 9:30, when he stuck his head in to ask what her orders were, she supplied them calmly in frigid voice. It was four o'clock before he managed to get a private moment with her.

He came with a fistful of papers and put them in front of her. "Willa, I was a brute. I sincerely apologize, I really didn't mean to - "

"Apologize! As though you'd trod on my foot?" Her voice shook. She stood and faced him, rage choking her. "You stay away from me, Jack Jordon. Don't come anywhere near me unless it's strictly office business. Do you understand?"

It was his turn to show discomfort. He flushed, then leaned in over the desk. "Willa, don't you see? It was like a commitment, a promise. You've got to marry me now!"

"You - are - a - monster!" she spat at him. "You don't
know what you're saying. I will never give one minute's thought
to marrying you! If you ever mention it again, I'll have you
thrown out of this office!"

"You can't mean that." His face was pale, a hard stubborn
look in his eyes.

She came around the desk. "I want you out of here - and
out of my life. Now!"

He moved back a few inches finally, then turned and walked
out.

She got through the week, each day a little easier than
the one before. He said "Good morning, Miss McConnell" and
"Good night," but otherwise made no attempt to approach her.
That his eyes, dark and sullen, followed her was beyond her
control. She felt relieved, reprieved, as though she had been
let out of prison. When she caught a glimpse of his face, it
was stony. He stayed at his desk, did a minimum of work and
spoke to no one. But he left her alone.

In the middle of the following week she met Harriet for
lunch at Mulvaney's. They had corned beef and cabbage and
Harriet talked about the opening of the Tea Room. Willa listened,
made appropriate comment, and did not mention Jack. After a
while Harriet brought the subject up.

"Your young man behaved very nicely at my dinner party,"
she began. When Willa said nothing, she went on. "Everyone
found him pleasant. He made very flattering remarks to me about

the house and the dinner." She speared a piece of beef and put it in her mouth. After a moment of chewing, she said: "Did you two get home all right? I mean, did you have a long wait for the train?"

"We had no trouble. We were back in the city by midnight."

"And did he - ?"

"He just took me home, Harriet." Willa didn't try to hide her irritation. "It was late, he took me to my place. Did you think we went carousing after we left Brooklyn?"

"Well! I'm sorry I asked," Harriet said. A few more minutes of eating and napkin work. "Is it - are you still seeing him?"

"If you mean are we going together, the answer is emphatically no!"

"I think you're making a mistake. He's charming, lively, good company. And very good-looking. And anyone can see he's interested in you."

"I don't want to talk about him. And I don't care a fig about his 'qualifications.'" Willa picked up her check, ready to leave.

It was two weeks later on Friday evening as she was about to put on her coat that she received a telephone call at her desk.

Without preliminary, Harriet said: "Willa, I want you to be the first to know this." A moment of strained silence, then: "Jack and I are going to be married."

The monologue that followed made only minimal sense to Willa, who listened, stunned, and tried to fit pictures to Harriet's

words. Jack had asked her help in persuading Willa to change
her mind, but Harriet had told him such a result was unlikely,
that Willa's decision was firm. "He was very angry with you,"
she said. "For some reason he believes you care for him and
that you'd come around. I told him I didn't think it would
ever happen."

Willa gasped. Then Jack hadn't told her the truth. The
shameful event was still a secret.

Harriet waited, but when Willa said nothing at all, she
continued. "This isn't easy for me to say, Willa, but I'll
try. I've said before that I thought him attractive, and if
you got the idea that I was taken with him, you were right.
Even knowing how he felt about you, and still feels about you,
I did something -- I asked him if he would consider me a
substitute."

Willa was speechless. Such a development had never, in her
most fanciful imaginings, occurred to her.

"He didn't really seem to be shocked. And after a while
he said he'd think about it, that he really liked me, that maybe
it could work out. I said my income could support us both,
that the tea room was going to be a success, we could manage
it together..." Her voice had grown thinner and Willa heard
beneath the words how painful the confession was. But stranger
than the news itself was what it revealed about Harriet's
intimate fears: that she was not attractive to men, that since
none had come forward up to now to court her, a future as a
spinster appeared certain. That Jack Jordon had stepped into

Harriet's 29-year-old life from such a circuitous path was unfortunate, and with her memory of immediate past events, Willa saw the chances for happiness with Jack as very slim. It didn't appear, however, that Harriet would welcome advice now, leaving little to say.

"When - ?"

"We're going to Connecticut on Saturday." The difficult part over, Harriet talked fast. "We'll get married in New Haven and stay there a few days. I can't be away any longer because the tea room opens in two weeks."

"Harriet - I need to know - will he come back to work, or is he quitting his job here?"

"He's going to tell John Lake today that he will resign. Jack will be a big help getting my business started, Willa, he's really a very smart man." The last words were wistful, not Harriet-like. Neither spoke for a minute.

Then Willa said: "Do you really care for him?" It was the only thing she could think of to say.

"Yes, I really do."

"Then I wish you good luck." She put the receiver back on the hook and sat for a long time looking into a corner of the room, while her feelings and memories sorted themselves into a hopeless tangle and she had to get up and go for a walk in the park to clear her mind.

The Sunday morning ride out to Brooklyn started below ground,
then emerged into sunlight and the string of cars made its
elevated way over the warehouses and tenements and on east.
Willa watched the backyard scenes pass as the train lurched
and rattled, pulling into platforms and out haltingly, a trainman
calling out the stations in a bored voice. There were few
passengers. She sat at a window, hands in her lap. It was
chilly in the car, the trainman often forgot to close the door
after leaving the last station. She hardly felt the cold, or
saw the people getting on and off, her thoughts   running
ahead of her, to the big red house on Hendrix Street.

At Van Siclen Avenue she left the train and walked the three
blocks quickly. Harriet's house sat back behind its iron gate
and high bushes, aloof from meaner residences that had over
the years gathered around the old mansion. Harriet's windows
were always draped, giving the house a huffy, look-down-the-
nose air, like an elderly dowager before a crowd of riffraff.

Willa opened the gate and carefully closed it after her.
She climbed the steps to the wide columned porch, rang the
doorbell and steadied herself with a gloved hand on the jamb.
Alice, the housekeeper, admitted her, smiled a welcome and went
to notify Harriet of her arrival.

It was cold in Harriet's parlor. The room was never heated

unless 'company' was expected. With its high white ceiling,
pale Chinese carpet and mauve draperies the room seemed an
appropriate setting for Harriet's life, a frame for the things
she held most dear. There were so many cold marble surfaces,
so much plush and chilly blue velvet. Willa sat on one of the
brocade side chairs, erect, like a sparrow poised for flight,
and waited for Harriet to come down into her queendom and learn
how her life was to be changed.

There was the sound of firm steps in the hallway and Harriet
arrived, a violet fragrance trailing her into the parlor. Today
she wore a gown of pale lavender wool with a white lace collar
and long fitted sleeves. She looked regal.

All she needs is a tiara and a scepter and she could pass
for Queen Mary, Willa thought testily. Harriet squared her
wide shoulders and paused with one hand on the back of a chair,
smiling.

Willa stood. Her voice steady, she announced: "I'm in the
family way, Harriet. I want you to divorce Jack so he can marry
the mother of his child."

It happened in the eyes before the smile could adjust.
A look of steel and anger. In the silence they both breathed
heavily.

"So. You do want him, after all."

"I don't want him any more than I did before. But I will
not be mother to a bastard." She spoke the words with no sense
of melodrama. It was a straightforward statement of intention,
sounding correct and proper in her own ears.

Harriet's voice rose. "Why didn't you think of that before you got into bed with him?"

Willa sat down again, feeling slightly dizzy. "Is that what he told you? That we just went to bed together?" She hadn't thought this would be easy, and the nausea of early pregnancy cancelled any small advantage Harriet's anger might have given her. "Harriet - Jack took me against my will, by force!"

Harriet blinked, then surprisingly took a step back and sat down on the cherrywood sofa. Behind her pinched expression she seemed to be making a rapid course reversal. Suddenly her chin trembled and a frightful smile grew on her face. She leaned forward. "He's no good, Willa. He won't be any better for you than he's been for me. He doesn't care about anyone but himself and how he can use people for his own ends. He's a selfish, miserable excuse for a man, and all that pretty front is - is just a sham, a fake." The words now tumbled out of her, a spillway out of control. "I've learned about his life before he went to work at American, about the woman he lived with, who gave him money, paid him to be her companion. He bragged about the life he'd had, all he had to do was visit her bed once a week. Until she threw him out."

Willa was very pale. She hardly heard her own words. "Did he marry her?"

"No more than he married me," Harriet answered bitterly. "It's been a lie. We never got married in New Haven, we've just lived together these past three months. Willa - " She reached for Willa's hand, then drew back quickly. "I told him he'd never have to work again, that I had money enough for all our needs, and why should he suffer rejection when he could have a fine life, with me. He said we'd tell everyone we had eloped, gotten married out of town, while he thought it over." Her voice cracked and she angrily pulled a handkerchief from her sleeve. "I should have known that all this was just to punish you, Willa. To make you relent. That was why he wouldn't go through with the marriage. He thought he could still find a way to change your mind."

Willa's hand shook as she touched Harriet's arm gently, without speaking.

"He's a weak selfish man, Willa, and you'll be making a terrible mistake if you think he'll be a decent husband or father."

"I have no choice."

Harriet said sharply, "Of course you do. You don't have to have this baby. There are ways - "

The answer was flat. "Never."

"Then you're a stupid fool!" Her eyes blazed.

Willa stared at her hands, limp in her lap. "I know. But it's what I have to do."

"You'll lose your job, you'll have the same awful life Jennie had. Jack will never be a provider, you and the baby will end up just as your mother did, in a tenement somewhere..."

"I could have fought him." She looked up, her eyes lifeless. "I could have found a way to stop him. I didn't. I let it happen. Now I have to take my medicine."

"Dear God!" Harriet wailed. "You'll be sorry for the
rest of your life!"

Now they held onto each other, feeling for the first time in
their lives a sorrow and sympathy that was genuine and a revelation
to both women. After a long anguished moment, Harriet drew
back.

"Well, then, let's be practical. You're going to be a mother.
You're going to be poor, that's certain."

Willa smiled bleakly. "I don't think I'm cut out to be
much of a mother, Harriet. Least of all to Jack's child."

"So, there are provisions to be made. I have the money
to take care of everything you'll need, when the time comes.
And since it's not likely now that I'll have a chance at
motherhood myself, I'd like to propose a plan to you."

Willa married Jack at the marriage license bureau in
Manhattan City Hall two weeks later. He was elated, accepting
her reversal as the right and desired outcome of his choices.
He promised to find a good job at once so they could move into
an apartment of their own and start life as a proper married
couple. For Harriet he now showed open contempt, and explained
his side trip into her bed as the result of a broken heart.
Willa, in refusing him (he said) had driven him into another's
arms. Hearing this tale, Willa's last nagging doubts were
swept aside. He could be dealt with, single-mindedly.

On their wedding night, suffering pregnancy's discomforts

and with the memory of its origin vivid in her mind, Willa lay on the bed in her furnished room and endured Jack's husbandly performance, dry-eyed and in silence. This time there was no orgasm.

Chapter V

1937-1941

After Jack's death Willa, always thin, grew thinner, coughed a lot and her face became pale and waxy. Bee suggested she stop smoking, that it might get rid of the cough. Willa's answer was "Mind your own business," and the next time Bee saw her there was a cigarette in her hand.

"Why won't she give it up?" Bee asked Harriet. They were chopping apples and dates for a Thanksgiving pie. The kitchen smelled wonderfully of cloves and cinnamon, oranges, cranberries and sweet pickles.

"Willa has been stubborn all her life," Harriet said. "Once she's set on something, there's no changing her mind. No way at all."

Bee sniffed. "That's stupid. How about if you talk to her?"

Harriet turned away abruptly and wiped her hands on a towel. "Finish this while I roll out the pastry. And just forget about getting your mother to change her ways. I tried, Bee. I tried. It didn't work."

89

Graduation Day, June 1937. After the ceremonies Harriet
hosted a dinner at Papa Vittorio's, enhancing the occasion
with a bottle of chianti. At eight she drove them back to the
apartment where she emptied out a suitcase of gifts for Bee.
When she left, Bee gave her appropriate thanks and waved her
car down the street, then turned to her mother.

Willa's look was direct and without apology. "There's a
good movie up on the Avenue," she said. "I'll treat."

A graduation gift? There was no way she could have bought
a fraction of what Harriet had dumped on the bed - a wool
cardigan, silk stockings, a handsome leather pocketbook, two
pairs of goves and a jazzy make-up kit that Bee had been eyeing
for some time. It was the invitation that was important.
Willa's gesture was to be respected.

"I've got enough for a soda afterwards," Bee told her mother.
They put on sweaters and walked up to Flatbush Avenue. The
film was a Jeannette MacDonald and Nelson Eddy romance,
"Maytime," and it made an opportunity for a few needed tears.
It had been an eventful day. There were goodbyes to friends
and a couple of teachers who had liked her and helped her
through bad times with math and bookkeeping. And there was her
graduation dress, made by Harriet's seamstress, far too elaborate
and expensive. The looks from the other girls told Bee what
they thought of it. And at last, the prospect of being free,

90

turned loose on the world, where her own choices would determine her life. She was out of their hands - Willa, and teachers, Harriet, rulemakers and principals. The thought was a heady one.

The night was warm and they strolled in a strain-free silence. Not close like friends, but in step at least. Willa smoked as she walked but tonight Bee decided not to notice.

At Loft's there was a wait for two seats at the soda fountain. Willa used the time for another cigarette, and Bee stared at the candy display in the window. White boxes and little plastic brides in lace. June was for beginnings. Also for endings. Childhood officially over, there was no need for a Momma any longer. Was there any chance her mother might want a friend?

"What comes next?" Willa asked when they were seated and had ordered black-and-whites.

As a woman-to-woman opening, it was exhilarating. Bee said: "Get a job, of course."

They sucked straws, not looking into the mirror behind the counter where eyes might meet. Traditionally, it was the only way they had ever managed a conversation, talking to a plate or a newspaper or a wall.

"What kind of work are you thinking about?"

"Anything to earn a buck." It was the wrong answer, of course.

"That's no way to talk," Willa said sharply. "And don't be so flip about something as important as earning a living."

"Well," Bee said into her soda, "Harriet's given me a couple
of names, places to go and put in a job application. Clerical.
Even if I took the right courses in school, I still don't have
any experience, so I'll have to start at the bottom."

"No college ideas, then?"

"No." Did Willa have any ideas on the subject? No one
in her family had gone to college, and it had never been talked
about when Jack was alive. Another four years of educational
incarceration, however, held no appeal for Bee. As it had to
Willa, New York City called her to escape from "the sticks,"
from the stigma of living in the tenements of Brooklyn.

The evening ended and they walked home, in a silence that
held no threat or criticism. They said goodnight at their bedroom
doors and that was it. Graduation Day was over, for better
or worse.

A week later, when an interview at the Metropolitan Life
offices (arranged by a friend of Harriet's) resulted in a job,
Bee made up her mind to move out and begin living her own life.
Willa would get along. She still worked behind a counter -
Gimbel's was years in the past, but she had been hired by another
neighborhood ladies' wear emporium - and without the need to
support a daughter, her income would stretch a little farther.

Final separation could be handled without shock and certainly
without tears.

Lucille, also job-hunting, found work a few weeks later
and because it made sense on their small salaries, the two girls

became roommates. Bee had found a furnished 1½ room "studio"
on the third floor of a New York brownstone that had weathered
the Depression with visible scars, namely a speakeasy-turned-
bar-and-grill on the ground floor. Saturday nights would provide
raucous entertainment that summer, as fights broke out among
the patrons, spilling into the street, with drunken shouts and
obscenities echoing at the edge of the action. The neighborhood
was nondescript, a featureless Manhattan street with dingy store
fronts, trash in the gutters, pigeons, and grimy kids playing
stick ball. For a few dollars more they had been able to get
the front studio, a mistake soon realized when hot weather made
open windows imperative. Dust and noise and odors characterized
the neighborhood, and came freely into their small space.

Counteraction was called for. With their first paychecks
they bought slipcovers from a Hester Street pushcart for the
two shabby daybeds, salvaged curtains from a Greenwich Village
Second Hand Shop and bought a couple of nameless plants for the
window sill. Lu contributed a small revolving fan and Bee
brought two Woolworth's flower prints from her Brooklyn bedroom.
The carpet was threadbare, but when some bright rag rugs
(Salvation Army Store) were thrown down, the room came to life.

It took only twenty-four hours to realize they had a problem.
Roaches.

"Jesus H. Christ!" Lu exploded at 1 AM her first night in
the apartment, having pulled the light cord in the bathroom.
"Bee! Get up! Get over here! What'll we do?"

Her shriek brought Bee staggering to the bathroom door,

where Lu stood transfixed, white with horror. Everywhere, on every surface, every fixture, everywhere - roaches, scattering as light broke up their midnight gathering. Bee grabbed a towel, dropped it, grabbed a bedroom slipper and began killing. Lu, shaking with disgust and in tears, rushed around yelling, "What'll we do! What'll we do?"

The creatures loved the dark. Leaving the light on over the kitchenette helped a little, and they sealed the garbage can with masking tape every night before going to bed. A lesson learned early was never to reach into a dark cupboard or cutlery drawer without thinking. They despised them, fought them, crunched them underfoot (when they could get to them fast enough), shuddered, squealed, pounced and swatted. The awful things kept coming. Eventually, squashing roaches became a pastime, not the savage hunt it had been at first. The hardware store down the block sold them something guaranteed to stem the tide but nothing, absolutely nothing, made an inroad in the population.

"I think the building grows them," Bee said, hoping it sounded like humor. "No matter how many we kill there's always the same number every night."

Willa and Lu's mother came from Brooklyn on a Saturday to see the apartment. Harriet declined, giving no reason. The women sat, took in the shabby wallpaper, the cracked sink, the things the girls believed they had hidden from sight, and sighed. Refreshment was crackers and lemonade. Each visitor had brought a housewarming gift: Stella's was a bunch of tulips and a coffee pot. Willa presented a package of dish towels.

"Who are your neighbors?" Willa wanted to know, as she searched for an ashtray.

Bee pushed a saucer her way. "We don't know anybody here yet. There's an old lady in the back apartment on this floor, but we've only seen her once or twice. Upstairs I think there's a herd of elephants, from the sound of it." She grinned to soften the picture. "And of course, the gin mill downstairs is pretty...lively."

"But we really love it here!" Lu said quickly. "Just see how nice we've fixed it up. Isn't it homey?" She sent a worried glance Bee's way.

Stella smiled. "You kids deserve a lot of credit. You got guts, I have to tell you. But promise us you'll let on if the going gets rough. After all," she looked at Willa, "you're our brats and we want to help if we can." She pushed damp hair out of her eyes and gave each girl a hug.

They left soon, fanning faces red with August heat, and the girls went back to roach-hunting and trying to live on what was left over after rent and carfare. Cooking a meal on the hot plate meant canned beans or Campbell's soup, and it became a Friday night practice to meet after work and eat a good hot dinner at the Automat: a chop, two vegetables, dessert and coffee for a dollar and a half - a morale lifter after the penny pinching of the rest of the week.

Every other week Bee was persuaded down to the Village to meet Harriet for dinner. They went to The Jumble Shop or Mama's for Italian and, once in a while, to a very expensive restaurant on lower Fifth, where the menu offered roast lamb and asparagus with Hollandaise. Harriet never mentioned the breakaway to Manhattan and seemed to be taking it with good grace. Bee told her in oblique ways that she still figured in her life.

Harriet had aged well. She was only a little grayer and a pound or two heavier each year. She took care of herself, with improvement classes at Elizabeth Arden's beauty salon and a judicious choice of foundation garments to encase her growing bulk. She continued to run her business and over the years it had gained a local reputation as the place to go for afternoon coffee and pastry in the Washington Square area. There was a waitress now, as well as the old Irish woman who had been her kitchen help from the beginning. It still looked to Bee like a Victorian boudoir, pinks and lavenders, doilies, bentwood chairs and flowering plants, all original decor, unchanged.

Time had also granted Bee a favor. The gawky twelve year old of the infamous confirmation picture in Harriet's album had filled out into womanhood at size 10. Taller than Willa at maturity, Bee could qualify as "willowy," had clear skin that was Irish-rosy, and eyes that were Jack's, not Willa's green-gold but blue. She had had light hair as a child, and this had deepened to a rich brown, thick and with a curl of its own.

One evening a few months later Bee sat with Harriet in the Tea Room, talking over coffee. The help had gone, the place was dark out front. They sat in the kitchen, playing with the idea of trying a new restaurant down the block. Lu had a date,

Bee really didn't want to go back to the apartment to Franco-
American canned spaghetti and deli cole slaw, all there was
in the refrigerator. Harriet's voice, always a better indicator
of intention than her words, had let it be known when she phoned
Bee at the Met office at noon that there were things to talk
about. Now she was making a thing about where they should eat,
her usual smoke screen for what was really on her mind. Bee
considered going home for the canned spaghetti. At least there
wouldn't be questions and excuses to come up with for something
done or not done to Harriet's satisfaction. It couldn't be
neglect. She saw Harriet far more often than she saw Willa.

"Why don't we go to Mama's?" Bee said. "It's dependable
and the service is fast."

"You've got a date for tonight?"

"No. But I should get back soon. It's shampoo night and
the hot water cools down after nine." A half truth.

"Let's try the new place. I like to be adventurous."
Harriet untied her apron and hung it on a peg.

"Okay, let's give it a whirl." Bee picked up her coat and
handbag. "Down the block?" Easier to give in than debate any
longer.

They ordered veal and Bee sipped water and waited. Harriet
finally met her eyes and stopped fiddling with things on the
table. "Do you remember, oh, way back when we talked about
the - that summer in Connecticut when I - when you - "

Bee held up a hand. "Of course I do. You were telling
me you would be a lonely old lady some day and might need a

caretaker." This had to be lightened up. Harriet feisty or Harriet devious could be dealt with. Harriet maudlin was something else. "Listen, you're never going to be lonely or need a nurse or any of that old folks nonsense."

"Not now, Bee, but the time will come..."

"I'm right here. I'm not going anywhere. If you need me I'm a phone call away. Just because I didn't want to move in with you right out of high school doesn't mean I'm out of your life."

Harriet sat taller, mollified. "I'm glad to hear you say this, Bee. You know how much you mean to me. I know I can count on you, that you won't let me down, ever." She lifted a handkerchief and patted her eyes. "You're all I have, Bee."

Bee reached across the table and took her hand. "Nothing to worry about. We'll probably never be out of each other's lives, Harriet." There was too long a history. Obligation on one side and pseudo-motherhood on the other didn't really add up to affection. Plainly, Harriet wanted to believe they did.

The veal arrived and Bee smiled and appreciated and they parted in peace with a routine hug.

Back in the apartment, Bee sat propped up in bed and sent her memory back to that summer: both of them painting the porch, walking the seashore, the evening cocktail hour with guests, and stuck in there somewhere, the promise. And how was that day different from this one? They were both older, of course. The undercurrent of anxiety Bee had felt and had tried to dispel by reassurance was the difference. Back then, the promise had been extracted from a child. Was Harriet thinking now that the time had come to call it in? True old age was years away. Harriet was active, mentally as sharp as ever, and of course, financially secure. There was no need for caretaking for the foreseeable future, if there was such a thing. Her mention tonight of that summer was a trip into sentimentality, an attempt to reweave the bonds that seemed to have weakened when Bee established independence by moving into the city.

At the Met, Policy Loans was drudgery. Bee collated requests for loans with all prior policy activity, stamped everything with new numbers and passed the packets on to the next division where appropriate letters were written and the packets passed on for processing. All this completed, everything left the department and traveled to wherever final disposition of the requests was made. During the early months Russell Leahy, her immediate superior, had been the main problem. Skirts were fashionably short and legs, once nylons came into the picture, were better to look at than ever. Russell thought of this as one of the perks of his position. No woman in the office wore slacks to work - skirts and blouses, tailored suits, dresses, were regulation. Rules were many. A female must remain unmarried while she worked for the company. Jobs being hard to get post-Depression, quite a few women kept their marital status a secret. "Stupid rule," Mag Devans told Bee. "A holdover from the days when whatever jobs there were went to family men, not single women." The Met hadn't caught up with the times, she said.

Mr. Leahy was bald, paunchy and convinced he was part owner

of the world, or at least that part of it called Policy Loans.

Rumor said he was having an affair with his secretary, but

shortly after Bee started to work in the department the woman

left suddenly. Soon it became evident that Mr. Leahy was looking

for a replacement. A dozen times a day he made a casual stop

at the big table Bee shared with two other new employees, leaned

in, winked, and moved on. When he was far enough away, they

grinned at each other and shook their heads. But he was the

boss, he held the power of the paycheck over them, and to his

face they showed proper respect.

After a few weeks of this a blonde seventeen year old was

hired as office messenger, throwing Leahy's libido into high

gear. He forgot the girls at the collating table and took off

after the newcomer without breaking stride. It was an education

and an entertainment for the rest of the office to watch her

fend him off as she skipped around on her errands. Young as

she was, she knew how to handle herself. And after a while he

saw the folly of his behavior, perhaps, because he calmed down

and went back to the business of managing the office.

As 1941 marched on, more and more servicemen appeared in

the city, and dating became an activity that Bee and Lu discussed

seriously. A mid-town service club run by a group of patriotic

business organizations provided advice and free coffee for men

on leave, and a casual stroll past it any given afternoon

produced the predictable result. If it was a corporal or a

private (and Lu was catholic in her choices) it would be lunch

at Nedick's - a hot dog with orange soda and a doughnut. If
her date wore a few more stripes, they went to Child's and a
movie afterward. A lieutenant meant theater tickets and drinks
at the Astor Bar on Times Square.

"It looks so easy when you do it," Bee said. "I can't -
flaunt myself that way. I guess I'm shy, maybe. Shyer than
you, for sure." She threw a sofa pillow at Lu's head. "How
come you know so much about men? About - all that stuff?"

Lu laughed and tossed the pillow back. "It's not flaunting.
It's, well, if you want a date and there are a lot of
good-looking guys in one place, you go there. That makes sense,
doesn't it?"

Bee looked at her soberly. "That's what I mean. It's putting
yourself on display. It's asking them to notice you. It's
not like meeting someone and liking him and then he shows
interest and asks for a date. It seems so calculating."

"Experience is what you need, Bee. How many guys have you
gone out with since we moved to the city? Two, I think."

"Two," Bee admitted meekly.

"And the last one, you went to the museum over near the
Park and looked at stuffed animals, right? What kind of a date
is that?"

"It was fun," Bee said defensively. "We bought chestnuts
and took them into the Park and walked around the lake..."

"He should have taken you to a good show and a dinner at
a nice restaurant. He was a sergeant, wasn't he? And it was
the first week of September, yes? Meaning he'd just gotten

paid and could afford it. You settled for - peanuts!"

"Chestnuts," Bee said in a low voice.

After they laughed and the conversation went on to other things, Bee thought about this. The young serviceman she'd met at the Automat had been quiet and nice-looking, had suggested the Museum hesitantly. She felt he had expected a refusal, had been refused before, was unsure about how to approach a girl, and this made him seem totally safe. Caution was the watchword. War was going on in the rest of the world and soldiers asking for a date would be asking for a lot more than a casual evening on the town. And then she remembered the other date, the lieutenant she had met in Times Square at the Chock Full O'Nuts counter. He had asked her to have dinner with him, taken her to a narrow little place on West 46th Street where she ate snails for the first time. He had a warm smile and a blonde crewcut and his brass had a fine shine, very military.

"How are the escargots?" he said, mopping up with chunks of bread. "I learned to eat them in Quebec - that's where my wife comes from."

"Wife?" Bee said, around the mouthful she was trying to swallow.

He hadn't stopped talking. "She left me two weeks ago, went back to Canada. She said she couldn't face army life, separations, no stability." He put down his fork and stared at the empty shells on his place. "I think she's going to divorce me."

Bee coughed, and waited for him to pull himself together.

After a short silence he said: "I didn't expect it to happen this way when I went into officer training. I thought she'd like army life, traveling and all that. But now," he showed her a tight grin, "we'll all be in the soup in a matter of months, maybe weeks. I really can't blame her for wanting out, can I? I didn't know I might be getting myself into a war."

The bill came and he fished for change for the tip. "Like to walk? We need to work this off..."

A perfectly safe invitation. No threat from any direction. He had a sweet smile, a firm but gentle hand on her arm as they crossed Columbus Circle and headed into the Park. The raw wind off the river died in the trees and he reached for her hand as they moved along the path in the icy dusk. Bee felt a sudden rush of sympathy for this sad young man whose pain was obvious in spite of the grin and the light words.

They found a bench in a sheltered spot and huddled close to keep warm and he told her about where he came from and then he went on about being so, so lonely, and when he reached an ungloved hand up under her wool skirt and whispered that he had a room over on 80th and would she like to go to bed with him, sympathy died a quick death.

"That's enough of that!" she said, shoving his arm away, her voice so loud it startled her. "I should have known better than to listen to all that - that garbage about your wife and the war and - " His face blurred in the dark and he sputtered something in protest. Bee stood up, brushed her skirt back into place and left him sitting there putting on the glove he'd removed to fumble her.

Two weeks after the holocaust at Pearl Harbor, Phil Shepard
and Bee discovered each other in Washington Square. It was
five o'clock, the twilight magical down there on the edge of
the Village, the Arch a majestic presence, the air still. She
had stopped to sit on a bench for a moment before meeting
Harriet. It was deep winter in the park. Sidewalks rang like
iron under the high heels of women as they hurried past, fur
collars high against the cold, breath mist circling their heads.
Trees were bare and frosted, huddled into each other, enduring.
In the handsome old residences along the north side, lights
were coming on. Bee imagined a scene out of the last century:
long-skirted women in furs walked delicately along the iced
pavement, turned aside to enter glowing doorways. Carriages,
not this honking traffic, lined the curbs, the breath of horses
steaming into the dusk. A romantic time.

Christmas about to happen, there were wreaths on the doors,
giant bristly things with huge red bows, and here and there
a shining tree could be seen through parted drapery.

Bee shivered. I'm twenty-one and I love New York and there's
got to be romantic things coming up for me! War was in the
air. What better time for love to find her, for sweet embraces
and soft tears at parting?

Running to hail a cab at the corner, he lost his footing on a patch of ice and landed on his rump at her feet. He was in uniform, and she guessed tall, from the length of him as he lay there catching his breath.

"Are you hurt?" Bee jumped up and extended a hand. "If there's anything broken, better just stay where you are - "

"No, I'm fine, just fine." He got to his feet carefully and ran his hands over his knees. "Just embarrassed. It happened so fast."

He had a nice face, not "gorgeous" (Lu's criterion) but passably good-looking. They sat down on the cold bench and he rubbed his hands together. "This is almost as cold as my home town," he chattered.

She asked the obvious, not eager to continue the conversation but being polite.

"State College, in Pennsylvania. That's a town in the western part of the state."

"Stationed nearby?" There was a single gold bar on each shoulder. It seemed discourteous to get up and walk away.

"In between. I'm here on leave, shipping out soon." He frowned up at the bare trees. "New York's a lonely place."

Well, she'd heard that before. She stood up. "Glad you're

okay. And good luck."

He got up too, wincing. "Wait - I need a few minutes to

- after all, that was quite a bump I took. Would you have a

hot chocolate with me? Over there?" Pointing to the lights

across the square.

"I'm sorry, I'm meeting someone..."

"Listen, pretty lady, I'm not being fresh, I'd just like

to talk for a few minutes, somewhere out of the cold. No plans

to take up your evening, just a hot chocolate and goodbye.

How about it?" A smile crinkled his eyes and he looked like

a kid, a big nice kid.

She was late getting to Mama's and Harriet was peeved.

When Bee told her about the incident in the park she said with

the usual Frost frostiness, "They're all alike these days.

Just because they wear a uniform they think every girl in the

city will fall at their feet." She patted a napkin across her

broad front and tucked it under a button. "You watch out, Bee,

and take care you're not talked into anything you'll be sorry

for."

"It wasn't like that - he was kind of sweet and we talked

about places he'd been, in the army, and then he said thank

you and we went our separate ways." No need to tell her they

had exchanged other pertinent information, like how to get in

touch. Bee had been impressed with Phil Shepard. He was a good

person, her instinct told her, not a man with only primary urges

on his mind. He had some unexpected ideas about drinking (he

said he'd never tasted liquor) and politics (he said he came
from a staunch Republican family). Since Bee enjoyed a highball
now and then and believed she came from a staunch Irish-American
Democratic family (*Willa* had voted for Al Smith) she only nodded
and smiled at this revelation.

She went back to the apartment and thought about the
encounter and the possibility that he might get in touch. He
had said he had ten days before his orders to ship out were
confirmed. And ten days could be a long time or a short time,
depending.

He called her at the office the next morning, and without
time to consider all angles, she *had* only a Yes when he asked
if he could take her to dinner when she finished work.

Three days later, over linguine and garlic bread at Luigino's
he asked her to marry him.

"But - I hardly know you!" she said, appalled at the cliché
but unable to think of anything else to say.

He smiled uncertainly and fiddled with his fork, blinking
at her. "I guess we have lots to talk about before I can expect
an answer."

"I rather think so!"

"I ship out - " He stopped short and they both started to
laugh.

" - in five days and you want something wonderful to
remember," she finished for him. "Phil - are you serious?"

"We could have a honeymoon here in New York, then I really

would have something worth coming back for." His eyes were
pleading and his face had reddened. "Do I sound as foolish
as I think I do?"

She looked into his young, earnest face, felt the pressure
of his warm hands and knew there was safety here, and a need
for love, and none of the casual sentiment she had been hearing.
Was this her sweetheart? Her fate? If the hollowness in her
stomach meant anything, he was.

"I think," she said in a faint voice, "we do have a lot to
talk about."

He told her about his parents, his schooling, his army
training. He said he was twenty-four years old and had a sister
named Genevieve, who still lived with his parents. He told
her about his first girlfriend, whose name was Marilyn. He
said she looked like Betty Grable, but he'd never made love
to her. In fact, he said, he had never made love to anyone,
but had read books on the subject and would try to be good at
it. Bee laughed uncertainly at this confession, willing to
take it at face value because he seemed to have trouble making
it. When he finished she squeezed his hand and they both felt
more at ease.

Pasta and wilted salad greens and a dish of melting ice
cream between them - she hadn't tasted much of anything since
they had been served. She told him about Willa and Jack and
Harriet, about Connecticut and Jack's death and Lucille and
the roaches.

When they left he hugged her as they stepped out into the

cold.

"I'm going to love you, Bee Jordon, so much - so hard - you just give me a chance!"

It was awkward and sweet, like the kiss he finally gave her at the door to her apartment. He made it last a little too long, probably from what he'd seen in the movies, or maybe that's what Marilyn had taught him. She didn't care. She returned it with real feeling.

They didn't get married that week. She persuaded him that it needed more thinking over. And by the time he got his next leave they would know for sure if it was what they wanted.

He sounded miserable when he said: "I suppose you're right. Without a doubt, you're right. But it's the hardest thing anyone has ever asked me to do. If I don't get back soon - you could meet someone else, you could forget me - I don't want that to happen, Bee."

"It doesn't mean I don't care about you, Phil. But this is a big step and we've only known each other for a week and a half." In another minute she'd fall apart like a rag doll in the rain. "There won't be anyone else, I'll be right here waiting for you."

He didn't ask the crucial question. Lu had said he would undoubtedly ask her to go to bed with him. "And with your attitude about sex - " Lu grinned.

"What do you mean, my attitude?" Bee said irritably. "Just because I'm tired of G.I. Joes with nothing else on their minds - am I a prude?"

"Don't get your dander up," Lu said. "If you're in love and want to wait til there's a ring on your finger, just tell him. If he cares about you, he'll respect your wishes."

Chapter VI

1942

Bee's life now took on formal adult shape and she moved out into the main stream of serious relationships where love was a matter of consequence. Phil Shepard was always in her thoughts. They wrote daily letters. He had been sent, not overseas, but to an army post in South Carolina and was engaged in preparing infantry troops for duty out of the States. He wrote her that he felt let down, having anticipated the big jump, but as soon as he realized this would expedite their wedding plans, he stopped grumbling.

Lucille moved out a month later, having found a modeling job at a minor fashion agency, with a small increase in income. Her social life was active, and the situation in the studio apartment could no longer accommodate it.

She was apologetic. "It's not the roaches, Bee, really. It's just - well, I need some private space for my own life. You understand, don't you? And I'm only a phone call away, and we're going to stay friends, like always, of course."

The new living arrangement, if hard on Bee's budget, came at the right time. Anticipating Phil's next leave, she made some stabs at re-arranging the place: new curtains, a small folding table that could be used for dining, a pair of brass candlesticks. She put the two daybeds together and bought a bedspread that covered both. Then, self-consciously, shoved them back against adjacent walls and told herself to stop thinking along those lines.

He had been gone for six weeks when Bee looked up from her desk one afternoon to find him standing in front of her. The shock wore off after two cups of coffee in the cafeteria downstairs, where he held her hand and pulled out a tiny white box.

"I was going to mail it, but then this chance came up suddenly and I grabbed it. I knew we could at least say hello, and maybe..." His eyes were dreamy all of a sudden. She let him slip the ring on her finger and they both stared at it for a while.

"It's beautiful," she told him, leaning against his shoulder as they sat at the counter, where everyone who saw them understood what was going on and there were smiles all around. The diamond was small but had a real sparkle. He explained that he had brought a trainload of men up to the New York Embarkation Center to be shipped out, and had only one night in the city. Bee went back upstairs to Policy Loans, said she had a terrible headache and grabbed her coat. Sly grins followed her as she ran for the door.

They took a cab to her apartment and once inside the door, fell into each other's arms.

"Bee, I've missed you - so much - " he groaned. "Do you have any idea how much I want you?"

She clung to him, shivering. "I know, Phil, I know. But we've got to be - "

His kisses smothered anything she might have said. She dropped her handbag and he pulled her coat from her shoulders and they moved toward the bed, clutching each other, kissing frantically. "We shouldn't - it's better to wait - " She knew he couldn't hear her, knew it was useless and that it was going to happen. And then resistance crumbled.

It was over quickly, with a sweaty gasp and a moan and nothing of the Big Bang the girls in the office had told her, with giggles, would happen. But he was tender and sweet, lying next to her, and said he loved her four or five times and she began to feel it had been, even if awkward, appropriate in the circumstances.

There was no question of Phil's finding a hotel room. They slept with arms around each other and when he left at 5:30 the next morning she sank back into pillows and dreamed for two hours before getting up to shower away the strange new products of love on her body.

The time had come to break the news to Willa and Harriet. This required an agenda. Top of the list, mention of his name occasionally. Next, prepare to introduce him on his next trip to New York. Third, show them the ring, and duck. Prediction: Willa would react in one of two ways. She'd be indifferent or

full of admonishings and warnings. Harriet? She would cry
"Betrayal!" for starters, then sulk for a while, then regroup
and try to figure out a way to divert Bee from her selfish path.
These ploys might have worked a few years ago, but Bee had
developed a reasonably strong will of her own. She was in love.
She had a fine marriage in her future, to a fine young man.
She would become an Army Wife, making a home in various military
posts around the country, a route some of her co-workers had
already taken. <u>Surely my family will stand with me in this?</u>
<u>Surely?</u>

In letters they discussed Bee's continuing to work, which
Phil disapproved of but gave in when she pointed out the
advantages. For the moment, she could keep *her* job at the Met
and they could put aside her earnings for furniture and so forth.
There was a chance, he said, that he would be sent to a post
in Mississippi, and once that was confirmed they could make
marriage plans. He had told his family, who were very anxious
to meet Bee. Meanwhile, he'd be able to come to New York for
a weekend soon, to meet Willa and Harriet and set dates for
the rest of it.

The war was heating up. New York was a center of military
activity. No social occasion took place without uniforms present
and no conversation lacked mention of the conflict going on
across both oceans. Popular songs about the Air Corps, the
Marines and *OTher* patriotic tunes filled the air.
It was exhilarating, a kind of dancing-on-the-edge-of-disaster
feeling everywhere. Bee had begun to worry about the possibility

that Phil might be shipped out, be put in harm's way. Then came

a happy surprise. During a routine physical examination, he

was found to have a minor vision defect. Since the army

certainly wouldn't want him shooting a rifle or commanding others

to do so if his eyesight wasn't reliable, he told her, he could

look forward to stateside assignments for the duration. Anxiety

subsided and Bee's thoughts centered on the coming May 30th

holiday, for which Phil had put in a leave request. She plotted

the scenario for introducing him to Willa and Harriet.

It went this way:

BEE: There's this really nice lieutenant I met...

WILLA: Oh? No more enlisted men?

BEE: ...a few weeks ago...

WILLA: Where?

BEE: ...and we've been dating...

WILLA: How long?

BEE ...and I thought maybe you'd like to meet him...

WILLA: When?

BEE: ... so I'm going to ask Harriet to have us all over

for dinner one of these Sundays..."

WILLA: Just let me know when.

BEE: Like Memorial Day weekend?

That had been relatively painless. To acquaint Harriet with

the facts required a little more finesse, since her stake in

the outcome was more sensitive. She came uptown after the

Tea Room closed and they met at Sasha's Garden, a Russian place

near Carnegie Hall. Bee was just finishing her first Martini when Harriet came in.

HARRIET: Is this just a sociable thing, or have you got

something to tell me?

BEE: Harriet, I want you to ...

HARRIET: I have a feeling it's something I don't want to

hear.

BEE: I just want you to ...

HARRIET: You haven't quit your job, have you?

BEE: Will you let me finish a sentence?

Silence, while Harriet studied the menu with great interest.

Bee beckoned a waiter and told him to bring another Martini.

HARRIET: I'll have one too.

BEE: I've been dating a really nice guy, a lieutenant,

and I'd like him to meet my family. That's all. He'll be

here for Memorial Day weekend. How about if I bring him

over to the house, and Willa too?

HARRIET: Is this serious, or just another fling with the

army?

BEE (sharply): He's more than a casual date, he's important

to me. I want you to like him.

HARRIET (sourly): We'll see. So I'm to understand you're

making plans?

BEE: We're thinking about it.

HARRIET (looking up from the menu, with a stiff smile):

Fine. I'll do a lamb roast and you can help me make pies.

Why is it, whenever I try to get a step ahead, she pulls

right around in front of me? So much for schemes and breaking/

the news gently. I don't have the talent for it.

There remained, of course, the actual revelation of the wedding plans. If Harriet could be soothed into accepting the situation as beyond her control, it would be a lot easier for everyone. Far back under happy anticipation a queasy memory trickled into Bee's overflowing cup. She didn't examine it.

They took the BMT out to Flatbush and made wedding plans on the way. She had done her best to prepare him, listing the probable sequence of events and what to watch out for.

He looked at her soberly. "Looks like you've been ping-ponging between your mother and Harriet most of your life. Which one are we to pacify here?"

"Harriet. Willa's easier."

The hoped-for meeting with Phil's parents hadn't been possible. Aside from a honeymoon week, he had no leave to look forward to for a while, and Bee planned to work right up to resignation date.

When he said he'd like to get married in the town where he grew up, in the church his folks attended, a quiver started in Bee's stomach.

"That may cause some ripples," she said. "Harriet probably expects to direct the ceremonies herself, at her church. Be prepared for a minor ruckus."

He had an arm around her as the cars lurched and swayed along the tracks under the river. The car lights flickered off briefly and he nuzzled her neck and said: "We'll manage,

Bee. It's our wedding, isn't it? If Harriet's feelings are hurt we'll give her something to do, like mailing out wedding announcements."

They both laughed. The idea of Harriet with pen in hand working down a list of Phil's friends and relatives was too strange.   "Seriously, she's a force to be reckoned with and when she's crossed, watch out. You're making off with her baby. You may never be forgiven."

"Tough sugar," he said flatly. Phil cleaned up army language in her presence.

They walked six blocks to Willa's apartment, hand in hand in the May dusk, hardly seeing the sidewalks or traffic at the crossings. Being in love, Bee reflected, is the sweetest thing that has ever happened to me!

Phil got a cool backhand from Willa. "Nice to meet you," she said, omitting his name. "Bee told me about you. Come in and sit down while I get my coat and hat."

He reddened a little and rubbed the back of his head, but said nothing. They stood there until Willa came out of the bedroom.

"Does Harriet want us to bring anything?" she asked as they left the apartment.

"No. I went there last night and helped her make pies."

"How many?"

"Three."

"Anyone else coming for dinner?"

"She didn't say."

"Three pies is a lot for the four of us."

Phil walked between them, his eyes swivelling with each bit of dialogue.

They took the streetcar to Harriet's house. It was a nostalgic ride for Bee, the trip she had taken so many weekends in her childhood, the same rattling car, the same drab and dingy neighborhoods. While Phil made an effort to draw Willa into conversation, Bee let her thoughts travel back a decade. There had been wonderful weekends spent with Harriet, not just shopping and household chores, but a kind of companionship she had with no one else. It's true, she thought, what I told Harriet - that we'll never really be out of each other's lives.

It was 7:30 when they walked through the gate on Hendrix Street, right on time. Harriet approved of punctuality. They had chalked up a plus. Alice opened the door and ushered them in. Willa moved into the front parlor at once and Bee and Phil followed.

Dr. and Mrs. Carter Plumb stood talking to Harriet, sherry glasses in their hands. I might have guessed, Bee thought. She has looked around for something to load the dice in her favor and found it, to my embarrassment.

The introduction sounded like this:

"Bee, do you remember Father Plumb and Mrs. Plumb? Of course you do! Lieutenant Shepard - (Phil extended a hand) - Bee was confirmed at Saint Andrew's, went to Sunday School there for many years." She beamed at the men, and turned a look of bland innocence to Bee. Willa had lit a cigarette and picked up a glass of wine. Whether she heard or not, she said nothing.

So now it was plain what was going on. Harriet understood that
something had been decided that was not in her favor. To salvage
what she could, and possibly to influence the outcome, she would
steer the conversation in the direction of her church as the
wedding site. After all, it was Bee's alma mater, speaking
religiously. Surely the young man would agree it was the only
place to hold the ceremony?

Bee had no fond memories of the church, and to have the
wedding performed there, in that old brown mausoleum, would
color the festivities drab and dull. She had the choice now
of submitting meekly or braving it out. There was no way Phil
could grasp the undercurrents in this meeting, the obligations
involved, the pressure being brought to bear. He had asked
her to come to Pennsylvania to be married, and she had agreed.
That was all he knew. She would leave it that way.

She took Willa upstairs to the bathroom and had a talk with
her.

"Are you going to marry him?" Willa asked, pulling on her
cigarette.

Bee waved the cloud of smoke away and sat on the edge of
the bathtub. "Yes. And I need your help with Harriet." This
was probably a futile request but had to be asked.

Willa coughed, doused the cigarette in the toilet and sat
down on the lid.

"You can see what she's doing," Bee went on. "She's going
to try to run the whole thing from here, the wedding by Dr.

120

Plumb and catering by Harriet's Tea Room."

Willa's response was a surprise. "We can't let her do that, can we?"

"N-no, I guess we can't."

"So let's see what can be done. What plans have you made?""

Bee told her about Phil's family and that he wanted to be married in his parents' church, with all his relatives and friends gathered round. "He's got so many - it wouldn't be easy for them to come here."

"Am I to be invited?"

"Well of course! Why, sure!" Reckless with surprise, gratification choking her: "You'll come down on the train, you - you'll stay at Phil's house, I'm sure his folks have room, and we'll -- "

Willa held up her hand. She looked at Bee for a long moment, her eyes unfocused as she weighed a few things in her mind. "All right. I'll see what I can do." She got up and left the bathroom and Bee sat on the rim of the tub, blinking.

She stared down at the sparkle on her hand, which Phil had urged her to put on when they arrived. No one, obviously, had noticed it yet. Had Willa seen it while they were talking? She got up and followed her mother down to the parlor and into the dining room where the table, resplendent in Limoges and sterling, displayed Harriet's bounteous hospitality.

Seating had been arranged to keep Bee from intimate contact with Phil. He was on Harriet's right at the end of the table, and beside him Mrs. Carter Plumb bubbled and twittered. Bee

sat at the foot of the table, past Willa and past Dr. Plumb,
a mile away and directly across from Harriet's piercing gaze.

Harriet glanced down the table every so often, sweetening
her smile with a coy tilt of the head, keeping up a low
conversation with Phil, who nodded and looked at his plate.
Bee was furious. The table was long enough so that conversations
going on across its middle effectively blanked anything from
the opposite end. Mrs. Plumb and Willa were talking about
something. Phil's
soft answers didn't carry and Harriet leaned over her napkin
or raised a fork and Bee couldn't hear a word. She hadn't had
time to alert him to whatever plan Willa was hatching.

Suddenly Willa stood and sent a solemn glance around the
table. Fixing her eyes on Harriet, she said: "My daughter and
her young man, here, (faint nod in Phil's direction) have asked
me to announce their engagement." She swivelled toward Bee's
end of the table. "As the prospective bride's mother, I am
honored to make this announcement."

Harriet's indrawn breath punctuated the second of silence
before Dr. Plumb got up and raised his glass.

"May we be the first to offer congratulations to the happy
couple." His wife stood, Willa lifted her glass, Phil looked
blank. Harriet's expression was unreadable, then she slowly
got to her feet and lifted her wine glass an inch off the table.
Phil came around and kissed Bee's cheek and raised her hand
for all to see the ring. Willa leaned in for a quick peck,
an incredibly smug expression on her face, then went back and

tapped her glass with a fork.

"I believe their wedding plans will take them to
Pennsylvania, where the groom's family lives, and honeymoon
plans, of course, are their own business." She sat down and
drank thirstily from her wine glass. The Plumbs exchanged glances
but kept their congratulatory smiles in place and began talking
to Harriet, whose eyes were riveted on Willa. In the supreme
happiness of the moment, Bee almost felt sorry for both of them.

Wind out of sails or not, Harriet plowed through the rest
of the evening with dignity, even to the point of offering good
wishes as they left. She hadn't looked at Willa again, and
they hadn't spoken to each other. At the door she laid a hand
gently on Phil's arm and said some words suited to the occasion.
The coldness in her voice and the steel in her eyes weren't
lost on Bee.

The three of them parted in mid-Brooklyn, and Bee and Phil
went back to Manhattan.

"I'm not sure what was going on this evening," he said as
they took seats on the train."but am I safe in assuming
everything's okay now?"

Because she needed to believe it was true, Bee said: "It
will be. Not having the wedding here will be hard on Harriet,
she's so used to having a hand in whatever goes on in my life,
but I think with Willa's help we've made our point. It's our
wedding, and it will take place wherever we want it to."

"Will they come to State College?"

"I've already asked Willa and she'll come. Harriet? Maybe

she'll come around if you charm her. Tell her it's important for her to be there. Right now her nose is out of joint and she's mad at me and God only knows what she feels about Willa."

The momentous weekend was over. At Penn Station they parted with a passionate embrace and some breathless kissing and he went back to camp. She watched his tall figure stride off down the ramp to the train, her throat thick with pride and happiness. He was so good to look at, so dear and sweet and handsome in his uniform with its bright insignia and Sam Browne belt, shoes polished to a blinding shine, everything about him so much what she wanted, had waited for, had wondered if it ever would happen to her.

At work she was put through the usual office "shower," fifteen girls, two supervisors, champagne punch, a decorated cake and a collective wedding gift - a set of luggage, the appropriate gift in this year of war and military marriages. Lucille had been invited, and after the party, said she wanted to treat Bee to dinner. They went to The Brass Rail, near Times Square, had drinks at the bar where Lu flirted idly with a young officer, then turned a serious face to Bee.

"I have to ask," she said. "Are you absolutely sure this guy is who you want to spend the rest of your life with?"

Bee's smile was more answer than her soft, "Absolutely."

"I'm your best friend, you know, and I can ask this kind of question. Did you - have you - ?"

Bee blushed. "Yes, we did, and it was wonderful, just heavenly!" 124

"Your first time, right?" Lucille smiled back.

"Of course. And maybe you can't believe this, but it was for him, too."

"No kidding?"

"I know, army life and all that. But I believe him. He's never fooled around, and that makes me so glad I didn't, either."

Lu shook her head at her cocktail glass. "In this day and age, really. Makes me wish sometimes that I hadn't."

By mid-June Phil wrote that he had found a small furnished apartment. It was a few miles outside Camp Shelby in Hattiesburg, Mississippi, to which he had been posted shortly after he returned to camp. He had put a deposit on it and suggested that she set the date so he could ask for leave and alert his parents.

Harriet and Bee were on speaking terms once more. She didn't call so often, and had ignored Willa ever since the announcement dinner, and Bee hadn't touched on the touchy situation. The rift was healing.

As soon as she had set the date, Bee phoned. "Harriet, Phil and I have decided on the first Sunday in July. We wanted you to be the first to know. He's going to call you tonight, to ask you something important."

She waited a few seconds before answering. "Oh? Well, I expect I'll be here. Unless I go out to dinner."

"He'll call at six." Bee waited. "Harriet, this will be the most important day in my life. Are you going to give me your blessing?" It wasn't really what she wanted to say, but it was what Harriet wanted to hear.

"You have my best wishes for your future happiness," was the stiff answer, and Bee could tell nothing from the tone of her voice. If that was the best she could do under the circumstances, it was acceptable.

Chapter VII

The Wedding - Willa and Harriet

The suitcase Willa had borrowed from Stella Engle was too
big for the few garments she thought necessary for the trip:
a dark blue dress with white collar and cuffs for the church
wedding, a raincoat, a wool sweater, a nightgown and slippers,
underwear and stockings. The brown two-piece suit she wore
for the journey could, with a change of blouse, fill any gaps
in her wardrobe. She had acquired it, after careful deliberation,
from the racks of a Flatbush Avenue second-hand clothing store.
It was clean, simple in style, and showed no signs of prior
ownership. (Willa had expected to find a button missing, pulled
threads at the hem, wear at the elbows.) Five dollars was not
a small sum for her, and when she discovered no defects but
a garment in good condition and with a fair expectation of
usability, she was pleased. Her old blue silk blouse was still
wearable, and she added a white cotton one to the suitcase for
insurance. Shoes, a small straw hat and her serviceable patent
leather handbag completed the outfit. In the July heat gloves
would be unnecessary and an extravagance she could not justify
for appearance's sake alone. To fill the space in the suitcase
she added two bath towels and a Sunday newspaper.

She left Brooklyn at 8 AM on Friday morning and arrived in Manhattan with almost an hour to fill before meeting Harriet at the Information Booth in Pennsylvania Station. Two weeks had passed since they had last held a conversation. The arrangements for this trip had been made over the telephone, in short sentences, with no hint of apology or contrition, explanation or forgiveness. Willa found a seat on a bench in the waiting room and pushed the suitcase under her knees.

Harriet prepared for the trip in much the same way, although with a larger wardrobe to choose from. Two black leather suitcases contained her clothing for the weekend: a lavender silk dress to be worn for the ceremony, created by Tilly Mendelson, the seamstress who, some years earlier, had sewn Bee's high school graduation dress; three summer cottons with matching shoes, a light coat for cool evenings, a shawl of pale rose cashmere and three pairs of gloves - kid, cotton and Italian lace. There was also a nightgown and peignoir in pale green satin, underwear, hosiery and a beaded silk handbag to carry to the church. A taxi cab was called and drew up in front of the house on Hendrix Street. The driver came up onto the columned porch, respectfully tipped his cap and gathered up the bags, while Harriet waited at the cab door.

They met at the Information Booth. Willa nodded briefly, Harriet offered a fractional smile, and side by side they followed the redcap down the platform ramp and boarded the train, as preparatory grunts came from the engine up ahead and steam surged and spurted from beneath the cars.

Harriet broke the silence. "I understand Bee's best friend Lucille won't be able to attend," she said, settling into the seat. She smoothed the skirt of her gray silk traveling suit, tucked her handbag between hip and window, and folded gloved hands in her lap.

Willa said, "Her fiancé's ship is coming in tomorrow and they haven't seen each other in six months."

"A shame. Bee must be terribly disappointed." Spite disguised as honeyed concern, Harriet herself having only recently suffered a portion of disappointment.

Neither had been given detailed information about the wedding plans. Other than the names of Phil's parents, the church, and the hotel where, at Phil's insistence and expense, they would be staying, they knew only that the ceremony would take place on Sunday morning and the evening before, a reception would be held and presided over by the elder Shepards.

Harriet offered another subject for conversation. "What with the war and the state of morality these days," she said with a sniff, "it's probably rare for a bride to come to her wedding night a virgin. I believe it's true in Bee's case, however, from what she's told me."

Willa's eyes widened at "virgin," a word Harriet had never used in her presence. She took a paper handkerchief from her bag and blew.

When the disturbance subsided, Harriet went on: "I do hope she'll be married in white satin. I've always thought of her in a long gown, with a train and a lace veil."

Willa strongly doubted that Harriet had envisioned any such thing. To be that noble, to accept that Bee would leave her and go off to start her own life, was not in Harriet's nature. For her to suspect, then plan to manipulate the situation was far easier to believe. Willa coughed and searched her handbag for another tissue.

"I wish I could feel absolutely sure that this - this young lieutenant what's-his-name will always take care of her and be good to her. It will be a shame if anything goes wrong with this marriage."

Willa came to life. On a train travelling away from home and familiar territory, she was somehow released from certain constraints and felt an impulse to bring up matters that had long lain dormant. Harriet wasn't simply making idle conversation. It was clear that she was drawing a comparison between Bee's marriage and Willa's of twenty or so years ago, once again to rub in the fact of a bad choice.

"No reason for it not to be," Willa began. "He seems to be a steady, reliable young man."

"But you know that wartime marriages - "

" - are as good as any others, as long as the couple has a good foundation to build on. They didn't rush into this, and Bee's an adult now. I think we can trust her judgment."

"Oh, you do. Well, I'm not so sure. She hasn't had much in the way of an example."

"You mean Jack and me." Willa said nothing for a few minutes, realizing that the residue of Harriet's ill feelings toward her needed to come to the surface. But a change had crept into the relationship and restraint had been weakened. She said: "I think it may be time to have a talk with her, to tell her the whats and whys of her parents' marriage. She has a right to know who Jack was and how he came to be her father. And it might help for her to understand where you fit in, Harriet."

Before the last words were out Harriet stiffened, one hand white-knuckled on the arm of the seat. "That's a very bad idea, Willa. You can't dredge up past history, certainly not that kind of history, just as she's getting married: How inappropriate!" Her voice trembled.

Willa was gratified by Harriet's reaction. "You may be right," she answered after a pause, exhilarated at having come out ahead in the exchange. "I'll have to think about it." She settled herself more comfortably and drew a deep breath.

Harriet stared out the window, blinking rapidly as she fought the anxiety Willa's suggestion had created. It was a threat, but was the intent malicious? Possibly Willa herself didn't know, believed she was speaking innocently. Whichever, it would put her, Harriet, in an awkward position if the facts of Jack's place in her life - and the details of that long ago drama - were to be revealed. For Bee to learn these things would tarnish the halo Harriet had worn for so many years.

"I think I'll go to the washroom and have a smoke," Willa said. As she left her seat she turned and smiled down at Harriet. In the washroom she lit a cigarette and sat on the bench provided for waiting. Their conversation in the last half hour must be examined for usefulness and, much as Harriet had done, she thought about how to turn it to her own advantage. She did not plan to disrupt the happy occasion with a sensational revelation, but Harriet would not know this. From having been so long subordinate, Willa's skills as a plotter were rusty. Better not to use them until a need became obvious. She stayed in the washroom through another cigarette, then returned to her seat.

Conversation lagged. As lunch time approached an invitation was issued to share the meal in the dining car and politely refused. Willa produced a sandwich wrapped in waxed paper when Harriet had gone, and bought a cup of tea from the aisle vendor. Lunch on lap, she stared at the passing landscape and thought about Jack and how, if it came to that, she could make Bee understand why it had happened. Through the years she had kept her attention on daily duty, coping with hard times, not looking back, accepting as just deserts the path her life had taken. Has the time come, she wondered now, to think about the past and consider whether any lessons should be passed on? How much should she reveal in order to demonstrate the justice of her actions?

The campaign of quiet, inexorable revenge that Harriet had embarked on when Willa and Jack were married had worked well for many years, helped along, if not by Willa's participation, at least by her indifference. She had known what was happening from the beginning. Harriet's machinations came as no surprise, nor did Jack's gradual deterioration. Between them, moving

along parallel paths, they had managed his downfall. She stopped
at that word, not liking the sound of it. He had simply walked
away from his obligations, that was it, and since strength of
character was not in his makeup, he had taken to drink as the
easy answer. She had given him no reason to expect an active
wifely partner, and had continued the pattern established on
their wedding night: patient endurance of his attentions with
nothing offered in return. Only once had he rebelled, had
shouted at her in frustration, "How can you lie there like a
Goddamned stick - not moving, not saying anything? You're like
a - a corpse! I'm trying to make love to a corpse!" and flung
himself out of bed and out of the bedroom. She had turned her
head on the pillow and gone to sleep. Nothing he could say
or do had shaken her from that resolution. For a while, when
Bee was small, he had made earnest attempts to win her regard,
if not her love, staying with a decent job, coming home every
night enthusiastically and making much of his baby daughter.
Willa observed his efforts as she did his lovemaking - from
a cold distance. As time went on, Jack began to understand what
was being done to him by the two women, but with hope still
flickering that Willa might be induced to turn to him some day,
he stayed where he was and the bottle filled the emptiness.
After a while he no longer cared what plots were hatched to
pull him down. On the periphery he watched what they wanted
him to see and so long as he had a place to return to that had
Willa in it, he forced no issue.

Should any of this be told to Bee? Now, or in the future?

Willa found it hard to see herself making such a confession.
Even with the passing of time, there was residual pain and
humiliation, and guilt. Although Jack certainly bore most of
the blame, she had always brooded on her own weakness and
believed it to be the root cause of the event. This admission,
which would have to go along with the other details, would be
a painful one.

A summer rain had begun to fall and for long minutes Willa
watched its slanting silvery veils as she traveled through the
countryside thinking about the past.

In the dining car Harriet had a seat near the window. The
car was crowded but approaching passengers, seeing her large
presence, went by and took seats farther down the aisle. One
couple, in animated conversation, started to slide into seats
across from her, but on meeting her frosty stare, quickly removed
themselves. She ordered an omelette and coffee. While waiting
to be served, she went over in her mind the conversation of
a few minutes ago. What sudden surge of courage had propelled
Willa into such an adversarial position? In all the years behind
them there had never been a dispute over guardianship of Bee.
The original plan had worked well. If changes were occurring
that meant a challenge to her status, they must be resisted.

The omelette was delicious and the coffee hot, and for the
moment anxiety rested and she enjoyed the meal. Food consumed,
she rose with what dignity the swaying dining car permitted
and returned to the next car.

When Harriet took her seat at the window, Willa offered
the next conversational gambit. Since she had no intention
of spilling the beans anyway, agreement could be made to look
like capitulation, providing her with a small advantage and
lulling Harriet's fears.

"I've been thinking about what you said before, and you're
right. It would be a bad time to tell Bee about the three of
us, on the eve of her wedding. If all goes well and the marriage
gets off to a good start, old problems shouldn't be on her mind."

Harriet waited to hear the right words.

"What I mean is, this kind of thing could alienate her from
both of us. I'll give it more thought. Maybe some time - "
Willa let her voice trail off.

Understanding wasn't slow in arriving for either of them.
Willa saw that, aside from the relish of having jarred Harriet's
complacency, nothing would be gained by further threats. On
her part, Harriet saw the wisdom of restoring the peace.
Silently, patiently, she would nurse the soreness of Bee's
defection, never allowing it to heal completely. Time was on
her side. Something, at some time in the future, would open
the door for her and she would reach in and snatch Bee back.

Arriving in a driving rainstorm, Willa and Harriet were
met with umbrella and taxi by Bee and Phil and escorted to the
Benjamin Franklin Hotel, where a large comfortable room had
been reserved for them. There were flowers on the dresser with
a note of welcome from Phil's parents. Phil explained with

an embarrassed laugh that an unexpected inundation of back-country relatives had filled his parents' home to overflowing. Even Bee was now sharing a room with an elderly cousin, he told them.

"Well now," said Harriet, running her fingers over the drapery, "we can do something about that right away." She picked up the telephone and asked for the Desk. "Yes, you can tell me if you have a single available, preferably on the fourth floor, near my room, for the next two nights."

Bee caught her arm, with an anxious look at Phil. "Wait, Harriet - "

"Nonsense. I'll get you a room here near us, you'll have a couple of nights with your family before - "

Phil's quiet voice cut in: "Bee's doing fine at my folks' place, Harriet. She and my mom are having a great time exchanging recipes." He leaned in at Harriet's eye level, smiled warmly, and gave her a little hug. "I know all about the cooking lessons you gave Bee when she was growing up. She's going to be the best little cook in the world!"

Harriet put the phone down.

The bellboy, struggling in behind them, deposited the bags and pocketed the coin Phil gave him. There was a moment of silence.

"I hope she remembers at least half of what I taught her," Harriet said crustily. She turned her back and began to take things from a small leather case. They watched as she lifted out a thick cream-colored envelope bearing an inscription in

purple ink, and propped it against the lamp on the dresser.
No one had any trouble reading the calligraphy:

BERTHA HARRIET JORDON

Satisfied that she had made them take notice, she said:
"I suppose flowers have been arranged for, and all the church
details taken care of?"

"Yes, Harriet." Bee was watching Willa, whose face was
flushed. The cigarette she had immediately taken from her purse
dangled from her free hand as she lifted her suitcase to the
bed, then turned to look for an ashtray. Phil got one from
the night table between the beds and handed it to her.

Harriet sighed. "Well, it looks as though there's nothing
left for me to do. I think, Bee, you might have included me
in the planning."

"But - there wasn't time - " Bee said quickly. "It's Friday
and the wedding is Sunday and - " she hesitated, "it's just
that it was easier to do it from here..." Now heading down
a path full of thorns, she stopped abruptly.

Willa came to the rescue. "You kids certainly have a lot
to do. Why don't you run along and leave us to unpack." She
made shooing motions toward the door. "Call us in the morning
if we can do anything to help."

Harriet went back to unpacking her toilet articles.

Gratefully, Phil took Bee's arm. "Sure, Willa. My folks
are anxious to meet you. They want all of us to get together
in the morning. We'll call first thing."

They left quickly. 137

Smoke circling her head, Willa began pulling things out of her suitcase and arranging them on hangers in the closet. For the moment she had nothing to say, and instead began, very softly, to hum a tune. Harriet sent her a long smoldering look and once her own clothes were sorted into drawer and closet, went into the bathroom and shut the door.

"I think there's something we have to accept," Willa said as they sat at dinner in the hotel dining room. "We're just guests at this wedding, not among the planners."

"That's simply not true," answered Harriet in an aggrieved voice. "We're part of the wedding party, Bee's only relatives, and we should have been given a part in the arrangements."

"Things seems to be moving right along without us," Willa said.

They continued their meal in silence, Harriet eating lobster and asparagus, Willa corned beef hash and mashed potatoes.

The next morning at nine Phil called their room from the lobby. "Mother and Gen - that's my sister - want to invite you ladies to have breakfast at our house."

"We'll be down in five minutes." Willa's voice was dry, businesslike. She hung up and finished her minimal makeup. "Harriet, they're waiting for us."

"Oh, bother! I wanted to find a hairdresser - "

"Your hair looks fine." Willa put on her dark green sweater and patted her own hair before the mirror. "Let's not keep them waiting."

Harriet's eyes flashed. "Keep who waiting? That brassy young man who's - who's taking Bee - "

" - who's taking your baby away from you?" Willa said. "You'd better get used to it, Harriet. She's left us. She's his now." She tucked her handbag under her arm and walked to the door. "And don't go grinding your teeth. You can't do a thing about it."

Throughout the day, during which the two families met, took notice of their differences, and laid groundwork for getting along in the years of in-law status about to begin, Harriet prudently held her tongue. There was a lavish breakfast: fresh strawberries, scrapple with eggs, preserves, pancakes with honey. Her ruffled feelings somewhat soothed, Harriet warmed the hearts of her host and hostess with her appreciation. If she glanced coldly in Phil's direction now and then, only Bee noticed.

With her hand in his throughout the meal, Bee sat and glowed around the table, not eating, blissful. The agenda was revealed, the program for the wedding rehearsal gone over, everything but the bride's gown made known. Local custom dictated a pre-wedding reception, to be held in the church function rooms late in the afternoon. When it was over, Harriet proposed that everyone meet in the hotel dining room and be her guests at a dinner for the wedding party. Bee was delighted and relieved that Harriet was behaving appropriately. Willa's unsmiling presence was no more than she had expected.

When the two women from New York retired to their room at midnight, they were weary and a little cranky with each other.

Luckily, sleep overtook them before anything hurtful could be said, and the wedding morning dawned without need for reparations.

Calvary Baptist Church sat among trees, its shaded flagstone walk bordered with pansies, its doors and windows open in the summer heat. Noon sun bathed the town in gold light. Inside, guests fluttered paper fans and talked quietly, waiting for the bridal party to assemble. Willa and Harriet, benched alone on the bride's side, stared straight ahead at the tall vases of flowers banking the pulpit and the railing in front of it. Above in the choir gallery, an organ played familiar music softly, and a small woman in pink organdy stepped from behind a curtain and sang about perfect love in a sweet tremolo. Across the aisle and back some rows a thin little voice piped up: "Where's the bride, Momma? You said there'd be a pretty bride." Adults hurriedly shushed the child and amused glances flew between them. Harriet frowned and sat tall in her lavender silk and pearls, lace gloves clenched in her lap. Beside her, Willa looked every inch the poor relation in her plain navy blue.

The wedding march began and all stood. When Harriet pressed a handkerchief to her emotional sniffles, Willa shook her head and moved an inch away. Then the bride and her attendant began their slow and careful walk down the aisle, preceded by a little girl carrying a basket of flowers. From a side door Phil and his cousin Duke stepped forward and the two parties met in front of the minister.

Tall and lovely in a simple white dress that skimmed the floor and a short veil gathered at the back of her head with a sprig of orange blossoms, Bee came to take her place beside Phil, handing her bouquet to Genevieve.

The service began. The surprise came when the minister lifted his head and asked the traditional question: "Who giveth this woman...?"

Bee turned, took Phil's hand in hers and faced Willa and Harriet. "We ask Willa Jordon and Harriet Frost to act in this capacity," she said with smiles for both of them. Flustered by this unexpected request, the women murmured the response, their hands blindly reaching for each other across years of fretful contention, jealousy, and the ungraciousness of a relationship without love.

Chapter VIII

1942-1943

The plan to ask Willa and Harriet to "give the bride away" had come to Bee suddenly, while she and Phil talked over the risks involved in putting Willa and Harriet in the same hotel room. Lacking a father or other male relative, she saw it as a logical solution, a clever way to keep both women on an even footing. A good move, Phil agreed.

Although bridal protocol would be carefully followed, Bob and Renee, Phil's parents, had quietly taken over the expenses of a wedding reception. Had Phil dropped hints about Willa's situation? Bee didn't question him about it, but she was grateful for his understanding. If they hadn't offered, the gap would have been filled by Harriet and she might have done something monumentally inappropriate. Keeping Harriet out of the preparations might have been a tactical error, but it made sense logistically to initiate the plan from Phil's home town. Wartime had softened the hard edge of wedding tradition anyway, and Bee could plead distance and convenience if she had to defend herself. One question: would Willa feel anything at all because her mother-of-the-bride prerogatives had been taken over? Not likely.

Bob and Renee were sweet, but a little stuffy, by New York
city standards. Phil was touchingly anxious to have their
approval of his choice of wife, and in a haze of happiness Bee
gave them her best smiles and everyone hugged and it was a lovely
wedding, all considered, with no major hitches and good feelings
all around.

Four days for a honeymoon, a leisurely trip southward, on
down into Hattiesburg, Mississippi, where Camp Shelby would be
Phil's post for the immediate future. Since it now seemed
unlikely that he would be sent into combat, they could make
plans to set up housekeeping. His status could change, however,
and beneath their high spirits lay a thread of uncertainty that
surfaced from time to time. Wartime restrictions applied,
naturally. Rent was high near a military post, and landlords
made their own rules. Gas was rationed, meat too - and the
post commissary wouldn't be a New York style A&P, he warned.

Bee's introduction to southern customs came swiftly. "White"
and "Colored" drinking fountains were the first shock, discovered
when they stopped in a small town just over the Mason/Dixon
line. There were others to come. Somewhere in North Carolina
where they stopped for breakfast, she encountered "brains 'n'
eggs" - a delicacy that produced borderline nausea and sent her
to the washroom to rinse out her mouth. Phil was laughing when
she came back to the table.

"Waaaaal, Ah declare!" he clowned. "Li'l gal, you gotta
be f'om up Nawth, if'n y'all ain't heared of brains fo'
breakfast!"

"It's disgusting," she said, and went back to the counter
for toast and jelly. Hot black coffee helped to banish the
taste and after a while he stopped kidding and they went out

to the car hand in hand.

The heat was intense. By noon Phil's khakis were limp and wrinkled and he had tied handkerchiefs to the steering wheel because it was too hot to touch. He promised, giving her a sticky hug, that one of her first lessons as a wife would be to learn how to drive. She was thrilled. Drive a car? The question had never come up before. In New York, with income just above the poverty level, it had been out of the question - and unnecessary, besides. Harriet, usually anxious to impart useful skills, had never offered to teach her.

Arriving in Hattiesburg on a blistering afternoon, Phil and Bee checked into the Forrest Hotel and showered away the dust and perspiration of the long trip. Then, still hot but somewhat refreshed, they fell on the big double bed. With more enthusiasm than control, Phil came within minutes, then lay back breathing heavily. Bee glanced at him, wondering if she should say something, then remembered Lucille's advice. It wasn't unusual, she had said, when partners were inexperienced, and could be expected to improve with practice. And, she had added, "There are ways to help him along, if you know what I mean. Any time I can answer questions, Bee, just get in touch." Bee had giggled. "So, you're an encyclopedia on sex now." She wasn't sure what "help him along" meant, but if it came to a crunch, she could probably figure out something to do.

A new word had entered her vocabulary - orgasm - but when she used it to tell him how delicious it was, he frowned. His own climax arrived in silence, with only a shudder or a low grunt to let her know what had happened. Not sure yet what was expected of her, She kept quiet when they made love, and if a groan of pleasure was unavoidable, she tried to stifle it.

Coming to terms with Phil's reluctance to talk about their lovemaking was first on her list of marital duties, she realized. A concession, easy to grant. His upbringing, undoubtedly, was to blame. Bob and Renee had struck her as very conservative, traditional parents, and the kind of casual sex talk that Bee heard all around her, living in a big city, was probably never heard in a small rural town. Phil's desire for her was apparent in many small tender attentions, and he seemed genuinely concerned that she enjoy herself too. A good beginning had been made, she felt, and the future would take care of itself.

After three days at the Forrest, they moved into their furnished apartment: two rooms, bath, back door entrance (it was a private house, whose owners had converted the first floor into two miniscule apartments). The wedding gift Harriet had put into the fat cream-colored envelope was a check for $500. Rather than spend it to brighten the shabby furnishings, they decided on a weekend in New Orleans, a classy hotel and the best restaurant the city offered.

Hattiesburg didn't offer much in the way of entertainment. There was a movie house, a few restaurants where one could get a decent meal, and a couple of department stores selling farm wives' fashions and baby carriages. There were no bars or cocktail lounges – Mississippi was a dry state. This didn't matter to Phil, an abstainer, but occasionally Bee longed for a tall Tom Collins in the August heat, and had to settle for lemonade.

The rigors of rationing were felt now. Back in New York, Harriet had suffered little. Buying modestly for her Tea Room, she was eligible, nevertheless, for the perks of a restaurateur – namely, samples of butter and eggs, sugar, cold meats (all on the rationed list) delivered in the form of "thank you for your business" gifts along with her weekly order from the food purveyors. Portions of these luxuries had been passed on to Bee.

They ate macaroni and cheese and salads, fresh greens and local fruit, and the once-a-week liver dinner was bravely endured. Sunday meant a visit to the Officers' Club dining room, where fried chicken and shrimp were on the menu, finished off with pecan pie and ice cream.

Gas rationing was the real hardship. Phil was given restricted use of a service vehicle, not to be used for pleasure. With the few gallons allotted for personal use, they could drive around town in the old Chevy, but a trip to the countryside had to be planned for. When she mentioned looking for a job in town, Phil wasn't enthusiastic but she persuaded him that she needed to get out of the apartment. She had explored what limited shopping was available, and a matinee at the movie house was no fun alone. "Something to do" would relieve the daily boredom and a part time job might fill the bill. The idea had a short life. Local merchants and businesses wanted little to do with Yankees. This attitude was illustrated vividly one morning on a town bus.

Seeking the library where she could get reading material for Phil's overnight duty, Bee boarded a crowded bus and took the last available seat just behind the driver. At the next stop a fragile old black woman climbed in, fumbled for change and almost fell as the bus sped from the curb. With no second thought, Bee jumped up and took her arm, then pushed her toward the seat she had just left.

With a look of fright and horror, the woman pulled her thin arm free. "No, ma'am! We'all don't sit here - we sits back there - " Amid hoots of laughter from the seats at the far end, she hobbled away without even a thank-you. Surrounded by frowns of disapproval from the "White Only" seats and some muttering about "You Yankees," Bee got off at the next stop. <u>No wonder I can't get a job in this town</u>, she thought, embarrassed and angry. <u>My 'northern-ness' sticks out all over me.</u> As a child of the Brooklyn streets where different colors and ethnic backgrounds were the norm, she had never experienced such distinctions.

They talked about this that night at supper.

"It's a southern attitude, impossible to change," Phil said. "You'll have to get used to it. I know - " He stopped her as she was about to say she would never get used to it.

"Phil, this is the twentieth century, not the 1860s! These people here think they're still slave owners!"

"Colors don't mix in Mississippi. It doesn't have to affect us - we're army."

It was true. The army didn't cohabit with local populations. It did what it could to keep from offending but it went about its business and its members, from every state, brought with them and lived by their own customs and attitudes. There would be clashes, inevitably, and Phil didn't want to be drawn into them. It would be Bee's job to fall into step, not question the customs, and for his sake deal privately with her feelings of distaste.

The driving lessons started in September and she took to it at once. Getting a driver's license presented no problem. Directed to the State Police shack outside of town, she was asked four or five questions, got two wrong, and was given a big smile and official permission to operate a motor vehicle in the state of Mississippi. No road test, no written exam. Fee, fifty cents.

The Chevy, not a thing of beauty but serviceable, became her getaway car, always watching the fuel gauge to be sure there was enough gas left for the weekend. Driving Phil out to camp in the morning, she would stop for coffee at the PX, usually meeting some of the other young wives, and then have the rest of the day to herself. She discovered a tiny local history museum, providing a couple of days' entertainment, then a miniature golf course a few blocks from their apartment. Without Phil's company, the diversions lacked real flavor, but she managed to pass the time and an hour before he came home she did her best, with limited materials, to present him with a tasty dinner.

Her driving skills grew rapidly. She loved the exhilaration, the feeling of power beneath her feet. She was twenty-two years old, married, and now a legal driver. What more proof of maturity was needed?

In the middle of September Phil was tapped for the job of Club Officer at camp, involving the management of the dining room, card rooms, and bar. There being no place in town to procure liquor (and no Officers' Club could function without it), a scheme had been devised to insure a steady supply. The source was in the next county, sixty miles away, in a warehouse behind a roadside diner, twenty feet from the state line. The sign above the door read:

HEALSBURG FEED & GRAIN

Inside, the building was an illegal liquor depot that supplied all the thirsty of the state of Mississippi, including the military establishment. The weekly run in the Chevy, conducted in secrecy late at night, brought twenty cases back to the Club bar, the trip made possible by the officers themselves, who pooled gas rations and filled the Chevy's tank. Phil packed the cases in the trunk, in the back seat, and under Bee's legs in the front seat. Hurrying along in the small hours of the morning, they slunk in behind their apartment and covered the evidence with blankets. After two hours' sleep, Phil would leave for camp at daylight to deliver the contraband, leaving Bee murmuring a sleepy goodbye.

"What would happen if a cop stopped us?" she asked. "Would he have any jurisdiction? Would we end up in the county jail?"

"Don't ask," he advised. "Probably the Club would deny everything and we'd be on our own. Who knows - courts martial?"

This wasn't very funny.

"Don't worry, I'm careful. The country roads are deserted late at night, anyway. Who's to see us - a few local moonshiners?"

Bee giggled. "How come they don't get a drinker to do the run? You couldn't care less about the stuff."

"Kind of ironic, isn't it?"

Phil's per case profit, offered by the Club members who financed the adventure, was socked away toward the purchase of a new car, the Chevy's springs and general health having been affected by the illegal activity.

One night at the warehouse they were invited to partake of the commodity they had been transporting. There were a couple of slot machines in the back of the big room, and while Phil negotiated a sale, Bee began pumping dimes in, with little luck. Seeing Phil in low conversation with one of the men, she wandered over.

"They want us to stay and have a drink. Someone here got married, there's leftover cold cuts and potato salad and booze. I said we had to get back."

"Oh, please, Phil - can't we stay? Just a little while?"

His look said it wasn't what he wanted to hear, but she pressed him. An occasional evening at the Officers' Club was, so far, all the social life they had, and not a lot of fun.

It had meant, for Bee, learning how to play bridge with women whose husbands often far outranked Phil. In the firmly entrenched pecking order among military wives, Bee knew her place was at the bottom, as a second looie's wife, and no one had much to say to her. For his sake, on those evenings, she nursed one rum and coke throughout the bridge game.

So they stayed and ate and Bee had three drinks and got dark looks from Phil, which she deflected craftily while trying to fill a fourth glass. He took it away from her, said his goodbyes and pushed her out to the car.

"You made a pig of yourself in there. What was that all about?"

"Sweetie, don't get mad. Maybe I'm not used to it any more. I really do know how to hold my liquor." She lolled against his shoulder, missing his angry look. "Let's go home and play house ..."

"Play?"

She decided not to hear the annoyance in his voice. "You know, in bed. Let's go home and play around til morning."

He was rigid with anger now. It might be a good idea to move away. She told herself: I'm not drunk, just tipsy. And why can't I suggest some fun in bed? Aren't I his lawful wife? His honeybun? His soulmate? Why is he being so hateful? On that sour note she promptly fell asleep, to be shaken awake a few hours later and dragged into bed and left there. Phil drove the car out to camp and delivered the cases of whiskey and Bee was left alone, carless, to think about her sins.

When she woke around noon, what she thought about was Phil
and his attitudes. Three months of marriage and he still hadn't
loosened up. He disapproved of drinking, so she mustn't show
any interest in it. He had funny ideas about making love, so
she shouldn't try to initiate anything, but wait for whatever
he wanted to do. It was getting to be tiresome. "Will he be
furious tonight, for what I did - will I get a lecture, or black
looks, or will he just sulk?"

She showered, took out a pretty dress, did her hair in a
soft pony tail with a silver ribbon, left her legs bare but
put on white sandals, and rubbed perfumed powder on her breasts.
He'll have to be stone to resist this, she told herself in the
mirror, grinning. She'd think of something tender, whispery,
but charged with emotion, like: "Sweetheart, I'm awfully sorry
about last night, I don't know what got into me. It won't ever
happen again, I promise..." all the while leaning against him,
arms creeping up around his neck, lips near his ear. If he
didn't relent after that, he'd be a marble statue.

She didn't need any of it. He called to say he had been
asked to trade duty night by one of the other men and would
see her tomorrow. Another day without the car. More punishment.
Anyway, he hadn't yelled at her or even mentioned the previous
night. Pull back and count your blessings.

Hattiesburg and Camp Shelby lasted six months. There was
a small scare in early January when Phil thought the army might
have changed its mind and was planning to ship him to Germany,

but his orders were changed at the last minute and he was posted
to Camp Davis, in North Carolina. Since they had acquired few
household furnishings, aside from portables like a toaster,
an iron (Willa's wedding gift) and an electric percolator,
packing was easy. Bee looked around the little apartment with
some sadness. Small and shabby though it was, there was
something of themselves in it, their first love, the first days
of their marriage.

The northeast trip in the old Chevy, which, in spite of the
whiskey run, was still alive, was uneventful. A new car would
be the first big expense they would face and high on their list
of priorities. Bee prepared herself for new experiences with
military living, and, of course, with a new set of army wives.

They arrived in Wilmington with four suitcases late on a
Saturday night, to hole up in a hotel and search for a place
to live. Phil signed in at camp and Bee started combing the
rental services, putting their names on list after list, even
paying a visit to the nearest Baptist church to let it be known
they were desperate. The town seethed with servicemen and their
families, all looking for living space. Restaurants were crowded,
lines were long, food expensive. After two weeks of searching,
they were accepted as being safe and sober enough by a young
couple with a small child, who had a furnished room to rent
on their top floor. Hoping for an apartment, at least, Bee
hid her disappointment and they moved in. There was the usual
hot plate, a tiny refrigerator and a private phone line. The
room was big and airy, windows looking out on the garden in

back. Their landlords, Lila and Pete Morgan, were friendly and outgoing, a first real taste of "southern hospitality," something that had been blatantly lacking in Mississippi.

The Morgans asked them to share family activities; backyard cook-outs, even a birthday party for the little boy. Bee found a part time job at the post library, checking books in and out, typing, keeping the stacks neat and tidy. The boredom of Hattiesburg forgotten, she relaxed in the glow of friendship and good feelings. And it was there in the spring of the following year she found out she was pregnant.

Current movies depicting life in the service often showed a young wife announcing her "condition" to a surprised and elated young husband, and Bee planned to pattern her own announcement on this. It was a time for babies, and she felt right in step. The only anxiety that disturbed her was the fact that she and Phil hadn't discussed this eventuality. He liked children, obviously, because the Morgan's little son could always charm him into a smile and a hug. But in a year and a half of marriage they had yet to talk about starting a family. Now it was academic.

Rather than deliver a speech, she decided, she would just drop the news casually into conversation, maybe at dinner, or breakfast, or maybe as they were getting ready for bed, or maybe at ....

"Sweetheart!" she crowed as he walked in at five o'clock on the day the doctor had given the word. "We're going to have a baby!" 154

He blinked, dropped his jacket on the floor and reached for her, swinging her up and around the room, skirt flying, right out of the last wartime movie she had seen.

"Bee! I can't believe it! Incredible! Our own baby!" He put her down carefully, then rushed for the telephone. His hand shaking, he gave the operator the number. "Hello? Hello Mom? It's Phil - with wonderful news! We're going to have a baby! Sure - Bee's fine - want to talk to her? Here - "

Bee was delighted. Just as it should be, a blessed event that pleased everyone.

Chapter IX

1943-1945

Bee had been writing to Willa and Harriet regularly, getting
in return Willa's sharp advice on how to be a good wife and
Harriet's pleas to "Come for a visit, even a short one. I miss
you so much!" Now it appeared that she would be going back
north to have the baby. The army hospital was full, booked
for months to come, and the local community hospital was out
of the question. Everyone was having babies. The doctor at Camp
Davis suggested she might want to leave for New York five or
six weeks before due date and locate hospital accommodations
there, where chances were better. Ecstatic about his impending
fatherhood, Phil wanted to do everything to insure Bee's comfort
and safety, even if it meant he would be absent when the great
event took place. He said he would be able to arrange for an
emergency leave once the baby was born, perhaps for a week,
but she would have to rely on Willa and Harriet for last month
care and for transportation to the hospital.

Such wonderful things were happening! Bee read reams of
maternity advice at the post library, took vitamins, paid
attention to diet and chatted with other moms-to-be in the PX,
picking up useful information from second-timers, like the luxury

of diaper service, the availability of formula, what to do for colic in newborns, and teething problems.

Nausea was occasional, usually when she was in the neighborhood of motor oil or gasoline - her stomach turning queasy at the first sniff. Other than that, early pregnancy gave her no trouble.

Two days before Thanksgiving she boarded the train in Wilmington, after a happy but tearful farewell, and went back to New York for the second most important event in her life.

Harriet met her at the train. Willa was working and hadn't been able to take time off. She was due at Harriet's for dinner, and had even been invited to spend the night, a concession on Harriet's part, since having Bee to herself after a long absence would have been expected. Bee was genuinely glad to see them. Still Dowager Empress, Harriet clasped Bee to her bosom and smiled and smiled all through dinner. Willa was something else. Her face was pinched and pale, she seemed to have lost a lot of weight, and there was sickness in her eyes. The cough was worse than when Bee had last seen her. Harriet watched her throughout the meal and when Willa reached for a cigarette she said: "You can do without for one night, Willa. Bee's pregnant. Maybe she'd rather not breathe smoke."

Two small pink patches appeared in Willa's cheeks and she blinked with irritation, but put the cigarette away.

"First, I'll take you to see Dr. Hammel," Harriet said. "He's reliable, doesn't believe in all that nonsense about eating

for two, getting fat and having trouble losing it afterward.
I've already talked to him about you. There's a room reserved
for you at the hospital. I'm sure you'll like him."

Nothing had changed. Harriet was in charge.

"How does your husband feel about the baby?" Willa asked.

Nothing has changed, Bee thought wryly. Both of them still
can't bring themselves to use his name. What was the matter
with these women? Why couldn't they acknowledge that she was
grown up, had a husband, who had a name?

"He's very happy about it," she said, calm and friendly.
"We're both happy about it."

"Have you picked out a name yet?" There was a gleam in
Harriet's eyes.

"We'll name it after Phil, if it's a boy."

"And if it's a girl?"

"Phil said I could choose any name I want."

Neither of them asked if she had chosen yet. Smart of them.
I wouldn't tell them anyway. It's my choice and my secret.

Bee stayed with Willa during the week, having the small
apartment to herself while her mother went to work. She took
long walks in the Brooklyn streets, bundled into a heavy coat
and mittens against the early December cold. Weekends, repeating
the pattern of her childhood, she spent with Harriet, this time
in a big bedroom on the second floor, not the tiny cubbyhole
of early days. She shopped for groceries and helped prepare
dinner and they talked long and seriously about the future.
For Bee, the feeling of déjà vu was overwhelming. Except for

the swelling and ungainly bulk of late pregnancy, she was young
Bee Jordon once again, watching Harriet pull her everlasting
strings of influence, and under the thumb of admonishing Willa,
whose ill health was making her testy and hard to live with.
Harriet went with her on the weekly visits to Dr. Hammel, where
she was examined, poked at and advised about exercise and diet.

December, cold and raw in New York, with Christmas
approaching and the depressing prospect of spending the holiday
far away from Phil. Even his frequent phone calls cheered her
only briefly, leaving her more than ever with the feeling of
being alone.

Harriet planned a festive celebration and Bee went along
with it half-heartedly, helping to decorate the big house, make
cookies, wrap gifts. It was only a small group that assembled
when the day arrived: Willa, Harriet and Bee sat at the long
table with two old friends of Harriet's who happened to be in
the city for a visit. The meal, prepared with all of Harriet's
talent and enthusiasm, was a work of culinary art which went
largely unappreciated except by Harriet herself. Willa had
no appetite, the guests were dieters and at the moment Bee had
no taste for celebration. Gifts were distributed over liqueurs
in the parlor. After offering appropriate thanks, the party
dribbled to a finish and they all left. Bee refused Harriet's
offer and called a cab. She and Willa rode in silence back to
Flatbush.

Most of the time she was uncomfortable, walked with tilted
gait, trying for balance. For hours she sat at one window or

another, watching hail and snow and rain and dark skies, waiting.
Delivery had been promised for early January. By the middle
of the month she had had enough and became grouchy and
complaining, snapping at Willa and Harriet, feeling deeply sorry
for herself. Phil got short answers then he called, but wisely
was patient, and she loved him for it, while giving him
monosyllables in a sulky voice.

Labor started at dawn, waking her from a troubled dream.
The pains were deep inside, stretching muscles, spreading a
fierce ache throughout her body, subsiding only to begin five
minutes later. It was Saturday. In minutes Harriet was ready
to leave, all bustling efficiency, and Bee gladly let her direct
operations. They arrived at the hospital in plenty of time.
Because no sense of urgency was conveyed either by the nurse
who undressed her or by the fact that the doctor took his time
arriving, Bee assumed she might be in for a long labor. Lucille
(now living in Rhode Island but in occasional phone contact)
had been, once more, a fountain of information, having had her
baby just before Christmas. It was all too true. Twenty-four
hours of regular, intense pains with frequent "peeks" by nurses
and doctors as they watched for the head to appear wore her
out. At the end, as she was wheeled into the delivery room,
she managed to smile up at the serious faces around her and
make a joking remark that was ignored as they called for the
final "Push!". She wasn't allowed to be present, however, at
the moment of Anne's birth. They covered her face with a rubber
mask and she went into limbo for the rest of it.

Phil came to New York two days later and stayed for the week at a hotel in Manhattan, refusing Harriet's offer to use her place as a base. He wanted to be free to come and go, he told Bee, to stay with her late into the evening and to take his meals at local restaurants. He said he didn't want to talk to anyone about his brand new fatherhood, or think about Harriet or Willa and what part they would play from now on. In addition, he had convinced Bob and Renee that their presence wasn't necessary, that he would see to it that they met their grandchild all in good time.

Bee's top floor room had a view of the glades of Prospect Park, only bare trees in snow, but nicer to look at than dull green hospital walls. When the floor nurse suggested she try to walk the distance to the nursery, she pulled herself up and into the satin robe and slippers Harriet had brought and, hugging the wall, made it on Phil's arm to the viewing window. Together, holding hands and leaning against each other, they stared at the tiny form in the hospital crib.

"Isn't she lovely?" Bee breathed, her eyes shining with tears. How had she produced such perfection? Where had this exquisite little thing come from? A miracle, absolutely a miracle!

"The most beautiful baby I've ever seen!" Phil said solemnly. He pulled her close, his own eyes overflowing.

It was a time of happiness and hopeful plans, the beginning of parenthood, of life as three. They walked slowly back to

Bee's room, arms around each other, and Bee told herself there would never be another day as happy as this one, never.

It was the next Saturday before Willa came, a bouquet of spring flowers in one hand. "Are you all right? Could I see the baby?" she asked, a strange shyness in her voice.

"Of course! Phil will take you down to the nursery. I'm supposed to stay in bed." Bee took the flowers and smiled at her mother. "Glad you could come, Willa."

"I had to wait, they wouldn't let me off on a weekday."

Phil took her arm, grinned at Bee and led Willa off down the hall.

At the end of the week Phil came to the hospital to take them to Willa's, along with the gift boxes Harriet had delivered every day, He told Bee he had bought a crib and some other baby furnishings and stored them with the Morgans while he searched for a larger apartment. It would only be a matter of a few weeks, he promised, until he could send for them to return to North Carolina.

That night after he left for camp, Bee cried for hours while Willa paced the floor with tiny Anne, who howled her newborn lungs out against her grandmother's shoulder. It was one thing to have come north to have the baby, because circumstances dictated it. It would be another thing entirely to be left alone post partum, to do all the "firsts" without Phil, like give her her first bath, soothe her through her first colic, see her first tiny smile. Willa was a help, but her stern

unemotional mothering consisted mainly of "You'll spoil her
if you pick her up every time she cries." Harriet's effusive
approach was equally irritating. She cooed and sighed, leaning
over the bassinet, arms outstretched for immediate rescue in
case the baby showed signs of distress. There was no way to
curtail these attentions, and Bee gritted her teeth and tried
to make the best of it.

There had been stony silence when she told Harriet the name
she and Phil had decided on. Deliberately, they had left out
a middle name, knowing that any choice would lead to words with
the two women. Anne was a beautiful baby, and Bee nursed her
in a trance of happiness, rocking her in Willa's old rocker,
crooning lullabies into her tiny ear. Afternoons, she walked
through the park, wheeling the handsome new carriage - again,
a gift from Harriet.

It was March before Phil wrote that he'd found an apartment.
By then Bee had had enough and wanted only to get back to being
wife and housewife, and now, joyously, mother. Her world was
overflowing with good things, nothing but sunny skies, and once
the miserable war was over, the future would be safe and secure.

A few days before leaving New York, Bee went shopping with
Harriet for baby clothes, Anne riding on her hip in a canvas
baby sling. In Macy's Infants Department they sat in comfortable
chairs while saleswomen distributed baby garments along the
counter top.

"If you'd rather." Harriet said, looking across a pile

of pink things, "I'll be happy to indulge you with diaper service
for the first few months. You'll have your hands full enough
without having to do that messy job."

"You've given me so much already, Harriet. I won't mind
washing diapers, really I won't."

"Whatever you say." Her amiability in the face of their
impending departure took Bee by surprise. Had she finally come
to terms with the new status? Was Harriet, at last, going to
treat her like an adult?

On the way back to Brooklyn in the car, Harriet introduced
the subject Bee had hoped to avoid - where they would resettle,
once the war was over.

"No, we haven't talked about it yet. Phil may even want
to stay in the service, make it a career. All I can tell you
is we'll think about it when the time comes." Harriet would
be looking for a promise to return to New York, but it was too
early for any decision. Bee eased her back into talking about
the Tea Room, and her weekend activities as Block Captain for
the local Air Raid Warden's office, something each neighborhood
was now involved with.

With the trip back south only a few days away, there was
packing to do, arrangements to be made for shipping the nursery
equipment Harriet had bought - a hundred small chores and no
time to deal with Harriet's emotional state.

"I'll stay with Willa tonight and tomorrow night," Bee
said. "You can come for us Sunday morning and we'll stay with
you until train time."

Harriet pulled up to a red light and turned her head. "Willa's not well, as I'm sure you've seen." It was the first time this topic had come into conversation since Bee's arrival in December. She had tried to get Willa to say what was going on, without success.

The traffic light changed and the car moved slowly forward. Eyes on the road, Harriet continued: "I know she wouldn't want me to tell you this, but I'm going to, anyway. You should know before you go back down south."

Was this something serious? Really serious? Suspicion had nagged at Bee once or twice in the past weeks, watching the deepening pallor. "What should I know before I go back?"

"She wouldn't see a doctor for a long time, and when she did, finally, the diagnosis was a malignancy in her lungs."

Bee was stunned, heart suddenly racing. Anne fussed against her shoulder and her hands shook as she tried to calm the baby. "Is she - what's she doing about it?"

"That's just it," Harriet answered. "She never went back to see him, and nothing I could say would change her mind."

"You mean - she's just going to let this go on? Not get any kind of treatment?"

"Treatment? What kind of treatment do you think there is? Don't you understand what malignancy means?"

"Well, yes, of course I do. It means she's got something bad, but to ignore it - what's the matter with her, Harriet?"

Anne cried louder and Harriet lifted a hand from the wheel and patted her. "Shhh...., sweetheart."

"We've got to make her go back. This is ridiculous - a grown woman, acting like an irresponsible kid!" Bee's eyes filled with sudden tears and she brushed at them angrily.

"Maybe you can do something with her," Harriet said.

"You can be damn sure I'm going to try!"

The news was a bomb, and the feelings it generated had to be dealt with fast. Time was running low, she had three days to work it out. Why hadn't this been mentioned before? Why was it dumped in her lap now, at the last minute? A chilling thought answered the questions: Harriet had kept the information back until this moment, hoping it would force cancellation of the trip back to Wilmington. Of course she was capable of such a thing. Nothing had changed, had it? Harriet used information to further her own ends, waiting to create advantage out of anything that came her way. ABout to confront her, Bee had a second thought. Talk to Willa first, don't take everything Harriet says as gospel. Wait and see what the facts are.

"I'll talk to her."

"Good luck," Harriet said, with a quick sideways look.

It was Saturday night before Bee found an opportunity. Anne was asleep, the bags were packed, everything ready for departure. Willa had put in a day behind the lingerie counter, arriving home pale and tired. Bee had a drink ready for her, supper on the stove, a firm speech shaping up in her mind. She would browbeat, bully, if necessary, but she would force Willa to face her situation.

Willa reached for a cigarette and Bee didn't stop her.

One more could make little difference now.

Without preamble, Bee said: "Harriet told me how sick you are, and I want to know why you aren't doing anything about it."

Willa exhaled slowly, her green eyes beginning to glitter, a look Bee remembered from her childhood,   signifying that wrath was building. She tapped her cigarette over an ashtray, then lifted the glass and took a long pull at the whiskey and ginger ale. A spasm of coughing caught at her throat. Bee waited until it subsided.

"Right this moment," Willa said in a cold, steady voice, "I probably hate Harriet Frost more than I ever have before. More than I did at the beginning, more than I did when Jack died, more than all the times she has made me feel I counted for nothing."

"You hate her? What are you talking about?" Bee stared in disbelief. "Harriet's been your friend since high school - she's been a fairy godmother, given us everything - for years!"

The laugh that bubbled in Willa's throat wasn't pleasure and brought on another bout of coughing. When it passed she said: "That's the way it was planned. She got what she wanted. So did I."

"What do you mean?" What had happened to the firm resolve to make Willa shape up and do the right thing? Five minutes into the conversation it had taken a different turn - God knows in what direction it was headed now. Bee watched her mother get up and splash more whiskey in her glass. There was a flushed,

defiant look on her face, telling Bee that some boundary was
about to be breached.

Bee held out her glass and Willa refilled it.

Willa sat down once more and cupped the glass in her hands.
"I'm going to tell you about Jack and me, and how Harriet fits
into what went on a long time ago." She met Bee's eyes, a gesture
unusual enough to cause Bee a moment of alarm. "I never wanted
to get married," Willa went on, "least of all to Jack Jordon.
He cost me a career, a fine life, a lot of things I had planned
for myself. He killed everything I hoped for, and I hated him
for it, and hated myself for letting it happen."

Bee's mouth had gone dry. She drained her glass and got
up and filled it with water from the tap.

The story began the night it happened. Bee could hear the
"it" in Italics as Willa dragged from memory the events of that
evening, starting with the dinner party at Harriet's. When
she got to the final scene in her furnished room in the Village,
she bravely recounted it all, from the first pleading cry to
the last savage forcing. She called it rape, but qualified it
with her own inability to fight him. Bee listened, fascinated,
wondering what she would have done in such circumstances,
fantasizing the act in all its steaminess, seeing her mother
reach for something to hit him with, then go into a kind of
trance while he did what he had planned to do for so many weeks.

The shock was Harriet's part, that she had been in love,
or thought she was, with Jack and had lived with him, unwed,
for three months. Harriet, in bed with Jack? It was a picture

to bring giggles, at any other time. But it had been tragedy, obviously, to young Willa, and Bee quenched her amusement.

The arrangement for her upbringing filled the gap in her understanding of Harriet's beneficence. That Jack had stayed, not walked away from them, was harder to understand. What had kept him there? A hope that wouldn't die, that his wife would finally accept him, even care about him? His drinking, however, was no mystery. He had been emasculated, truly, by Harriet's anger and contempt, made a eunuch by Willa, and had his child taken out of his control by both of them. It made a kind of weird sense, now, as her mind filled with scenes she had never examined: Willa as mother, cold and unresponsive, because she wanted no part of motherhood, but something else - a different life. When she got pregnant all that she had planned for became impossible, or so she saw it. The child she didn't want she gave to Harriet, who wanted motherhood. And because revenge for Jack's rejection drove her all her life, Harriet tightened her hold on Bee year by year.

Despising Jack, bitter toward Harriet, indifferent to her child - what a barren, frozen life it had been for her mother. The times she lived in frowned on motherhood out of wedlock. Bee stifled an impulse to point out how unnecessary the sacrifice had been. Today, in the nineteen-forties, such scruples were, if not unheard of, more often given only lip service. What Bee saw as a sad little melodrama, Willa had viewed as a major disruption in her life and a crisis of conscience that could only be resolved one way.

Willa came to the end of the story, made herself another drink and lit a cigarette. They looked at each other in silence.

"I'm glad you told me this," Bee said finally. "But it's water under the bridge, isn't it? I'm sorry it happened to you that way, that you felt you had to do what you did, but Jack's not here any more and I'm married now and Harriet, well, Harriet will have to get along without me. I can understand," she began to choose words carefully, "why you hate her, or say you do, but you two have been through a lot together and probably will always mean something to each other. I think she told me about your sickness because she thought I could help you."

"She had no right."

Bee shrugged. "Anyway, we're back to the original question, which is what are you going to do about your health, and how soon?" It sounded callous, in her own ears, to put aside so casually the painful confession Willa had made. But they had to get back to the current problem because what Harriet had said was obvious. Willa was seriously ill, and time was running out - for both of them. Bee wanted to get on with her life, free from worry over Willa's condition, wanted not to be saddled with anxiety and frustration, both of which she had had her share of, growing up with these women in charge of her life.

Unexpectedly, Willa said: "Bee, I may not have been demonstrative when you were a child, but I want you to know - I loved you, as much as I could, and I think Jack did, too, in his own way."

Willa? When, ever, had anything remotely resembling love been
shown by either of them? Did she now, after all these
revelations, want Bee to answer that she, too, had been a loving,
if undemonstrative child?

"Willa, listen to me. I have to leave on Monday morning.
Don't let me go back to Wilmington with this worry on my mind.
Will you see a doctor right away and find out what can be done?"

Willa's gaze went past Bee, once more expressionless, and
she got up and took her glass to the sink. When she came back
she looked at Bee coolly, nothing at all in her face. "I'll
keep in touch. Now, let's see if you've packed everything."

A month after Bee returned to North Carolina, Phil received
orders transferring him to Fort Benning, in Georgia, and once
more they pulled up shallow roots and made the move, this time
with baby Anne and a hired truck full of nursery furniture.
Bee settled in to more formal army life, Phil having received
a promotion to first lieutenant. She was included in the wives'
charity affairs, bridge tournaments, club suppers and other
gala entertainments. A small, protected island in a sea of
uncertainty and distant violence, they pretended that none of
it really touched them, that the next card game or cocktail
party was a matter to be taken seriously.

In Brooklyn, with Harriet, Bee had learned about air raid
precautions and underground shelters and black-out curtains
and enemy subs off the coast of Massachusetts, but the newness

of motherhood had shielded her from real understanding. The war was far away, and its local symptoms - rationing, practice sirens in the night - only minor inconveniences. Here, in Georgia, social activites were a more immediate concern than headlines in the news, and alarming possibilities grew out of catching the attention of the General's wife more than they did from reports of overseas battles.

And then suddenly (it seemed to her) it was over. D-Day and VJ-Day and parades in the streets, men returning from war, families being reunited, a new era of peace about to dawn, and something to be decided: should Phil stay in the army, remain in the protective cocoon, or should he return to civilian life, and if so, where?

PART TWO

Chapter I

February 22, 1949

Dear Bee:

Another Christmas has come and gone without you. How
many times have you come to New York since Anne was born? Twice,
I think. Two years ago for the funeral and once for a week
at Easter. Have you any idea how lonely I am, with Willa gone
and you so far away?

Now that the war is over and your husband is out of
the army, what's really keeping you out there at the edge of
nowhere? Let me tell you what I'm thinking about. First, as
you must be aware, I've made a Will and you are my only heir.
The house in Brooklyn will be yours when I die, and if I don't
sell it, the summer house in Connecticut, too. Second, I have
a proposal for you. Come to New York and live with me in this
big old house. I just rattle around here, it needs young folks
to bring it to life. Since closing the Tea Room, my time is
my own, and if you should be thinking of returning to work,
Bee, you'd have a built-in nanny to take care of Anne. I want
you to think about this seriously, and let me know how the idea
strikes you.

Love, and hugs for Annie from her Aunt Harriet.

ITALICS

On a November morning Willa had been taken to Kings County
Hospital in an ambulance, after collapsing at her job. When
Stella Engle learned about it twenty-four hours later, she tried
unsuccessfully to call Harriet, then, not knowing how to reach
Bee and Phil, called Lucille in Providence. By the time Harriet
heard the news, Willa had passed into coma. Harriet's arrival
at the hospital was twenty minutes too late. She made
arrangements with a funeral service, ordered flowers and made
the phone call to Pennsylvania.

Bee went to New York for the funeral, said the proper words,
blew her nose, thanked Harriet and Stella and went back to State
College, to Phil and Anne.

It was easier, away from the scene, to think about her
feelings.

(Italics) What, exactly, am I supposed to feel? Relief that
her sickness is over? Sorrow that she died alone? Remorse
because I haven't been much of a daughter? Yes, I do feel relief
that it's all over. She suffered, obviously, and as to dying
alone, well, alone is what she always wanted. And remorse?
Yes, remorse. Maybe I could have made more of an effort to
be what she wanted, or at least to get a communication going.
The times we could talk to each other stand out like ink blots
on a blank page. I gave what I could, in the face of her lack
of interest. I'll try to remember the one or two positive times,
like Graduation Day and the movie we went to, and the day Jack

was buried, when I almost gave her a hug. But now I have to
get on with my own life, and see what I can make of it.
(end Italics)

The letter lay on the kitchen table where Phil couldn't
miss it when he came down to breakfast. It wasn't the first
in this vein Bee had received, but this one, she felt, had clout.
Since returning to civilian life Phil had resisted every
suggestion that they leave State College. He felt at home there,
had put in time learning a new business and wanted to stay where
he was, settle in and raise his family in familiar surroundings.
When Bee pushed the subject into conversation, once in a while,
he said: "How could I justify such a move to my father? You
know he plans to get behind me when I go into business on my
own. I owe it to him to stay here, where he can be part of
it." Shepard Heating & Air Conditioning: Phil had great hopes
that it would provide him with a substantial income and some
local prestige. He had done his homework, and with his father's
support, would soon be able to stand on his own feet.

And so the discussion would teeter on the brink of argument
as Bee pressed her own case, and sometimes would spill over
into angry words. She didn't feel a part of small town life,
had made few friends, and thought often about New York, and
Lucille, and the good times they'd had together. And now there
was substantial merit in Harriet's latest proposal.

"Just read it before you say anything," she coaxed when
he glanced suspiciously at the envelope. "This one isn't like

the others, Phil. She's offering something real - not just crying the way she usually does." She slid eggs from the pan, picked up two pieces of toast and put the plate in front of him.

"Harriet has a one-track mind," he said. "She wants you back in her clutches, and Anne, too. And she's so used to getting her own way she can't handle anything like refusal. So what's she come up with to sweeten the pot?" His expression was sour as he picked up the letter and started to read.

Bee waited, holding back an impatient answer. Before he came to the end, she broke in: "Think about it. Harriet is making me her heir, I'm to get all that property, and she has all kinds of investments, and the money from selling the Tea Room. Phil! It could mean a fortune!"

"At what price? We'd have to live with her forever. Can you see me getting along with Harriet, with her petty schemes, the way she manipulates people? Be realistic, Bee, it couldn't work."

About to rush in angrily, Bee stopped, hearing a faint hope in his last words. If he'd said "It absolutely can't work" or "I refuse to consider it" she would have a job cut out for her. But "It couldn't work..." was less firm, less adamant.

"Give it a little more thought. Maybe something could be worked out if we went up there and looked around. Brooklyn's a big place. We could find an apartment - I think that would satisfy her." She smiled placatingly. "And let's talk to Bob and Renee. They can help us decide."

He looked at her over his coffee cup. "And I suppose she'll cut you off without a cent, if we don't do what she wants," he grunted, and stood up. "Don't get your hopes up about this, Bee."

For two days Bee said nothing and went about preparations for a cook-out planned for the weekend. In the kitchen, Anne hopped from foot to foot around her mother, pleading to be allowed to help, getting in Bee's way as she gathered baking supplies and thought about how to approach Harriet.

"Momma! Momma! Let me do it!" Anne pushed at the knees standing between her and the table where bowls were lined up. "I can mix, Momma! I know how!"

Bee said: "Anne, don't get in the way, I have to get this done before your father comes home."

"But Momma - " Anne whined. "I can do it - "

"No, you can't!" Bee said. "Now go play somewhere!"

"You're mean!" wailed Anne, tears spilling over. "You never let me do anything!"

Bee poured cake batter into tins, working around the child, who stood her ground, yanking at the apron above her.

"Here. You can lick the bowl."

"Don't want the bowl. Want to help!"

"Oh, for God's sake! Here - you can put the pans in the oven."

With both hands on the oven door handle, Anne pulled it open, took the cake tins and carefully slid them onto the shelf. Peering in with satisfaction, she turned a wet smile up to her mother. "See? I can help!"

"Now go - find something else to do. I have a lot of work
to finish before supper."

Misery forgotten, Anne trotted out of the kitchen.

The front door slammed and Phil called out: "I'm home. What
smells so good?" He came into the kitchen and took Bee in his
arms. "Who's the best cook in the state? Who, I ask?"

"It's lemon cake. For the cook-out on Sunday, and maybe
some cookies, if I can find the time." She moved away from
him, wiping her hands on a towel. "Supper won't be ready for
a while. Want a drink?"

"I'll have a glass of milk." He opened the refrigerator.
"You go ahead - I know how much you like the sauce."

"For God's sake!" Bee said for the second time in minutes.
"What's that mean? Am I a lush or something? Just because
I like a drink before dinner - "

"Don't be snarly, honeybun. I was just kidding." He grinned
at her and poured milk into a glass. "Remember when I used
to call you that? Way back when?"

"Just let me get on with what I'm doing because if I don't
get these things in the oven soon I'll have to do it after we
eat and I really don't want to spend the evening in the kitchen."

Phil's smile faded and he finished his milk and left the
room.

(Italics)

I can't believe this is all there is, that sex is fifteen
minutes of silent groping in the dark and two minutes of sweaty

178

intercourse. If I say "fucking" - that word from my Brooklyn
street background that comes more readily to the tongue, Phil
will give me his pinched stony stare and I will have to withdraw
the filthy word and apologize. How do I communicate my wishes
without using the recognized, commonly accepted words? I'm tired
of saying meekly, "Let's make love tonight, Phil." I want to
do more than "make love." I want romance, I want soft lights
and low music, not silence and darkness.

He says: "Be quiet, Bee," if I begin to moan. He says:
"Someone might hear us." Who's to hear? Five year old Anne,
asleep since after dinner? "We might wake her," he says. And
so it goes. In any case, it's over soon. No sweet words in
my ear, no tender touching, no kisses below the chin. It hasn't
changed since the first week of our honeymoon, when he promised
"to do better." And all I have to tell me it should be different
are a few casual references from Lucille, remembered from back
in our city days: "If he does his job right, you'll be in
Heaven," and "Don't say no to anything new until you've tried
it. There's more to sex than just a hump in bed, Bee." And
the girls at the Met: "Once you've had it, you'll know why
we call it The Big Bang." (end Italics)

By constant reminder of the inheritance, Bee finally wore
down Phil's objections and they went to New York a month later,
leaving Anne with Renee and Bob. He made no firm promise,
but agreed to hold the decision until he saw how things went.
Meaning, Bee knew, if he could manage to get along with Harriet
at close range. She had been able to persuade Harriet that

they would need their own place, but assured her they would look for something not far from the Hendrix Street house. Overjoyed at their return and confident she could exert enough pressure to make them stay, Harriet conceded the point gracefully. Over a lavish dinner on the night they arrived, she was quietly helpful with current real estate information and newspaper classified ads.

After four days of following every appropriate lead in nearby communities, they came up with nothing. Picky post-war landlords made it clear they didn't want families with children and/or animals, but were holding out for elderly childless couples with no bad habits or pets.

Bee phoned a few acquaintances from the past, but they knew of nothing, and after offering sympathy for her efforts, said goodbye quickly. Then Harriet suggested they move beyond the borough and try Long Island. New bedroom communities were springing up all over Nassau and Suffolk counties, and the owners were less particular about tenants' family status than the ones in the city.

An ad in a Westbury local newspaper turned out to be as close to their needs as they had seen so far, and exhausted by the week of hunting and dealing with hostile landlords, Phil capitulated and they signed a two-year lease. Thirty miles from Brooklyn and beyond the immediate range of Harriet's attentions, it satisfied Phil and Bee was happy and hopeful for the future. The big step had been taken.

Harriet was ecstatic, full of advice, everything from picking up the cost of moving to eternal baby-sitting. Hasty plans were made over coffee Sunday morning and they left for home on the noon Greyhound from Manhattan.

While Phil dozed behind a newspaper, Bee pressed her forehead against the cool glass and watched New Jersey slip by, then into Pennsylvania, through little towns and wooded areas, and thought about what the move would mean. Phil would have to get a business started, of course, and money would be tight for a while, but with Harriet as back-up for Anne's care, a job for herself wouldn't be out of the question. Details to be arranged later. She was tired of being only a housewife, and going to work was a stimulating possibility. In the bright glow of recent events, Bee put out of her mind dissatisfaction with Phil as lover and daydreamed Phil as president of a successful business, provider of a house in Manhasset, two cars in the garage, Anne in private school, a swimming pool in the backyard. And herself? Young society matron? Realistically, better go back to finding a job somewhere and helping out with the household expenses. Time later to daydream the future.

The move was an easy one. Most of their furniture survived and only a few additional things were needed to make the little Westbury cottage cozy. As promised, Harriet came forward with many offers of help, most of which were gratefully accepted. Phil kept his temper when small things went wrong and when Harriet's officious manner set his teeth on edge. She was trying. He gave her A for effort.

Armed with references from former business associates, Phil

endured a number of interviews, promoting himself and his skills
with the necessary show of confidence. Starting on a commission
basis in a new territory, he knew, would take guts and stamina,
and the little nest egg his parents had given them to help
through the first barren months was a lifesaver. The company
that took him on held out the promise of a salaried position
within six months, if he proved worthy, and after that they'd
talk about a partnership arrangement as a future possibility.
Gratified at this appreciation of his qualifications, Phil told
Bee they could look forward to being on an even keel by the
end of the year.

The initial tension and anxiety were relieved. "Thank God
for those engineering courses I took in college," Phil said.
"If it hadn't been for the war, I probably would have a degree
to show these guys."

"You've got something better. You've got three years of
hands-on experience. That should count for a lot."

"We'll see," he said.

Bob and Renee came to see the new home on Walnut Street
and while struggling to hide their disappointment over the move,
shyly wished them luck. Bee watched Phil's face for signs of
regret but he kept a noncommittal grin as he talked to his
father. Bee promised frequent visits with Anne, and they left
with smiles and hugs for all.

Their section of Westbury was a young community, modest
income couples starting their families now that military service

was behind them. Bee moved eagerly into the new routine of summer
weekend cookouts where the men gathered in companionable knots
around barbecue grills and women sat together at trestle tables
with Tom Collinses in their hands and little ones tugging at
their slacks, of dogs on leashes and ice cream trucks and lawn-
mowing and the drive-in on Saturday nights with a blanket for
Anne and hamburgers and beer at intermission. Her sponsor in
neighborhood initiation was Maddie Whitlock, who looked so much
like old friend Lucille that it was startling. They liked each
other at once. Maddie had two youngsters, 4 and $2\frac{1}{2}$, a husband
who sold truck tires, and a benevolent mother-in-law. On a
playground bench, while the children explored the possibilities
of friendship in the sandbox, Bee and Maddie exchanged views
on education and current events and sex and the cost of living,
and Bee told her how much she resembled an old friend, and Maddie
said how about introducing me to my look-alike? The conversation
started Bee thinking about Lucille and she tried the Providence
number still in her address book and found Lu and her husband
and son living just outside the city. He was a pharmacist and
she was modelling for a local art school. Bee invited all of
them to Westbury for a weekend (bring sleeping bags for the
kids) and Lu said she'd see if it could be worked out soon.

Maddie had a casual attitude toward housework that Bee found
comforting. Piles of clothes on chairs and couches, waiting
for laundry sorting; dishes perpetually in the sink, windows
crayoned and toilet paper festoons in the kids' room. Phil's
fussiness about dust and disorder were still irritations and

it was relaxing to spend a morning at the Whitlock's where such
things didn't matter.

The first hurdle to overcome, once she had decided to go
job-hunting, was to find day care for Anne. The original
proposal from Harriet that she keep Anne in Brooklyn while Bee
went to work was out of the question. Bee walked with Maddie
to the market, Anne and the little ones tagging along, and asked
her for advice.

"How do you find a daytime sitter reliable enough to take
on an 8-hour day," Bee asked, "without paying out as much as
you're bringing in?"

"You're thinking about a job?"

"We need extra income. The move took a chunk out of our
savings and Phil's only on commission. At this point it's not
a choice - it's a necessity."

Maddie pulled Jimmie up from a spill and kissed his scratched
knee and wiped away tears. From a crouch she looked up. "A
few of the women in my church are getting a baby sitters' club
together, where you earn hour credits toward your own needs
by sitting for the others." She stood up and brushed dust from
her skirt.

"How could I fit into something like that? I'll be working
full time. If I take only part time work, it's hardly worth
it."

"Let me think about it. Maybe I can come up with something."

The next day Maddie called with an offer to do the job
herself, at a reasonable rate, taking Anne in to play with her

two, making the project hardly any more trouble than it already was, and giving her an appreciated chance to earn a little spending money. An ideal solution. In September Anne would be in kindergarten half a day and only need care for a few hours. With high hopes, Bee phoned Harriet.

"I'm Mrs. Shepard, here to see Mr. Quigley," Bee told the red-haired receptionist. The office was a long sober room with old fashioned furniture and a dark brown carpet, anything but cheerful. There were five desks in a row, three of them empty. Young men in dark business suits were bent over catalogs at the other two. Neatly lettered across the door at the far end was:

PARAMOUNT REAL ESTATE

Edwin Quigley, Esq.

"I have a ten o'clock appointment," Bee added. A thought amused her. This could be a replay of that first job interview at the Met - like this, a result of Harriet's string pulling. Ed Quigley, broker and attorney, lived in a restored brownstone off Washington Square, in the city. His wife had been a regular for morning coffee and pastry at Harriet's Tea Room and had recently called her to say that Ed was looking for a secretary for his office in Mineola, out on Long Island, having lost one to the lure of Florida and a Marine sergeant stationed there.

The receptionist flipped the intercom switch. "He'll see you right away, Mrs. Shepard." She waved toward the back and returned to her paper.

He was as neat and sober as his office, a short stubby man
with a pencilled mustache and close set eyes behind thick
glasses. He moved away from a window and sat at the desk. He
didn't ask her to sit down.

"My wife tells me you're Harriet Frost's niece."

"Not exactly. Harriet more or less raised me. We're
family."

"You're looking for a job. What's your experience?"

"Nothing in real estate - sir." It seemed a good idea
to be respectful. "I worked for the Metropolitan Life Insurance
Company a few years back. Recently, because my husband was
an army officer, I did secretarial work on a military post.
I have the usual office skills, still in pretty good shape."

He pushed some legal-looking papers across the desk. "Ever
see any of these?"

She glanced down at them. "Contracts for real estate sales
and purchases?"

"Yes."

"No, I haven't. But I'm a fast learner, Mr. Quigley. I
type 75 words a minute and take shorthand. I'm sure I can fill
the job - sir."

The contracts went into a drawer and he gave her a narrow
smile. "I run a tight office, Mrs. Shepard. I pay well and
I expect a lot in return. There will be overtime expected of
you every so often and I like my employees to be punctual. We
sell quality homes, meaning expensive ones, both here and in
other areas, and I want my office to reflect this. We have

four salesmen and one other attorney besides myself. We work
hard and we don't horse around, the way a lot of our competitors
do. You'll find out what that means as you go along. Think
you'd fit in?"

Sounds dull as dishwater, but I can live with it. "I'm
sure I can - sir."

"Fine. Sit down andlet's talk."

Phil grumbled, but not convincingly. His protest that
he "could provide adequately" for his family should have sounded
as empty to his own ears as it did to Bee's.

"Phil, be realistic. If we don't generate more income soon,
we're going into debt. Right now we need whatever I can bring
in."

"What about Anne?" he said sharply.

"Taken care of. Maddie and I have an arrangement already
worked out. And in September Anne will be going to kindergarten
for half a day." Because she knew him well, she saw that this
was an ego thing, that taking charge of the problem and bringing
the solution to him as an accomplished fact tarnished his self-
image as Head of the Family. Well, so be it. She saw no reason
to tell him the job had come about through Harriet.

"When do you start?"

"Next week."

He went back to his newspaper, not asking her what her salary
would be.

(187)

"We've been invited to a party down the block," Bee said
later. "We're supposed to wear costumes, it's for next Saturday
night."

"I'll be working."

"Please, Phil - I want to go! Can't you take one night
off?"

He said shortly; "I don't see how. We need the money, you
said so yourself."

"But it's only for one evening. You can forget about air
conditioning for a while and have some fun."

"Why do you keep harping on fun? Everything has got to
be fun with you! Fun isn't on my mind much these days, Bee.
I'm trying to persuade myself I did the right thing by leaving
a good solid business to come here and take my chances with
a new - "

She broke in: "Just see if you can manage it, please."

"Don't get your hopes up," he said.

She watched him for a long moment while he flipped pages,
his face flushed and angry. Then, unable to hold back: "That's
been your favorite expression for some time. I suspect it applies
to just about everything I can expect from you, right?"

"And what does that mean?"

"Think about it." She turned and left the room, clamping
her lips shut on a vivid and explicit expression to describe
his performance in bed.

Chapter II

1949-1950

(Italics)

If I spend too much time thinking about how to enjoy myself,
he spends too little. Nose to grindstone day after day, he's
just not companionable any more, we're not friends, we don't
spend enough time together. Damn it, I'm entitled to some fun!
I put in a lot of time keeping the house neat, I spend hours
marketing, doing the laundry, planning meals for my family.
I'm entitled! Add to that the bucks I'm bringing in to help
with the budget... And certainly it's not unreasonable to ask
for a little physical affection once in a a while. What is
happening to this marriage that started out so perfectly?

(end Italics)

Coffee at Maddie's on Saturday morning was an established
neighborhood custom and Bee accepted the invitation eagerly.
Connie Bianco with her three year old, Liz Waite (no children,
four dogs), Jeanie Pelosi and Bobby, five; Maddie herself with
her young ones, comprised the kaffee klatsch - the kids pacified
in the backyard with cookies and Kool Aid. Everything of
significance that occurred in the neighborhood was discussed

and evaluated in Maddie's kitchen.

The upcoming party was a source of endless speculation: who would come, who would come as what, who would back out at the last minute because a kid was sick, and on and on. There were some sly glances exchanged when certain names were mentioned, male, usually, and Bee waited to be cued in. Husbands were always a topic of conversation, especially those who could be counted on to make passes after a few drinks. Bee made mental notes of a name or two - men who, she was told, would take "a free feel" if she let them dance too close. She was titillated: her first neighborhood party and the sexual undertones made it exciting.

"Is any of this serious?" she asked, looking around the table. "Do these guys expect something, or is it only horseplay?"

Jeanie laughed, not happily. "My Joe is one of them, unfortunately." A round of laughter, then she went on: "I don't think he means anything by it, he's a guy with an overdeveloped libido, is probably what it is. Not that he can complain. He gets plenty at home. So why does he do it? Male ego, wouldn't you say? How many women can he impress? I just look the other way. He's not going to walk out on me, he loves his kid too much."

The cups were refilled, pound cake passed around, and Bee listened, fascinated, while they took on another husband, discussing his proclivities with great relish. Harmless, she told herself, all of this is just play-acting. These men couldn't possibly be as horny as described. But in the light of the conversations going on around her, she looked forward to the party and the chance to check it all out.

She dragged the old Singer out of the hall closet and checked it for function. Aside from a missing needle, nothing appeared to be wrong. Search of a sewing box produced the right needle and with a little dusting and a couple of squirts of the oil can, the machine was ready to operate. It had been Willa's, dredged up from Harriet's basement where it had been stored after the funeral.

The party invitation had specified "wear something of your own creation" and "keep it inexpensive!" The moth-eaten roulette table cover had come from a local Second-hand Shop and would yield enough material for a brief skirt, using the center number columns. "Odd" and "Even", cut out, would be sewn over a black lace bra. The rest of the costume consisted of a red net scarf to which she glued plastic poker chips, a wig of bright yellow yarn, and black mesh stockings. <u>This is a classy outfit!</u> she told herself in front of the hall mirror. False eyelashes and a smear of glittery eye shadow, a couple of "beauty marks" done with a black eyebrow pencil, and a gaudy rhinestone necklace completed the costume. The reflection thrilled her. She felt like a kid on Hallowe'en.

"You look like a Sixth Avenue prostitute," Phil said. He had refused to wear a costume, saying it was a bunch of nonsense, adults cavorting around in ridiculous clothes. When she pleaded,

he said angrily: "Bee, drop it. I'm not going to make a
spectacle of myself in any damned costume."

"Come for just a little while," she had coaxed. "It's only
down the block. Have a coke and something to eat and then you
can slip out and come home." She walked around in front of
him. "It's a party for couples. Maddie and Tom are going.
I can't go alone."

She had bought a rubber mask for him, a wrinkled baggy-eyed
face with stubble. She brought it out now, trying to joke about
it. "Here - will you please wear this crazy thing?"

Maddie's mother-in-law had agreed to watch the children.
They dropped Anne off and walked to the Barnett's house in
silence. Phil marched beside her, rubber mask in hand, his
face set and stony. Bee pulled up short at the front door.

"We're not going in like this, Phil. You've got to get that
expression off your face." She grabbed his sleeve. "What's
the matter with you, anyway? You look like a sulky child!"

"You want to know something, Bee? You're a ball-breaker."

He had never used such language before. Since the early
days, he had kept profanity and off-color words out of his
conversation. She burst out: "That's a rotten thing to say
to me! Just because I want you to lighten up and enjoy
yourself!"

"You don't have any idea at all, do you, what I'm going
through these days?" On the front steps he turned, sliding
the mask over his face. "Here, is this funny enough for you?"

The door opened. Bee pushed ahead of him, unwrapping herself from the raincoat, and went to stand in her glittery costume

at the entrance to the Barnett's playroom. Gratifyingly, everyone

noticed and a few men whistled in appreciation. She strutted

into the crowd, leaving Phil at the door, the mask once more

in his hand.

It was two hours later when food was being put out that

she gave a thought to his whereabouts. When she located him

he was sitting in a living room chair, mask on the back of his

head, talking to one of the husbands about car repair. The sight

suddenly infuriated her. With alcohol firing her mood, she

fixed her hazy attention on Betty Barnett's next door neighbor,

himself well into over-indulgence, and moving in with a wide

inviting smile, rubbing her body against him, pushing both of

them into a nearby couch. Laughing, they rescued their spilled

drinks and struggled to their feet.

"Hey, you gorgeous hunk!" she babbled, "what's this I hear

about the size of your - "

"Hold on there, just a minute - who told you - ?"

"All the wives on the block are talking about you, Wally.

Wanna show me if it's true?"

Wally grabbed her around the waist. "Let's go get another

drink and talk about this," he said, and together they stumbled

down the hall toward the kitchen. Bee's laugh drifted back

to where Phil, his face white, sat slumped in his chair.

Tom Whitlock dropped onto a low stool next to Phil and held

out a bowl of peanuts. "Nice party?"

Phil frowned. "Is that a comment or are you asking me for

an opinion?"

"It's just a little too loose for me," Tom said, tossing a handful of nuts into his mouth. "I'm no prude, but these neighborhood orgies tend to get out of hand."

"Yeah."

"What is it with suburban wives, anyway?" Tom nodded toward a ballerina in a pink tutu and tights, her chubby body bouncing against her partner as they danced to the throbbing Latin music from the record player. "Soon as they come in the door they forget the guy that brought them and head for somebody else's husband."

Phil put some peanuts in his mouth, chewed quickly and swallowed, then coughed as the salty bundle hit his windpipe. Tom reached over and pounded his back. Then his eyes slid around to Maddie, propped against the doorway to the dining room, chatting quietly with a middle-aged woman in a black velvet cape and satin slacks. She raised her glass as he nodded and they smiled at each other across the room.

"Not your wife," Phil said in a tight voice.

"No, I guess not," Tom said after a moment of silence. Then, as though having an afterthought, he said: "She apparently gets what she needs at home."

Phil sat up suddenly. "What the hell does that mean?"

Tom held out the bowl again, not looking at him. "Nothing, Phil. Don't get riled. You put in long hours — maybe you need to spend more time with Bee. Just an observation, not a criticism."

For a few tense seconds Phil glared at him, then sank back
as though air had been let out of him. "I'm edgy, working too
hard. Bee's gone a lot and I worry about her. We've got
problems, just like everyone else, and maybe she does take one
too many once in a while, but - "

"She's a good kid, Phil," Tom said.

"It's - oh, hell - what I mean is - Bee doesn't go chasing
men, she's just kidding around. She flirts a little, nothing
serious, absolutely nothing serious about it. She likes
attention, that's all, and maybe I haven't given her much
lately." He heard himself talking too much, embarrassing Tom.
He took another handful of peanuts and held them in his cupped
hand, staring at them.

"Sure, Phil. She gets a charge out of coming to a party
all decked out and the men all give her the eye - it doesn't
mean anything, not a damn thing." Tom's voice trailed off and
they both looked out through the smoke at the gyrating bodies
as the music came to a surging finale. He got up, held up his
empty glass and started for the kitchen. "She's really a good
kid, Phil," he said over his shoulder.

Twenty minutes passed. Bee came back unsteadily and glanced
at the dancing couples. A full glass in his hand, Phil was
leaning back with eyes closed. He hadn't even finished his
first Coke. In the smoky, noisy room he was the only person
not in costume, the only person sitting by himself. Phil, her
husband, the party pooper, never into the spirit of any party,
a misfit. She took a deep breath, grabbed her raincoat from

the hall tree and ran out the door and down the path to where Wally waited in his convertible.

The party was breaking up when she returned. Wally pulled up to the curb, let her out and went to look for his wife. She looked around for Phil among the guests straggling across the lawn.

"He went to pick up Anne half an hour ago," someone called out.

She waved vaguely at the departing partygoers and set off down the sidewalk toward home. He was sitting in the darkened living room, slumped back in his chair. She started to tiptoe toward the stairs when he spoke.

"Where've you been?"

She stopped. "I went for a drive with Wally."

"Wally?"

"Wally Marks. The Hunk, he's called."

Phil's voice was tired, subdued. "I got fed up and came home. Sorry."

Bee looked at him defiantly. "I went off in a man's car, I didn't come back for over an hour. Is that all you're going to say to me?"

"What should I say?"

"Don't you want to know where we went and what we did?"

"If you have to tell me, sure."

"Damn it! What if I tell you we went over to the park and made out. Would it matter to you at all?" She was talking too loud and he frowned, pointing toward the stairs. "How do you know I haven't cheated on you?" she finished in an furious whisper.

"Just answer to your own conscience, Bee," he said. "If you're the same girl I married back in 1942, you haven't done anything you can't tell me about."

"We went up to the Deli so he could buy cigarettes, then we sat and talked for a while, then we came back."

"Now can we go to bed?"

"Sure. It was a great party, wasn't it? We had a wonderful time, didn't we? We should do this again some time, yes?"

"Be quiet, Bee." He headed for the stairs.

Bee flung her coat on the couch and followed him.

Holding Bee's hand in a five year old grip of steel, Anne dragged her feet along Walnut Street to the intersection with Grant where, in the Parkside School kindergarten, her first encounter with state education would take place.

"I'm almost six," she had insisted many times during the previous week, "and everybody goes to first grade when they're six. Why do I have to go to kindergarten?"

"You aren't six yet," Bee said for the fourth or fifth time, "and until you're six you have to go to kindergarten. We'll see what happens in January. Just don't pester about it, will you?"

They crossed the street and mounted the steps to the front door.

"Will I have to play with finger paints? Will there be any

crayons? What if I have to go to the bathroom? What if I get sick and throw up? What if - ?"

"Stop whining, Anne. You'll get all the answers when you meet the teacher." She glanced at her watch. "Hurry, now, I don't want to be late for work."

Anne pulled back suddenly, choked, and put her breakfast on the rubber matting in front of the entrance. Two other women went through the door hurriedly, dragging their interested youngsters past the smelly pile. Red-faced, Bee grabbed tissues from her handbag and began to mop Anne's wet face. The child retched and brought up another curdled mess, then stood shaking as her eyes spilled over.

"Momma," she wept, smearing tears and saliva with one hand and clutching at Bee's skirt with the other. "I couldn't help it, it just came up - "

"Sh-shhhhh..." Dabbing furiously at the new white sweater and conscious of disapproving looks as more parents and children came up the steps from the street, Bee whispered: "It's all right, stop crying, we'll find a bathroom and clean you up."

"Momma!" The cry rose. "Don't make me go in there, Momma! Not today - I'll just get sick again!"

A janitor was approaching with mop and bucket. Bee grabbed the sticky trembling hand and went quickly back to the sidewalk.

"I'll go tomorrow, I promise." Anne hurried to keep up with her mother. They were waved across the intersection by a school guard and headed back along Walnut Street. Bee said nothing, tight with frustration. At Whitlock's she swung up the path and knocked at the door. There was no answer. "Damn!" she said and went around to the back. A note was taped to the kitchen door. "Tom - you forgot your lunch, it's in the fridge. I'm spending the morning at your mother's."

"That does it!" Bee exploded. She looked around, saw Anne fleeing across the lawn toward home. With nothing left to do, she leaned against the door and watched the child scurry up her own path and stand, hand on knob, waiting for her mother to follow.

The phone call to Quigley's would have to wait a while. She filled the bath tub, added some baking soda and told Anne to get undressed. "Soap up real good, your hair too, and call me when you're clean." She went to the kitchen to re-heat the breakfast coffee. The clocked showed 9:30. If Maddie hadn't gone off with her children, the delay would have been minimal. Nobody's fault, just rotten luck. A day of work missed.

When she called, one of the salesmen answered. "It's my daughter," she told him. "First day at school trauma. She upchucked all over herself and I had to bring her home."

"You sound surprised," he said with a laugh. "It happened to both of mine. Panic attack at being away from Mommy. She'll be okay in a day or two."

"A day or two? How much time do I have to give to this nonsense? I'm missing a day's work, my sitter is off somewhere - will you let Ed know?"

"Sure thing."

She thanked him and hung up. The coffee tasted bitter and

she had already glanced at the morning newspaper. She wrapped
Anne in a big towel, rubbed her hair dry and told her to get
dressed. Subdued, Anne said little, watching her mother
anxiously, and put up no resistance when told to lie down for
half an hour. Bee picked up a magazine and took it to the living
room to wait out the morning.

At the end of a lengthy conversation about Anne's first
days in school, Harriet told Bee she had decided to put the
beach house up for sale.

"Why?" Bee felt a little surge of regret and nostalgia.
"You've spent so many summers there, how can you bear to give
it up?"

The heavy sigh meant another 'I'm getting old' speech.

"It's not the same, going there by myself. When I was younger
and you went with me, it was a happy place. Now it's lonely.
I'm getting on in years, Bee, it's just too much work. Besides,"
she paused. "Someone's interested."

"Who, Harriet?" Bee knew her part well.

"His name is Maurice Greenwood, he's an art collector, has
a gallery in Manhattan. I've bought a picture or two in the
past and I mentioned the house to him and said I was thinking
of selling it."

"Can he pay what it's worth?"

"He's able to, certainly. If someone can do the right job
of selling."

So that was it. "Are you thinking of me?"

"You loved the place, Bee. You'd make a good salesman.
And, killing two birds with one stone, I could give Ed Quigley
something in return for hiring you. He can handle the legal
business and the sale - all it needs is for you to take Maurice
up there and show him the house. I know you can make the deal
attractive. How about it?"

Bee thought for a minute, looking for something subterranean
in the proposition. Fact #1: Harriet had maneuvered her into
a useful position in a real estate office. Fact #2: Harriet
had a house for sale. Fact #3: one hand was preparing to wash
the other. Nothing devious or underhand, just straightforward
financial strategy. Bee let her wait a little longer. Then
she said: "I think I can do that for you. Phil's working out
in Patchogue this week, probably through Saturday. If you'll
take Anne, I'll show this guy around the place on Saturday and
see what I can do to promote your deal."

Harriet's thanks were profuse. They settled the details.
Bee could use Harriet's new Chrysler - white sidewalls, black
leather inside,   very expensive. Suspicion:
was there something going on under the surface? Which brought
her to fact #4: Harriet stood to gain, not only by Bee's
salesmanship, but in some other way. Did this art collector
figure in some scheme she was cooking up? Time would tell,
as always.

"I'll bring her in after breakfast, then go and pick up
your arty friend."

Phil was late, dinner was cold, Anne was cranky about

something so Bee put her to bed early, resisting a plea for a story. When he came in at ten, she heated up the cold pasta and meat sauce, poured a glass of wine for herself and an iced tea for him.

"Harriet has a job for me this weekend," she told him.

He shrugged and turned a tired face. "Will it take up Sunday? I thought we might do some family thing, like a picnic or - "

"Only Saturday." Bee felt a pang of conscience: maybe an effort was called for here. "She's decided to sell the beach house and wants me to take an interested buyer up there and show it. I'll drop Anne off with her early Saturday, and we'll be back here by evening."

"Sell? I thought she was leaving the Connecticut house to you."

"That was iffy. The Brooklyn house, that's for sure. In writing, along with the other stuff she's promised me - us." She didn't tell him about Harriet's offer of the new car for the day, and wasn't sure why she didn't. While he folded his newspaper and wearily got to his feet she put the dishes in the sink and the wine bottle back in the cupboard. "A picnic would be nice," she said. "It's warm enough for Jones Beach. Anne would love that. I'll pack a lunch."

He was halfway up the stairs, yawning. "Great...." His voice faded.

"Nothing doing, fella," she said under her breath. "You have a husbandly duty to do tonight, so don't think a big yawn

will get you out of it." When she slid into bed next to him
he grunted and turned on his side away from her. She stroked
his back - naked, because he wore only his shorts to bed, winter
or summer. She let her hand roam over his shoulder, touching
his cheek, stubbly after ten hours on the road.

He moved with irritation. "Let's go to sleep, shall we?
I'm bushed."

She brought her hand down and around his waist, slipping
under the shorts, moving it across his belly, knees tucked cosily
behind his, then pulled closer and made a line of kisses along
one arm, still silent, moving her body against his.

"Not now, Bee!" He jerked away. "Can't you see all I want
is some sleep? Can't it wait for another night?"

She held her breath, not answering, because if she did it
would be something too sudden, and very angry. Then she said:
"Is it because I had a glass of wine? Is that why you don't
want me near you?"

"For God's sake, Bee - "

"You haven't touched me in over three weeks. What's wrong?
You can't be tired all the time."

"Can't I?" His voice came alive and he turned over and
sat up. "Want to hear what I went through today? A stupid
customer called in an emergency and I drove all the way out
to Greenport to find out it was just the guy's wife had pulled
the plug and forgot she did it. And that was only the beginning.
Stuff like that happened all day, petty errands, insane phone
calls, and wasted effort. I didn't earn a penny. And I don't

feel like making love and if you're going to take it as meaning
I don't care about you or that I'm through with sex - think
what you please. We can talk about it when I've had some sleep."

He pulled the blanket to his shoulders and turned his back
once more. She lay there until the now familiar disappointment
and anger began to die and memory gave her a recent scene at
Quigley's. Only a week on the job and she'd gotten a whistled
once-over from Andy Pacello, one of Ed's salesmen. He had waited
until they were alone in the office to make his move. "Don't
work so hard all the time, honey," he said, sidling up to the
desk and hooking a knee over a corner. He leaned down so his
smile was inches from her face. "Ed's gone for a couple of
hours. How about you and me stepping over to Clancy's for a
little libation?"

Bee glanced toward the receptionist. This wasn't something
Ed Quigley should hear, and the girl might be the kind who
reported infractions to boost her own stock. If the "honey"
was offensive, the invitation was tempting. She pulled the
last sheet of a long legal document from her typewriter. A drink
was just what she needed. "Sure. I'd love to go."

They sat at the bar in dim light and she batted back his
sly sexual banter and they drank Martinis while a juke box played
Belafonte calypso. She liked what she was doing. It was
harmless, hurt nobody, and made her feel good. She appreciated
the male attention, even if it came from such a dubious source.
A little bit of casual flirting, going nowhere, would lift her
spirits for the moment, allowing her to feel girlish and free.

And of course she wouldn't mention it at home.

Since there was no place to park on Madison Avenue, the plan was to pick him up in front of the gallery at 9:30 on Saturday morning. From Harriet's description, she expected someone middle-aged, ordinary-looking, and not very tall. He wasn't tall, probably a couple of inches taller than she was. The rest of it didn't altogether fit, either. She estimated he was in his forties, and in no way ordinary-looking. A quick glance as he got into the car told her he had dark shining eyes under heavy brows, a small neat beard and hair that was salt and pepper, beginning to retreat at the temples. City traffic didn't allow for any closer examination.

They chatted about Harriet. She heard a suggestion of a foreign accent, not in his speech but in the way he phrased sentences. She couldn't place it but liked the flavor. He said he lived in Scarsdale, had a wife and   a young son. He wanted a seashore place where they could spend the summer months while he ran the gallery in New York, driving up weekends.   -All nice and straightforward, spoken in a warm, pleasant voice. Bee got on the Thruway quickly and they rolled along in moderate traffic, keeping up casual conversation. She concentrated on the sheer enjoyment of driving the big car, and didn't pay a lot of attention to what either of them said. It was 11:30 when they pulled into the driveway in front of Harriet's cottage and parked in the semi-circle.

For a moment they sat there, looking at the house. She let him take it in without saying anything. The day couldn't have been more helpful - incredibly blue sky, a few puffy clouds, a breeze heavy with the scent of flowers, the house newly painted, looking clean and inviting, hedges clipped, scrub pines deeply green behind the low picket fence that ran up the side of the property. A post card by Norman Rockwell.

They left the car and strolled along the flagstones that meandered around the house to where the garden parted and a path led down to the water, a path Bee had taken so many times on so many happy days: her feet tingled with remembrance. On the porch where she had spent hot mornings with a paint bucket there were rockers and a wicker couch. Harriet's caretaker in the nearby town had done his job well - everything looked attractive. They sat to enjoy the view. She could almost taste the lemonade she and Harriet had sipped, and the salt on her lips was a sea memory as real as the sun on her arms.

She narrowed her eyes and leaned back, remembering how it was to be twelve, without worry, a little fish who came out of the water only long enough to eat and sleep, in bliss for two long months in the summer.

"You're far off somewhere," he said in a quiet voice.

She blinked back to the present and said dreamily, "Somewhen, I think. I was twelve the first year I came here with Harriet." It occurred to her that he might not want to listen to reminiscences, and she stopped. "Want to walk down to the water?"

He smiled and for the first time she really looked at him, liking his craggy face and warm eyes.

"It can wait. Tell me about your summers here." He settled back and propped his feet on the low railing. He seemed to belong to the scene already - sun and sand and shady porch, waves and blue ocean and his relaxed, slightly rumpled figure on the calicoed couch.

"I was a city kid, this place was heaven to me. It was all so clean, smelled so good!" Did this sound gushy? Should she be talking to him like this, telling about something she felt deeply? Not since Lucille had she done this. Was it his obvious interest, the way he bent to listen?

He must have sensed that she was self-conscious and began to talk about himself. "My son's name is Karel, and he's eleven. He's had cystic fibrosis most of his short life, and it will probably only get worse. I want a place to bring him to, where he can have a semblance of a normal life, the beach, the ocean, all this - " He waved toward the water then turned with a tranquil smile. "He's a brave boy, for all his limitations. His mother has the care of him, because I have to be in the gallery. Summers in Westchester can be sweltering. I think he'd be happy here, the way you were happy, Bee."

He had used her first name. Why did it give her such a lift? She smiled at him, the day suddenly magical as they looked into each other's eyes. She had to break the spell before she said something goofy, like "Mr. Greenwood, let me show you the attic insulation." She led the way down the path, trying not to skip.

The moment was enchanting, transcendent. She felt urgently, vividly, a woman. Without turning, she could feel his eyes on her and knew he liked what he saw. Heat waves shimmered above the sand, like silk in water, rippling between sea and sky. Sandpipers darted before them, spearing lunch from the tide line, then scattered into the air to complain about human presence.

"I never thought to bring sunglasses," he said, squinting. "Nor a thermos with something cold."

"There'll be cubes in the fridge. We can have ice water." She shucked her loafers. Barefoot, she ran to the water's edge and turned to call: "if you're to be a beach person, even part time, you'd better come and sample the water!"

He dropped his jacket and took off his shoes. With waves sucking at their feet, they stood and looked out over the emerald water, not talking any more. He picked up a shell, bleached by water and sun, and asked her to tell him about it.

She told him about quahogs and how to make chowder with them, as they sat on the wicker couch, knees not quite touching. And after a while she took keys from her pocket and opened the door and they went in to inspect the house.

Chapter III

1950

It had taken little effort to persuade Maurice Greenwood
that the cottage would meet his needs: once she had shown him
through it, pointing out its many charms, he had made his
decision to buy on the spot. Bee drove back to New York and
this time the black Chrysler under her hands didn't lure her
attention away from their conversation. She told him about
the little shore front town, the fishing jetty a mile east of
the house, where to pick blueberries in the fields, how to
recognize poison ivy. She cautioned him about dune grass, how,
if you trampled it, eventual deterioration of the dunes would
result. She explained about starfish and periwinkles and other
fauna of the sea's edge, remembering all the while how all of
it had shaped her childhood. And behind it, always, Harriet's
presence. Was it only because of these remembered gifts that
she kept Harriet in her life? Somehow, this day had made her
think about it, reach for an understanding she had never thought
she needed.

He told her about his gallery, an enterprise that had come
to reality five years ago, out of his own life-long passion
for collecting, here and in England where he had lived

before the war.

When she returned him to the Madison Avenue corner at four o'clock they said formal goodbyes. He shook her hand and thanked her and waved as she drove off into traffic.

Her eyes were shining when she recounted the day's happenings to Harriet over a cocktail in the parlor of the Hendrix Street house. To see Harriet's face during the report, one would have thought it had all happened to her, so genuinely pleased and gratified did she look.

Signing of the contract of sale took place three weeks later in Ed Quigley's office. The Greenwoods arrived early, as Bee was gathering papers to put on Ed's desk. Maurice introduced his wife Albertine. She was a small woman with a round, sweet face and pale eyes. Her handshake was firm, however, and she did not appear ill at ease in spite of the darting glances, which always returned to Maurice. Their son Karel was a slight, blond child who sat silently during the proceedings. Once he whispered something to his mother, then smiled at Maurice and reached for his hand.

The occasion was friendly, good wishes were expressed and a few questions asked and answered satisfactorily. When it was over, Ed thanked Bee and walked with the Greenwoods out to their car, pausing to chat for a few minutes. Harriet went

back to Brooklyn with all her anticipations fulfilled and
signified her thanks a few days later by sending Bee two tickets
to a current Broadway hit, for a Wednesday night in the following
month.

When Bee showed them to Phil, his reaction wasn't a surprise.
"It's just like her to forget I never have a weekday evening
free any more."

"Maybe she couldn't get Saturday night tickets. It's a
popular show."

"Why don't you ask Maddie to go? Tom doesn't mind baby-
sitting."

Bee thought for a moment. "I think I'll try to reach Lu
in Providence. We've been trying to get together for a couple
of months and nothing has worked out. This would be a fine
time to do it. She has family still living in Brooklyn, she
could visit them and we could have a night in the city, dinner
and the show. If Maddie would sit Anne for the evening."

"Whatever you want..." He wasn't listening.

Looking at him as he bent over a pile of invoices on the
table, she saw the tiredness in his body like an aura hanging
above him, and a pang of compassion stirred her memories: Phil,
tall and jaunty in his uniform, holding her hand as they walked
slowly along the train platform where he would catch a train
for camp, leaving her to wait anxiously for his next leave.
The remembrance was bitter-sweet and passed quickly.

Impulsively she said: "You look really beat. It would do
you a lot of good, relax you, if you'd let me fix you a drink."

She hurried on before he could give her an angry answer. "Only enough to warm the tired bones. Medicinal, not just booze."

He stared at the papers in front of him. She couldn't see his face. He could be ready to blow up.

"You know," he said, "you may be right. I need something, for sure. If you think - "

Astonished, she moved quickly for a glass, splashed some scotch into it and added tap water. "Here, just sip it, let it warm you going down."

He drank slowly.

"Doesn't that feel good?" A breakthrough had been accomplished, she wasn't sure how, but understood that caution was needed. He shuddered as the alcohol reached his stomach, but bravely swallowed once more. When the glass was empty, he handed it to her and went back to his papers.

<u>Don't push it</u>, she told herself, watching him discreetly as she rinsed out the glass, then poured a shot for herself. <u>Let him feel it, let him find out it won't kill him to take</u> <u>a drink. Don't ask questions, wait until he says something.</u>

Fifteen minutes later, work finished, Phil got up and stretched. "Done," he announced. "I'm sleepy. Guess the scotch did help. I don't feel as tense as I was an hour ago. I'm going to bed." He looked at her apologetically, a strange new look. "Sorry - I just can't keep my eyes open."

"It is relaxing, isn't it?" Bee smiled with relief. Count your blessings, one victory at a time. <u>Maybe after this he'll</u>

6

be more sociable, maybe we can even have a drink together, a
happy hour, time to sit and talk - if he can ever forget about
work for fifteen minutes. She followed him up to bed and when
he kissed her, sleepily, she kissed him back. Lying next to
him in the dark, she thought: if I can persuade him to get down
off his high horse about liquor, other areas could become
accessible. He might even show a little more enthusiasm for
sex.

On Friday afternoons Ed Quigley left for home early to
avoid the weekend traffic jam, and Bee could relax and spend
the remainder of the afternoon in casual conversation with the
salesmen. Andy Pacello, on the make as always, had to be
discouraged now and then, but he took it good-naturedly and
still asked her to join him for a drink at Clancy's. It had
never gone beyond the spur of the moment invitation, the
meaningless bar talk, the careless flirting exchange that seemed
to repay him for the money spent.

A few weeks after the contract signing Bee sat at the bar
with Andy, listening idly to his complaints about Ed and the
way he ran the office, and looked up to see Maurice Greenwood
coming through the door. She watched him, her pulse quickening,
as he detoured away from the bar and took a seat at a small
table against the wall. He hadn't seen her yet. With a tug
at Andy's sleeve she said: "Excuse me - the guy who bought the
Connecticut property just walked in. I think he wants to talk
to me." She left the stool and walked over to Maurice's table.

"Maurice?"

He stood and put out his hand. "Bee, how nice to see you.
I stopped over at the office hoping to find you in..."

She sat down when he motioned toward the other chair. "What
brings you to Mineola? Did you want to see Ed? He leaves early
on Fridays..."

"Will you have a drink with me?"

"But I'm - "

"With the fellow at the bar? He's one of Ed's salesmen,
isn't he? Just go over and tell him we're talking business.
Can you do that?"

When she had done as he asked, she came back and sat down
again. "Are we talking business?"

"We can, if you'd like. I'd rather we talked to each other.
There's nothing more to do about the sale, is there?
Everything's moving along as it should, yes? The deed will
be passed and then it will be history. What I don't want to
happen is for us to lose contact."

A waiter approached and Maurice ordered, then turned back.
"Am I mistaken when I assume we both want to get to know each
other better? Does it sound incredibly obsessive if I tell
you I can't get you out of my mind, that I want to talk to you,
be friends with you, so much that it keeps me awake at night?"

This couldn't be happening. The words were almost casual,
compared to the intensity of his eyes.

"H-how can we be friends?" she asked, unable to look away.
She knew her chin was trembling. The drink was in her hand

before she knew she had picked it up.   "I don't think - it's
not - " She stopped as he lifted the glass from her hand and
set it in front of her. He took both her hands in his, and
their warmth and strength calmed the unbelievable moment.

"It's, I mean, it just doesn't happen like this," she said
with a shaky smile. "There's no sense in it, we shouldn't be
saying these things."

"I don't ask for my life to make sense any more, Bee. I
only ask that it give me some small return for what I've
invested. We have to talk. Will you call me at the gallery
when you can take a few hours away from the office? I'll pick
you up wherever you say. Only, do it soon. Whatever this is
between us won't wait."

She reached for the glass and took a long drink. "I'll see
what I can do," she said.

His eyes were full of amusement as he said: "Use this phone
number, it's in my private office."

She put the card in her sweater pocket and they both stood.
She took his offered hand. The contact was electric, impossible
to break.

"Soon," he said, gently disengaging his hand.

When he left she went into the Ladies' Room, avoiding Andy's
questioning look. Thoughts flew in circles, always coming back
to the question: if this is on the way to being a love affair,
how can it be carried on when both parties are married, have
children, jobs, responsibilities, and all the rest of it? Would
it be a matter of slipping into a motel now and then, or would

he make provisions for intimate meetings with a little more dignity? Does he know how to do this? Because I sure as hell don't! How could he be sure her part in it would be secure, that an angry husband wouldn't show up with a pistol in his hand? She knew that these questions were being asked too soon, but they churned in her mind and wouldn't stop.

Work at Quigley's suffered while she debated the "shall I?"s and the "I shouldn't"s. One moment she felt guilt, the next elation; asked herself how on earth she could even be thinking about doing this, then, how long would it be before they went to bed? She forgot a few important dates on Ed's schedule and had to scurry around to repair the errors. She took notes at a conference and they didn't get typed for two days. Her mind was a-blither, feeding on the vision of Maurice's eyes when he said: "Soon..." and every so often Phil's face, stern and disapproving, slipped into her daydreams and jerked her back to reality. Her stomach was in a state of perpetual mild ache. Through it all she hadn't the slightest idea how to go about arranging to meet him. He had said he would pick her up, which probably meant he would drive out from the city. Or did he mean for her to drive in and meet him somewhere halfway? Or take the train? Or what?

Another Friday arrived and opened the door for an immediate decision. Ed had flown off with his wife for a long weekend. Phil had a meeting with his associates to talk about a partnership, that would run until late Friday night. Anne had been invited to spend the night with the Whitlock children and

go to the circus with them on Saturday. The field was clear.
At three o'clock all the important typing had been done. Andy
Pacello had his head buried in the business news. The other
men, taking advantage of the lull, had left to begin the weekend
early. Her heart pounding, excitement drying her throat, Bee
called the number Maurice had given her. When he answered she
said abruptly: "I'm free for the evening."

He said at once: "I can pick you up in an hour. Is there
a drug store near Ed's office where you can wait?"

"Two blocks east. Coast Pharmacy. On the corner. I'll
be there."

If he had begun a conversation, discussed arrangements,
asked questions, she would have crumbled. But he had been formal
and short. She went into the washroom to freshen her face and
comb her hair. Her mirrored eyes looked back solemnly, none
of the anxiety showing. When she applied lipstick, her hand
trembled, but only a little. Now that the moment had arrived,
she was unexpectedly calm. No panic now, no coy girlishness.
Be yourself. Talk to him calmly and don't stutter. Something
important is about to happen. Don't goof up.

She left the office with a wave to Andy, who looked up and
grinned. He would take her early departure as a chance to sneak
a few hours off because the boss wasn't on scene. Let him think
that. He wouldn't say anything, because he did it himself.

When she got into the MG he reached over and squeezed her
hand, then pulled away fast, rounded the corner and headed for
the Parkway. She sat back, all decisions now out of her hands.

"Are you all right?" Maurice asked when they had moved into the Friday afternoon stream heading east. "No questions raised about leaving the office early?"

"No one was there, except Andy, and he'll probably go home soon. Ed's in Florida."

"And your own situation?"

"All clear." It sounded like a weather report, not information that was to lead to an assignation, probably in a motel out on the Island, one of the "hot pillow" places used by suburban cheaters. She dropped the lid on such thoughts and turned with what she hoped was an easy smile. "My car is in the town parking lot down the block from the office. If I'm home by ten, I won't have   have to answer questions."

He took her hand, holding it firmly for a moment. Neither spoke. The MG rolled along at a steady 55 and a few minutes later made an exit at the Babylon sign, sped half a mile in light traffic and pulled into the parking lot in front of a small sedate-looking restaurant. In subdued neon over the entrance: "Sandoval's Fine Seafood."

He chose a booth away from the door, with flowers and a soft light on the table.

"A drink?"

"Yes."

"I believe the occasion calls for something more than a Martini." He hadn't smiled at her yet but when the waiter left to get a bottle of champagne and a cheese board, his eyes held her with an intensity that made her catch her breath. I shall

remember this moment for the rest of my life. This loving look
will stay forever in my memory.

He spread Brie on a piece of dark bread and put it in her
hand. She ate, sipped wine, watching him.

"So," he said finally, brushing a few crumbs from his tie
without embarrassment. "It has come to this, Bee Shepard. We
have to find out if the attraction we feel is superficial or
has real substance. Tell me how it appears to you."

She hesitated for only a tick of time. "I don't know what
to call it, but you're right. It exists, and if we don't watch
out, it is probably headed for something serious. I feel," she
stopped, then went on bravely, "as though a fire has been lit,
down deep somewhere, and I don't ever remembering being so -
warm."

He laughed,   the sound   full of joy. "What a fine
way to tell me!" Now he lifted his wine glass and drained it,
with a gesture urging her to do the same. They looked deep
into each other's eyes,   drinking
champagne as though they were drinking water, unaware of anything
around them for long moments.

After a while he said: "Let's have something to eat. They
have great swordfish here. And a salad?"

She nodded. Would it be possible to eat? Would the fierce
ache in her stomach allow food? It was worth a try, but it
would hardly matter if she couldn't eat - certain formalities
must be gotten through and a meal was evidently one of them.
Maurice's appetite, however, appeared to be unaffected. In

fascination she watched as he applied himself to his dinner
and talked around mouthfuls.

"My day isn't as circumscribed as yours, of course. There's
a young man in the gallery, an aspiring artist, who takes my
place when I have to be elsewhere." He gave her a sudden sharp
look. "Am I beginning to sound like an infatuated schoolboy?"

"N-no. Not at all."

"Of course I am. We aren't yet comfortable with each other.
I'm as uncertain as you are. I don't know how you feel about
me, or how to make this easy for you. But we're going to be
lovers, Bee, no doubt about that."

She shivered, unable to control the wave of panic that came
from somewhere below her ribs. "Maurice - you must, I mean,
I need - what I'm trying to say is that you will have to help
me - " She took a drink of water, altogether discomposed.
"Will you hold my hand until I'm able to say something sensible?"

His hands folded over hers.

"It's something I have absolutely no experience with, is
what I'm trying to tell you. I'm a suburban housewife and mother
of a five year old. I shop and do laundry and gossip with
neighbors over coffee and run a house on not very much money.
I have a routine kind of a job in a routine kind of a business.
I also have a husband who - who - " It wasn't possible to bring
Phil into this. "I've never done anything extra-marital beyond
a little casual flirting, and I haven't any idea how to do what
you say we are going to do," she finished, lowering her eyes
but leaving her hands in his.

218

it - yet. For the moment, the long, delicious anxious thirsty
moment before they went to bed, Maurice was hers to dream about,
fantasize, hold in her thoughts and share with no one.

Lu arrived at her mother's apartment on a Sunday night and
called to set up the date. The Wednesday evening tickets to
"Guys and Dolls" showed an 8:30 curtain time. Phil would be
working until nine or ten that evening, and would pick up Anne
at the Whitlock's when he got home.

Bee phoned the gallery and told Maurice the situation.
"I'll ask for a few hours off for personal time on Wednesday.
As long as I let Ed know ahead, there won't be a problem."

"Can you be in the city by one?" There was no emotion in
his voice, no eager, aching desire. Passionate expressions
would come later. Telephones were for passing on information,
nothing more.

"I'll take the train from Mineola and call you from Penn
Station." The cool words were a lie. Her heart was pounding
in her ears.

She parked the car in the depot lot and caught the 12:30
to the city. Staring out at the passing Queens scenery -
warehouses, junkyards, the endless cemeteries in the distance
- she listened to the questions in her head that had no answers.
Was this to be the moment of truth? Would he have a bedroom
somewhere to go to? Would she have to creep past a grinning
desk clerk to arrive at the private love nest? Anxiety conjured
up one that had to be faced: if this adventure should come to
light, she stood to lose a lot. Was it going to be worth it?

I

He met her in front of Penn Station and directed the cabbie to an address on Riverside Drive. "A friend of mine has an apartment there," he explained. "He's in France now. Before he left I told him I might need a quiet place to bring a lady to, and he gave me his key."

She needn't have worried. Again, something to get used to. He would never bring anything but discretion and dignity to their meetings. This is a sophisticated gentleman, who knows how an affair is carried on. This will never be a "hot pillow" romance. She was safe. He cared about her feelings, and about appearances.

He took her hand in the elevator, held it as they stepped out and while he opened the apartment door. Five rooms, full of antiques, tall crowded book shelves, thick oriental rugs and heavy, dark draperies. She had seen rooms like these in the movies. Suddenly he pulled her against him and gave her a reassuring hug.

"My friend is an editor in a New York publishing house. He collects books because they're his business, which explains the thousands you see here."

She started to say something but his lips covered hers and all thought fled. When the kiss ended they stepped back to look at each other.

"There's a bottle of wine in the refrigerator and some cold lobster. How about lunch?"

She found her knees once more attached and reliably stable. Still holding hands, they went into the kitchen and together took out plates and silverware, wine glasses and food.

"How can I eat?" Bee asked, "when all I can think about is what will happen in a little while?"

"Taste the lobster, Bee. Time is on our side, we don't have to rush. The wine is for the butterflies in your stomach."

Warmth spread through her, tensions eased. They ate and drank and talked a little, eyes meeting with pleasure, hands touching when free of fork or glass. He put the dishes in the sink, ran some hot water over them and, picking up the wine glasses, led her back to the bedroom.

Tall windows looked out on the Drive and beyond, to the river and the New Jersey shore. She pretended interest in the skyline as he talked about it. When he turned from the windows, releasing the drapery cord, the light softened into dusk and her anxiety faded. There was a lamp on the small table at bedside. He turned it on and they sat on the bed and when the kissing began it was deeper and more intense than before.

"Maurice..." she said against his lips.

His hands as light as a caress, he began to undress her and in a little while she lay in his arms and there was nothing between them. He stroked her hair and kissed her eyes and again her mouth, a deep and sufficient kiss, cradling her head in his hand.

"Your mouth is sweet and clean, like a child's," he said against her hair. She clung to him, fingers tight on his shoulders, tense with need and old memories: Phil, and sudden plunging heat, finished in minutes, nothing satisfied, no hunger answered. _Oh, let this be different!_

He moved back and stroked her face. "Gently, sweetheart, this isn't work. Let me pleasure you for a while. Be still now, don't move, enjoy what I do." His hands were expert, not demanding, not hot and hurting, and he brought her slowly and deliberately to orgasm. She gasped, arching to his body when release came. He held her close and they lay together, resting. Then very gently he directed her hand to his own need. She had no precedent for this. "Should I - do you want me to - ?"

"Of course," he said with a soft laugh. "Here, hold me, don't be afraid. You won't hurt me, just be firm - ah, yes, that's what I mean."

Time passed in bliss, and after a while they propped themselves on pillows and sipped wine, bodies warm and close undercovers. Then he was ready again, and this time gentleness wasn't in his hands or mouth. With strong, hard thrusts and a drumming in his pulse that she felt as though it were her own, he came in minutes, bringing her with him, and they finished in a rocketing joyous climax, then fell apart, glistening with sweat, not moving, speechless.

When she could speak she said in a rush, "Oh, I love you, Maurice! I do love you!" and clasped her arms around his neck. He raised himself on an elbow, delight in his eyes, then said softly: "Bee this is fine sex, but we can't call it love yet. That may come, but for the moment, let's take this gift and use it well."

His words left her without any of her own. Not love? What

were they doing in bed, then? What did all this glorious desire
signify, if not love? A phrase rang in her head: did he now
think of her as just a "good lay"?

"I didn't mention it before but I should now," he was saying
as he gathered her sheet-draped body into his arms once more.
"I always have contraception at hand. You're not to worry."

She needed to laugh. "Are you always so practical?"

It suddenly didn't matter that he hadn't told her he loved
her. That may come, he had said, and if it meant that he was
almost in love, on the verge of loving, it was close enough
to satisfy her for now. She kissed him again, lingering over
it, then pulled away and headed for the bathroom. The evening
with Lucille was ahead. She had better cool down with a quick
shower.

Chapter IV

1950-1953

Anne says: "Tell me a story, a long, long story, Harriet, okay?" Her voice and eyes beg for 'yes', a word she seldom hears from her mother, the telling of stories an investment of time Bee has not cared to make. (Bedtime for Anne comes at eight, two or three hours before her father returns from his Long Island appointments, therefore she has only rarely asked him for the favor.) It is easy to persuade Harriet, and hoisted onto the broad lap, leaning against the wide bosom, Anne settles herself in comfort to hear about Rapunzel and The Three Musicians of Bremen.

The story winds down and Harriet mentions bedtime but can be talked out of it by Anne's coaxing. They go into the kitchen where Harriet heats milk for cocoa, and when it is ready she says: "As soon as you finish this, you must go to bed."

Anne nods impatiently. "Tell me what everything was like when you were a little girl..." She is endlessly fascinated by tales of times gone by, incredulous about a world with none of her familiar surroundings and pastimes. No Good Humor trucks driving through the neighborhood? Horses pulling streetcars?

Movies where nobody talks? Harriet makes up stories about how little girls a hundred years ago lived and amused themselves. Harriet says she will teach Anne how to crochet, knit, sew. Anne is not enthusiastic. She thinks more along the lines of learning how to skate, ride a bicycle, play tennis.

"Love me?" She holds Anne close, nuzzling her neck. "As much as I love you?"

"More!" Anne squirms contentedly on Harriet's lap. "And I'll love you forever, I promise!"

Harriet's eyes fill at the memory this promise calls up. She hugs Anne fiercely. <u>This one shall be mine, as Bee should have been</u>. They sit cosily for another half hour, sipping cocoa, then Anne yawns and gives in when Harriet says, "Time to tuck you in." Brushing of teeth and prayers (it won't hurt her to learn, Harriet has told Bee) then a hop under the covers, a kiss from Harriet and the light turned out. Anne burrows into blankets, safe and warm, knowing that here she is loved.

Harriet goes back to the living room, sinks into the deep soft chair under the mellow light from the Chinese lamp and thinks about the future, how she can shape events to weaken Phil's influence, which must be done if Anne is to belong to her.

Bee's life now settled down around the center that was Maurice Greenwood. Phil, Anne, Harriet, the job at Quigley's, Lucille and the Whitlocks, made up the periphery where thoughts lighted briefly, not staying with anything very long. At the

core, never out of her mind, was the first rendezvous in the
Riverside Drive apartment. She played it back daily, moment
by ecstatic moment - at her typewriter, at the wheel of the
car, at the kitchen sink doing dishes, only blotting it from
her mind when Phil's presence broke the enchantment. Guilt
pangs were fleeting, anxiety momentary and easily put aside.
She did what needed to be done to run the house, satisfy Ed
at work and give Anne casual attention, while nursing, underneath
duty, the joy of delicious moments with Maurice.

Phil's partnership negotiations were going forward and there
would soon be changes, he hoped, in the long hours of travelling
and the selling routine he had been following. He had achieved
salary status quickly, having put forth monumental effort to
show his employers that he meant business, was dedicated and
serious and a hotshot salesman. The other members of the firm,
the Bentley brothers, Tim and Mike, and Flora Angelini, the
sixty year old accountant whose husband had founded the company
and whose money had kept it going after his death, welcomed
Phil with a cocktail party in the Patchogue office of A & B
Heating/Air Conditioning, to be known as ABS Air Conditioning,
Inc. by the end of the year.

All of their savings, as well as the remainder of the money
Phil's parents had given them, were going into this partnership.
Phil was edgy and not very talkative.

Bee went along and made conversation, had a few drinks and
watched her husband struggle with a pineapple daiquiri.

"Tastes like an ice cream soda," he whispered to her after

Flora had refilled his glass. They moved toward a table strewn with dips and crackers. "Not that I'm getting into drinking, but these people expect it."

Bee smiled at him absently. Another time she would have paid attention to this changing behavior, his new and tentative experiences with alcohol, so out of character. But her mind was elsewhere. She was treading water at this party, keeping a conversation afloat, making comments without tapping her thoughts.

Phil said: "What's with you, Bee? Mike just asked you something about North Carolina and you told him you'd never been there."

"Sorry, I was thinking about something else."

"May I point out," he said, "that these people are going to make or break my future? That it will be a big plus for me if they like you too? Give it a try, Bee. Put something into it."

"Sure," she answered, unchastened, not losing her smile. She accepted another drink, filled a plate with chips and sat down next to Flora, winking at Phil as he moved away. Thanks, his eyes said, it's the least you can do in the line of wifely duty.

Wind died, storm clouds broke and a winter sun hurried to the horizon. Bee had come home early from Quigley's to drive Anne into Brooklyn, an invitation for a weekend visit from Harriet. Bundled into their coats, they were about to leave

when the front door opened and Phil came in, bringing a gust
of icy air. He peeled off his bulky muffler, glancing at the
overnight bag Anne carried, then at the hopeful look in Bee's
eyes.

"No, Bee, don't ask me - I can't do it." He turned away
abruptly. "I've got a meeting in Hempstead in an hour. There's
no way I can drive to Brooklyn and be back in time."

"Okay! Okay! I'll do it myself!" She pushed Anne ahead
of her toward the door.

" -- and it won't be over much before midnight. It's dinner
first then getting together with the lawyers, so don't expect
me home early."

"I never do," she said as they went past him and out the
door. Anne turned to wave goodbye but the door had closed.

The half hour drive, stretched to an hour because of road
conditions and 5 o'clock commuter traffic, gave Bee time for
thought. Unexpected freedom, a whole evening without
accountability, had been dropped in her lap. It was Friday.
Maurice usually stayed until eight at the gallery. If she called
from Harriet's, a meeting might be possible, even if it meant
only a drink somewhere and an hour of holding hands. She could
pick him up on Madison and they could drive to ...

"Momma, I asked you - "

Bee pulled the car out of the slow traffic and headed up
the exit ramp. "I didn't hear you, Anne. I've got to think
about driving now, don't bother me with questions."

"I just asked - "

"Wait til we get to Harriet's, then you can ask me," she said, her mind filled with possibilities. Would he be free too? By some miracle, would they have a place to go to, to be alone? Weekly meetings were the ideal - more likely, it would be two week intervals, occasionally even longer, as logistics could be worked out.

In Brooklyn, snow banked by the plows gleamed white in the frigid dusk. She found a parking spot a few doors from Harriet's house and they ran up the steps to the porch. Anne rang the bell, stamping snow from her boots. Alice let them in and helped them out of their coats.

"How bad is it out there?" Harriet asked, hugging each in turn. "Are the roads icy?"

"We had a real snowstorm!" Anne supplied details with enthusiasm. "It's piled THIS high in front of our house!"

"She doesn't have to drive," Bee said. "It's fun for her."

Hands above her head, eyes shining, Anne squealed: "I never saw so much snow in MY WHOLE LIFE! Maybe we could make a snowman in the backyard tomorrow? Could we, Harriet?"

"We'll see. Now take your bag upstairs and unpack. Put your toothbrush and stuff in the bathroom."

Bee said: "I have to make a call. Can I use the hall phone?"

"Of course. I'll put on tea."

She let it ring a dozen times before putting the phone down. Maybe I dialed the wrong number...maybe something's wrong with the phone...maybe the storm... Frantically, she dialed again.

Voices down the hall told her Harriet and Alice were getting tea things together. She turned and cupped her hand around the instrument, but there was only the steady unanswered ringing.

"Anything wrong?" Harriet asked as Bee came into the living room and sat down.

Some message of distress must have been received. Not smart. Cool down. She gave Harriet a bright smile and accepted a teacup and napkin.

Harriet's eyes narrowed. "What's the problem?"

"Nothing at all. I couldn't reach my friend, she's probably not home from work yet."

"Your face is flushed, your hands are shaking and your voice is two pitches above normal. There's got to be a problem."

Bee stared at her and nothing that would make sense occurred to her to say. "I'm fine. I just want to go home before the roads get any worse." She put the cup down and got up to leave.

"Sit down and tell me what's going on," Harriet ordered.

Disappointment flooded and spilled over. Not yet comfortable with deception, Bee gave up, came back and sat down.

"Are you seeing another man?"

Five seconds passed before she could speak. "Yes. Yes, I am."

"Is it Maurice Greenwood?"

Startled, Bee said: "What makes you think it's Maurice?"

Harriet's eyes twinkled. "Just a lucky guess. I think you had better tell me about it."

"But - Anne's here, I can't let her hear anything --"

Harriet went to the foot of the stairs and called: "Annie?

Momma and I want to talk for a while. There's a present for you on my bed. Play with it until I call you."

A delighted chirp from above and a door closed.

"Now, I want to know everything," Harriet said as she refilled their cups.

Haltingly, Bee told of the events of the past few months. They had been together four times, and only two had provided privacy and the opportunity to make love. Bee found that she couldn't give details: the intimacy, blissful and new, could not be shared with anyone. She told Harriet only that a love affair had started and that it would be very important in her life. She said she hadn't any real notion of how to conduct herself or how to set up conditions to make meetings easy, but that it was necessary for her to learn. Uncertainty was going to be a big part of it. Maurice could arrange to be free, but couldn't always give much advance notice. And disappointments like tonight had to be endured.

When the awkward confession was over, Harriet reached out and put her arms around Bee. "I'm glad you told me, and you know if there's anything I can do to help, I'm here for you." The embrace was brief. Above it, Harriet's eyes glittered and her cheeks were pink.

"I'd better leave," Bee said. "There's no point in going into the city - he's probably left the gallery."

She moved toward the door and Harriet followed, touching her arm tenderly. "I'm offering more than just a shoulder to cry on, Bee. Count on me for any help, any time."

Bee drove slowly back to Westbury, her thoughts in a tangle of disappointment and worry, overlaid with astonishment. Harriet hadn't been shocked or even really surprised and there had been no hint of disapproval. What was in her mind? A frightening thought: had a wrong move been made? Did the precious secret now belong to someone else - someone with a reputation for using such knowledge for her own good? Better to cut information off, give Harriet's questions vague answers. The confession had come too easily, lured on by Harriet's interest. Now a lid would have to be put on it. Definitely, a lid.

She took leftovers from the refrigerator and made a light supper for herself, pacing the kitchen while the food warmed, sipping a scotch and water. On one hand, relief. On the other, regret. It was comforting to have confided in someone, but Harriet would not have been her first choice. If it was a mistake, and time would provide the answer, proper steps would be taken. Harriet was full of sympathy and eager offers of help. Her feeling for Phil had never been in doubt, and these offers had to be colored by satisfaction at learning he was being deceived.

After supper, she wrapped herself in a quilt and curled up on the couch with a book, reading a little, thinking over her situation, mourning the evening's lost opportunity. After a while she dozed off, then woke suddenly when she heard the front door close, a sharp rattling noise that meant Phil didn't care whether she was sleeping or not. She sat up, ready to point out his discourtesy, then noticed his flushed face and

- - -

blurred eyes as he stumbled against the table at the foot of
the stairs.

"I'm home," he said.

She looked at him.

"I'm also late," he added with a smug grin. "Later than
I said I'd be, if you want to know the truth." He peered at
his watch. "It's almost two in the morning."

"Really. What were you drinking?"

He belched, delicately patted his lips and leaned over the
end of the couch. "Been drinking over at Heb - Henley's Bar
with my friends, and some other guys. You looking down your
nose at social drinking all of a sudden?"

"Not daiquiries again?"

"I seem to recall some scotches. Quite a few. Isn't that
what you started me out on?"

"I didn't start you out on anything, Phil. Were you drinking
before or after the meeting?"

He giggled, a loose high sound that set her teeth on edge.
"Before, during, and after."

She pulled back from his reaching hands. "Go on up to bed.
I'll bring you an ALka Seltzer."

"Don't want an Alka Seltzer. Just bring me your beautiful
body."

"Forget it, Phil. You wouldn't know what to do with it."
She headed for the kitchen.

He called after her: "Oh, I know, all right! Question is,
do you remember how to do it?"

She stopped in the doorway, not turning. "What's to remember? A couple of minutes of thrashing around in bed, then you roll off and it's over. Is that what I'm supposed to remember?"

His face slackened and he closed his eyes, groping his way to the foot of the stairs. He turned when she held out a glass.

"Drink this."

He took it.

"Now go to bed. I'll be up later. I want to clean up the kitchen."

He gave her a sour angry look and started up the stairs while she watched him, much the same look on her face.

Grade school wasn't the trauma kindergarten had been. Anne was making friends, adjusting to school regimen. Bee was happy for the added freedom of a full-day session that allowed her to set up a stable routine for seeing Maurice. In anticipation, he had arranged with his editor friend for use of the Riverside Drive apartment on a regular basis - one afternoon a week, if Bee could manage it. Another piece of good fortune came her way when, a few weeks into the new year, Ed Quigley approached her with a proposal. He planned to open a branch office in Manhattan in the immediate future, near his home in Washington Square, with the eventual goal of closing the Long Island business and concentrating his efforts in the city. Would she be interested in transferring her secretarial duties to New York? Five full days weren't required. For the present, Monday, Wednesday and Friday would meet his needs. To clinch the offer, he told her that as compensation for the cost of commuting he would continue to pay her for five work days and might even (to be decided later) throw in some help with travel cost. The offer told Bee she had made herself valuable, and she said she'd talk it over with her husband and let him know soon.

Mentioning it to Phil, she kept the details vague, saying she had promised Ed three days, with a possibility that a fourth might be needed from time to time. Anne would still stay at the Whitlocks after school on the days Bee was working, and this seemed to satisfy Phil. And every so often she dropped a casual remark about shopping at Macy's, meeting friends for cocktails - thus stretching the time she could spend away from home.

They both knew the marriage had lost its flavor, was on hold, going nowhere. Phil's long-standing reluctance to discuss intimate matters kept him from bringing his feelings into conversation, and Bee, once early twinges of guilt subsided, waited hungrily for the afternoons in the city and gave only lip service to housewifery. They met for meals, occasionally, talked in superficials, and kept up a semblance of amity. One aspect of the situation brought them together in an area without conflict. After the first barren days with ABS Air Conditioning, Phil was now making money. They were pulling out of debt. Bob and Renee, still concerned and with continued offers of assistance, could finally be retired as parental sponsors. It was a good feeling, and Bee, in a spurt of kindliness, praised Phil for his long and dedicated efforts.

Improved finances provided a subject for conversation, which, without it, would have died. When ~~she~~ THEY learned that their landlord might entertain an offer to buy, Phil agreed to investigate. The house had been built on an expandable plan and when the negotiations got underway to purchase it, they plotted an addition and other improvements to make it more comfortable. The discussions filled dead time for Bee, and she welcomed them.

In bed, she kept carefully distant from him. Comforted and complete in her new love, she now thought of sex with Phil as a betrayal and kept herself frigid, making no move that could be interpreted as encouragement. Phil made occasional overtures, stroking her back, edging his knees close to hers as she lay on her side away from him. Once in a while, after a drink or two, he would force the issue, and she would give chilly permission. When it happened, the memory, like a bad taste, stayed with her until the next time she saw Maurice.

"Do you know how I feel?" she asked him. "Letting someone else touch me that way?"

"Sweetheart, he's your husband. He's touched you that way for a long time before I came into your life. Of course it isn't the same as it is with us, but it's not tragedy, now is it, really?"

She wanted him to tell her she was his alone, and when he refused to make it a serious subject to talk about, she stopped telling him when it happened.

He never brought Albertine or Karel into their conversations,

except to mention that his son was well or doing poorly. He
kept their love affair apart, allowing no other events or
considerations to intrude. It was successful, he said, a miracle
to be appreciated, not tested. Politics might be discussed:
he was a marginal radical, a renegade Democrat who had drifted
to the left out of disillusionment with his party. With McCarthy
rampaging in Washington, he wisely kept his views to himself
and only with her felt free to express them. Bee was
non-political, at base uninterested, but listened because she
loved to hear him talk. He introduced her to other interests
of his. He took her to the Museum of Modern Art, leading her
carefully into understanding of what she saw. Where she would
have giggled in someone else's company, she kept quiet as he
gave her lessons in art history, told her how to look at
paintings, pointing out nuances she would never have caught on
her own. In music he bought recordings for her, composers whose
names she knew dimly but whose work she had never experienced.
She discovered Bach and her sense of order responded to his
works. She heard Mozart's symphonies and was delighted.
Beethoven's sonatas touched her, but she wasn't able to say
why - mentioned only their "power," which sounded cliché even
as she said it. Maurice told her what to listen for, and after
a while she found a deeper and more satisfying response. Once
he allowed her to view an exhibit in his own gallery, paintings
and sculpture done by friends of his, leaving her alone with
the art, staying in his office with the door closed. It was
like doing homework, and the idea titillated her as she strolled

past marble and ceramic and tall hanging canvases.

When he asked her what she thought of the exhibit she told him: "The ones Michael Dade painted are like - almost - music. They flow the way music flows. I liked them best. The sculptor, well, he has too heavy a hand. That big piece in the middle of the gallery could have been carved by a bulldozer." She stopped and thought a moment. "But maybe that's why he chose granite - because he had something heavy to say."

He laughed and hugged her. "You're on your way, Bee. Before long you'll know what you're looking at, and how to respond - and maybe why the artist created it."

"You give me so much. You make my life rich," she told him.

Once, shyly, he brought one of his own early works for her to see, a vibrant painting with brilliant, slashing strokes. He propped it against the wall in the Riverside Drive apartment and stood beside her while she viewed it.

"Why haven't you kept at this?" she asked him. "Why are you selling art instead of creating it?"

He answered at once: "I got it out of my system years ago, when I was faced with the reality of making a living. I'm not that good, Bee, just passably good. And much better at assessing the work of others. One does what one's good at, yes?"

Never longer than four or five hours, their afternoons were divided between adventures in the city and the hours in bed. Lovemaking was essential, as needed as food and water. Things she had never known about became as natural as breathing.

She knew his body more intimately than she knew her own, and relished the freedom with which she could express her feeling for him. It was a revelation, a blossoming of something she hadn't even known was there inside her. In turn, he held back nothing that would enhance their pleasure. Bee was happy, without shame or shyness.

"I think I could give up every other thing in my life," she said, "but this."

"That's a pretty wide statement." He laughed, squeezing her hand across the cafe table. "I'll take it to mean this love affair brings you joy."

Beyond my wildest dreams, she wanted to say. Instead, she blinked back tears and squeezed his hand and held onto it.

He was in her thoughts constantly. She speculated, asked herself questions, turned over and over in her mind the few answers she had. She knew he was forty-five years old, was Jewish, and had a wife and a son with cystic fibrosis. She knew his political leanings, his tastes in food, art and music and his buried desire to be a painter. Did these things add up to a whole man? What were the real questions? At the top of the list: where did she fit into his life? He had sought her out, had made the initial move. What need did she fulfill for him? And what now kept his interest? She was a wife and mother, not very sophisticated. Up to the time he had taken her in hand she had had no experience with the things that filled his life.

(Italics)

He tells her often that he likes her looks, that she has a sweet face and a fine figure and is cheerful and fun to be with. And lately, that she is a magnificent bed partner. That is his doing, of course, but she is a quick learner. So the basis for this fantastic love affair would seem to be sex. Maybe, hopefully, not only sex. But sex was the primary reason they were together. Recognizing this didn't affect her love for him. If this is his need, I am here and happy to meet it, with joy and thankfulness. Coming to this conclusion, she is satisfied and waits without anxiety for him to say the words she says so often: "I love you! You are all I care about!"

(end Italics)

Chapter V

1954-1956

Another Long Island winter, arriving with snow, sleet, and temperatures in single digits. Bee's position in Quigley's new Manhattan office had matured. She successfully passed the required state exams and was now licensed to sell real estate. Her first important sale between a city home owner and a determined by tight-fisted buyer from another state had boosted her value in Ed Quigley's eyes and he honored her efforts with, not only the earned commission but a substantial salary raise for her secretarial skills. Combined, the financial rewards provided her with a badly needed new car.

"It's a VW bug," she told Phil. "You know what good mileage they get. It will be great for commuting. I pick it up next week."

He said: "Congratulations," with a stiff smile, not having been asked to go along when she bought it.

Anne asked if this meant she now could have a real bicycle, a two-wheeler. "We're rich, aren't we?" She postured in front of them. "Dad's a big shot at ABS, isn't he? And you're going to be selling houses like crazy."

A sudden wrench of memory - Willa's voice from her own

childhood - made Bee turn angrily. "No, we're not rich, and don't let me hear you talk that way again. It's time you learned something about how we get the money we have. It doesn't fall out of the sky. We work damned hard to get it."

Anne pouted. "I thought maybe I could get a bicycle..."

"We'll see," her mother said. "But don't think you're entitled to it because we're a little better off that we were before."

With dark looks at both of them, Anne left the room and stamped her way up to her bedroom, where she slammed the door with a resounding bang.

"If you had a little more time to spend with your daughter," Phil remarked, "you might bring her down to earth. She thinks she can have everything she wants just because she wants it."

"Phil, I'm as busy as you are and my day is as long as yours, and I give her as much of my time as I can. She gets this way after a summer with Harriet, if you've noticed, and it takes time to bring her back to normal."

"You're letting that woman raise our child!" he burst out, throwing his newspaper to the floor. "Anne pays more attention to Harriet that she does to us, and I'm sick and tired of it!"

Anne had spent two summers with Harriet at a resort hotel on the Maine coast. No other children on scene, her interest and attention had been held by tennis lessons, sailing lessons and weekly riding instruction at a nearby stable. In September, returning to Westbury with a suitcase full of new school clothes and a stylish hairdo, she had been "a pain in the behind" and

needed "an immediate dose of cold reality" - Phil's words -
when she complained about having to return to "the sticks."
Over Bee's protest he had delivered a lecture, sending Anne
storming out of the house to look for sympathy at Maddie's.

He bent and swept the paper up and dropped it on the coffee
table. "You spend all day in the city, you waltz in here at
seven or eight o'clock, or even later. Is that any way to bring
up a child? She needs a mother! Why in hell can't you manage
to stay around here long enough to give your family proper
attention?"

"I neglect my family?" Bee shouted. "Meaning you, too?
Meaning I neglect you, Phil? Is that what this is all about?"

"You're damn right it is!" He faced her, their angry eyes
inches apart. "You haven't given either of us a thought worth
mentioning in months. What in hell is so fascinating about
New York? That two-bit real estate job with Quigley? Don't
ask me to believe that's all you're interested in."

He stopped suddenly, then grabbed his jacket and went toward
the door. "I'm going for a walk. I don't know when I'll be
back."

(Italics)

Don't panic now. He hasn't asked any questions I can't
fend off. He's mad and needs to blow off steam, but he doesn't
have the guts to come right out and ask if I have a lover.
He will never do that, because he's afraid of my answer.

(end Italics)

She heard the front door close and turned off the television.

It was after midnight. He had been gone three hours.

"Coming to bed?" he asked.

"Not yet."

A moment of silence. "I see."

(Italics)

What do you see, Phil? Do you really see anything? Have you ever made the slightest effort to see me as I really am? Is the answer to our problem as simple as this: two people with different needs, who have never been able to talk about them, about what's going on in this marriage? I'm not a towering intellectual, I'm an ordinary woman who knows something vital is missing from her life and has gone out to find it. If I could have asked you to help me, maybe things would have turned out differently. And I think that, pretty soon, it will be too late.

(end Italics)

Visits to Hendrix Street were still obligatory but less frequent, usually tagged onto an invitation for Anne to spend a weekend. On these occasions Bee drove her to Brooklyn and stayed for a brief chat, during which, inevitably, Harriet asked questions about Maurice and got the answers Bee had prepared.

"He's fine, Harriet."

"And you?"

"We're still together, still 'an item,' as the newspapers say."

This appeared to satisfy and the conversation would move

on. Harriet's pleas to spend time with her, to come for dinner, to see her more often, had cooled somewhat, now that Anne could be lured into the city to go shopping, take in a Broadway show, a dinner at a fancy restaurant. Bee felt relieved. Phil's response was increasing irritation, and he let her know how he felt.

Lucille had become a sympathetic confidante, after her initial surprise. "You, doing something extra-marital?" she had said. "Out of character - or at least, the character I grew up with." It was their high school days replayed. In long phone conversations Bee recounted the events of her last city meeting with Maurice, up to but not including the moment they went to bed. Lu didn't press for details, but gave close attention to the reports. Bee told her about her disappointment with Phil and their crumbling marriage and how Maurice had made life exciting once more. Lu held back advice, offering comment only if asked.

Bee's decision to tell her had not been planned, but had slipped out without intention, she believed. She was glad she had done it, valuing the opportunity to talk freely, which of course could never happen with Harriet. "You're such a help," she said into the phone as she lay on the couch sipping scotch and water. Phil was out, Anne had gone to spend the night with a friend. The evening was hers. "Being able to talk to someone, without having to fib - "

"It must be a strain," Lu said. "But it sounds as though it's worth it. I envy you, in a way."

245

"You're not telling me - ?"

"Absolutely not! Nothing is wrong with my marriage. It's Rock of Gibraltar solid. But romance? Well, it does tend to simmer down as the years roll by..." Her voice trailed off wistfully.

"Listen, friend, don't complain. I'd give a lot if I could have a Rock of Gibraltar in my bed!"

They both giggled like teenagers. Bee felt comforted. Lu was, as usual, on her side in all things. The phone calls and occasional visits, when Lu could get down to the city, were good moments. Mentioning it to Maurice, she got his unconditional approval.

"In this kind of situation, having a trusted confidante is healthy - someone who doesn't preach caution or morality. She sounds like a true friend," he said.

She didn't tell him that Harriet, too, knew of the affair.

In February Karel's fevers and coughing took a bad turn and Maurice left the gallery in mid-afternoon every day for two weeks. Bee suffered the deprivation, keeping her voice resolutely cheerful when she had him on the phone.

Then, a piece of unsettling news. Maurice told her his good friend was making other plans and the Riverside Drive apartment would no longer be available. "He's getting married, giving up his European jaunts for a while," he said. "It only means we'll have to find another place, Bee. You're not to worry. As soon as my home situation eases I'll put my mind to it."

With nothing else to do, she accepted this and began to look for possibilities on her own. Out on the Island, of course, were the motels - where no questions were asked as long as the fee was paid. The idea was distasteful, after so many months of secure, comfortable arrangements. It was a last resort, and she didn't mention it when she talked to him.

Easter week, Anne's school to be closed and Bee with two important sales to consummate at Quigley's. There was a fortuitous call from Harriet.

"How would Anne like to go to Washington with me, to see the cherry blossoms? I've reserved a room at The Mayflower, we can leave Saturday morning. I'll have her back by the end of the week."

"You've saved my life," Bee said. "There's no way I could be away from the office, unless I want to lose two substantial commissions. And Phil - he's got no time to be with her. Thanks, Harriet."

"As always, happy to be of service. Bring her in when school's out on Friday. We'll have a couple of hours to shop before we leave."

"She'll love it," Bee said.

She filled the week with work, of which there wasn't any lack when Spring arrived at Quigley's. A lot of people, geared up by Spring fever, wanted to look at houses, most often in the country outside New York, and Bee was expected to take them

on their explorations. The three days she had agreed to give
Ed had risen to four, not unexpectedly, leaving only one day
to spend with Maurice. But as Karel's condition worsened, he
was unavailable on Fridays, her only day off. She tried to make
the best of it, watching the calendar, fixing on a probable
date for the long drought to end, and forcing herself to be
content with daily phone calls to the gallery.

When she drove to Brooklyn to bring Anne home after the
Washington trip, Harriet commented: "You don't look very happy.
Anything wrong?"

Bee shook her head. "Nothing. Well, not really."

"Maurice?"

"Lack of Maurice, rather. I haven't seen him - his son's
been sick. And where we've been meeting isn't available.

"It's not over, then?"

"Of course not!" Bee said sharply. "It's just - I have
to be patient, that's all."

"Never one of your strong points," Harriet chuckled. "Count
your blessings, Bee."

Anne came in, draped herself over Harriet's chair and thanked
her profusely for the trip.

"We'd better get going." Bee stood up.

"Keep in touch," Harriet said.

Two weeks later Harriet called. "I've joined an old folks'
travel group," she said, "and we're going to London next week.

I expect to be there a month, driving around the Isles, doing the theatre thing at Stratford. How about letting me have Anne for a weekend before I leave?'

"Sounds fine. Phil can drive her in on Friday, his hours are better nowadays. Once in a while he has time for his family."

There was a short silence. Bee waited to hear the second reason for the call.

"You can do me a favor, Bee. I've given Alice a vacation - she hasn't had one in over a year and needs a rest. If I leave the housekey with you, will you come by once a week, see that everything is all right here?"

"Well, sure. Glad to help."

Another brief pause.

"Harriet? Is there something else you want to ask me?"

"I just had a great idea. You and Maurice - I mean, perhaps you'd like to meet at my house while I'm away."

This time the silence built while Bee listened to a small voice telling her this was Harriet at her conniving best - or worst. But the temptation was strong. If she accepted the offer it would give Maurice a chance to spend a few hours away from his home situation and would be good for both of them. "I'll think about it."

"I'll give the key to Phil on Friday."

"Why is Harriet going to Europe? I'm going to miss her terribly." Anne used adverbs frequently, her vocabulary having recently been expanded with words like "fantastically," "awfully," "terrifically," and so on. Phil's eyes were on the road, concentrating as he pushed through Friday traffic. At the mention of Harriet's name his face, which Anne could see only obliquely, told her she had displeased him again.

"Well, I am!" she said rebelliously. "How come you always get mad when I talk about her?"

Maneuvering into position behind a truck, he didn't answer.

"She's always doing nice things for us - like buying me clothes and all that. And the trip to Washington..."

"I don't want to talk about Harriet." His voice cut across her words and she pulled away and leaned against the door.

Harriet met them in a dust smock, her white hair pinned back and a smudge on her nose. She gave Anne a hug and offered him a cup of coffee, along with an envelope. "Here's the key for Bee. I'll be grateful if she could drop in and see that all's well here while I'm gone. This neighborhood - " she waved a hand toward the front windows, "has gone to pot these last few years. God knows what kind of people live on this block. I worry about leaving the house empty."

In the front parlor, suitcases, a steamer trunk, hat boxes. In the dining room, a pile of small bags and cases, dust covers on the furniture, shades and draperies drawn. The rooms already looked abandoned. Departure date only three days away, Harriet was a bustle of activity.

Anne sat on the sofa in the living room, staring at the lifeless TV screen, and chewed her lower lip. In the kitchen,

Phil had poured another cup of coffee and now brought it to stand in the doorway, observing Harriet as she bent to count bags.

"When are you coming home?" Anne's sulky voice broke the silence.

"In about four weeks." Harriet moved into the front parlor, still counting. "Will you come to the boat to meet me?"

"You bet," Anne said, with a quick glance at her father. "If I can get anyone to bring me." When Phil turned to frown at her, she bounced on the sofa, pounding a small cushion. "Nobody's ever home any more. Mom's always working and he -" she pointed, then stopped when she saw his face.

Harriet smiled as she moved past Phil, not looking at him, marking off items with a pencil. She stopped at the sideboard where she glanced in the mirror, caught Anne's eye and winked.

Phil dropped his cup on the table, hard. "Watch your tongue, Anne. I'm your father, not 'he'."

"Let her alone, Phil, she doesn't mean anything, It's the way children talk these days." She handed a piece of paper to Anne. "Will you run down to the corner and get these things from the drug store? And have a soda while you're there. Your father and I want to talk." She took money from her apron pocket.

Anne jumped up and dodged Phil's angry looks.

When she had gone he said abruptly: "Isn't it time you stopped messing around in our lives?"

Harriet continued her rounds, dropping the faint smile.

"What do you mean by that?"

"Anne is turning into a selfish, complaining brat, and I think it's your influence that's doing it."

Her eyes blazed at him. "If you're shirking your job as her father, someone has to step in and fill the gap! That child is starved for affection, and little enough she gets at home!"

"You have a hell of a nerve, taking me to task about my job as father!" Rage choked him. "You've interfered ever since we moved to the Island. I want you to back off and let us raise our own kid!"

The smile came back. "Instead of accusing me, wouldn't it be more appropriate to take a good look at yourself? Your success rate as a parent - or as a husband, for that matter - is obviously pretty low."

His face flamed and he pointed a shaking finger at her. "Our marriage is none of your damned business!"

She hadn't stopped. "It's plain as the nose on your face that Bee is unhappy. And if you don't know that an unhappy wife begins to look around for - "

"Are you going to tell me Bee is - " He was unable to say the words.

"I wouldn't blame her if she was!" She dropped the pencil and leaned over the table toward him. "She's got plenty of opportunity, hasn't she?"

"You're a vicious woman, Harriet. I won't stay here and listen to any more of this garbage." He was sputtering and knew it. He pushed past her and headed for the door.

In high gear now, she called after him: "It could happen right here, couldn't it? What's to keep her from bringing someone here - ?"

Her taunting tone followed him until he slammed the door and ran down the steps and got into his car.

253

Chapter VI

1956

Dragging her feet and staring at the ground, Anne moved
across the lawn toward the front door, her school bag banging
against her knees. Daily homecoming after two hours at the
Whitlock's, never a lot of fun, was today a special misery.
Report card time. No A's or B's. Only C's and one D. Remarks
by Miss Cooperman on the back added to the discomfort.

"Anne is a volatile child, sometimes appearing depressed,
sometimes very lively. On occasion she is aggressive, causing
a problem in class. Overall, however, she is a bright girl,
learns easily (when the subject appeals to her) and is capable
of better grades than these. Perhaps we can talk about this
at the next teacher's conference. I'd like to know more about
her home situation. We should be able, together, to come up
with an answer for her spells of depression."

The "D" in General Attitude had been given, she was sure
now, because of the incident with Billy Hewitt. It had happened
a couple of weeks ago. She had bombarded him with "Teacher's
Pet! Teacher's Pet! Billy Hewitt is Teacher's Pet - dog!"
after he had walked off with the Social Studies Quiz prize,
a straight A, the only one in the class, earning wide smiles

and a lettered certificate from Miss Cooperman, which he had pasted up on his locker for everyone to see. It had rankled, all this fuss over a dumb quiz. And Billy Hewitt, already getting all the attention because his answers were always right, now had something else to brag about. It was sickening. Anger had simmered for a week. She glared at him, stuck out her tongue, called him "Teacher's Pet!" in a loud voice whenever their paths crossed. He grinned and gave her a push as he passed, then darted out of her reach, laughing.

Then on a Monday morning she had encountered him at the door to the classroom and they jostled each other to be first into the room. In sudden fury, Anne had shoved viciously and Billy had gone down in a heap, books and papers flying across the floor.

That's it, I know that's it, she told herself as she opened the door with her housekey. If he wasn't such a cry-baby, hadn't yelled that his arm was broken, which it wasn't, only scraped, Miss Cooperman would have believed it was simply an accident. But Billy Hewitt was a fink, he had made a big deal of it, and Miss Cooperman had given her a penalty, two extra hours of homework, and promised to let her parents know. The card she held in her hand proved that she had meant what she said.

She dropped her school bag on a chair in the living room, peeled off her jacket and flopped down on the couch. For a few minutes she stared at the lifeless fireplace, in deep ashes from a fire a week ago. Who would come home first? Bee? Or Phil? She had to make plans. If her father showed up first

(once in a while he came home before dinner) she would say:
"Dad - here's the report card - just sign it - hurry, I've got
to go over to Celia's, we're doing homework together." It might
work. For Bee, it would be best in the morning, as she was
leaving for work: "Oh, Mom - I forgot to show you this last
night - just sign it on the back - bye, see you tonight."

Could she bring it off? Depending on how distracted they
were, depending on who was most tired and didn't want to talk
to her, depending on how convincing she could be -- . Of course,
eventually, at the conference later in the month, a lot would
come out but maybe by then things would have calmed down and
the incident with Billy dropped from memory. Don't count on
it, just maybe.

"Phil, could you possibly take Anne's teacher's conference
next Monday? I have to be in Teaneck all day."

"If I have to," he answered, looking up from a stack of
papers.

"Well, good. Thank you." She had expected resistance.
"It's at four, in her home room. Miss Cooperman."

"Is it about the report card?"

"And other things, I should imagine. She's giving the
teacher a hard time. Maybe you can find out what's going on."

"Miss Cooperman? Sorry about this - I had to drive from
Patchogue." He was late for the appointment, catching her as
she was about to leave.

256

"Oh. I guess I can give you a few minutes." She went back into the room and sat stiffly at the desk, letting him see her annoyance. A middle-aged woman, not the young teacher he had anticipated. She waited while he took off his coat and settled into a chair.

"I'm Phil Shepard, Anne's father."

"I know."

"The report card was a disappointment, naturally, but we'd like you to tell us more about how she behaves in class and why you think she's such a problem."

Miss Cooperman leaned forward. "Mr. Shepard, Anne's not a problem to me. She's a problem to herself. First of all, she works too hard to get attention - from the other children as well as from me, often aggressively. And when she's corrected, she retreats, won't talk to any of us. She's full of ups and downs, not able to handle correction properly."

"We don't see any of that at home," Phil said. "She acts like a normal child, no extreme behavior and certainly no periods of depression."

"Has she a brother or sister?"

"No."

"Does she have good relationships with other children she plays with?"

"As far as I know, yes."

Miss Cooperman glanced at a chart on her desk, then looked up. "Please accept this question in the spirit it's given. Does she have a healthy relationship with you and her mother?

Does she confide in you, ask for help with school work, things like that?"

Phil looked over her head at the wall clock, then met her eys briefly. "My wife and I both work, Miss Cooperman. It won't go on forever, but having two incomes makes a difference in the quality of our family life. Inevitably, there isn't a lot of time to spend with Anne. She's well cared for, we see to that, but our jobs take us away from home a lot."

"Is she - ?"

"She isn't a neglected child, Miss Cooperman. You can't lay her behavior problems at that door."

"I'm not implying that she is. Let me go on. Does she express affection openly with you, give you hugs and kisses, enjoy your company?"

He answered quickly: "Of course, A normal amount, not excessive, just - normal."

"Maybe she needs more than a normal amount, Mr. Shepard. I understand your situation and I'm not suggesting you should change it. I do believe, however, that Anne needs to know, in demonstrable ways, that you love her. Wait a minute - " She stopped him as he was about to speak. "I may be out of line here, but I do it for Anne's sake. She's a smart little girl, can be an A student if she gets on the track and isn't pulled off it by the need for constant attention."

Phil stood. "I appreciate your taking time to discuss this," he said formally. "I'll pass on your comments to her mother."

There was a brief silence, then she held out her hand.

"Thanks for coming."

"I spoke to Miss Cooperman today."

Anne was on the couch in front of the TV, a bowl of popcorn in her lap. "So?"

"We talked about your grades, and about your behavior in class." He sat down beside her.

"What did she say?"

"Never mind what she said. I want to know why you're giving her such a hard time. And what's this about being depressed?"

Anne grunted, not looking up.

Phil took the bowl from her hands. "Anne, listen to me. Is there something you'd like to talk about, something that worries you?" It was an awkward beginning, but he couldn't find any other way to bring up the subject. Clumsily, he took her hand. "Do you think we're bad parents?"

She looked away from the screen, pulling her hand from his. "No. Nothing's bothering me. What do you mean, depressed?"

"Miss Cooperman thinks maybe you don't get much affection at home." He attempted to put his arm around her, but she shrugged it off.

"What does she know, anyway," she answered, peering around him at the screen. "Could I please watch my program?"

"Maybe I don't spend a lot of time with you," he went on, moving away. "Would you like me to take you to a movie tonight? How about that - a movie?"

"Sure. Now can I watch?"

He bent and kissed the top of her head, then hugged her hard, patted her shoulder and stood up. She turned and watched him leave, her eyes puzzled.

It was a Disney movie about animals, and she let him know it was for a much younger audience, groaning at the dialogue, shifting restlessly in her seat.

"Sit quiet and watch, Anne," he said, his arm over her shoulder. When she tried to shake it off, he tightened his grip, his fingers digging into her arm. "It's the kind of thing you should be watching at home, not that other stuff," he whispered. She slid a sidewise look at him, but didn't answer.

When the film ended and the lights came up he blinked and rubbed his eyes.

"I bet you fell asleep," Anne said huffily. "I should have too, it was a dumb movie."

"Let's go get a soda," he said. "Then I have to get you home, it's almost ten."

Anne ordered a plate of chocolate ice cream and Phil sipped a Coke.

"Feeling better?"

"What do you mean?"

"Not, well, sad, or anything?"

"I feel fine. The movie wasn't much fun, that's all. I'm twelve, you know. That kind of thing's for kids."

"Suppose next time we go I let you choose. That is, whenever I can take a night off, of course."

Now she grinned at him. "That'll be the day, won't it?"

She licked the spoon and dropped it in the dish. "Let's go.
Next time I'll pick, okay?"

     Enduring the long abstinence, Bee was short-tempered at
home and work, giving abrupt answers and absent-minded attention.
The pattern of one afternoon a week with Maurice hadn't been
changed for a long time, except for an occasional period when
one or the other was unavoidably away from the city. Bee found
it hard to concentrate and Ed Quigley pointed this out to her
when a client complained that he'd been given only casual
attention, in effect brushed off after a single office visit.
She brooded about the situation, felt deprived and let down,
and because it occupied her thoughts, neglected other things.
     He called her at Quigley's at noon on Friday. She was at
her desk with a prospective buyer, staring into the distance
as he and his wife thumbed through catalogs.
     "Bee - I can come to the city for a few hours this afternoon.
Can we meet somewhere?"
     She caught her breath, then cupped the phone in her hands.
"Yes, yes. Let me think. Let me - " A phrase flashed by her
- Harriet's offer of the house - "Can you get over to Brooklyn?"
     "Of course. Where?"
     She gave him directions and the address, told him she had
a key and the house was empty. "I'll meet you there at
one-thirty." She hung up and signalled to the salesman nearest
her. "Sir - would you mind? Mr. Drew will be glad to answer
your questions." She raised her eyes hopefully. Bill Drew nodded

and she grabbed her coat and bag and ran out.

The door closed behind them, Maurice opened his arms and she walked into them. Tears starting, she said: "It's been an ice age, it's been a desert..."

"I know, I know. It couldn't be helped."

"There's a big wide beautiful bed upstairs. We're alone. Harriet is in England. I can't wait any longer."

There was a frenzy in their lovemaking, a hunger that nothing seemed to quiet. She cried wildly at one point: "This mustn't happen again - being apart is like being dead! I need you, I need you..."

Finally exhausted, they slept. Still embracing, they woke when it was almost dark, got up and dressed quickly, touching each other often, then went downstairs and made coffee and sat in the living room to drink it. It was almost eight o'clock when they left the house, with no firm plans for another meeting, but the possibility of next Friday afternoon here at Harriet's.

"What's this I hear about you and Anne going to the movies? She said you took her to see a Disney film that was 'yucky'."

"She watches too much junk on TV, Bee. I tried to show her something decent."

"She hated it. Why didn't you let her choose?"

"I told her she could, next time."

Surprised, Bee said: "Is this to be a regular thing?"

"Not a regular thing," he said testily. "I just thought

it might be something we could do together."

Bee slid a look at him. "Is this because of what Miss Cooperman said, about her not getting enough attention at home?" They had talked, briefly, after the conference.

"You sound like Harriet." He turned away abruptly. "She told me Anne is starving for affection and we have only ourselves to blame if she acts up." He stopped on his way to the door and turned with an angry glare at her. "I gave her a piece of my mind."

"Miss Cooperman?""

"No, Harriet. She's too damned officious. I told her to back off." He started up the stairs. "You going to check out her house this week?"

"Why, yes. As a matter of fact, I went by last Friday. Everything was all right. If Ed will give me a little time, I'll try to go again this week." She hadn't expected him to remember about the visits Harriet had asked her to make. Had her answer been believable? Casual enough? When he nodded and went on up the stairs she was relieved.

Alone, she listened to the late news for a few minutes, dreamily, the prospect of Friday at the Hendrix Street house filling her thoughts. With Karel's crisis over for the moment, Maurice had promised there would be no more long gaps, no more "barren deserts." Harriet would return in two or three weeks, and they would have to find another place. She would leave it to him to find a replacement for the Riverside Drive apartment. When she finally climbed the stairs, she felt relaxed and at peace, the center of her world once more at rest.

Phil was reading. He looked up as she came in and went to the closet for her robe. Something told her to move into the bathroom quickly, to run a tub, cream her face, fill half an hour with busy work. Phil's intention hung in the air and tonight she couldn't go through with it. Not now, not so soon after she and Maurice had come back together, not with another Friday just ahead. Not tonight.

When she came out of the steaming bathroom, toweling her hair, he got out of bed.

"Let me help. You used to like me to rub your hair dry." He took the towel before she could turn away.

"It's almost dry..."

"Just for old times' sake, Bee, let's pretend."

About to ask 'pretend what?', she thought better of it and bowed her head. While he toweled vigorously she stood still and said nothing. There was something terribly sad in his "..for old times' sake."

When he finished he dropped the towel. Suddenly his arms were gripping her, holding her against him. She could feel his body tremble as he pleaded: "Please, Bee, don't say no tonight, don't move away from me again. I need you - I feel so alone - "

About to pull away, she stopped. What was happening? Some kind of reluctant, belated compassion for him? Was it that she didn't want another argument, bad feelings, not talking to each other for a week? The tiny hesitation had given him

the advantage, whatever had been her reasons, and now it was
too late.

His kisses were frantic, he clutched her shoulders and pushed
himself over her, his hands rough and demanding. Long habit
held her body rigid, without warmth, only the woodenness that
had been all she could give him for the past three years. He
acted blindly, thrusting his body at her, his breath hot against
her face. When it was over, she moved to the edge of the bed
and turned her back.

Long moments of strained silence passed.

"I guess that's the best you can do, isn't it, Bee? You're
not there for me any more, are you?"

She couldn't give him an answer. There was nothing that
would reassure him or soften the harshness and cruelty of the
moment.

With one arm over his eyes, he lay still against the pillow.
Bee didn't move either, stiff and miserable, waiting for sleep
to come and wipe from her mind what had just happened.

For the next two days Phil followed his business rounds
in a fog of depression, keeping up a minimal appearance of
interest and enthusiasm as he talked to clients and processed
their orders. Hard words, full of contempt, rang in his memory:
What's to keep her from doing it right here? Harriet's voice,
cutting into his thoughts, left him staring at papers on his
desk, then lifting his eyes blankly to the window where a Fall
wind blew leaves across his vision. By Thursday he knew he

had to find out. If he drove into Brooklyn at noon he could park down the street behind other cars and watch Harriet's front gate. But not in his own, recognizable, station wagon. The Patchogue office provided a car for emergency use - a courtesy when a salesman's car had to go in for repairs. No questions would be asked if he borrowed it for a day. The decision made, he felt a measure of relief. One way or another, the gnawing questions would be answered.

Friday was Long Island misty, overcast sky a gray blur as wipers swept the glass. He kept his speed at 45, in the far right lane, not trusting anything faster in his state of anxiety. He told himself "this is a wild goose chase" and "nothing to worry about - I trust her - she wouldn't do such a thing - " but pictures continued to form in his mind: Bee would show up (alone) and give the place a quick once-over, then leave (alone) in her own car. Then the mental scene would shift: Bee getting out of a strange car, a tall man holding her elbow, both walking toward the house, laughing. In his mind he was sitting at the wheel, hands clenched, watching, then jumping out, running across the street to confront them, Bee turning in surprise, then panic, the man wheeling to face him, the moment when his fist connected with the man's jaw...

He swallowed hard, wiped his forehead with a cold hand and pulled up onto the exit ramp. It was 1:30. How long would he have to wait? Should he stop and get a container of coffee, a doughnut? His teeth chattered. No. What a ridiculous picture! Jealous husband sips coffee and munches doughnuts while waiting for his guilty wife to appear with her lover.

On Hendrix Street he crept along the blocks until he was five doors from Harriet's house, slid in behind a black Buick and turned off the engine. 1:45. She could come any time. She could show up at 3:30 or 4 or even 5 o'clock. He could wait for hours or know the answer in minutes. He prepared himself to wait, leaning back, eyes on the rear view mirror, making a deliberate effort to calm his breathing.

At 2:15 her VW pulled up to the curb in front of Harriet's gate and she got out, alone. At the front door she took out a key and was about to put it into the lock when something drew her attention. Turning, she watched as an MG came to a stop behind her car. A man in a gray raincoat, collar turned up, no hat, got out and went through Harriet's gate, up onto the porch where Bee waited. They kissed. Bee opened the door, took his hand, and they went in.

For long moment Phil sat and stared at the closed door, not thinking about anything. No anger, no shock, nothing. Then, all of a sudden, he felt a frantic need for the coffee he had rejected earlier. In this neighborhood of private homes and churches there were no lunch counters, no corner deli's where he could buy it. He would have to abandon his vigil and leave the block. This would be the best thing anyway. It could be hours before they came out. Hours before they finished what they were doing in there. Hours of sweaty groping at each other on one of the big beds on the second floor. Hours of gasping and moaning and - and - bodies rubbing together, legs tangled, arms clutching, lips - lips -

He jammed the car into gear and pulled out fast and headed out of the area. Not lunch, not coffee. What he needed now was alcohol. Something very strong, something that would kill the picture blazing in his mind, strangling his thoughts, something he could dive into and lose the memory of that door closing on his wife and the stranger she had kissed.

When he reached Patchogue the office was closed. He left the car in the parking lot and got into his own wagon and went back to the parkway. Two exits short of Westbury he angled off to Old Country Road and found a bar and went in.

The clock over the bar showed 6:30 when he finally pushed his stool away and left the place. He wasn't drunk, only groggy, as though he'd missed a night's sleep. His mouth was furry and he searched his pockets for a mint. Finding none, he abandoned the idea and headed for home.

There was a note in Anne's handwriting on the kitchen table. "Mom's staying out late again. She said to warm up the baked ham and macaroni for supper. I already had some. The rest is in the oven."

He pulled a bottle of scotch from the liquor cabinet and poured some into a tumbler, took it into the living room and drank it slowly, wincing as the raw liquor burned his throat. After a few minutes he switched on the television and stared at a news program. When it was over a comedy came on, something about parents whose kids were putting things over on them. He

had trouble following the story and when it came to an end he
went back to the kitchen and poured another drink.

Anne had not come down to greet him. Sitting in the dark,
the TV off, he felt abandoned, left somewhere at a great
distance, in isolation, cut off. The feeling frightened him.
He shivered, drank some more whiskey, stood up and made his
way uncertainly to the stairs. Climbing slowly, one hand on
the railing, he was surprised to find himself breathing heavily
when he reached the top. He went past the bedroom door and
on down the hall to where light showed under Anne's door.

She had pillows piled behind her head and there was a book
on her lap. The bedside radio was wailing "ah needs mah baby's
love..." She looked up as he came through the door.

"I'll turn it down - " she said quickly, reaching for the
knob.

"Never mind. It doesn't - I don't mind." He came unsteadily
toward the bed. She moved aside and he sat down and stared
at the door.

"You want something, Dad?"

"No. I just want to sit here for a minute."

"Here?" She frowned. "Why?"

He turned and with a visible effort focused on her face.
"I'm just - lonely."

She saw his flushed face and the rank alcohol odor reached
her. She leaned away from him and scowled. "You smell like
booze. I hate it. It's a rotten smell."

"I can't help it," he said. "I've got a lot on my mind.

Booze helps. Not that you can understand that, I suppose."
He inched closer, blinking at her. "You have any idea what
it's like to be lonesome? Like nobody every comes near you
any more, like you're poison?" He looked at his hands. They
were trembling.

Anne said quickly: "Nobody says you're poison, Daddy. What
do you mean, nobody comes near you? We're here - Mom and I.
We're here, well, sometimes. You're not all alone."

"You mean that?" His voice slurred. "Could you tell me,
could you say, 'I love you, Dad?' Could you say that?"

"Sure - sure, I could say that." She tried to move back,
away from him. "I love you, Daddy. I love you."

His eyes filled with tears and he reached for her, pulling
her against him. "Anne, baby, you're my little girl, I love
you, I wouldn't do anything in the world to hurt you."

She tried again to move away but his arms held her.

"I love you so much -- " With a clumsy, jerking movement
he pulled her to his lap, her head against his chest, and his
hands began to tug at her nightgown. She tried to wrench herself
away but he was too strong. With one arm he held her waist,
the other fumbling at his own clothes, eyes closed, his voice
only a whisper. "Annie...I'm not going to hurt you, I love
you..."

"Daddy!" She struggled as his hands gripped her body and
swung her around to straddle his lap, her nightgown up to her
hips. "What - Daddy! What are you doing?"

"Sh...shhhh..." he whispered, stroking her back. "I just

want to hold you, close to me...don't pull away, baby, I can't take any more of that..."

When she felt the heat of him against her she gasped and went rigid. Before she understood what had happened his body convulsed and his arms went limp. He was shaking, the whiskey smell heavy in the air around them. He looked up, his eyes glassy now, sweat streaking his face. She fell from his knees and rolled away, then scuttled backward to the wall.

More angry than frightened, she cried out: "You're not supposed to do - things like that! I'm your child!" Tears coming, her face crumpled and she began to rub at her thighs with the nightgown.

It was as if her voice were coming down a long tunnel, the sound hollow and far away. "I didn't mean to hurt you, baby, I couldn't help it..." He got up slowly from the rumpled bed. Leaving behind him the steamy smell of his madness, he stumbled down the hall. In the bathroom he stripped, balled his damp shorts and dropped them into the hamper and got into the shower. When hot water boiled out of the shower head, he took it full in the face. Then, dripping, he stepped from the stall and pulled a towel around his body. Unable to focus on anything farther away than his own hands, he felt his way along the wall to the bedroom where he dropped to the bed and into oblivion.

271

Chapter VII

1956-1957

For a week Anne struggled with the mystery of her father's behavior, unable to put out of her mind his plea for affection and cry of loneliness. The rest of it couldn't be called up without fearful anxiety. She rejected at once the idea of going to her mother for an explanation. Bee wasn't there for answers to mysteries, for questions of emotion or puzzlement. Bee was the one to go to for new shoes, for help in solving a math problem, or for a raise in allowance, not someone to take your fears to.

She stayed out of her father's way when Bee worked late, spending nights at the Whitlock's or with a school friend, coaxing an invitation on one pretext or another. On the evenings when it was impossible to avoid him (with Bee home at dinnertime, the three of them around the table) she kept her attention on the food, not looking up, and went to her room as soon as she could. Bee commented on her "sulkiness." Phil said nothing.

Then Bee made a Sunday evening date to meet a friend in New York for dinner and a movie, and Anne, in bed with a cold, waited in dread for Phil to approach her.

Once again he told her that he wouldn't hurt her, that she

was his baby and he loved her. "I only want to be close to you, to hold you in my arms. It's something we can do together that will keep me from being so lonely." His voice was thick with alcohol and strain. "We mustn't tell Mom, she's too busy to think about us. We've got each other, Annie, haven't we?"

When he sat at the foot of her bed and his flushed face moved closer, she cringed into pillows and watched him fearfully, afraid to resist. He pulled her close, whispering, then gripped her arms and lifted her over his lap. As before, it was over quickly. She fell back on the bed, tears spilling over, not daring to cry out. He leaned to stroke her head. "It's all right, sweetheart, just go to sleep now..." then moving jerkily through the door, closing it behind him.

Harriet's letter arrived on a Wednesday, letting them know she would be on the returning Queen when it docked. Bee was expected to do chauffeur service. "There will be a lot of luggage, best to pick up my car from Hendrix Street and drive to the pier."

"It's a Saturday, isn't it?" Anne asked. "Can I go with you?"

"I don't see why not," Bee said genially. "It's a chance to see one of the biggest ships in the world. Something to brag about at school, huh?"

"I don't care about that - I'm just glad she's coming home. I missed her a lot."

Bee shrugged. "We'll have to get started early. The ship

starts unloading passengers about nine, she says."

Not meeting her mother's eyes, Anne said: "You think maybe I could stay overnight with her? You could come get me on Sunday...."

"She's got a lot of unpacking to do, She'll probably rather be alone."

"I can help with it."

"We'll ask her. But don't pester the minute you see her."

The ship had been docked since before dawn. When Bee finally found a parking space the passengers were beginning to disembark, trickling down gangplanks to congregate in the customs shed. Anne caught sight of Harriet first and her face lit up. "There she is! There she is!" She tugged at Bee's arm.

It was late morning before they loaded the last of Harriet's bags into the trunk and back seat of the car. The three of them sat in the front and Bee headed for Brooklyn. Harriet hugged Anne close and they smiled at each other. Bee watched the road, her thoughts busy with the possibility of seeing Maurice soon. He had called Quigley's yesterday to let her know he had found a place for them to spend a few hours together - at least once or twice a month, maybe more often. Things had to be arranged, he said. He was getting the details worked out.

Harriet's housekeeper had removed the dust covers and aired the rooms. The refrigerator was stocked with necessaries, and a bottle of wine, cooling on the bottom shelf.

Bee was persuaded to stay for a while to hear about the

adventure and Anne, bouncing with excitement at being allowed
the overnight, ran upstairs to make her bed and find her
toothbrush and nightgown.

In the living room Bee and Harriet sat with Chablis and
crackers. After only a few minutes of casual talk Harriet asked:
"How's Maurice?" When Bee didn't answer at once, she said: "I
hope my key was of use while I was gone." She smiled over her
glass. "Do I sound like a lewd old lady, arranging for such
extra-marital assignations? You'd be right if you said I
wouldn't have done it when I was a young woman. But times have
changed, and I'm proud to say I'm no stick-in-the-mud when it
comes to accepting change. Besides, you know I want to help,
in any way I can. I can see what life with Phil is like..."

Bee looked at her thoughtfully. The words, as always, had
the ring of sincerity, but also, as always, Harriet hid her
reasons and it was necessary to look deeper for motive. Hard
to reconcile this free and easy attitude with the churchgoing,
prayer-teaching Harriet of her youth.

"He's fine. And yes, we did come here once or twice while
you were gone. But he's found a place for us to meet
occasionally. I feel -- " She stopped, then shrugged and gave
Harriet a weak smile. "I still feel uncomfortable talking about
him, even at this late date. It's, well, it sounds like an
undercover conspiracy, like the CIA or something, when I talk
about where we meet, and how often. Do you see what I mean?"

Harriet poured more wine. "Don't pin the scarlet letter
on your blouse, Bee. You're doing what you have to do to live

with a bad situation."

"You're looking at a real Mata Hari. You wouldn't believe how I have to manipulate things to make it all possible." She leaned over and gave Harriet a peck on the cheek. "One of us will drive in tomorrow evening and pick Anne up."

"I've got a raft of presents for her - and even something for you, if you've been a good girl."

Bee laughed. "Yeah," she said.

Harriet's intuitive nature, alert always where Bee or Anne was concerned, told her this was a child different from the one she had said goodbye to 6 weeks ago. Anne's eyes never quite met hers, conversation didn't flow freely and came to an abrupt end if Harriet didn't keep it alive. They worked together unpacking bags and suitcases, hanging clothes in closets, putting lingerie away in drawers. Anne gave appropriate thanks for the gifts but something was lacking, a warmth, a real pleasure in receiving them.

"How is school? You've got a new teacher, haven't you?"

"Mr. McClintock."

"You like him?"

"He's okay."

"What will you be doing for fun this year?"

"Well, there's softball, and - " Anne dropped a blouse and when she picked it up their eyes almost met. She quickly reached for another garment in the big suitcase. "And - well, I think there'll be a couple of field trips."

Silence built while they kept busy. Harriet arranged things on her big mahogany dresser, sliding a glance at Anne once in a while. "Are you feeling all right, Annie?" she asked finally. "Maybe you've got a cold coming on. You look - " she pressed a hand to Anne's forehead and bent to look into her eyes, "kind of washed out."

"I'm fine. Really, I'm fine."

"Sure?"

"Really fine." Anne produced a bright smile then turned back to the job.

"Then let's go down and see what Alice fixed for dinner." Harriet could bide her time. Children weren't skillful when it came to hiding big problems. Something would give her a clue and she would find out what the trouble was before long. They went downstairs hand in hand and when she heard Anne's tiny sigh of relief, Harriet squeezed her hand.

The new meeting place was a hotel room in mid-Manhattan. Maurice had hung an art exhibit at the hotel for one of the VIPs on the Banquet Staff and over drinks after the opening, the arrangement had been made. The VIP himself planned to use the room for a similar purpose once a week: a day's use could be arranged by a phone call.

"Somewhere deep down inside I think I'm still a prude." Bee's smile was without humor. "This is beginning to look like a -- "

"I know, I know." Irritation sharpened Maurice's voice.

"Let's try to think about us, Bee, not about where we are."

The room was large, with heavy dark furnishings, draped windows, a refrigerator/sink area along one wall, a table and two upholstered chairs, a couch and a queen-size bed covered with brown satin. It depressed her to look at it. She moved over to stand with him at the window, and reached for his hand. The day was somber, its cold somehow right here in the room with them. She shivered. "I think - " knowing caution should shape her words but suddenly not caring, "I would be happier if we had a place of our own, where we could be free of outside things. It's always been like this, using someone else's place, someone else's bed. I can't help it, I wish it wasn't like this."

"This is all I can do now, Bee. We have to be careful, not make unreasonable demands of each other."

"I've never asked for anything, Maurice."

"I know you haven't." He pulled her against him. "Let's keep it that way."

Christmas arrived, was somehow celebrated, Bee and Maurice, as always, apart for two or three weeks while their families engaged in holiday activities. Anne's birthday, in January, came and went with less than usual attention. She had a cold, a fever. Friends were called and the party postponed. Bee was able to get home for dinner on the birthday evening, hurrying in with an armful of presents she had picked up as she passed through Hempstead. These were accepted listlessly, and left unopened as Anne coughed and sneezed her way upstairs, having eaten little. Bee followed her with a hot lemon toddy, tucked her in and promised a party for the next weekend. Anne turned her face to the wall and pulled the blanket over her head.

279

Chapter VIII

1958

(Italics)

Maybe it's not a good idea, probably can't be arranged and
conceivably could do immediate damage to our situation. But
I want to do it, more than I've ever wanted anything. After
all these years of one-day stands, of never being totally care-
free, never spending a night together - now at last there's
a chance for us to have a whole week together, to play like
kids in the sun. We deserve it! Always careful, taking no risks,
protecting the innocent "others" in our lives. This will be
our reward for good behavior, earned by long and noble effort.
Don't think about whether it's a good idea or a bad one, think
about how it can be arranged and how to avoid consequences.

He's taking Karel to Miami again, to the specialist at St.
James Hospital, for a week of consultations and treatment.
Albertine is going to Boston to visit her sister. I can take
the next flight to Miami and be with him for seven whole days!
A week of nights together, hours of nothing to worry about,
no precautions to avoid being seen, no edging past a doorman
into someone else's apartment. He isn't very enthusiastic about
it, understandably. His main concern is Karel, as it should

be. A sick child occupies one's mind, leaving little room for anything else. The boy has been this way all his life, and may never get better. What Maurice is doing now is last straw grasping, and I have a duty to be there for him, give him support and affection.

It's hard for me to think coolly about this. The prospect of a week of freedom is intoxicating. Of course there will be compromises. I must be prepared to spend some time alone. Not too steep a price, really. But first I have to find a convincing reason to give Phil for making the trip. Something will have to be set up, maybe with Andy Pacello. We've done favors for each other in the past. He's not the most endearing character I know, but he's useful. It will mean having drinks with him, listening to his jokes and putting on a show of camaraderie. If he'll help me cover for this leave of absence, I'll owe him a big one.

Phil can manage with Anne for a week; all he has to do is be there at dinner. She can get herself off in the morning and Maddie Whitlock will check on her after school. I'll leave plenty of food in the fridge, clean clothes, all details taken care of in advance. I'm used to planning this way - but never before for a whole week. I'll do whatever it takes - anything - to have this week with him. We'll have long, loving nights together, I'll never ask for another thing, if I can have this. Never.

(end Italics)

281

On Saturday a week later, when Bee had an appointment to show a Tarrytown property to a client, she suggested at breakfast that Phil take Anne to the movies for the afternoon.

"There are a few decent ones to choose from - no more 'yuckies,' Anne. How about it, guys? I won't be home til after seven. You can grab a bite to eat out or bring some Chinese in."

Reaching for her bag on a nearby chair, she missed the anguished look Anne gave her father and the frown he returned.

"Sure, we'll think about it." Phil brushed crumbs from his lap. "I've got some paper work to do. We can decide later." Over Anne's head his eyes were blank when he looked up. "See you whenever you get home."

"Shouldn't be too late." She took her coat from the hall closet and wrapped a muffler around her neck. Smiling absently in their direction, she went out the front door.

"Do I have to go?" Anne asked, staring at her cereal bowl.

"Not if you'd rather not."

Anne weighed the choices. If she went with him, it would be a stiff, uncomfortable afternoon, always watching for a sign - if he held her hand too long, or gave her a hug that was too tight. On the other hand, if she refused the invitation, she would have to come up with a good reason to be out of the house all day. A Saturday could be long and if she stayed home she knew he would start drinking after lunch, and then...

"I'll go," she said, moving quickly around him as he left the table. "I'm going over to Joanie's now. She has a new puppy. I'll be back in time."

Phil went into the den, took papers from his briefcase and spread them on the desk. For a few minutes he looked down at them, seeing only lists of incomprehensible figures, his eyes fogged and unable to focus. Tugging at his insides, an appetite that wouldn't let go, that made him tremble suddenly, made his voice shake and sweat begin along his spine. Away from the house, he could fight it, holding his attention on business, forcing himself to think only of the day's work. But when he came home at night it was waiting for him as soon as he stepped through the door. First, the sour memory of the afternoon of waiting and watching on Hendrix Street, then Bee gone all day and into the evening, liquor in the cabinet, Anne upstairs listening to the radio, doing her homework, curled up on the bed, bent over her books.... He closed his eyes, saw her in her nightgown, hair damp and body warm from the shower, and desire toppled every other thought. His body throbbed with it, his mind fastened on his need with a force he couldn't resist.

It took three or four drinks before the voice in his head stopped telling him how monstrous his actions were, how depraved. When the curtain finally fell he was able to make it up the stairs and into her room, to block from sight her fear. "You're my baby, I love you so much," were the words he had to say to make it all possible. And, "I could never hurt you, I just want to be near you, to hold you..." closing his eyes as he pulled her body against his. The one thought that kept self-hate from overwhelming his waking hours was the fact that, even in the strangled moment, he had not penetrated her. Contact alone was his need, and it brought relief quickly. How many times had he gone to her room this way? Not a half dozen, surely. Probably only two or three. The memory faded afterward, retreated as his throbbing pulse calmed.

All right, it would be the movies today. No chance to do anything else. No chance to hit the bottle right after lunch. He would let her choose the movie, then maybe they'd eat out or maybe pick up some take-out on the way home. Maybe, even, he would be able to look at himself in the mirror without loathing next morning.

Leaving the movies at five, Anne and Phil stopped at China Moon for Egg Foo Yung, noodles, and Shrimp Chow Mein. The afternoon had been without tension. Phil had not reached for her hand, had done and said nothing to cause anxiety, and Anne relaxed, laughed a little and began to hope it was over. The weeks since he first came to her, a nightmare in the beginning because of the real fear that he would hurt her, had become more confusing than frightening. Always gentle, stroking her head, calling her his baby, he gave the appearance of a loving daddy, one she could recognize. But what he did after that, the strange, hot sensation of his body, and then the gasp and she could fall away from him - was the mystery she had no answers for. Boy and girl stuff, talked about with snickers at school, gave little information. Sex talk was mostly sly whispers,

and provided nothing to help understanding. Some of the girls,
having recently experienced the onset of "the curse" were more
specific about bodily functions. But she had no idea where
to find an explanation for what her father did when he came
to her room.

A Saturday night dinner together was rare, and as they ate
they talked a little, stiffly, unaccustomed to the intimacy.
Anne watched her parents furtively, gave a minimal smile to
Bee's comments about her renewed appetite and, instead of
streaking for the stairs as soon as the meal was over, hovered
around the table and listened to their conversation.

"There's a good chance I'll have to do a big favor for Andy
Pacello soon," Bee was saying. "One of his Westchester clients
wants to have the firm do an evaluation of his Miami estate,
and since he's up to his neck in appointments, I may be tapped
to go down there."

Anne had dropped into a chair and was staring at her.
"You mean you're going away? To Miami? In Florida?"

"It's not settled," Bee answered. "Who knows, Andy might
be able to go himself. I won't know for a few days."

"When, though?"

"I told you, nothing's definite. I can't tell you yet."
Maurice would fly out on a Saturday. If all went well, she
would be on the Sunday AM flight to Miami.

Phil picked up a newspaper and went into his den without
comment. Nothing told her, one way or another, what his feelings
were. It was rarely that he even met her eyes nowadays. Relieved

that no further explanation was called for at the moment, Bee
stacked the dishes in the sink and went into the living room
to watch television.

Her face pale, Anne slowly climbed the stairs to her room.

(Italics)

Someone up there loves me! I've been able to work it all
out, lining up a plausible itinerary for Andy to give any random
caller, arranging for a leave of absence with Ed Quigley, who
didn't even want to hear where I was going, only that I have
someone to cover for my appointments. I have a seat on Delta
to Miami for Sunday at 8:30 a.m. Maurice will be at the airport
to meet me and I have a single room on the same floor as his
at the Meridian. My suitcase holds a bathing suit, shorts and
a slinky nightgown. A week of bliss lies ahead. How lucky
can I get?

Tonight, Thursday, I'll break the news at home. Phil hasn't
shown any interest in my comings and goings for months. If
he questions or calls my office, my back-up will swing into
action with convincing answers. I've been a good girl! I haven't
hurt anyone, both our marriages are still intact, and I have
given myself and my lover pleasure and happiness. This week
is my reward.

(end Italics)

Anne was at Whitlock's baby-sitting the new twins when Bee
got home. There was a note from her on the kitchen table: "I'll

be back in an hour and I'll be hungry." It was after eight, traffic had been awful, weather worse, the drive from the city a nightmare. Her nerves were frayed. A drink would help, then she would be able to tackle the question of what to cook for supper.

Phil lay on the couch, his eyes closed, an empty glass in his hand. The TV was on, without sound. A troop of mounted men galloped across a desert and for a minute Bee watched the screen, hearing in the silence Phil's heavy breathing. Then she looked down at him and sudden, blazing rage welled up. Slumped, sprawled, his shirt open at the neck, one shoe on the floor beside the couch, he looked like a rag doll that had been dropped from a great height. She wanted to jab him, poke him, strike his body in some place to cause pain, jerk him upright, slap his eyes open. How dare he lie there, drunk, while she had spent the last two hours struggling through traffic that barely moved, on icy roads that could spin the car out of control... Before the urge to strike him became irresistible she turned and hurried from the room, flinging her coat and gloves on a chair as she passed. At the sink, running cold water through lettuce, she told herself to simmer down, forego the temper tantrum. Happiness is hours away, don't jeopardize it. She poured scotch and added ice cubes and sat at the kitchen table waiting for the alcohol to soothe her anger.

As she was sliding chops into the broiler a few minutes later she heard a noise behind her. Phil stood in the doorway blinking and rubbing his chin. 287

"I didn't hear you come in," he said.

"Of course you didn't. You were out like a light." She closed the oven door and walked away from him, drowning anger with a long pull at her drink. Then, "Dinner will be ready in twenty minutes. You've got time to clean yourself up." She didn't try to keep the insult from her voice.

"Knock it off, Bee. I had a drink, that's all. I'm not drunk. I've been home for two hours, nobody here, and I just dozed off. Don't nag, okay?"

Reaching for cups and plates, she didn't answer.

He sat down. "How was traffic?"

"Terrible. I left New York at five. It took me two hours just to get through Queens." His inquiry had the sound of attempted peace-making. She went on: "It's probably going to be this bad tomorrow too. I may go in late rather than buck rush hour." Keep it casual. Just an exchange of opinion and information. It's been this way for months. Better than open argument, but a strain, too, trying to keep everything looking normal. "By the way, it looks as though I'll be flying down to Miami after all. That job for the client in Westchester has materialized and Andy can't get away. It means something important to the firm, so I've told him I'll pinch hit for him." The front door had slammed and Anne came slowly into the kitchen. "I've got my plane ticket, just need to throw a few things together and catch the eight-thirty flight on Sunday morning."

"I'll drive you to the airport, if you'd like," he said.

"That would - be nice." She was surprised by the offer.

"Anne can come along, too."

"I don't want to!" Anne said. "Don't bother me on Sunday,
I don't want to go to the damned airport!" She turned her back
to them and began picking at the salad piled in a wooden bowl.

"Well, what's got you in a tizzy?" Bee asked.

"Leave her alone." Phil stood up, avoiding Bee's eyes.
"Let's not get into any more arguments. Let's just eat and
stop hacking at each other. All right?"

Phil backed the station wagon out of the carport and hit
the horn.

"Got to go now," Bee said. Anne was standing at the dining
room window, twisting a paper napkin in her hands. The remains
of a hurried breakfast were strewn across the table. "I thought
you might change your mind - you could have stayed in bed if
you don't want to come to the airport."

"I don't want to go - I told you!" The napkin was a pile
of white scraps at her feet. "Just go. You'll miss the stupid
plane."

Bee hesitated, hand on the doorknob. "Maybe you'd like
to kiss me goodbye?"

Not turning from the window, Anne said: "No. You're only
going for a week, not a year."

"Suit yourself," Bee said. A small sharp burst of memory
made her hold back at the door for a few seconds. It passed,
and she said, "See you next Sunday," and closed the door behind
her.

289

The car pulled away and Anne continued to stare at it until it turned the corner. Then, blinking back the tears she had kept Bee from seeing, she went to the telephone and dialed Harriet's number.

Maurice was standing in the crowd at Gate 14 when she came off the plane. He was tired, she could see, but his smile was welcoming and he kissed her warmly.

"I'm glad you could come," he said as they headed for the baggage carrousel. "A week ago I didn't think it such a great idea, but the way things are going, it will be good to have you with me."

"How's Karel?"

"Not doing well. His fevers are more frequent and the 'cleaning' doesn't last long. I'm hoping these people can do something for him."

"What about recovery? Do they have any idea how long it will take?"

He didn't answer at once, the struggle to handle it apparent on his face. She squeezed his hand as they walked.

"We've pretty much given up that hope, Bee. C.F. isn't something you get over, like chicken pox. The doctor here wants to have him under observation for a few more days, but it's obvious that he isn't very optimistic."

"And - his mother?" As always, it wasn't easy to talk about his wife.

"She's worn thin," he said bleakly. "She had to get away,

or I'd have two invalids on my hands."

The hotel wasn't on the beach, but a few blocks away, and not one of the luxury palaces from the Sunday Travel Section. It was low key and comfortable. The guests were quiet and elderly for the most part, sitting around the pool, sipping their drinks and talking in low voices among themselves. Her room was down the hall from Maurice's, a precaution they weren't sure was necessary but had taken anyway. She didn't expect to spend a lot of time in it. Karel, of course, had a private room at the hospital, where Maurice would spend a large part of the day. She had made plans for this: there were a couple of paperback novels in her bag, the beach beckoned, and the evenings and nights lay ahead.

Two days passed before they made love. Sunday night had been dinner in the hotel and a walk along the beach, then Maurice pleaded exhaustion and after a goodnight kiss, went to his room. Bee put her satin nightgown back in the closet and took a book to bed. Monday night he was called to the hospital when a crisis occurred, then stayed for a consultation with the doctors. He got back to the hotel after ten, again tired and disheartened. She didn't show him her disappointment.

About to step into the shower on Tuesday morning, she heard a knock at her door. She grabbed a robe and hurried to open it.

Holding a paper sack of doughnuts and two containers of coffee, he came into the room. "You're being a good sport about this, Bee," he said. "I've had a talk with Karel's doctor and know he's doing everything that can be done for the moment."

There was gray stubble on his chin and his slacks were wrinkled. She took the bag and dropped it on the dresser. "Coffee later." She put her arms around him. "First things first."

An hour later they lay against the pillows, holding hands, glowing with the warmth and bliss of the moment, not talking. She marveled, silently, at the strength of passion he could show after all the many, many times they had done this. Why did it never become routine? How come it didn't cool, grow boring? With Phil, it had. In spite of all her efforts to keep it alive, nothing got better, expectations died, and the marriage fell apart. What was it here, with Maurice, that was different? The sex, certainly. Phil had never mastered the art, whereas Maurice was talented and innovative and made each time a delight and a surprise. It was more than sex, of course. They had things in common to talk about - to share. Maybe that was the secret of the affair's success.

"I love you," she said into his neck and his arms tightened around her and the kissing began again, deepening at once and bringing the familiar heat and desire. "You are my lover, my sweetheart, the center of my life..."

When they finally got around to breakfast the coffee was cold and the doughnuts unappetizing.

"How about a Bloody Mary at the pool?" Maurice said, pulling on his socks. "And a plate of fruit and some caviar and..."

"Enough! Stop right after the Bloody Mary!"

"You're a lush, you know that? A luscious, lascivious lush!"

Banter, love talk, after moments of high emotion and incredible ecstasy. As much a part of their lovemaking as the act itself.

Maurice went back to his room and Bee took her interrupted shower. She had just finished toweling her hair when he returned. A sharp knock on the door, then his bleached face, blank eyes staring at her as though seeing a stranger. He stood there, rigid, one hand on the doorjamb.

"He died, and I wasn't there. This morning, at ten. They called me at nine thirty, but I was here."

"Karel?" She stopped breathing and a pulse began to hammer in her throat.

"I've called my wife, she'll fly out tonight and we'll make - there will be - arrangements to make when she gets here."

"Oh, Maurice..."

It was instantly gone, but she had seen it. The spontaneous, swiftly killed flash of rejection, of _stay away!_ that looked out at her for a tick of time. She froze, waiting for what would come next.

Not touching her, he said: "I know you'll understand. I can't - it's best if you leave now, Bee. I'll get in touch, eventually."

"But - my return flight. It's for Sunday."

"See if you can change it." With a thin smile he backed away, turned and went down the hall. In shock and bewilderment, she watched him go into his room and close the door.

What in God's name do I do now? What's going to happen to me? To us? Why won't he let me stay until she gets here?

I can help, be here for him to lean on, talk to. Why is he
pushing me away like this?

She wasn't able to change the plane reservation and, afraid
to take the chance of seeing Maurice and his wife together,
kept to her room except for quick trips to the coffee shop to
bring back food. He must have known she was still at the hotel,
but he made no attempt to see her or talk to her. She could
only guess at what was happening.

Karel's death, even if the doctors had forecast it, would
be a frightful blow. They would draw close, no matter what
previous distance had been between them as man and wife, and
she didn't want to see it, even across a hotel lobby or on the
other side of the street. To catch a glimpse of the sorrowing
parents, heads together as they comforted each other, was more
than she could bear. For all the time they had been lovers,
she had banished such scenes from her mind, seeing Maurice as
belonging only to her. It was what made the love affair possible
and created the make-believe that held it together.

For the rest of the week she stayed in the room, reading,
brooding, in misery.

One day, one loving morning, was all there had been before the
roof caved in. He could have left the next day, as soon as
Albertine arrived. Or he could still be at the hotel on Friday,
or Saturday, or even Sunday, while arrangements were made to
take the boy's body home. She stood at the window, looking
out over the busy Miami street, feeling as though life had

stopped happening, that she had gotten off the track and could only wait on the sidelines until someone came to tell her how to get back on.

"Before I go another block," Harriet said as soon as Anne got into the car, "you'll tell me what this is all about. When you father gets back from the airport, what will he think? Did you leave him a note?"

Anne shook her head. "Please, just take me home with you. You can call him when we get there. I - I can't talk to him any more."

Harriet moved into traffic and headed for the Southern State Parkway. She noted the tear-streaked face and, remembering the anguish in Anne's voice on the telephone, asked no more questions. "Come and get me! I can't stay here!" The cry had been sheer panic.

At the Hendrix Street house Alice had made hot chocolate and muffins. She put them on the dining room table and disappeared.

Cup in hand, Harriet said: "Now. Will you tell me what happened? I can't kidnap you like this - I'll have to tell your father something."

"I'm so scared -- "

"What are you scared about?"

"You're the only one I can talk to - Mom's gone to Florida for a week - and I'll have to stay home with Dad and - and - I can't! I can't stay in that house!"

"What do you mean?"

Anne jumped up, knocking over the cup of chocolate. "He - he does things to me when we're alone in the house!" Her voice was shrill, her face flushed. "He gets drunk then he comes to my bedroom - and he does things to me!"

The hot chocolate trickled from the table top to the floor and made a puddle at Harriet's feet. She sat absolutely still, seeing only Anne's tear-smeared face.

"My God," she said softly, and reached out and took Anne's hand and pulled her into her arms. "Oh, my baby, my baby..."

Anne sobbed and clung to Harriet, her body trembling.

"Can you tell me - what he does, Anne? Can you tell me?"

Half an hour later Harriet led Anne upstairs and told her to lie down, to take a nap, not to worry, everything was going to be all right.

"Do you have to tell him that I told you? I can't ever go back there if you do. Do you have to?"

Harriet drew her hand from Anne's frantic grip and leaned over to kiss her. "I'll only tell him that you're here, that you don't feel well and will be staying here a day or two."

"Can I stay til Mom gets back? Please?"

"Wait til I talk to him. Then we can decide."

At the telephone table in the hall Harriet tried to control the shaking of her hands. When it continued, she put the instrument down and went to the kitchen where she took out a bottle of sherry and poured some into a glass. Her stomach was churning, her thoughts a tangle: disgust, first, then anger.

29

Then, slowly, with a widening of her eyes, elation. Phil's fate was now in her hands, irrevocably. With one telephone call, everything would fall into place. It was an intoxicating moment and she savored it, sipping sherry, her eyes alive with anticipation.

Phil answered after the first ring. "You've got her there? What in hell - ?"

"Calm down," Harriet said pleasantly. "She's here and she's safe."

"Will you tell me what this is all about or do I have to come in and choke it out of you?"

"She called me, after you left for the airport, she said that she couldn't stay in that house another minute. Does this suggest anything to you, Phil?"

"What do you mean?"

"You know exactly what I mean. She has told me everything!" Excitement overwhelmed her. "Phil Shepard, you are a filthy monster and don't deserve to have a daughter! And if you don't do just what I tell you to do, I'll tell Bee the whole story and she'll dump you like the bag of garbage you are!"

"You bitch!" His strangled cry burst from the phone. "Let me talk to her - what did she say- ?"

"No, you can't talk to her. I'm keeping her here until Bee gets back from Miami. Don't try to come for her, I'm going to see that she's safe until then. Now, here's what you're going to do, Phil Shepard, and this will be done my way, not yours!" 297

Chapter IX

BEE - PHIL - HARRIET

(Bee)

The skies opened up as the plane coasted in for a landing
and for a few tense moments I held my breath. I could see
nothing through the streaming glass at my elbow. In the
terminal, at one of the rain-spattered windows, Phil would be
watching and a wave of nausea hit me at the thought. A week
ago he had been that part of me I could do little about, a
condition of what my life had become. Now, with the anguish
of the past week blurring my vision like the rain on the window,
I pleaded: let him not be waiting, let the storm keep him away,
let me find a cab and go home alone. I have to get myself
together before I can talk to him.

He was there, of course. Weather wouldn't jog him out of
his husbandly role. You don't let your wife fend for herself
in the airport, you get there when her plane comes in, you carry
her luggage, hand her into the car and take her home. Even
if there is nothing to say, nothing between the two of you any
more, you do your duty.

This is all that is left of Phil Shepard, my wartime
dreamboat, my handsome suitor in uniform - only his officer-

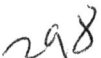

and-gentleman manners, often strained but still operating.

After a brief greeting we drove in silence, while I held
onto thoughts of the earlier Phil because they were less painful
than those crowding my mind.

After a while he asked: "Everything work out? Did you have
a chance to enjoy Miami?"

I answered, managed to say something about the beach, the
hotel food, the people at the pool, keeping my voice flat and
calm. We drove home through the drenched Sunday afternoon that
seemed a century removed from the one a week ago.

When we turned the corner into Walnut Street, I saw Harriet's
car parked at the curb. Jolted out of old memories, I turned
to Phil. "What is she doing here?"

"She's got some plan in mind for Anne and wants to talk
to us - talk to you about it." He finally looked at me. "I
told her you'd be back today, so she drove out."

"Plan? What kind of plan? Phil, I'm really not in the
mood to listen to her -. "

"She's thinking of sending Anne to private school, some
swanky place in Connecticut. I'll let her tell you about it."

"What's the matter with the school here?" What could have
brought this up? Had Anne complained again about her boring
life in the suburbs? Harriet, of course, could be wrapped around
Anne's little finger when it came to spending money. An idea
filtered through annoyance: it would certainly allow me more
freedom, because once Maurice's situation cleared, we'll be
back together. "Well, since she's here, I don't have much

choice. Let's go in."

She got up as we came into the living room, hugged me and
sat down again. "Have a good trip?" Her voice was cheerful,
her smile warm. "You must have had gorgeous weather down there.
This is really the best time for Florida. We've had nothing
but cold and rain."

"Phil says you want to talk about Anne. What do you want
to talk about?"

"I'll get to it, I'll get to it! Just sit and catch your
breath."

My patience was wearing thin. I dropped my coat on a chair
and went into the dining room. As I opened the liquor cabinet
Phil called out: "I'll have a scotch, if you're pouring. Harriet
- can we get you something?"

When she said No he made a show of coaxing her. "Hey, it's
cold outside. A drink will warm you up." She refused again
and when I came back with the drinks she was glaring at his
back. He took the glass and gulped, his face red and angry.

I said: "What's this all about?"

"It's about Anne's schooling." Harriet settled back. "She's
mentioned having problems, not getting along with her teacher
last semester, and now with the new one, Mr. Something-or-other.
She's not really happy there, Bee, and I'd like to make an offer,
to both of you." Neither of us said anything, waiting. "I'd
like to send her to an academy in Connecticut, a private school
that has a very fine reputation, where she'll get a first rate
education , discipline, and a lot of things public school doesn't

300

provide. It will be a good experience for her and maybe give her more enthusiasm for school." She stopped, her smile still in place.

I stared at her for a moment, digesting the proposal. The pluses were obvious. I looked at Phil, but he was staring at the headlines on the Sunday newspaper that lay on the coffee table.

"Well, what do you think?"

"Phil?" I said. "Shouldn't we talk this over before we decide?"

"What's there to talk about? I think it's a damn good idea." He didn't look up.

I turned to Harriet. "It's a very generous offer. Can we call you in a day or two? I want to think about it, and talk to Anne, too."

"Of course." Her eyes sparkled and she beamed at us. "She has a couple of months to go before school vacation. If you decide to let me do this, she'll have time to get used to the idea. Let's leave it at that. Call me when you've decided."

(Phil)

The skies opened up as the plane coasted in for a landing. Through the rain-spattered windows I watched it cruise down the runway and ease up to the terminal, my thoughts as blurred as the glass. I had considered not showing up, letting her fend for herself at the airport, carry her own bag, call a cab.

But that would have been childish. I had taken her there last weekend. I had no reason not to be there when she returned.

The week had been torture. The confrontation with Harriet on the phone had fractured what little peace of mind I had left. The bitch! The hateful, spiteful bitch! I could kill her with my bare hands, take her fat neck and squeeze and squeeze... She's gotten her way, finally. She will tear me apart in the process, but she's got what she wants. My daughter. If someone asked me how to describe what is happening, I'd say it's like that old Indian trick of pinning a man's legs to two bent saplings, then releasing them to fly up and tear him in half.

And the rest of it, the part of me that can't give up, still alive in spite of what happened, the insatiable need to touch her, hold her, her sweet breath in my neck, even her fear an excitement. How do I deal with that now?

These are the questions I can't answer. Who am I - the filthy monster Harriet calls me? Or the man Bee used to call "an officer and a gentleman" and fell in love with back in wartime? Or am I just a sick guy who has taken a bad turn and needs help? Well, Harriet's got the reins, has held them from the beginning, and now she's got me to jerk around and she will get away with it because I can't let her tell Bee, I can't deal with it if Bee finds out.

My head was hot, ready to burst, more questions battering me. Had they met down there in Miami? Or perhaps been on the same plane? A whole week - of what they had done in Harriet's house. All that was necessary was to have told a few careful lies, falsify details, and she could have pulled it off.

I asked her how she enjoyed the trip.

She told me about the hotel, the food, the beach, the pool, in a flat, calm voice. No way to tell what was going on behind it. We drove home through the drenched Sunday afternoon that seemed a century removed from the one a week ago.

When we turned into Walnut Street I saw Harriet's car parked at the curb. My stomach lurched, and suddenly my mouth was dry, parched.

"What's she doing here?"

I said: "She has some plan about sending Anne to a private school. I told her you'd be home today."

"Phil, I'm tired from the trip and I really don't want to listen to her."

I got out of the car and went up the walk. I heard her slam the car door and follow me.

Harriet came toward us as we entered. "Well! Have a nice trip?" she asked Bee. "The weather must have been gorgeous. We've had nothing but cold, freezing rain since you - "

Bee interrupted, plainly losing patience. "What is it you want to talk about?"

Harriet kept her smile. "I'll get around to it in a minute. Why not sit down and catch your breath?"

Instead, Bee went into the dining room and I heard bottles clink together as she took one out of the liquor cabinet. I asked her to pour me a scotch. Harriet's eyes lit up with malice and she said No, without the "thanks" when I asked her if she

wanted anything. I couldn't look at her. The self-satisfied
expression sent a wave of nausea over me and when Bee handed
me the glass I drank it fast.

Harriet launched into her speech about Anne's problems coping
with school and how wonderful this fancy academy was, with tennis
and riding lessons, lots of extras, beefing up her offer so
Bee would say yes. With my help, of course. It surprised the
hell out of me when Bee turned to me and asked what I thought
about it.

So, Anne will be told and the three of us will decide whether
to accept this "kind and generous offer." I know what my job
is: to swing things Harriet's way if the other two are undecided.
And all I can do is go along, let her run the show, or Bee will
find out what I've done and there's no way I can live with that.

(Harriet)

I had gone only a mile before the clouds opened up and
a torrential downpour flooded the Southern State Parkway.
Windshield wipers did little to clear the glass, which now fogged
over. With visibility down to almost nothing, I pulled over
to the shoulder and up onto the low bank. Other cars were doing
the same, hoping to wait out the sudden cloudburst. Anne sat
beside me, silent, the tension in her body almost visible.

The respite would give me time to think further along the
lines I had prepared to present to Bee. Phil, of course, would
make no objections. Not if he knew what was good for him.

30

Once more I felt a glow of deep satisfaction, remembering the phone call, and his angry, frustrated scream when he knew that I knew. Come September, Anne will be in school in Latchfield, where I can visit her regularly - long walks along the river, a movie in town, dinner out. First, however, I must see to it that Dr. Hamell examines her. I can tell her it's a requirement before enrolling at Latchfield Academy. She mustn't be frightened, she's been through enough already. I really can't take her word for it that he didn't actually - that it wasn't - oh, that evil man! I could strangle him with my bare hands!

When the rain let up I moved back into traffic and went on my way, reaching over once in a while to pat Anne's shoulder and smile encouragingly at her. When I turned into Walnut Street I could see they weren't home yet, the station wagon was gone. We got out and I used my key to let us in. Anne disappeared quickly up the stairs and I went into the living room to wait.

They came in and I got to my feet. "Welcome home! How was the trip? Hope the weather in Miami was better than what we've been having." And did Maurice enjoy it, too?

Bee answered, a little curtly, I thought. "Phil says you want to talk to me about Anne."

"Yes, I do. But sit, catch your breath, and I'll get to it in a minute." This might take a little time, but that was on my side, too. I can be generous and let them think it over, let Phil do the selling job he knows he has to do. "No, thanks," I said to his offer of a drink, watching him redden under my gaze. He gulped down the straight liquor and I knew my presence

305

made him jittery, nervous. I settled back on the couch. "Anne

has told me about problems at school, the teachers who don't

like her and how hard it is to please them. When summer vacation

is over in September I'd like to send her to Latchfield Academy,

In Connecticut. It's a fine school, has a reputation for high

standards, discipline, and lots of fun extras." I leaned

forward. "Just what the child needs to re-kindle her enthusiasm

for school."

Bee's expression told me nothing. "That's a very generous

offer, Harriet. Can I take a few days to think it over?"

It was time to leave. I got up and reached for my fur coat

and gloves. "Of course. Nothing has to be decided right away.

End of semester is a few months away. Let me know when you've

decided."

Phil would have to apply only minimum pressure, since my

offer, if accepted, would free a lot more of Bee's time to spend

with Maurice. All taken into consideration, everyone would

benefit. I gave Bee a quick kiss and left.

Anne would be safe now. If Phil dared to do anything more

to her, she would tell me and I would come down on him so hard

he wouldn't know what hit him. I'll call her every day, because

she'll be anxious. And in a few months we'll be going off for

summer vacation and she'll be out of the house. She'll be mine.

Chapter X

1958

The phone rang five times before Harriet answered. Anne
was close to hysteria. "Harriet! You promised to call me -
you said every day! It's Monday afternoon - why didn't you call
me?"

"Calm down, Annie. I had to do some shopping. I was going
to call you in a few minutes. Now, let me tell you what I've
arranged. When school is over you and I will drive up to
Connecticut to enroll you in Latchfield Academy. It's a nice
school - I'll tell you all about it before we go. There's all
kinds of things you don't get in public school - it will be
lots of fun."

"But - what about now? What about the rest of it, til June?"
Her voice was shrill.

"Your father won't come near you again, Anne. I promised
you that, didn't I? Do you remember what I said? You and I
will spend the summer in Maine, just like last year, and then
you'll start school at Latchfield in September. All you have
to do is be patient until school is over. Can you do that,
Annie?"

"How can I be sure he won't do anything? What did you say

to him?"

"Never mind what I said. I did whatever had to be done
to bring this to a halt. Remember this, Annie. I have
everything under control."

Spring finally drifted into summer, the semester was over
and the hot months stretched ahead. The Maine vacation, extended
this year to two months, helped a little to blot out the fears
that memory repeated over and over in Anne's mind. Harriet
had been right, though. Since that last time, he had stayed
away from her, hardly speaking to her, and hadn't come to her
room. But the possibility hung in the air, and when she caught
him glancing at her, she brushed past him quickly and ran for
the stairs.

On Tuesday following the Labor Day weekend, Harriet and
Anne drove to Latchfield, in the Berkshires, over winding country
roads, through fields and woods tinged with the first pale
yellows of autumn. At the academy they conferred with the
headmistress and Anne was assigned a room and the class schedule
given to her. She clung to Harriet, trembling, when it came
time to leave.

"I love you, Harriet," she whispered. "You've been so good
to me."

The words brought sweet memories, soothing the soreness
of Bee's defection and the bitter, sour anger Harriet felt for
Phil. She gently disengaged herself from Anne's arms. "Your
job is to make me proud of you, Annie. Show me you can get

good grades, that I've done the right thing by bringing you
here."

"I will! I promise!"

"Call me if you need anything, anything at all. I'll drive
up once a month - maybe even more often, if I can make it. We'll
go out for dinner, have some fun together."

They kissed and Harriet left. Her throat tight with tears,
Anne waved her down the flagged path outside the dorm and watched
her get into her car, then pull out into the campus road and
drive out of sight.

Nothing had been heard from Maurice beyond a perfunctory
call two weeks after Bee's return from Miami. He had asked
her if she was all right, she said yes, but before she could
ask when she would see him, he said, "I'll call you when I can,"
and hung up. That had been in February. She had tried to reach
him at the gallery, but was told he had not been in recently.
The young assistant, who knew her voice, said he believed Mr.
and Mrs. Greenwood had taken a trip, after the funeral. They
would probably be back the end of March. But when Bee called
after a four week wait, there was no answer at the gallery.
The phone rang and rang, and finally she put it down and went
uptown to see what had happened. A notice on the gallery's front
door told the public that it would be closed indefinitely and
to watch for an opening date later in the summer. Calling
Scarsdale was a terrible temptation, but she resisted it. There
was nothing to do but wait, as the empty months went slowly

by.

Then it was July. With Anne gone, life was simpler. At the office she worked hard, made a few good sales, and evenings, tired and unhappy, ate dinner and went to bed early. Phil, retreating more and more into his private misery, buried hmself in paperwork and didn't approach her for sexual attentions. He spent weekday evenings out at Patchogue calling on clients. On weekends, there was little conversation and meals together were rare. Sunday nights Phil kept a bottle of scotch at his side and watched endless TV programs. Bee was in bed by ten. Some time in the early morning hours he came to bed, and if she was awake, the smell of liquor made her turn impatiently to the wall, letting him see her resentment.

Time dragged on, hope of hearing from Maurice all but died. She walked mechanically through the September days, saw Anne briefly in October when she came down to Brooklyn to go to a concert with Harriet. They kissed each other, made casual talk: Anne thanked her for the allowance check just received, Bee asked about recent exams. Anne's goodbye was cool, her eyes blank. Bee said: "Don't forget to write."

The day before Thanksgiving Bee received a call at the office. Maurice's voice was strained.

"Can you get some time off next Tuesday? I'll meet you at the Lexington, in the bar. Two o'clock?"

"I'll be there." She knew better than to keep the conversation going. But what did this mean? A meeting in a bar? That he didn't want to be alone with her? Or make love to her? After all these months? All the doubts and anxieties flooded back. He was only calling her to break it off, didn't want to take her where they could be alone, just the Lexington bar, where he could do it casually, where she wouldn't cry or plead or make a scene. That was it, the reason he didn't want to see her alone. It was all over. She went into the Ladies' Room, past the sly glances of the salesmen at their desks, and turned on the water in the basin and cried, long shuddering sobs that left her weak and pale and without makeup at hand to restore her appearance. After a while she dried her eyes, splashed cold water on her face and went back into the office. A few minutes later she told the receptionist she had an appointment with a client, and left.

The holiday brought an invitation from Harriet to have dinner in the city. (Anne had elected to spend Thanksgiving Day visiting a schoolmate's home in New Haven.) Bee asked if it meant Phil, and Harriet huffed a little and said, "Of course, if you want to bring him."

"Are you inviting anyone else?'

"Just the Vinsons, you know them, from St. Andrew's. I thought we'd go to Luchow's - "

"Phil hates German food, Harriet. I think we'll pass this time. I'll call you next week and maybe we can get together."

To recognize the holiday, she bought a small turkey, baked a pumpkin pie and produced a bottle of wine. Phil refused it, staying with scotch and water. They spent the evening with newspapers and a book. In bed she dreamed of past love, of

recent bitter loss and departed ecstasy, and spent a restless
night.

On Saturday she called Lucille. After a number of rings,
there was no answer at the Providence number and she put the
phone down and looked up Lu's parents' number in Brooklyn.
Lucille answered on the first ring.

"Lu! Am I glad you're in town! I have to see you - it's
a long story - can we get together while you're here?"

Lu broke in: "Bee, hold on. What's wrong? Of course I can
see you. We're here for the weekend with the folks. How about
tomorrow morning? Come on in and we'll go for breakfast
somewhere. Okay?"

"He's going to leave me," Bee moaned, her hand on the coffee
cup unsteady. The food she had ordered sat before her,
untouched.

Lu patted her shoulder. "Of course he isn't. Don't even
think it. He's had a really bad time. He's counting on you
to understand and be patient."

Tears about to spill, Bee said: "It's been so many months,
almost a year. How long does it take to get over such a thing?"

"Stop the waterworks, Bee. You're feeling sorry for
yourself. Moaning and groaning isn't going to help. Has he
called?"

Bee told her she would see him on Tuesday. "In a bar, Lu!
That's all he can come up with after all this time - a bar!"

"You mean you have a date with him? Well, lady, if I were

you, I'd hold off the recriminations until he can explain."

Bee mopped her eyes and stared at her friend. "Do you really think this will pass? That he'll come back to me? And - what about his wife? Won't he - ?"

"He's been standing by, as he should. Ask yourself, Bee, would you get over it in a few months? Losing a child?"

"Of course not." Lu's admonishings, not quite what she had expected but a kind of wake-up call in the corner of misery she had crawled into, were making sense. Maurice had been shattered by his son's death, his wife probably devastated, and they had been hanging together for mutual comfort. It didn't mean that he had forgotten their love affair. As he had always maintained - it was a separate part of his life, it didn't touch the rest of it in any way.

Lu smiled warmly. "You'll see him on Tuesday and things will be worked out. You get that stiff upper lip in place, kiddo!" She stood and reached for the check. "Call me after you've seen him. And don't cry over spilt chickens until they hatch."

Bee laughed shakily. "Thanks, as always, Lu. I'll call."

Tuesday arrived at last. It had been easy to arrange the afternoon off, the time between the holidays not busy at Quigley's. She put on her best - a close-fitting turquoise suit with a while silk blouse, black pumps and the soft cashmere coat she had treated herself to after her last big sale. She had her hair done and made up her face with great care. On

313

the uptown bus, she felt like a martyr going to the lions, and stared out at the passing streets in mounting anxiety.

The bar was crowded. She plowed through a jostling bunch near the door and made it the far corner, where she ordered a double scotch and leaned over the table, fighting panic.

She looked up and saw his familiar rumpled figure edge past the mob congregated at the bar. He saw her at once and made his way over. Would he sit down, or would he tell her they had a place to go and to follow him?

He shook his coat from his shoulders and took the seat across from her. His face was gray, tired, but his eyes came to life as he reached for her hands. "I'm glad you could come."

"Nothing could have kept me away," she said, trying to smile. But it was useless. Tears welled up. "Oh, Maurice..."

"Shhh...don't say anything for a minute."

Bar noises closed around them. High laughter, staccato conversation, mounting decibels of liquored enjoyment that she tried to ignore. What he would say now would mean life and love, or the end of hopes, and if the worst happened here in this loud, careless place, she knew she would break down and howl her misery into the bedlam around them.

"How have you been?"

He couldn't be asking her such a question. "Is that all you can think of to say?"

"No, I have other things to talk about. Let me get a drink, you're ahead of me." He beckoned a waiter and asked for scotch, no ice. When the drink arrived he smiled for the first time.

"I haven't taken a drink in six months." Like a European, he sipped the alcohol, savoring it. Americans gulp their liquor, he had told her once. "How can they taste it if it drops into their stomachs without passing their palates?" She had laughed and told him he was a hopeless sophisticate.

She waited while he took another sip. Then she said: "Will you tell me what has happened since Miami?"

"Bee, I can't talk about Karel's death, or about the funeral." He stared into his glass for a moment. "I think I need to tell you about my wife, who has come through this rather well, I think."

Bee stiffened. His wife? He wanted to talk about her, now?

"She is an exceptional woman, Bee," he went on, meeting her eyes directly. "She was in a rest home, as it's called, briefly, but was able to come home after a month because the doctor said she was handling the situation better than he'd expected. As soon as she was strong enough, we took a trip. It's hard to remember, now, where we went or what we did but we got away for a while and found we could eventually talk to each other about it, and what it was going to mean for the rest of our lives."

"I think I need another drink," Bee said. The waiter was called and when she had a fresh glass in her hands she said, "May I tell you how sorry I am about what happened?"

"I know, Bee. Of course I know. Let me talk, don't ask questions." His voice wavered   but he cleared his throat and continued. "It will take a long time for me to forget where I was and what I was doing when my son died. And why I wasn't there for him, or for his mother." He held up his hand as Bee started to speak. "I'm not calling it guilt, that was never a factor during the years you and I were together. It's a final and inevitable acknowledgment of my failure to measure up to standards I always believed I had. It's like seeing myself stripped naked in a mirror, no more pretenses to cover up who I am."

"Pretenses?" She was having trouble following this.

"I wasn't pretending when I told you what you mean to me," he said, "but believing that I wasn't hurting anyone else, thinking I was being so careful and so far-seeing that I could make us a private world that touched no one else, with no price asked, that was my mistake. We thought we existed in a vacuum, I think. It wasn't so."

Bee's face crumpled. "We - were a mistake?"

"Let me finish." He took her hand again. "I'm living with a picture of myself that I don't like very much, and I have to find out why compassion went out of my life. What did I trade it for? And how was I able - it's a harsh thing to say, Bee - to get away with it all those years?"

"What is going to happen to us?" She couldn't get her own voice above a whisper.

"We're going to be apart. We're not going to be as we have been. Until I can pull out of this." He avoided her eyes for the first time.

316

She pulled her hands away, reaching for the scotch, spilling some as she sucked it from the glass. "You mean for good, Maurice? Is that what you mean?"

"I don't know. I truly don't know."

"Can we be together one more time? If I have that, maybe I can live with this, maybe."

"No, Bee. It would only make it harder for both of us."

"Maurice!" Panic took over. "You owe me at least a chance to - you can't just walk away like this!" Hysteria choked her. The long months of uncertainty and need that had built like flood waters broke through. "It's not fair! You can't mean what you're saying!" She gripped the edge of the table, half out of her chair. She bent toward him, whimpering. "You mustn't do this to me!"

Interested glances from nearby tables went unnoticed. She saw only his face and heard only her own voice.

"Bee, sit down. Let's talk quietly..."

"No!" She was on her feet, grabbing a napkin to wipe her eyes.

He reached for her. "You're right, this isn't the place to talk. I should have known it would be painful and should have made other arrangements. If you can meet me one day next week, I'll see that we have a place for the afternoon. Will that do?"

A spasm caught her shoulders and she blinked and sat down slowly. There was a faint promise in his voice, a tiny sliver of hope. She looked at him, thinking quickly. If she could get him into bed once more time, work the old magic he had taught her to use, tease his hunger in well-tried ways, he would come back to her. That would do it. She would use all the skills she had learned. She would have a week to plan, to create a banquet of delights, the sweet taste of love that had kept him with her would work now. It could not fail. "Tell me where to meet you," she said.

His eyes softened and relief brought light to his face. "I'll call you at the office on Monday."

When they said goodbye he kissed her gently and she walked away, dry-eyed, holding herself tall in her best blue suit and cashmere coat, handbag tucked under one arm, not looking back.

318

Chapter XI.

1958 - Winter

Early December in New York. Windy, raw days, wan sunshine,
a dusting of snow to remind holiday shoppers that a white
Christmas was always possible. Rockefeller Center's tall glowing
tree, skaters on the ice, hot chocolate in the cafés,
Thanksgiving having been only a minor hiatus in the target
festivities. In spite of its blatant commercialism, Bee had
always looked forward to the Christmas season, her heart lifting
to carols, evergreen wreaths, tinsel, sparkling lights. Back
in time, Christmas at Harriet's had been like that, a time of
warmth and wonderful presents, a cherished memory.

Maurice had agreed to one more meeting, just one more.
What if his mind was already made up? What if all her efforts
failed? She was sick with the what-ifs lining up before her.

Time dragged once more. Nothing went on at home. Phil
came and went with only a thin hello and a mumbled goodbye.
Another time she might have questioned his withdrawal, his
aloofness, but with the chance to see Maurice once more coming
up, she allowed no other thoughts to distract her. She talked
to Maddie, phoned Lucile to report the last meeting and the
hopes for the next one. She did grocery shopping on the way

home from the city and laundry when supper was over. At the
office on Tuesday she was thankful for a quiet day. She had
drinks with a few of the salesmen at a bar down the street,
trying for holiday conviviality and not succeeding.

He took her hand as they left the elevator and they walked
in step to the end of the corridor, where a narrow window looked
out at the river and the New Jersey Palisades on the other side.
He had been able to get the Riverside Drive apartment for a
few hours, he said, because his friends were on the west coast
for the holiday. The walk, the familiar view from the window,
the key turning in the lock, this little routine had always
been prelude to delicious hours, to pleasure she couldn't find
words for, to intimate talk that taught her as much as passion
did and freed her for a little while from the banality of her
life in Westbury.

Nothing had changed. Nothing would change. This, once
more, was home, where love would hold them together. He took
her coat and handbag and put them with his coat across a chair,
then took her hand again and led her to the sofa, across the
big dark room where they had always started their day together.
Now he would bring the bottle of champagne from the kitchen
with two tall thin glasses. He would pour the wine and they
would sit side by side, talking softly, looking into each other's
eyes as they drank, anticipation warming them. Then they would
go into the bedroom where slowly and lovingly he would undress
her, and she would sink back into pillows and wait for...

Maurice said: "What has to be done now, Bee, is not a punishment, but a necessary change that will happen to both of us. You won't find it easy to see it this way, and the pain will be considerable - for me as well. I'm making this decision, and I will have to live with it, remembering what you have meant to me."

His words were falling between them like a soft, deadly rain, smudging his face and making it hard to focus her eyes. She knew they were still standing, that her hand was still in his, but somehow there was no feeling in it, as though it had gone to sleep. She looked down at it.

"Come, sit here with me," he said.

Coldness had seeped into the room, was creeping around them on the couch. The sudden silence indicated she was expected to say something.

"Did you forget the champagne?" she said, glancing toward the kitchen.

"Champagne is for celebrations," Maurice said, from somewhere in the distance. "Not for what we must do here."

She shivered. "Aren't you cold?" What was happening to her plan, her strategy?

"We won't be seeing each other any more, Bee. This is the way it has to be."

"Forever?" Her voice sounded reasonable and calm in her ears. "Are you saying it's forever, Maurice? Or just a little while? Maybe you mean a little while longer, is that it? Maybe just until - "

"No, Bee, I won't say forever. But I can't say any more than what I've said. I don't know if we can ever be together the way we were."

She leaned to look into his face and blinked to clear her vision. He looks awful, she thought. How come his face is so white, so pinched? This is happening to me, not to him. Why should he look so miserable?

"Maurice, this is my death you're talking about, you know. Can you live with that? Can you?" Without warning she wrenched her hand free and struck him on the shoulder.

He caught her hand before she could strike again. "Don't do this! It's not your death! Don't make this into a damned soap opera!" He pulled her into his arms. "What we've had has been wonderful and happy. But we knew from the beginning it would never be more than it was, a love affair that was a joy for both of us."

She drew back, her eyes blazing. "Tell me, Maurice, if Karel hadn't died, would we still be together?"

Stunned, he stared at her.

"Tell me. Would we?"

"Yes," he said finally.

Like a sour regurgitation, misery and anger caught in her throat. "So that's it. It's because of him and because of his mother that -- "

"Don't say it, Bee."

" -- that you're leaving me. I never counted all that much, did I? Just filled a once-in-a-while need, not the real thing."

His arms came up again, but she shook her head. "Why shouldn't I say it now? What's for me to lose? It's over, you said so. I can say anything I damn please, because it doesn't matter any more!"

He stood up, and she stood with him.

"Don't let these be the last words between us, I beg you, Bee. You know what I feel for you, what I've always felt. Don't say it doesn't matter."

"What do you feel for me, Maurice?" She was shouting now. "You've never said it. Never said, 'I love you, Bee, I love you the way you love me.' You never had the guts to say it and now, when it's all over and I ask you -- "

"I love you, Bee. I love you dearly and probably won't ever stop. I love you in ways I've never loved another woman." He held out his arms and she saw the tears he tried to blink away. Her throat closed on the bitter words she had meant to hurl and she went to him because there was nothing left to do. What she had waited so long to hear had now been said. The words were like a curtain going down. She heard them bleakly, standing silently in his embrace. She had brought no tears for this day and seeing his, her anger dissolved.

Down on the street he hailed a cab and rode with her to Quigley's office. They said goodbye on the sidewalk,

and walked away from each other.

Chapter XII

1959-1960

For Christmas Harriet let it be known that she planned a
holiday party: a few parishioners from St. Andrew's - and Dr.
and Mrs. Plumb, of course - and some old friends from
Connecticut.

Phil refused to go. Bee said: "Anne has only a week's
Christmas break, and Harriet has theater tickets and shopping
trips planned for her. If we don't go to the party, we probably
won't see her until spring."

There had been one trip to visit Anne - a Sunday - which
Bee had made alone, Phil backing out at the last minute, after
a phone call to a Babylon client. She asked Anne if she would
care to drive to the shore to see Harriet's old beach cottage
but Anne declined, suggesting instead that they take in a movie
in town. Bee said, "Fine with me," although it really wasn't.
They saw a current hit, talked about it a little over hamburgers
afterward, and Bee went back to Long Island feeling she had
taken care of motherly duty adequately.

The year had passed slowly, the emptiness growing. Dreams
brought scenes out of memory, some happy, some full of anxiety.
Work at Quigley's had been heavy in early Fall, and this occupied

her time and thoughts, for which she was grateful. But always underneath anything she thought or did, was the soreness, the unsatisfied ache, of Maurice's loss.

Conversation between Bee and Phil had dwindled until it consisted mostly of greetings and goodbyes as they passed each other on various errands and business trips. They seldom sat down to a meal together, and the few evenings when they found themselves at home, Bee usually asked the Whitlocks to come over for a drink and stay for casual talk. Bee dutifully wrote to Anne every two weeks, enclosing a check for "extras." Phil sent a post card now and then, urged by Bee. They received a letter from Anne in October and after that, she stopped writing.

Maddie had tried, unsuccessfully, to get Bee to tell her what was wrong.

"Sometimes you look like a homeless waif," she said, having invited Bee for coffee on a Saturday morning, after a number of such invitations had been lackadaisically refused. "Things aren't going well, are they?"

"They're about the same. I'm coping."

"Don't you miss Anne?"

"Sure. Don't worry about me, Maddie. I'll work out of this. Just temporarily a little depressed, that's all."

"Because of Phil's drinking?" Maddie had never been one to dissemble. "It's not hard to see what's going on with him."

"That, too." Bee smiled without much heart. "Lately I don't know how he can work at all. For a guy who never took a sip

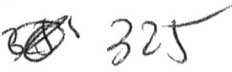 325

of alcohol, he's certainly gotten into the stuff in a big way."

Maddie didn't push for details and Bee was grateful.

Talking to Lucille was out of the question. Lu knew too much and her recommendation would be to bring misery out into the open, air it, let pain be talked about. An impossibility, for now. The hurt was still raw after eleven empty months and not to be examined in conversation, even with a best friend.

Harriet's Christmas party was planned for the 20th. She called Bee two or three times to make sure they were coming, asking Bee's opinion of the menu, describing the big Christmas tree she had put up early and was still decorating. Bee found the subject tiresome but kept responses on a friendly level, no longer listening, as she had done in the past, for undercurrents in Harriet's words. She didn't care, was uninterested in any schemes Harriet might be crafting. What mattered in life was over.

Phil finally agreed to attend the party.

The big house glowed inside and out with holiday cheer. The giant evergreen that Bee remembered from her childhood stood once more in the center of the formal parlor, a marvel of color, shimmering tinsel and heirloom ornaments. At each window fronting the street there was a holly wreath, and out on the covered porch that ran along two sides of the house, another smaller tree with blinking red and green lights and ropes of shining silver. Hidden somewhere in the long hall that led back to the kitchen and dining room, a record player murmured familiar carols. Sweet and spicy odors, the soft clink of china, glass and silver, and low conversation greeted Bee as she entered. It was a night out of the past, all the elements in place, as they had been twenty years ago and more, and like a warm cover it descended on her unhappiness and made it, for the moment, bearable.

Phil was searching for a parking space in the neighborhood and had urged her to go on ahead. She knew why. It would give him a few minutes with the bottle he kept in the glove compartment. During the festivities he would sit on the sidelines, mumbling answers if anyone spoke to him, nodding sleepily as it grew later. And some time during the evening, he would slip out to the car again, Harriet's egg nog and champagne not potent enough for him.

She found Anne in the kitchen, helping to prepare a tray of little sandwiches, skewers of cheese and cold meats, and bowls of crudités. They hugged each other perfunctorily, and Bee asked the proper questions: how is school, how are your grades, what are you doing for fun. Anne answered readily enough but without enthusiasm. She appeared to have grown an inch or more, the child's body beginning to shape subtly into a woman's curves. "Are they feeding you well up there?" Bee asked.

"You know cafeteria food, Mom. It's soggy and all tastes the same. We go out for pizza when we can't stand it any longer."

"Do you really like the school?" Bee asked, suddenly understanding that some motherly concern would be appropriate. "Have you made some friends?"

"Yeah, I like it. Some of the kids are okay. It's just a school, nothing special. Harriet thinks I'm doing all right, and that's what counts, right?"

"She's spending a lot of money to keep you there, Anne. I hope you show some appreciation."

Anne grimaced and wiped her hands on a dish towel. "Of course I appreciate it. It's a lot better than that fucking junior high in Westbury." She lifted the tray of appetizers and pushed past Bee and through the door to the dining room. "And the kids aren't as square as those morons back home."

Bee followed, preparing to take issue with the new vocabulary, but the dining room was filling with guests holding glasses and dipping into trays of hors d'oeuvres, Harriet beaming as she moved among them. Her silver hair, still piled in the style of her early days, was a crown to her regal gown of pale green velvet embroidered with sequins at the neckline. A faint scent of lavender (her "trademark", Willa had called it) trailed her through the room.

Phil had found a corner to retreat into, taking a glass of spiced cider with him. When he caught sight of Anne he allowed his eyes to stay with her as she passed with the tray. The look of bitter contempt on her face when she saw him was like a stinging slap.

"Hello, Anne," he said.

"Hello, _Daddy_," she answered, and moved on to offer the tray to guests standing at the fireplace.

Bee had stopped near the double doors, open now to make

the two rooms one for the party. She caught Harriet's arm as she passed. "What's going on with Anne? She's learned some pretty foul language at that fancy school." Watching Harriet's face, she went on: " She called her Long Island friends morons and used a four-letter word you would have washed her mouth with soap for using. And just now she said something obviously nasty to her father."

Harriet paused to smile at a passing guest. "It's just a teen-age phase. Trying out the adults to see how much it takes to rile them. Don't get testy about it. Youngsters need a little leeway. And what's a few bad words, anyway?" She patted Bee's arm.

Where does she get her expertise? Bee turned impatiently.

Harriet leaned in and whispered: "I want to hear about you and Maurice. The little boy has been gone for months. Are you two back together again?"

"I don't want to talk about him, Harriet. This isn't the time or place." The mention of his name brought hurt like a physical blow. She twisted away, heading for the kitchen and a towel to blot away the sudden tears before anyone saw them.

Harriet came after her. "Bee - I won't ask, if you'd rather not talk about it. But let me know if I can do anything, will you?"

It burst out of her. "You've done enough, Harriet!" Bee didn't even know what she meant by the sharp answer, but the need to lash out had been irresistible.

Unheeding, Harriet moved closed. "Listen to me. I've booked

a cruise to Bermuda, a stateroom big enough for both of us.
Will you go with me?"

Bee mopped at her eyes, leaned against a cupboard door and
looked at Harriet with angry suspicion. "Why do you want me
to go with you? What's this invitation doing for you?"

It was Harriet's turn to receive a blow. Her eyes went
cold suddenly, and her voice made Bee shiver. "All right.
I'll tell you what's behind it. You're trying to survive a
broken love affair, you have a rotten excuse for a husband and
a child who doesn't like either of you. None of this would
ever have happened, if you had kept your promise to me."

Bee looked at her in consternation. "What are you talking
about? Why are you bringing up all that old history?"

But Harriet was on a roll, her eyes snapping, her face
flushed. "I think it's time you stood back and took a long
look at your situation. I'm offering you a couple of weeks
to do it." She didn't try to hide the sneering smile that started
across her face. "I'm also going to give you a piece of advice
you'd be wise to follow. Divorce him. Unload that burden, then
come and live with me."

Bee stepped back uncertainly. What had brought Harriet
to this pitch? Had something happened that only she knew about,
that made it possible for her to make this offer? Think about
it, don't answer right away. Make her wait.

"Well?"

"When does it leave?"

"Middle of February."

"That's weeks away."

"Anne has to be back at Latchfied by the tenth of January. I'll take her back, then you and I can go shopping for cruise clothes. It'll be like old times, Bee." There was syrup in her voice, smoothing away the sharpness of moments ago.

"What about my job?"

"Tell Ed you need a rest. If he's got eyes, he knows you need one. Who buys houses in mid-winter, anyway?"

Bee picked up an empty wine glass and filled it from a bottle of cognac on the counter behind her. She drank it all, then turned to Harriet. "Let me take Anne back to school. I think I'd like to spend some time with her."

Harriet shrugged. "Why not? As long as you promise you'll go with me..."

It was Bee's turn to offer an enigmatic smile. "No promises, but I'll think about it."

For another hour she drifted from dull conversation to duller, to buffet to wine table, and at midnight drank an obligatory toast and wished a few people a Merry Christmas, then knew she'd had enough. When she saw Phil nodding over his lap, she went back to Harriet and told her they were leaving.

"He's halfway to comatose. I've got to get him home."

Anne waved idly from a chair near the fireplace, then turned back to the couple who were asking her about her social life at Latchfield. Bee wondered whether some of the new language would find its way into the conversation.

Never had the holidays been so flavorless. She was glad
when the season ended with midnight supper at the Whitlock's
on New Year's Eve. Maddie served only beer during the evening,
with an eye on Phil, and as the final hour of 1959 approached,
opened a bottle of champagne and poured for the four of them.

"Let's make 1960 a happy year for us all," she said
wistfully, looking at Bee, who couldn't find a smile to give
her. When they went back across the frozen yard half an hour
later, she knew she would cry into her pillow, facing the wall,
while Phil stayed downstairs with his bottle of scotch.

Anne's impending sixteenth birthday brought up the subject
of a driver's license as the new year began. For once, the
response was unanimous. Not yet. Wait another year. What good
would a junior license be anyway, up at Latchfield? No one
was going to buy her a car, and anyway, with that kind of license
an accompanying adult was required. "Take driver education,"
Harriet advised. "We'll think about the car for next year."

Anne grumbled, then stormed, felt schemed against, badly
treated, and let them know it. When they got into the car for
the drive to Latchfield she brought it up once more.

"I don't want to hear any more about it," Bee said. "It's
No, until next year. When you graduate, we'll talk about it
again."

Anne drew away, sulking, but Bee would have none of it.
"We haven't much time to spend together, kiddo," she said,
controlling irritation. "Let's try to be friendly and enjoy

it, shall we?"

The squall subsided and they were civil to each other for the two days before school re-opened and Bee had to return to Long Island. They shared a motel room and took walks, saw a movie, had dinner in town. Through it all Bee felt the strain Anne was under, the effort to be daughterly, to maintain a pleasant attitude and reasonable conversation. Some of the colorful words had been eliminated, but behind everything Anne said was an emotion held in check, and Bee couldn't find a name for it.

In the motel room Anne kept her portable radio tuned to a music station and this annoyed Bee, who had hoped for quiet. On Sunday Anne showed relief when it was over and Bee, with a pang of guilt, felt the same. They talked easily for the first time at lunch before she drove away.

"You've got to think about college soon," Bee said over coffee and apple pie. "Any ideas about where you'd like to go?"

"Not yet." Their eyes met. "How about you, Mom - did you ever want to go to college?"

Surprised, Bee answered: "Not really. It was the Depression, you know, no money for that kind of thing. I wanted to get a job and support myself." On sudden impulse she told Anne about the first little roach-infested apartment she and Lucille shared, and how they had tried to make it habitable with Salvation Army furnishings. Anne listened, looking at her hands, and nodded once in a while.

"Sounds grim," she said. "But you survived."

"I did."

They were silent for a moment. Anne pushed the pie away and signalled the waitress for another cup of coffee. "Harriet used to tell me stories about what it was like when she was a little girl. I always loved those stories."

Bee waited to see where this was going. Was Anne saying she would have liked to hear that kind of thing from her mother? And what could Bee have reported - what about her young life with Jack and Willa in the dreary Brooklyn tenements would interest Anne? Awkwardness suddenly dropped over them and brought to mind a picture of graduation night, the soda fountain at Loft's, and Willa's stern admonishings about the future. Eyes not able to meet, words just words, nothing like a communication. And, as it had done then, Harriet's invisible presence dominated the scene.

Anne looked up. "You never told me anything about when you were a kid. What was it like?"

About to give a short answer, Bee stopped. They came so easily these days, short answers. Grief had drowned any desire for conversation. "I guess there isn't a lot to tell," she said, and heard the apology in her voice. "Life wasn't much fun when I was a teen-ager."

"Harriet told me about Jack, but she said some funny things about him, like he was drunk all the time. Is it true?"

How to describe to someone whose short life held no experience of real deprivation? "He had a job, a menial kind

ot job, low wages, his life was unhappy, I suppose. Drinking
was probably his only entertainment. He wasn't cut out to be
a father, he never paid much attention to me, never talked to
me about anything important." Her voice died suddenly, as she
heard the words she had never said before. She reached for
the coffee, cold now, and drank quickly.

Anne said: "Did you love him?"

Ten seconds ticked by before Bee could say "No." She knew
Anne wouldn't stop now, that a wall had been breached and she
would want answers. Willa's confession - how could Anne ever
comprehend such a story?

"And your mother?"

Here's where it ends. Bee reached for her purse. "Anne,
we don't have time for this now. I've got to get back to
Westbury. We'll finish it another time."

Anne's lips quivered, but Bee had turned away and didn't
see. "I'll bet," she said to her mother's retreating back,
and grabbed her coat from a nearby chair.

Bee paid the check and they left the restaurant. A hasty
kiss on the cheek and she got into the station wagon and pulled
away.

Chapter XIII

1960

The next few weeks, while she cleared the decks at the office and finally told Phil about the cruise, were a strain, leaving her worn and tired and glad at last that she had agreed to go with Harriet.

Phil was silent when she gave him the news. She had expected a sour look, a sneering remark about Harriet's "generosity," but got none. He shrugged and asked if she wanted him to do anything special during her absence.

A week before the ship was to leave, Harriet brought up the subject of divorce again, as they sat over cocktails in her parlor.

"You've known from the beginning, of course, what I think of your husband, Bee. I don't care much for him, and I'm sure your feelings, now, are much the same."

Bee didn't answer, raising her eyebrows over her martini glass.

"So. Now there's the question of my Will."

"Question?"

"I told you when you moved from Pennsylvania that this house - as well as all other assets I have at the time of my decease

- would be yours."

Bee's attention sharpened. "And - ?"

"Yours, Bee. Doesn't that tell you something?"

"I suppose it tells me you're going to change your Will
to cut him out, then everything will come to me, right?"

Harriet nodded, watching Bee quietly.

"And if I don't divorce him, you'll cut both of us out,
right?"

Harriet fixed her eyes on something above Bee's head, perhaps
the Corot reproduction on the far wall, or the small humorous
Klee (not a reproduction) she had bought from Maurice a long
time ago. "I don't want it to sound like an ultimatum - but
I have to tell you that I feel that way now. I don't want any
of my money to get into Phil's hands."

"How much time do I have to think it over?" The final
scheme, coming clear at last. Harriet at her best/worst.

"We'll have three weeks together, Bee. There will be time
to make plans."

"I see." Tiredness closed over her like a blanket and she
had no more energy to follow the conversation. "I'll get back
to you."

January had been unexpectedly mild. Accustomed to the bluster
and ice of past Long Island winters, Bee found the sunny days
moved her thoughts easily to the Caribbean cruise. She went
shopping with Harriet, tried on summer dresses, shorts, swim
suits and sandals in a mood of accommodation. Snarling at

Harriet at Christmas had cleared the emotional air briefly, relieved the anguish that mention of Maurice had brought to the surface. Now she made an effort to show appreciation and Harriet received the implied apology and cheerfully wrote checks as they wandered from shop to shop.

At home, Bee talked little about the upcoming vacation, saying only that it would be a much needed rest and that she would be easier to live with after it. Phil had been making tentative overtures toward reconciliation, an occasional "Let's eat out tonight - you look tired." And even some cautious and clumsy attempts to get conversation going in the evening. Bee wondered whether Anne's absence had anything to do with this reviving behavior, but looked no deeper for reasons. Her emotional bruises were healing and the prospect of a fresh new scene, with no cares or strain, softened her and made her response to him easier. The question of divorce, and what to tell Harriet, hovered in the background of her thoughts, but she pushed it away and told herself she would give it attention after she had rested.

In bed, the problems had not gone away. She knew he wanted to touch her, move close, hold her against him, but because he didn't come to the bedroom before he had fortified himself with two or three drinks, her rejection was swift.

"Why can't you, just once, come in without whiskey on your breath?" she snapped in angry frustration. "Maybe we could - maybe you'd find me more receptive if you'd go without your precious booze!" It had been hard to admit to herself that the lack of sex was beginning to depress her, make itself felt in dreams at night, and the inescapable fact that it was right at hand, would take only a nod from her to start up again, made her furiously impatient with his fumblings.

Then one night after they had gone with Tom and Maddie to a movie and stopped for ice cream at Howard Johnson's on the Turnpike, Phil followed her upstairs, bypassing the liquor cabinet in the dining room. When she raised her eyebrows he said: "I'm trying, Bee. Maybe you could give me a little encouragement?"

The moment was fragile. The choice was hers, to let it happen or, once more, pull back and crush his small gesture toward reinstatement.

"Come to bed," she said, more gently than she had really intended, and because he liked it that way, she turned out the light.

He reached for her, timidly, and when her arms went around him in return, he trembled and pulled her close. They lay in an embrace for a long moment, silently, then she took his hand and guided it to her breast, holding it there, feeling its familiar grasping urgency. "Relax, Phil, I'm not going to push you away," she whispered.

"Bee -- " His voice was hoarse in her ear. "It's been so long, I've needed you for so long -- "

"Don't talk, just hold me, go slowly..." But something was wrong, she felt it. His need, frantic and hot a moment ago, was dying like fire under a sudden dash of water. For a

few seconds she continued to move against him encouragingly.
When he took his hand from her breast she stopped, aware suddenly
and with alarm that he was crying.

"Phil?"

"I can't, Bee."

"But - why?"

"I can't give you a reason. Maybe it's just been too long,
you've been too cold. I don't know how to -- " He turned from
her abruptly and got out of bed. "I think I need that drink."

She sat up, turned on the bedside lamp and stared at the
door. What had just happened? Certainly he had been in the
mood when they got home, and for sure when she turned to him
in the dark and reached to touch his body. She got up and went
into the bathroom. From below she heard the clink of glass and
bottle. Now, she thought as anger surged, he'll stay there and
get stinking and I'm going to take a sleeping pill so I won't
know when he gets back into bed.

Ed Quigley told her to take all the time she needed, she
deserved a decent stretch of it, having taken only minimum
vacation time in the past few years. On Friday she cleaned
her desk and re-arranged the client appointments, then said
goodbye over a chorus of "Bon Voyages" and drove home to Westbury
with, for the first time in months, a sense of pleasant
anticipation. Two days to pack, get the house in order, and
say goodbye to the Whitlocks, then Phil would drive her to the
pier on Monday morning, where she would meet Harriet and board

the Bermuda Princess. The answer eventually required of her
could be put off until rest and warm sunshine had worked on
her tiredness and lethargy. Divorce. She had thought of it
often during the early years with Maurice. How wonderful life
would be, had been a recurrent theme in her daydreams. If I
left Phil and Maurice divorced his wife we could live together
and ... But the dreams always ended with an unfinished sentence,
because cold reason killed the fantasy and she knew Maurice
too well to hope.

Phil had appointments for most of Saturday, and this gave
her the day alone to pack for the voyage, make a quick trip
across the lawn to have coffee with Maddie, and give the house
a fast clean-up. She turned on the evening news at six, made
herself a drink and sat down to wait for Phil. At seven he
hadn't called. Not unusual. Best to wait before starting dinner.

At seven-thirty the phone rang and she reached for it across
the coffee table.

"Mom?" It was Anne. "Mom?" Her voice broke off with a
choking sound.

"Anne? What's the matter? Anne?"

"Mom - you've got to come up here, come and get me!"

"Calm down - tell me, what is the matter? Are you hurt?
Where are you?"

"I'm all right, I'm not hurt, but something awful has
happened! They're going to kick me out of school! The
headmistress is going to call Harriet first thing Monday morning,
she says I can't stay here -- "

Anne's voice cracked and Bee heard the panic. "Wait a minute - you know Harriet won't be here on Monday, and I won't either. We're leaving on a cruise early on Monday morning."

"You can't go, Mom! I can't stay here, they won't let me - they'll tell her everything! Come and get me - now - I've got nowhere else to go!"

"All right, all right, be quiet now - tell me where you are. Are you in the dorm?"

"No. I'm phoning from outside. I'm in the cafeteria. You know where it is? I've got my suitcase with me. I'll wait right here. How long will it take you?"

Bee sighed as the immediate future shaped a scene in her mind. It was unlikely that anything was serious enough to alter the Monday departure plans. If Anne was having real problems at school, she could stay home in Westbury with Phil until they got back from the cruise. Then contact could be made with the school and whatever was wrong could be straightened out. "Stay where you are, Anne. Have a cup of coffee. I'm leaving right now - be there by nine-thirty."

"Okay - okay. I'll wait outside."

Bee hung up and ran to find paper for a note to Phil, but the front door opened as she was writing.

"Phil, I have to drive up to Latchfield. Something's wrong up there, Anne just called, she's in some kind of trouble with the headmistress and wants to come home."

He dropped his briefcase on the couch. "Now? You're leaving now?"

342

"I'll bring her back and we can talk about it later. I
told her I was going on the cruise with Harriet. She can stay
here with you until we get back, then we can deal with whatever
problems she's having up there."

She grabbed her purse and started for the door, car keys
in hand. Flinging a "See you around midnight," behind her she
missed the sudden white cold stare Phil sent after her as she
ran for the station wagon.

The drive up the Thruway into Connecticut bucked heavy
weekend traffic and it was almost ten o'clock when Bee pulled
up in front of the Latchfield cafeteria. Anne was standing
there, a bag at her feet. She picked it up and ran down the
steps and threw it in the back seat, then slammed the door and
burst into tears.

"Now." Bee made a swift U-turn and headed back to the road.
"Tell me what's going on -- "

"Hurry! Get me away from here - I don't want anyone to
see me -- " Anne rubbed a sleeve across her eyes and leaned
foward, peering out the window. "I'm in trouble - like I said
- and they're going to report to Harriet and have her take me
out of school What it is - " She gulped, caught her breath
and went on, "is - I got caught smoking, you know, a joint,
in the dorm, with a couple of girls. We're all suspended, not
just me."

"What? You mean - <u>marijuana?</u> You were smoking that stuff?"
Who smoked marijuana? Delinquents, bad kids, ghetto kids.

Not kids like Anne! Not Anne, specifically!

"Yeah. Kids are doing it, Mom. It's no big deal, it's like, well, booze, something to do at parties, to be sociable..."

"<u>You're into drugs!</u>" Bee's voice rose in a scream. The car wobbled as her hands momentarily left the wheel. "You - that's why you were expelled? Drugs? Oh, my God!"

She pulled the car to a stop on the shoulder and turned off the ignition. "You're only sixteen! How can you - where do you get that kind of thing? Who - how do you pay for it?"

Anne said shakily: "Harriet sends me extra money, I can get whatever I want out of her, you know that. And there's a guy who comes around, he eats at the pizza place we go to on Fridays..."

"This is crazy! I can't believe - what will we tell Harriet?"

"Mom, maybe we can figure out something she'll believe. But if they call her from Latchfield before we can get our story straight - "

"And your father - what can I tell him?" Bee's mind was a jumble of frantic questions. She turned the key and got the car in motion. "And I'm leaving on Monday - I can't get out of that."

"No!" Panic was back as Anne clutched at her mother's arm. "You can't go away, you have to stay with me until - "

"Harriet won't find out. We'll be on the ship before the school calls. And we'll be gone three weeks."

"Please - don't go and leave me with Dad!"

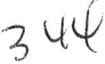

Bee bore down on the accelerator and they hurtled along the dark road toward the Thruway. "I have to go, Anne, Harriet's paid for the tickets, and I promised her."

Anne slumped against the door, snuffling and wiping her eyes, as they pulled into traffic and headed for home.

She opened the door and they came into the living room, Anne dragging her suitcase, glancing around quickly. "Where's Dad?"

"Maybe upstairs. I've got to talk to him, Anne. Maybe you'd better go up to your room and go to bed. We'll talk about this in the morning."

He appeared as she was making herself a cup of coffee in the kitchen. She told him to sit down and listen to what she had to say, then help her figure out what to do. The telling was done in a rush, and his face was pale when she finished.

"Only - only bad kids do this kind of thing, don't they?" he said. "What kind of school is that place, anyway, don't they have any control over the students?"

"Apparently it's something kids are doing - Anne says others have been expelled, too. Phil - I can't back out of this cruise now, Harriet's bought tickets and I have all those new clothes - and - I need this! I really need this, Phil! Can you take care of her while I'm gone?"

His eyes closed and he rubbed a hand across them. "So, you have to go. And you want me to - "

"You don't have to do anything, just be here - she can amuse

herself, all you have to do is see that she eats and - and
behaves herself until I get back."

Phil stared at her, then nodded. "Just see that she behaves.
That's all. Okay." He left the kitchen and she heard him
climbing the stairs. Relieved, she finished her coffee and
sat for a while at the kitchen table, waiting for anxiety to
subside and let her sleep.

In the morning she was up early. There was no sound from
Anne's room as she went down the stairs. Phil was in the kitchen
with the Sunday newspaper and a glass of orange juice.

"I think we can work this out," she began, "but what to tell
Harriet is the sticker. If she finds out why Anne has to leave
Latchfield, she'll be furious."

"She won't find out tomorrow," he said. "Maybe while you
are sailing the blue Caribbean you can prepare her for the news."

Bee bristled at his tone of voice. "You think I should
just cancel everything and stay home, don't you?"

"The thought occurred to me."

"Well, I won't. You two can manage here - I need to get
away, and this is the only chance I'll get this year."

"I've got to see a client this morning. Don't look for
me until late in the afternoon." He got up, folded the paper
and left the kitchen. Bee stared after him, and when she heard
the front door close she went to the window and watched him
back the station wagon out of the carport.

When Anne came downstairs Bee had a bowl of cereal waiting
for her, and coffee was warming on the stove. Rubbing her eyes,

Anne looked around the room. "Where's Dad? Is he here?"

"No - he had to go see a client. He'll be back later this
afternoon. Here, eat your breakfast and then we have to talk."

But Anne's appetite managed only a few spoonfuls, and when
Bee poured coffee, she drank only a sip. "What are you going
to do - will you stay home, or will you go with Harriet?"

"I've already told you. I just can't back out at this late
date, Anne. You know how Harriet is about these things. She'll
hold a grudge forever. I've promised. I have to go. But I
won't tell her anything about this. I won't even tell her you're
home. And while I'm away, I'll think of something. Because
she has to know, I'm sure you realize that."

"So I have to stay here with Dad while you're gone. That's
it, right? Does he know I'm here?"

"He knows you came home with me, and I had to tell him about
the - smoking thing. He was as horrified as I am. Oh, I just
can't believe -- " Bee broke off and began to pace back and
forth. "How could you do such a thing, Anne? How could you?"

"I can't finish this," Anne said, pushing the food away.
"I'm going back to my room."

An hour later, over a second cup of coffee, Bee was staring
morosely out the kitchen window, when she heard a sudden thump
from overhead, then a shriek.

"Mom! Help me - Mom!"

She dropped the cup and rushed toward the stairs, up and
into the hall. The bathroom door stood half open and Anne was

347

screaming, "Mom! Mom! I didn't mean to - "

She pushed the door open, slamming it back against the wall. Anne was writhing on the floor, her body thrashing from side to side, heels pounding the tub. Blood was everywhere - on the floor, on the sink, the bathtub, soaking through a towel Anne was holding to her wrist. A bloody razor lay on the bathmat.

She grabbed another towel from the door rack and dropped to her knees. "My God! Anne - what have you done?" Her own voice was shrill with shock. "What did you do to yourself?" She grabbed Anne's wrist and held it high, then wrapped the towel around it and pulled tight. "Just keep it up, over your head!" Scrambling to her feet, she raced from the bathroom, down the hall to the extension phone in her bedroom. Anne's cries followed her: "Don't leave me, Mom! Come back - !"

"I'm calling for help - I'll be back right away. Just keep your arm up!"

Probably the ambulance took a few minutes to get there, but to Bee it seemed that she had no sooner hung up than she heard the doorbell. Propping Anne, swathed in reddening towels, against the bathtub, she ran downstairs, flung open the front door, pointed upward and jumped back as medics, carrying a stretcher, started up the stairs.

A police car had pulled up into the driveway and a man in uniform came into the hall. "It's your daughter, ma'am?"

"Yes. Are they doing anything? Are they - will they - ?" She choked and grabbed the officer's arm. " - there's so much blood..."

"Better get your purse and coat, if you want to ride in the ambulance, ma'am," he said quietly. "They'll do what needs to be done, She's in good hands now."

They wouldn't let her see Anne in the ER, and she paced the waiting room a few doors down the corridor, fearful and in anguish. A nurse came in after a while, and told her she could see Anne briefly, before they took her up to the ward, then she would have to answer some questions and sign some forms. She refused the cup of coffee the nurse offered, knowing it would never stay down, feeling panic gripping her stomach.

Anne lay on a gurney, sheet-draped, her bandaged wrist across her chest. Her eyes were wide with fright and she whimpered when Bee leaned over her.

"Mom - I didn't mean to do it, I don't want to die - Mom, am I going to die?"

"No, Anne, no, baby, you're going to be all right, they're taking care of you."

"Don't leave me, Mom - stay here - "

"I'm right here. I'm not going anywhere."

In Admitting, Bee answered questions and signed forms, trying to read the fine print but unable to make sense of it. A policeman in plain clothes asked further questions, wrote down her answers. The staff psychiatrist talked to her, questioned her gently about Anne, and said she might need his services eventually. Bee struggled to hide her impatience, to cooperate, but every minute away from Anne was agony.

By early afternoon Anne had fallen asleep, exhausted, probably sedated, lying on her side, face to the wall. Bee's eyes flooded at the sight, and she leaned over the bed and gently stroked her daughter's hair, whispering, "You're going to be okay, I'll stay right here..."

At five she tried to reach Phil at home, but there was no answer. At five-thirty she tried again, then dialed Maddie's number.

"Bee? Where are you? I just got home from Jamaica - took the kids to see grandma. What can I do for you?"

"Have you seen Phil? There's no answer at the house - "

"I think I saw him drive away as I pulled into the garage. Why, is something wrong?"

"Maddie - something awful has happened, and I need to get in touch with him - are you sure he drove away?"

"Bee - where are you? What's happened?" Maddie's voice rose.

Hurriedly, avoiding details, Bee told her she was at Meadowbrook Hospital with Anne, and didn't know when she would be home. "If he comes back, Maddie - get over to him fast and tell him where I am."

"My God! Anne? But I thought she was - yes, yes, I'll watch for him and tell him as soon as I see him."

At seven she called Maddie again, but Phil had not returned to the house. "What can I do? Shall I come and get you? How is Anne? What happened?"

"Maddie - I can't answer your questions - I may have to

stay here overnight - what I need you to do is let Phil know as soon as he gets home. Will you do that?"

"Yes - but can't you tell me - ?"

"Not yet. When I get home, Maddie."

Anne woke briefly at ten, then sank back into sleep. Bee stayed at her side, refusing the offer of a cot in an empty room down the hall.

It was eleven before she remembered. She rummaged in her purse for change and went to the telephone in the hospital lobby.

Harriet answered sleepily. "I was just getting into bed. Why are you calling at this hour, Bee?"

"I won't be going with you in the morning, Harriet. I can't explain it now, it's too complicated. Something urgent has come up and I have to take care of it. I'm sorry - when you come back I'll explain. Have a good trip..."

"You can't do this!" Harriet squealed. "I've paid for the tickets - I've got a stateroom - what's happened? What's wrong? Bee, you can't just back out - "

"We'll talk when you get back. It's impossible for me to go with you - that's all I can say right now."

"Has something happened to Anne?"

"Anne's okay. Call me when you get back." She hung up and went back to the ward to sit beside the bed until morning.

Chapter XIV

1960

It was Tuesday morning before Anne could be released, and
Bee walked beside the wheelchair as a candystriper took them
down to the front lobby. She helped Anne into the cab and they
rode in silence back to Walnut Street.

"Can I stay in the living room?" Anne asked. "I don't want
to go upstairs..."

"On the couch," Bee said. "I'll get a blanket."

When she had propped Anne against pillows and tucked the
blanket around her, Bee sat down next to her. "We've got to
talk about this, Anne. I have to know what made you do such
a - such a dangerous thing. I don't want to hear that you're
sorry you did it, nor a promise never to do it again. I want
to know why."

For a long shuddering moment Anne stared at her mother,
her eyes filling. Then she said: "You really want to know,
Mom? Really? Even if it's pretty awful, even if you won't
believe me when I tell you?"

"What do you mean? What could be so bad that you had to
try to - kill yourself over it?" Instinct told her to go easy,
don't push, don't frighten her, but anxiety forced the words

out: "Tell me, Anne, what made you think you didn't want to live any more?"

"It's not just the school, not just the things I've done up there - it's what happened here, right here, back before I went to Latchfield!"

Bee sat back, frowning. "What happened here, Anne?"

"It was what Dad did to me, for years and years - upstairs in my bedroom, when you weren't home!" Her voice rose shrilly and she sat up and faced her mother. "He would put me on his lap and - and do - do sex things to me! He did it, Mom! He did it! I'm not making it up! And I had to tell Harriet so she'd come and get me, that time you went to Florida, and then she must have said something that made him stop it, and then - and then I went to Latchfield and didn't have to stay here anymore..." Wrenching sobs shook her shoulders. "And if you go with Harriet - I'll have to stay here alone with - him!"

Bee's mouth opened and she made an awful sound, a cry of fury and disbelief. "No - no! Stop it! Don't say such things! Not your father, Anne! He would never do - you're lying!" She reached out and grabbed the blanket and yanked it away. "How dare you tell such lies about your father? How dare you - "

Anne screamed: "I'm not lying! It happened - ask Harriet!"

Bee staggered up from the couch, dragging the blanket behind her. In the dining room she turned once to stare at Anne, then went into the kitchen.

The note was propped against the sugar bowl. She looked down at it, squinting. From Phil? She had called twice yesterday, receiving only the endless ringing.

Her hand shaking, cold shock blurring her vision, she picked up the note and read it:

"Dear Bee:

I won't be coming home for a while, maybe a long while, until I can pull myself together. It's been more than I can handle, these last few months, and I have to get away. I know this will mean you can't go with Harriet, but worse things have happened. She'll get over it. And this will give you a chance to be with Anne, something you haven't had much of lately. I've settled with the folks in Patchogue - they say if I ever want to come back, they'll welcome me. Meanwhile, I'll deposit money to cover the mortgage and other expenses, each month. Maybe later on I'll get in touch.

I love you and Anne, even if this doesn't sound like it."

He had signed it "Philip," the name his parents called him.

For a few taut minutes she stared at the scrawled note. Then the dam broke.

"You Goddamned son of a bitch! You've gone off and left me - walked out and left a pile of shit behind for me to deal with! You bastard!" She swept into the living room, waving the note. "You and your father! Between you, you've done a real job on me, haven't you? Now he's taken off, left me! My - my whole world is falling apart!" The last words were a strangled sob. She grabbed her coat from the hall clothes tree and ran from the house, slamming the door behind her.

She got into the VW and screeched around the corner and
raced toward the parkway, her throat tight with fury. At the
Jones Beach exit she sped across the coast road and into a
beach-side parking lot. It was empty, except for a maintenance
truck at the far end. She pulled up facing the ocean and killed
the engine. For two hours she sat, huddled in the front seat,
watching gulls and wind-tossed clouds and an occasional lonely
hiker heading for the boardwalk, while she tried to think about
Phil and what Anne had said, and knew she had to believe it,
in spite of everything in her that said it wasn't, couldn't
possibly be, true.

Much later she drove back to Westbury. The living room
was empty. Anne had fixed herself a cup of warm milk, the pan
was in the sink. Her bedroom door was closed, only silence
inside. Bee opened the door a couple of inches, enough to tell
her Anne was in bed, asleep. Then she went into her own room,
lay down on the bed and let the hard dry sobs shake her body
until she, too, fell asleep.

The alarm, which she had forgotten to re-set, rang at five
and she reached out blindly and turned it off, then went back
to sleep and woke at nine.

· Why even get out of bed? There isn't a damned thing left
in my life that I can do anything about, it's all a stinking
mess - if I had any guts I'd do what Anne tried to do - just
bow out, leave it all and go away for good.

She showered and got dressed. The phone rang as she was

about to sit down at the kitchen table with a cup of coffee.

"Bee? It's Maddie. What's happened? Did Phil come back?
Is Anne home? What can I do?"

"You want to hear the whole dirty story, Maddie? Pour me
a cup - I'll come over and tell you."

Maddie was shocked, disbelieving, when the telling was
finished. She took Bee in her arms and they both cried and
clung together, then she made another pot of coffee and brought
out some doughnuts, which Bee didn't want, but managed to eat
a few crumbs. It was noon before she thought about going home,
and only after Maddie said that Anne might need her, might wonder
where she had gone.

Tuesday came and went. Anne appeared briefly, made herself
something to eat and went back to her room. Bee sat in front
of the television set, a magazine in her hands, and barely looked
up. Wednesday she went to the bank to see what arrangements
Phil had made. The balance in the savings account hadn't been
touched. The checking account had a lot more money in it.
He had removed his name from both accounts. She was asked to
sign papers to reflect the new title. He must have settled
with Angelini and taken out his partnership money. She signed
where they told her to sign and went home.

She fixed something to eat for supper, and went up to ask
if Anne wanted to share it with her. But Anne's bedroom was
empty. Another note lay on a pillow.

"I don't want to live here any more. You hate me, Dad is
a monster, Harriet will hate me too, when she finds out. There
was some money in your dresser drawer - I took it with me.
Some of my friends are in New York and they've asked me to go
to California with them - they've got a van. I'll let you know
when I get there."

Bee took the note downstairs and got the bottle of scotch
from the liquor cabinet. When it was all gone, she closed her
eyes and went into limbo, sprawled on the living room couch.

Chapter XV

1960-1961

In a house-cleaning frenzy, Bee scrubbed and polished, took
down draperies, washed windows, cleaned closets, vacuumed, mopped
and dusted.

Anne didn't call. Ten days passed. Maddie advised notifying
the authorities. Bee said Anne had enough trauma to deal with
- being hunted by the police would make things worse. She would
wait. Anne had said she'd get in touch.

She found that she was repeating some of the indoor jobs:
mopping the already spotless kitchen tiles, dusting where no
speck of dust showed. She had cleaned the bathroom with bleach
and Lysol, scrubbed the fixtures and taken the bath mat out
to the trash barrel. Then she was sick to her stomach, bending
over the toilet.

Maddie came over each morning and when she left Bee went
back to the compulsive cleaning, polishing silverware,
re-arranging book shelves, taking things from one closet to
put in another. Phil had taken most of his clothes - suits,
shirts, underwear, socks - but there were still a few jackets
and other articles hanging in his closet. She took them all
out, packed them in cartons and shoved the cartons back into

the closet. She stayed away from Anne's room, would have locked it if there had been a key.

Two days before Harriet was due back from the cruise a letter arrived from Anne. It was short, saying only that she and her friends - Myra, Carri and Carri's boyfriend Mark - were staying a few days in New Orleans with Myra's aunt. "And Mark knows somebody in San Francisco where we can stay until we get a place of our own." The last sentence brought immediate tears: "Maybe some day you'll forgive me, Mom." Then, a P.S., "I guess you'll have to deal with Harriet."

Although it had not been arranged, Harriet would certainly phone when the boat docked, requiring transportation for herself and luggage to Brooklyn. Electing not to provide the service, Bee drove out to Montauk Point on Sunday. The day was chilly and stormy, and the farther east she drove, the darker the skies became. When she reached the little town at the tip of the Island, it was raining, hard driving gusts that clogged the windshield wipers with sand and rocked the little car in open stretches. She had hoped for a walk on the rocky beach, but instead found a small restaurant and settled for a lunch of chowder and homemade bread before a blazing fireplace. Drawing out her stay, she bought a newspaper and idled in front of the fire with it. There were few customers, the weather to blame, the waiter said.

The afternoon passed and by four she went back to her car and headed west into gathering dusk and, now, light rain. The

long silent drive gave her time to think about the coming
confrontation with Harriet. She couldn't see beyond a complete
break, a cessation of communication and shut-down of intimacy.
Would she be able to control the frightful anger that lay ready
to explode? Would she be able to listen to whatever explanation
Harriet would offer to justify her behavior? The appalling
facts would have to be brought out into the open. It would
take a monumental effort to remain calm and talk about them.

The miles swept by, she put on the headlights, and finally
left the highway and wound down into Westbury and Walnut Street.

The telephone was ringing when she opened the front door.

"Bee! Where have you been? I got in hours ago - had to
take a taxi all the way to Brooklyn. Where have you been?"

"Sorry. I'll drive in tomorrow morning. We've got things
to talk about."

Harriet's voice veered into sulky. "Can't you say you're
glad I'm back? At least?"

Bee hesitated over "No" but said instead: "Unpack and get
a night's rest. I'll see you in the morning about ten."

She put down the phone and went upstairs to bed.

Harriet came to the door to let her in. A steamer trunk
and piled suitcases sat in the middle of the parlor where they
had been dropped, obviously not yet attended to.

"I called you a dozen times," Harriet said. "You knew when
the ship was to dock. It would have been friendly of you to
meet me there."

Bee met her cool stare. "I'm not feeling very friendly toward you, Harriet."

"What's that supposed to mean?" The dark piercing eyes that had demanded and forced obedience for all of Bee's life now turned on her. "I don't like the sound of it."

"Don't try intimidation tactics on me. I think you'd better sit down while you listen to what I have to say." Bee took the other woman's arm and backed her toward one of the velvet side chairs, then drew another one forward for herself.

As if she understood something not yet under her control was about to happen, Harriet clamped her lips shut and sat down, not taking her glittering eyes from Bee's face. "It's about Anne." A statement, not a question.

"Yes, it's about my daughter. I think your celebrated intuition is telling you why I'm here, so let's get right down to it."

"Is she all right?"

"I don't know. She was expelled from school for smoking marijuana, tried to kill herself in my bathroom and the last I heard she's on her way to California with three other teen-agers."

"What?"

"Before she left," Bee went on conversationally, priding herself, for the moment, on her unemotional responses, "she told me about what Phil did to her, and that you have known about it for over three years."

"What do you mean - tried to kill herself?" Harriet was

trembling, her face drained.

"She took a razor to her wrist, but it was a clumsy try. I got her to the hospital and they bandaged her, and after that, she took off." The scene in the bathroom jumped full-blown into her mind, blood-spattered tub, bathmat soaked with it, the screaming, "Help me, Mom!"

Calm deserted her, as she had known it would. "Why have you remained silent all these years? Never saying a word to me - letting Anne deal with these awful things alone? If I'd known I could have found help for her! But you took her away!"

"Wait - just wait a minute - "

"No!" Bee shrieked. "It's all your fault! She could have died!"

Harriet jumped up and shook her fist in Bee's face. "And you're blaming me for all this? What about your part? Neither of you has an ounce of understanding or interest in that child! You've neglected her, pushed her aside, showed her she counted for little in your lives! That's why she wanted to kill herself - not my fault, Bee - all I ever did was love her!"

"You call that love?" Bee shouted her down. "You bought her, Harriet - just as you bought me when I was a child! It started out as a pay-back, didn't it? For what Jack did to you? And when Phil came into my life, you transferred all that spite to him."

Their flushed faces were inches apart. For the first time in her life, Bee met the furious eyes without turning away. "And that's why you fixed me up with Maurice, isn't it? To get me away from my husband. But it backfired, Harriet. Phil left me all right, but that's not going to send me back to you. And you've lost Anne, too. She wants no part of either of us. So all your machinations have come to nothing. You're going to be what you told me you'd be, back there when I was twelve - a lonely old woman - a sad, miserable, unhappy, unloved old old woman!"

Harriet sat down, her face pinched and white, hands to her mouth, staring in horror as Bee shook a trembling hand in front of her nose.

"I never want to see you again! You're out of my life forever!" She stumbled against a chair, turned and walked unsteadily to the front door, opened it, went down the steps and got into her car.

(Italics)

I write scenarios for myself and Anne, fantasizing a walk along the beach at sunset, hand in hand, talking softly, small confidences, tentative questions, light answers. I am full of mother love. My eyes are damp and my throat hurts because she is so beautiful, my daughter. She holds my hand and looks at me, talks to me. She tells me we are friends. Beneath the words something is taking root, something begins to exist where nothing has existed before, and will be permanent, will withstand. We are going to love each other, no matter who or what else comes into our lives. I am happy because we have found each other at last.

This is all making-believe, playacting, a wish, a dream.
She stopped saying "I love you, Mommy," when she was five.
Stopped looking at me when she was ten, and cut me out of her
life by the time she went to Latchfield. I knew only her
whereabouts, nothing more. And the terrible truth is that I
didn't care enough to ask.

This is how I would tell it to Maurice, who always listened
and who told me what things meant. But Maurice is gone and
there is no one to tell it to. I read it over and see that the
tone is maudlin, self-pitying. I tear it up, dropping the shreds
into the waste basket.

During the years when this imagined scene could have taken
place, I was otherwise occupied - with concern about myself,
my job, my friends, how I appeared to the rest of the world.
I bought clothes, dieted, make myself into a pretty woman.
I flirted with everyone, men and women alike. I wanted praise,
needed attention. And when Maurice came into my life, it seemed
as though I had it all. Love had found me, at last. It _was_
love, wasn't it?

I shall overcome this. I'm strong, I'm young, and I know
what I have to do. There is something of Willa in me, after
all.

(end Italics)

For two days Bee didn't go near the telephone, either to
call or to answer. Maddie came to the door once but was put
off with an excuse.

When she finally picked up the phone after five minutes
of ringing, she heard Harriet's voice: "Please - Bee! Let me
say - "

She hung up and left the house.

Two days after that, a letter.

"Dear Bee: Don't tear this up before you read it - "

She shredded it and put a match to the pieces.

It was three months before she heard from Anne again. Bee
had trusted that a letter would come, refusing to speculate
on what Anne was doing out in California, refusing to allow
fear to rise to panic.

There was a murky snapshot tucked into the envelope. In
the background, a store. A cafe? Coffee shop? A black girl
and a white girl, unsmiling, arms linked. Anne wore patched
jeans and a sweatshirt. The other girl was in ragged shorts
and a sweater, her bushy black hair pulled back with combs.
The note said: "This is my friend Sunshine. We have jobs bussing
dishes at this restaurant. So far I haven't had much success
making sense of my fucked-up life, but I'm hanging in there.
I live with Carri and her boyfriend in North Beach. Don't worry
about me, I'm not on the street or broke or starving. I even
have fun once in a while." It was signed "Saskia - my new name."

Bee looked at the picture for a long time, until at last
her heartbeat slowed and she could see the figures without tears.

Phil wrote in September, saying only that he had deposited money to her account. She could read the postmark: State College, PA. So he had gone back to his roots, back where everyone knew and respected him, back to Mom and Dad who were sure he could do no wrong. Bee acknowledged to herself a small hope that he had found a measure of peace. She had heard once from the Patchogue office, a note saying they were sorry to lose him and hoped he would do well wherever he decided to settle. They must have known she and Phil were no longer together, but, delicately, left out any mention of it in the letter.

In October, a card from Anne with little information, merely: "I'm doing okay."

And nothing from Harriet.

"She finally got the message," Bee told Lucille at Thanksgiving. She had been invited to spend the holiday weekend in Providence. Work at Quigley's had been heavy for six months, she was tired, and accepted the invitation gratefully.

The previous summer she had written a long letter to Lu, explaining what had happened, all of it, about Anne's attempted suicide and subsequent departure for the west coast. The last meeting with Harriet was glossed over.

Lu phoned right away, horror in her voice. "My God, Bee! That poor child! That monster of a father!"

Bee accepted her sympathy and the immediate promise of help or advice. A friend, a real friend, a confidante, someone to turn to. No recriminations, no pointing out   faults and errors of omission, no blame. Lu, Bee felt now, was the only person in the world she could depend on, and the loneliness of this condition depressed and worried her.

"About Harriet," Lu said as they cleaned up in the kitchen after the holiday feast, "you've lived under her thumb since you were a kid. You really think it's all over between you?"

"I feel like I've dropped chains, crawled out from under, made the break - free at last!" Bee laughed self-consciously. "Seriously, Lu, who knows? But for now, until my life gets back into gear, I don't want to see her or talk to her. Can you understand that?"

"Of course. I just want you to see the reality. Time wounds all heels, as the current saying goes - it also does heal, if you let it." Lu gave her a warm hug, then leaned against the kitchen sink and said tentatively, "And Phil?"

"How can you ask? You yourself called him a monster. You think I could live with him, get into bed with him, after what he's done?"

"He's a very troubled guy, Bee. He needs help. Not from you, maybe, but if you could suggest - "

"He's living with his folks in Pennsylvania. Let them get him some help." It was impossible to envision any circumstance under which she would approach him. The revulsion she had felt on first learning of his actions was still active, still raw and sore.

Lu was silent for a moment, wrapping left-overs in foil, re-arranging things on the refrigerator shelf to accommodate them. Then, wiping her hands on a dish towel, she said briskly,

"What are your plans - you'll stay with Quigley, I assume?
And the house - any idea what you'll do with it?"

"Maybe sell it, maybe rent it. I can't think about it now.
All I can think about, Lu, is Anne - and what kind of life she's
got out there in Beatnik town."

"We're taking our vacation around Christmas - going to try
out the slots in Reno. Maybe I can arrange a quick side trip
to San Francisco. Would you want me to look her up? See how
she's doing? It wouldn't be that much extra time - and I'd
like to help."

"But - I don't even have an address - "

"I'm willing to invest a day. She mentioned North Beach,
didn't she? And working in some kind of luncheonette? I'll
case the neighborhood, ask some questions, who knows? Maybe
I'll find someone who knows 'Saskia.'"

Early in December Anne finally wrote a real letter. She
told Bee she had a better job, and would soon have a room of
her own. Meanwhile, Bee could write to her at Carri's place.

"You've probably read about San Francisco, about beatniks
and drop-outs - everyone's writing weird poetry and wearing
crazy clothes, and the guys all have long - I mean LONG hair,
and there's lots of pot available, but I'm staying away from
it. I can't afford it, for one thing, and my boss says he'll
fire me if he smells it on me. So you can stop worrying. I've
met some great kids, we hang out together, eat together and
share whatever money we come up with."

After the 'Saskia' there was a P.S. that brought a heart-stopping pang: "I'd like to hear from you, if you feel like writing." Nothing about Harriet, nothing about Phil. But a small, tentative reaching out.

She called Lu and read her the letter. Lu asked for the address and promised to bring back some news. Then, quietly, asked if she had done any thinking about formalizing the separation. Bee said no, she hadn't. Not yet.

But she would need to write to Phil soon. The house would be put up for sale and when a buyer was found, undoubtedly he would be required to sign papers, etc. Rather than put it off, she wrote him a short note. With this behind her, she packed her personal belongings, sent the furniture to storage, and said goodbye to the Whitlocks. The three-room apartment she had found in the Village was in a quiet cul-de-sac behind a row of stores, furnished, one floor above the street. Ed Quigley hadn't pried, but there were questions in his eyes. She gave him a brief explanation, saying only that she and Phil had reached the parting point. She doubted if he would hear anything from Harriet. When, goaded by curiosity, she asked him if his wife had seen her lately, he shook his head. "She's gone off somewhere, Scotland, I think. The wife hasn't kept in touch..."

She wrote to Anne, sending a substantial money order, "to help with groceries..." The tone of the letter was calm, almost impersonal, no "Your mother loves you, come home!" Only a simple "I'm here, if you want to write, or need anything."

369

Chapter XVI

1962-1963

The apartment was stuffy, winter-sealed against the frigid wind that lashed the windows, leaving ice tracings on the glass. Christmas was only another cold New York day, snow hovering over the city, ready to dust streets and sidewalks and whiten Central Park. Refusing Maddie's invitation to come out to Westbury for a few days, Bee picked an expensive restaurant for her dinner and asked for a table near the window so she could watch the snow fall. To kill a lump in her throat, she ordered a bottle of champagne, bringing back painful memories. She drank two glasses, then waved it away when the waiter came to pour.

Now that Anne had said she was managing to get her life in some kind of order, Bee began to think about a trip to San Francisco. Lucille would return soon with news about Anne - where she was living, how she looked. After that, she could pack her bags. It needn't be an extended visit, only long enough to assure herself of Anne's health and safety.

Bee talked to Ed Quigley as soon as New Year's Day had passed. He wanted to know why California rather than the Virgin

Islands, mentioning weather. "My daughter is living in San
Francisco," she told him, and when he said something vague about
beatniks and how come she had permitted this relocation, Bee
said: "She's doing all right, has a job and a place to live.
I just need to see her."

"What about - did she finish school? That ritzy place in
Connecticut?"

"She got into trouble up there, Ed. Smoking something that
sent the headmistress into shock. She was asked to leave."

"Kids," Ed said, shaking his head. "What do they want
nowadays, anyway?"

Lu called to tell Bee she had seen Anne, briefly, on a one-
day jaunt to San Francisco with her husband. "She's thin but
apparently in good health, doing okay. I talked to her where
she works, a fish place. She's coping, even looked a little
glad to see me. Told me to say Hi to you." Lu paused, then
said: "Don't leave things the way they are, Bee. Tell her you're
coming."

The plane landed at San Francisco International just before
noon. She had written the date and time of her arrival but the
plane had run into delays in Chicago (a storm shutting down
operations temporarily) and then been re-routed, finally landing
three hours late. She caught a bus into the city and checked
into her reserved room at the Golden Gate Inn, off Union Square.
Anne had given her no phone humber, only an address, and Lu
had learned little more.

After a cup of coffee to steady her nerves, Bee called a cab and gave the Filbert Street number. She had no plans for opening a conversation: Anne would decide the direction it would take. She would answer questions, fill in blanks, but above all, she was here to listen. It wouldn't be easy. There was a wound that no stretch of time would completely heal. Too much damage had been done because the secret had been kept.

The taxi drew up in front of a shabby three-story house and Bee paid the fare and got out. A group of young people, lounging on the front steps, moved aside to let her pass. A girl said, "Hi," in a soft voice. There were no names on the panel of six mailboxes near the door. About to press a button randomly, Bee felt a touch on her arm.

"Looking for someone?" It was the girl who had greeted her.

"Do you know which apartment Carri lives in? Or Anne? I mean - Saskia?"

"Sure. Number three. But they're not here. Carri's gone off with her boyfriend for a few days, and Saskia - she works at the Fish Grotto over on Columbus." She pointed. "Turn right at the corner, it's about three blocks."

"Thanks." Bee went down the steps, offering a small smile to the group sitting there.

"Have a happy day," someone called after her.

It was a narrow grill-type restaurant, smelling heartily of fried fish. Six tables hugged one wall, on the other side a counter with stools stretched back to the kitchen door. There was one empty seat at the far end. Bee moved hesitantly through

the crowd and took it. She looked around anxiously through
the smoky haze, feeling uncomfortably out of place, her trim
gray suit and white blouse out of sync with the dress of those
around her. She ordered a cup of coffee and studied the
food-specked menu. Nothing in it sounded even vaguely appetizing
and she put it down.

"Mom?"

Bee turned quickly. Anne stood behind her, balancing a tray
of dirty plates and glasses.

"Anne...oh..."

"I'll be finished here in half an hour, then we can go.
Eat something, if you want." She moved away, weaving among the
patrons.

Bee watched until the kitchen door closed after her. Her
hand shook as she lifted the cup, spilling some of the coffee.
The man behind the counter swept a soiled rag over it and
refilled her cup with a grudging, "Okay, lady, accidents happen."

Anne's appearance was a shock. No more neat ponytail, her
hair was an untidy tangle that brushed her T-shirted shoulders.
She wore grimy jeans, patched, rolled to the knees above once-
white sneakers. But it was her face - paper white, without
makeup, shiny with sweat, a smudge across one cheek - that was
so startling. She had lost weight, looked thin and frail.

Bee glanced around furtively. The tattered jeans, wild hair
and T's or sweatshirts, none very clean, appeared to be in the
nature of a costume, or uniform. The boys all looked alike.
Shaggy hair, torn jeans, and here and there, a straggly beard.

Everyone smoked, and on each table there was a carafe of red
wine and the remnants of seafood dinners. Conversation was
a jangle of voices with, from somewhere, music (a guitar?) rising
and falling around it.

She held the coffee cup, refilled once more, with both hands
and told herself not to stare, not to draw any more attention
to her non-conforming appearance. Already there had been
sidelong glances from along the counter. She looked away,
avoiding eye contact, but felt unwelcome in this strange place.

They walked along Columbus Avenue in silence. Anne had draped
a fringed shawl over her T-shirt and slung a canvas bag from
her shoulder.

Flatbush Avenue. Graduation night, 1937. In step but
separate. Communication as inaccessible now as it had been
then. I've handed this down the way a woman passes recipes
on to her daughter. Why haven't I learned anything, all these
years?

She had expected the apartment to be as shabby inside as
outside, but the rooms, even the tiny kitchen, were clean and
uncluttered. Curtains at the front windows, a little ragged
at the hems. No carpet, a few small rugs. Along one wall, a
faded red velvet couch, two straight chairs, a metal table in
the middle of the room. She peered quickly into one of the
two small bedrooms. Mattress on the floor, covered with faded
blankets. Anne watched her while she took it all in, saying
nothing.

Bee took off her jacket and sat down on one of the chairs.

"My plane was late. Bad weather in Chicago."

"I figured."

"I've got a hotel room downtown, near Union Square."

"How long are you staying?"

"A few days." <u>As long as it takes.</u>

"I work 10 to 3, most days."

"Can we get together when you're through at the restaurant?"

"Sure."

Bee smiled wanly. "This isn't getting off to much of a start, is it?"

"I don't know what you want me to say." Anne looked at her shoes.

"Before I go back," Bee said, choosing words carefully, "we need to know more about each other than we do now."

"You mean, like a confession? Like, who did what and who's to blame?"

"I guess that's what I mean. Yes, that's close." She had expected only to "look in on" Anne, see that she was all right, then go home. But it wasn't going to be that way. They were going to have to tell each other the truth.

"Let's have a Coke, then, if we're going to talk." Anne went to the refrigerator and came back with a bottle and two glasses.

"Maybe - if you'd ask me some questions we could find a place to start. I'll give real answers, I promise."

For a few minutes Anne didn't answer, holding the glass with hands suddenly white-knuckled. She blinked, set the glass

on the floor beside her. "Well, now that you're here I guess
we've got a job to do. The first question. Okay, the first
question is the hardest of all to ask. How come you didn't
love me when I was growing up?"

It was like a blow to the heart. "Anne - you think - are
you sure I didn't?"

"As far as I could tell," Anne said, "you didn't. Oh,
I got fed and washed and dressed and sent to school just like
other kids. Like it was a thing you had to do because you had
a kid. Not because you were interested in me, not because you
cared." She got up and went to the window, pulled the curtain
back and stared out. Not turning, she said: "I'm trying not
to get angry, Mom. Just stay with me while I sort out how to
say things, okay?"

Bee said: "That's what I'm here for."

"I used to get so mad, I used to go up to my room and -
and cry because I felt so fucking unwanted!" She came back and
sat down. "Nobody in that house ever got a hug or a kiss, you
know that? We were all - just there, under the same roof, not
living together, not caring about each other - just like - like
zombies!"

Bee sipped the Coke, not tasting it, and set the glass on
the floor next to Anne's. "Maybe I can tell you something about
what went on that took my attention away from you."

Anne wasn't listening. "You're going to tell me you were
so-o-o- busy, your job was so-o-o important. You couldn't get
home in time for dinner, you were just never there!" Her

shoulders shook and her voice shrilled. "I was alone - all by myself - in that house. Until Dad - "

Bee reached out and pulled her close, cradling the tangled hair against her breast. There was no resistance. Anne was crying, in silent shuddering misery, as they held each other.

"Enough," Bee said after a while. "It's a start. Let it stop for today." She held Anne's hands as they got up together. "There's a lot you don't know, that you'll need to know to understand. And it's going to take more guts that you can imagine for me to talk about it. Can we get together tomorrow? Here?"

Anne freed her hand and brushed at her eyes. "Sure, Mom. Come about three-fifteen. I'll be here."

How can I talk about what I've hidden for so long? About Phil, and how what we had, once, died. About Maurice and about Harriet and how I let her run things, right from the beginning? And about Willa, where it all started. How much of it must I tell, to make her understand?

She put on a nightgown and creamed her face, staring into the mirror in the bathroom.

Oh God, she thought, do I have to do this? Wet with tears, her eyes stared back at her. I want her forgiveness and I can't get it until I've told her what I've done. If we can get past this, I think we can love each other.

Bee waited on the steps. It was three-thirty before Anne
came down the street. "It's Friday," she said, "always more
dishes on Friday."

They went into the apartment.

"How about some coffee?"

This time they sat together on the red velvet couch. Anne
got a fruit crate from the kitchen and with a flourish, spread
a dish towel on it. "Voila! Coffee table!"

Bee smiled. It was an ice-breaker, of course.

"If you can stand it, Mom, I'll just finish what I started
to say yesterday," Anne began. "I probably sound like a whining
bitch, but you said to be honest, so I've got to spill it all
out."

"I'm listening," Bee said.

"You went through the motions. I guess you thought you were
doing it right, but something important was missing. Even I
didn't know what it was, back then. All I know is - if it had
been there I would never had gone to Harriet when - when I needed
help. I wanted you to be motherly, like Maddie Whitlock. I
wanted you to fuss over me, but all I got was - you never treated
me like a child, Mom! You never kissed me and told me whatever
was wrong would get better, like a scraped knee, or something.
And I never saw you look really happy, you know that? Were
you, Mom? Were you ever real happy?"

Willa, the indifferent, the uninterested. The inattention
she had brought to the job of motherhood. The job she had never

wanted and never tried to learn. Had she ever smiled?

Bee pulled tissues out of her handbag. "I knew we'd need these," she said. "Once we almost got a conversation going, do you remember? When I drove you back to school? I started to tell you about my childhood, my mother - and I couldn't finish, I copped out, walked away without telling you the rest."

"I remember," Anne said.

"I think I can do it now, if you want to hear it."

Anne nodded, picked up her coffee cup and held it with both hands. "I can listen, too. Go ahead."

Bee started with Harriet because, of course, all the important events in her life could be traced to her influence. Risking Anne's impatience, she started with Willa and Harriet's early friendship, moved quickly to Jack and the role he had played with both of them, and then she told the story of Willa's seduction, remembering the words of her mother's "confession," when Anne was only weeks old. Anne listened, and after a while her own face reflected the emotions Bee was feeling as she recreated the times she lived through, back in the Brooklyn of the 1930s.

She told of the beach house, of the promise Harriet had extracted, and about Jack's death, and then Willa's.

It was an hour later when she finally brought Maurice into the tale, not dwelling on the romance, the loving, but on the things he had taught her, the ways he had made her life fun, and full of good things. And she found a way to tell Anne why

these things had not happened with Phil. The telling made her
think of him, bypassing the horror and remembering the man she
had fallen in love with long ago.

"How long were you in love with Maurice?" Anne asked.

I've never stopped. I will always love him. "The love
affair lasted almost five years. Then we - it ended."

"You don't see him any more?"

"No."

"Does that hurt?"

Unbearably. "I'll get over it. What is hurting more now
is what we're here to heal. Do you think we have a chance,
Anne?"

"Thanks for telling me all this, I mean, for getting me
to see what was going on. I was a little kid, I only saw what
was happening to me. And yes, I think maybe we've got a chance."

"Will you find out about some kind of - counseling, or
therapy - will you let me pay - "

"A shrink? You think I need that?" Anne grinned.

"It would be a good follow-up for what we've been doing
here."

"I'll think about it, Mom."

Two days later Bee boarded the plane for New York, waved
to Anne as she watched from the terminal window, and prepared
herself for six hours of sorting out, finding hope, losing dread,
and, just possibly, inching her way toward reconciliation.
Not yet ready to forgive, but ready to put aside anger and blame
and give compassion a chance to be born.

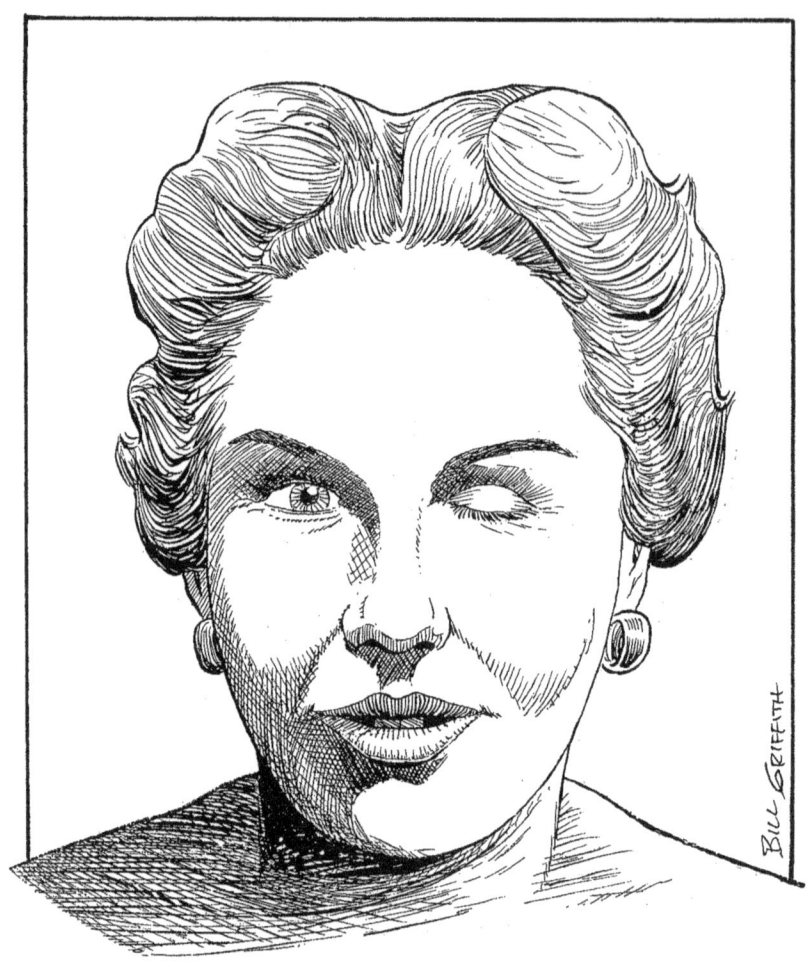

BARBARA GRIFFITH was born in Brooklyn, N.Y. in 1919.
She married James L. Griffith in 1942 in Hattiesburg, Miss.
She began writing in the mid-1950s while living with her
family in Levittown, Long Island. Her first published work,
"The Litttle One" appeared in the March 1959 issue of Fan-
tastic Science Fiction magazine. Throughout her life, she
conducted writing workshops and continued to publish
fiction and non-fiction pieces in magazines and journals.
Departed Acts is one of several unpublished novels.
She died in San Francisco, Cal. in 1998.